Ghost Warrior

by

H. Richard Slichter

1663 Liberty Drive, Suite 200
Bloomington, Indiana 47403
(800) 839-8640
www.AuthorHouse.com

© 2004 H. Richard Slichter
All Rights Reserved.

No part of this book may be reproduced, stored in a retrieval system, or transmitted by any means without the written permission of the author.

First published by AuthorHouse 11/19/04

ISBN: 1-4184-9320-1 (sc)
ISBN: 1-4184-9321-X (dj)

Printed in the United States of America
Bloomington, Indiana

This book is printed on acid-free paper.

This is a work of fiction; names, places and events are the product of the author's imagination and are used fictitiously. Any resemblance to persons, places and events are coincidental.

Cover design by Leslie Harris Studios

This book of short stories is dedicated to those valiant warriors who have stood by me through the many battles life has brought to us. Your courage to stand up for what you believe in and feel is right is acknowledged and appreciated.

H. Richard Slichter

ACKNOWLEDGEMENTS

Many thanks to my Costa Rican and Colombian friends who helped me so much with my ideas. Jose Diaz, Flor Diaz and Cristian Aldana, thank you so much for all the time spent helping me to translate this book into Spanish, to enable more readers to hopefully enjoy my story. Carlos Camacho, thank you. Your input was essential.

Thanks to my wife, Marie, for her understanding, patience, and endless hours of assistance. It will forever be appreciated.

PROLOGUE

Entering the world of the Navajo Ghost Warrior, one regains the ability to fantasize in a universe filled with contradictions, myths and legends. The book takes us to primitive villages located deep in the jungles of Colombia and then sweeps us into caves filled with ultra-technical advancements. The morals related in these tales of transparent simplicity, fierceness and indifference, not only transport us to an extraordinary world created by the author, but shows us a hidden and fascinating aspect of the eternal fight between good and evil.

Somehow the Ghost Warrior's adventures, accompanied by great doses of humor and irony, make us remember the adventures related by Miguel de Cervantes in "Don Quijote de la Mancha". In both books we find loneliness, insanity, loyalty and betrayal. This, accompanied by the ongoing fight for noble causes shared with the love of not Dulcinea but Angelita, brings us to a close alliance with the satire and themes of the movies and TV shows of our times.

With the unusual technique that we often see in movie scripts, the author takes us on a fast moving journey to the South American jungles of Colombia. This background, for the greater part of the book, provides a tropical, dangerous and sometimes mystical setting in which dominant and foreign customs sometimes are overshadowed by external forces which cause the innate goodness in people to become over powered by the forces of evil.

With less emphasis on location and greater attention to the diverse and often intense personalities of his characters, the author skillfully enables the reader to relate to their experiences and adventures. This fascinating, fast moving and often amusing book of tales carries us away from the everyday stress and fatigue of our world and allows us access to a world where our own battles against evil are fought by the Navajo Ghost Warrior.

Flor Alba Diaz
Criminal Court Judge
Bogota, Colombia
Retired.

CHAPTER I
MY GUARDIAN ANGEL

Cry for me, jungle. Cry for me today. For in the jungles of my mind I have fought the longest and deadliest battles of them all. Jungle, my jungle; cry for me no longer, for in your comfort I have found my angel....

What a night for a mission – dark, starless and quiet as death itself. The C-130 was flying at 20,000 feet, give or take a couple of hundred feet. Raul was a CIA assassin, or more specifically, a sniper who had been charged with assassinating "World Problems" since he was 25 years old. Raul, a full blooded Navajo Indian, was hired by the company straight out of the Marines, where he had been a government-trained sniper since the age of 17 when he had forged his grandfather's signature on the enlistment form. Raul, at the age of 17 was running; running at full speed from possible problems with reservation police.

Raul, along with his older brother Hector, were left orphans when Raul was 9 years old. Their father, 'the reservation drunk', had killed himself, as well as their mother, in a horrendous automobile accident. The idiot actually thought he could run his 1966 Chevy pickup into a bridge abutment at 85 miles an hour and walk away. Raul hated this man because he had taken his mother from him, and for this he prayed that the gods would scorn him and make him sit in shit for eternity. Hector never spoke badly about their father, but then again Hector never spoke badly about anyone because he was just a nice guy. Raul had thought he was weak for that. Raul was a fighter ever since he could remember, and Hector was a diplomat. Raul could remember how angry he would get at Hector, because more than once he had stepped into the middle of something that Raul figured was totally under control, and stopped him from fighting. Raul used to tell him, "somebody sticks a gun in your face, and what, you're gonna talk him to death?" "Little brother" Hector would say, "when that time comes, I'm going to order you to kill him."

"What the hell are you talking about?" Raul would ask, and each time Hector would get this really stupid look on his face, and say "I have no idea. Ask Grandpa."

Grandpa was Johnny Lightfoot, and Raul was closer to him than anyone in the world. Grandpa took both Hector and Raul after the accident, and brought them into his home. He told them, "now you are my sons and nothing more will harm you." Johnny Lightfoot was a Navajo chief by birthright, and the tribe looked to him constantly for guidance. Grandpa had been a war hero and was one of the famous "Wind Talkers" that had developed the code the Japanese could not break, and had helped the United States win the war- as Grandpa would say, the "the big war". Grandpa had strong medicine and many were convinced he could see the future.

Raul often thought, "Boy, was Grandpa so right, so many times". Grandpa had told him he could run from his people, but would never stop being Navajo. Raul had no idea what that meant, until one day a reservation police officer who had been fired by Grandpa, returned to their home and killed him. Grandpa had been head of the tribal counsel. Billy Dirtyface, the policeman in question, was back in front of the counsel, trying to explain once again why he had beaten a handcuffed prisoner to the point of hospitalization, for absolutely no reason other than Billy was sadistic by nature and this prisoner had pissed him off. Hence, in his mind, that was reason enough.

Everybody in the tribe knew Billy had killed Grandpa, but no one could prove it. So Billy, after a few drinks or a couple of snorts of cocaine, would make it a point to brag to Raul about how he had gotten away with murder, and there was nothing anyone could do about it. Big mistake. Hector was away at college and Raul had to right the problem on his own. On the day before he enlisted into the marines, Raul killed Billy Dirtyface and hung his body in front of Grandpa's house. Attached to the body was a suicide note, confessing to Grandpa's murder and asking the tribe's forgiveness. Raul had obtained the note by breaking one finger at a time on Billy's left hand until he decided to write it. Raul had thought very seriously about scalping the son of a bitch, but the suicide would have been a hard sell with Billy's scalp hanging next to him in front of Grandpa's house. Raul had to be smart about what he did, and smart he was.

Raul had always been infatuated with rifles and firearms in general, and knew he wanted to be a sniper long before the age of 17. And now with things as they were, what better time to sign Grandpa's name to the form he had, and run from the tribe, his home, as Grandpa had foreseen that he would do?

Now, many years later at the age of 44, Raul sat in the back of a C-130, thinking how smart Grandpa was and how much he knew about the future. Raul, an English speaking Navajo with a large Navajo vocabulary, had learned and become so fluent in Spanish from years of military duty in Colombia, that many Colombians actually thought he was a Colombian.

Hector, a short man of stature and about 40lbs. overweight, including the bushy mustache, had graduated college and gone on to become a boss in the CIA. Hector was very smart, and being "the diplomat" was still one of his outstanding attributes. He had majored in Latin American Culture, therefore was very fluent in Spanish, and more so, very much aware of what was going on in South America.

Hector had gone into government service right out of college. He moved up the ranks rapidly, to his current position of agent in charge of Latin American affairs, a job at which Hector was very proficient - and just plain good at.

Raul and Hector had kept in close contact with each other during Raul's military years, and though Hector was eight years older than Raul, he never acted like the "older brother." Instead, he would tell Raul how much he respected him and looked up to him for setting things right with Grandpa. All Raul would ever say is "whatever", and let the moment pass.

While in the Marines, Raul had become so proficient at his duty assignment that his Sgt. would tell him over and over that he was the best sniper he had ever seen. He remarked that his natural ability was so far beyond the norm that he was "off the charts," and could write his own ticket to his future.

Raul had done assignments for the CIA while in the military, and was very familiar with the company long before Hector asked him to come and work for him directly.

Raul's first response was, "Why?... I'm happy in the marines, why change?" Hector then used all the logic that he was so good at. He explained how much more money he would make from the company than as a soldier. Then after the money thing didn't really seem to be as effective as he would have liked, he offered with exasperation, "Work for me, and nobody will ever fuck with you as long as you live. Be your own boss, spotter, no spotter, whatever you want. Just do what you do so well."

Just as Hector had expected, Raul smiled and said something in Navajo that only Hector and he understood, and the deal was done.

Now many years later, Raul sat in the back of this airplane reminiscing in his mind about how many people he had killed in the name of 'what's right'. More dying faces than he could or would possibly want to remember. Grandpa had told him that the one thing in life he always wanted was for Raul to be a good and honorable man, and always do what was right. Now, Raul, a proud Navajo, was trying to decide what was right and what was wrong. He had run from his people because he killed Billy Dirtyface. Maybe that was wrong, but Grandpa deserved revenge. Now Hector gives him packages with pictures, names, and all the data needed to snuff out a life. "Granted, these are the shitbags of the world, as we know it, and I suppose if I didn't do it somebody else would have to." He would ask himself, "am I playing God? And are thoughts like that really warranted, this late in the game?"

"To hell with it. When the light goes red, just jump out and stop thinking so much." Raul sat back and started checking his equipment and waited. The problem with solo night jumps is how much time you have to think, even if you don't want to. And Raul didn't want think anymore, but…..

"What am I doing with my life? Shouldn't I be married with kids and living in some subdivision like everyone else? Look at me. I have loved one woman in my entire life and she was killed in a bombing. The story of my life; don't get close to anyone, they could get killed." Raul heard the bell; it sounded far away, but it wasn't. The light was red and it was time to jump. "God, I hate this part of the job more that anything. Jumping out of airplanes sucks."

When the door opened, the cold air hit Raul in the face so hard it took his breath away and his goggles pressed so hard against his face it hurt. Raul prepped to jump, and he realized that it was so dark that he couldn't get a fix on where he was. Not a star in the sky, and the moon was nowhere to be seen. It couldn't be darker. That was bad, but that was also good because he could get on the ground without being seen, or shot in the air. Raul was out of the plane when he felt the prop wash, the strong wind created by the props when the plane ascends too quickly after the jump. Normally, that wouldn't be a problem, but in this case, Raul realized there was a problem. The strong winds he had jumped into had pushed him into a wooded area. "Shit! I'm going to land in those fucking trees. Just what I needed."

What seemed like a lifetime later, Raul was hanging in a tree, 25 to 30 feet above the ground. "What now?" Raul thought, "I have maybe two hours before some troop of guerillas wanders by, and sees me stuck in the tree. Let me think, what would they do? No brainer, they will shoot me and that's that. Now that I know I have no option, 'here goes!'." And at that moment, Raul cut the cords on his parachute, falling some thirty feet to the ground.

Raul heard the crack as his left leg broke on impact, and at that moment the pain was so severe he thought he was going to pass out. He, in fact, started going in and out of consciousness, without realizing it. Raul looked down at his leg, and in horror saw what damage had been done. The bone just below his left knee was protruding out of his pant leg. His leg was covered in blood, and some other things that had come out of the wound, that he really wasn't sure of. What he was sure of was that he was really fucked now. He couldn't walk; in fact, he couldn't even stand up. The first thing he thought of was, "get on the radio and get some help here". Great idea, except his radio lay about three feet to his right in about four separate pieces, and was not up to manufacturer's specs. He tried using his cellular phone, but in the forest reception was not even an issue. It just didn't happen.

"What are my options?" he thought. "I don't have any options ... what's that noise?" he asked himself. "Someone's coming and I can't even move out of the way or hide." As Raul reached for his pistol, he felt the whole world go into slow motion and he passed out again.

Raul started to wake a few minutes later, and the first thing he felt was a terrible tightness in his left leg, almost like someone or something was standing on it. He could feel the sweat running from his armpits down the side of his body. His face was cool and damp. "That's strange", he thought; "almost like someone is wiping my face." Raul thought he could hear a voice way off in a distance. It sounded like a woman. But his mind was probably playing tricks on him. When he opened his eyes, his first reaction was to hold his breath for a moment. Kneeling down next to him was an angel; not really, but the closest thing he had ever seen to one. The woman was holding his head in her lap, and wiping his face while humming. When she noticed that he was awake she said, "Be quiet, and lie still. This place is full of troops and I'm trying to figure out how to keep you alive". She didn't need to concern herself about him talking, he thought, because he was speechless. This woman was gorgeous; long black hair that reminded him of ribbons of silk running down the back of her petite, but obviously very strong body. Her eyes were as dark as onyx, but they sparkled and gave off this aura of strength that was incredible. Her skin was light brown, actually not much different than his, and he thought she was probably mid- twenties. Finally she spoke, told him her name was Angelita Marques and that she was going to dig a hole next to where he was lying, and push him into it.

She then looked at him for the longest time and remarked, "You look like a Colombian, but also you don't, so what are you, and where are you from?"

Raul thought for a minute, and answered her in Spanish. "I'm a Navajo Indian from the Northwest corner of New Mexico, and my leg is killing me."

"What can I do?" she asked.

"Tell me what's pressing on my leg."

"I put a rope around it, just above your knee to stop the bleeding. Two or three more minutes of bleeding, the way you were, and I would be burying you now instead of trying to hide you." "Here", she said, "take one of these pain killers I found in your pouch."

Raul took the pill, and promptly passed out again. When Raul awoke this time, he found himself in the hole Angelita had dug, covered completely with leaves and anything else she could find. He also discovered that she had put his pistol in his right hand.

Through the branches and leaves she had placed on top of him he could see that she was standing about twenty feet from him, and was talking to three men in uniforms. These were not military men, but instead para-military guerillas. Raul strained to listen to what was being said, and it didn't sound good at all.

"What are you doing out here in the forest all alone?", the man in the center questioned.

Raul could see that the man was standing too close to Angelita, and was trying to intimidate her. Angelita stood her ground and answered, "I am on my way home from my daily walk, why?"

"You are out here all alone, just walking in the jungle? How old are you?"

" I'm 32, why? What's that got to with anything?"

"Don't you realize how dangerous it is out here for a beautiful woman like yourself to be alone? Anything could happen. You could be assaulted, or raped, or even killed and nobody would know. "

Raul prayed the pain would stop; he didn't want to pass out again. He knew Angelita needed him, and he wanted to be there for her. He would kill these three clowns in a heartbeat. Nobody was going to assault his angel.

The man in the center seemed to be the only one talking. The other two were just standing there, undressing Angelita with their eyes.

Angelita very calmly smiled and asked, "what makes you think I'm out here alone?"

"Because, my cute little girl, I don't see anyone else here with you, and that's going to make you all ours."

" You're not looking in the right places." Angelita replied.

"What are you talking about?", the man in the middle asked, wiping the sweat from his face and licking his dry, cracked lips.

"Very simple," she said, "my brother is sitting in a tree, watching us with a high powered rifle in his hands."

"Really," he said, "and I should believe that just because you say so?"

" I really don't care what you believe. But I will tell you that he spent some twenty years in the military and was an army sniper, and a very good one. Secondly, the first move you make against me will be your last- and I promise you that." The two men on either side of the self-appointed leader became very nervous, and started looking around, moving back and forth.

One of them spoke. "Why don't we just leave? This woman is not important to us."

"Because", the man in the middle said, "she's lying and I'm going to teach her a lesson."

As soon as the man in the middle grabbed her shirt and tried to rip it off, Angelita pulled a 6 inch knife from a holder on her back and plunged it into the man's chest as hard as she could. The man froze in surprise, with a grimace on his face. He looked at Angelita and began spitting blood from his mouth just before he fell dead on the ground. The man on the left, the one closest to Raul, grabbed for his gun and Raul got off one shot from his hiding place. The Glock 40 cal. bullet hit the man in the left temple just above the ear. The man screamed in pain as bone fragments and blood splattered on the face of the other man. It was at that time that Angelita and Raul both realized that the other man wasn't a man at all; he was just a boy of about 15 or 16 years old, and scared to death. The front of his trousers were soaked with urine, and he was crying and pleading for no one to kill him. Angelita grabbed the boy by the shirt and slapped him on the side of the face. She took his gun, which was later discovered didn't even work, and told him to go home, burn the uniform, and go back to being a boy again. The boy thanked her and promised her he would try, and ran off.

Angelita returned to where Raul was buried, loosened the rope on his leg for a moment to maintain blood flow, and told him she was leaving to get a doctor and a horse. She wanted to get him out of the jungle before more troops came looking for him. She gave him another pill, and put a rag in his mouth so he wouldn't cry out in his sleep and give up his location. She kissed him on the forehead and left. Raul must have had that 'what was that for?' look on his face, because she just smiled and said, "thank you, I've never had a Navajo Indian save me before. In fact, I've never even talked to a Navajo Indian before. Are they all as handsome as you?" Two or three minutes later she was gone and Raul had drifted off again.

Raul had Angelita's face burned into his mind, and he knew this woman was special. At that moment he didn't know how special, but time would show him. Raul wasn't sure why, if it was the drugs or the pain, but Grandpa was standing in front of him, and he was telling him something.

"Grandpa, what is it? I can't hear what you are saying."

"Raul, the great spirits of the Navajo have put you here, and you are tested once again. This woman is right, and you must make decisions now."

"Grandpa," Raul asked, "am I going to die in this hole, lost in the jungles of Colombia?"

"Faith, my son, there are many miles left on your journey to the land of the great spirits; the woman will return, and you must keep her close, she is important to the Navajo."

"Another Grandpa riddle," Raul thought. "What could he possibly be talking about now?"

The next vision Raul had was of him, dressed as a war chief, sitting on top of a painted horse. "These visions are crazy," he thought. "I've never had dreams like these before. What's going on here?" Then the realization hit him like a 2 by 4, right between the eyes. All of these years of working for the company, and never a scratch on him. This was the first brush with death – up close and personal. What was he being told? What was he learning that he wasn't even aware of? Time, the hunter of all souls, as Grandpa would tell him, knows all, sees all, and will give you the vision, when it is right for you. Just before the dreams faded into the dark realm of deep sleep, he had one last glimpse of himself as a Chief in full headdress, sitting atop a magnificent war horse, overlooking an ongoing battle with the U.S. cavalry. "What's up with that?" he thought.

Raul had lost track of time, and had no idea how long Angelita had been gone, but awoke with a start when he heard voices and felt someone touching his now really sore leg. Angelita was back and had a man with her; an old man. "My God", thought Raul, "this man has got to be 90 years old". The medication he had taken had worn off and Raul was really starting to hurt, and hurt a lot.

"This is Dr. Sanchez; he is the closest thing we have to a medical doctor in our area".

"Great" thought Raul, "he's probably a horse doctor, but my options are down to zero."

"Not just horses," Angelita responded to his look. "But pigs and chickens and goats and cows; all kinds of animals. He's a vet."

Raul tried to remember if he had made that crack out loud, or if was he just thinking it. He was sure the latter was correct, which meant she had read his mind - and if that were the case he definitely needed another one of those knock-out pills.

Dr. Sanchez assured Raul that he would do the best he could under the circumstances; however, the break was a compound fracture and setting it with the patient in a hole in the middle of the jungle made matters more difficult. Raul was then given a small flask with some unknown liquid in it and told to drink it. "Drink this?" he snarled, "it smells like it came out of the ass of a cat," Angelita smiled. "She has a sense of humor," Raul thought. "I like that."Angelita told him it was an opium derivative, and it would help with the pain he was about to experience when Dr. Sanchez set his leg.

Raul did as he was told, and while he was waiting for it to kick in asked, "Angelita, where is your brother? I thought he would be helping you."

"No", she said. "He's too busy."

"Too busy?"

"Yes, he's a trial lawyer in Bogotá."

As he was drifting off, Raul asked, "what about the sniper thing?" And the last thing he heard before the deepest of sleep hit him was his angel laughing and telling Dr. Sanchez that the only thing her brother took shots at were prosecutors.

Dr. Sanchez was looking intently at the sky, watching a group of buzzards circling and asked, "Do you know why those buzzards are circling above us?"

Hesitantly she answered, "Yes sir, I do."

"And why would that be?" he asked, raising an eyebrow.

"Well sir, I think it has something to do with the two dead bodies in the bushes over there."

"That explains the foul smell in the air," he replied. "So tell me," he said, "why might you know of dead bodies in the bushes, or shouldn't I ask?"

"They are, or were, guerillas, and one of them tried to rape me, so I killed him."

"And the other one?" he asked.

"The man in the hole shot him in the head."

"While he was lying in the hole with a compound fracture?"

"Yes, sir, and it was a really good shot, I might add."

Dr. Sanchez looked at her for a moment and said. "My dear, I think that we must hurry and get this man out of here. From the looks of his clothes and the very fancy rifle lying next to him, he came here with death on his mind. Is he an American?"

"No, he said he is a Navajo from New Mexico."

"What is a Navajo? I have never heard of such a thing before."

"He is an Indian, and a very good looking one at that, don't you think?"

There lay Raul, all six feet, 210 pounds of him. A well built man with shoulder length jet black hair he usually kept in a pony tail. Probably the most unusual feature about him was his pale blue eyes. Nobody in the family had, or could think of a reason why his eyes were pale blue. Grandpa used to tell him that the spirits made him special and gave him those eyes so everyone would know it.

The only thing Raul knew for sure was that after a few years of being picked on and called an outsider by his schoolmates, he took up the art of karate and while in the military mastered, quite skillfully, some ancient forms of Asian combat. Thus he was very seldom "picked on" for anything.

When Raul woke up again he was on a door, being dragged through the jungle by the horse that Angelita had brought back with her. The doctor was nowhere to be seen. Angelita was walking the horse and humming again. The music coming from her was beautiful to him, and that mixed with the quiet sounds of the jungle, made Raul think he was in paradise.

Nightfall came and they were still walking through the jungle, and he had never felt more tranquil in his life. What Grandpa had told him kept repeating itself over and over in his mind. "This woman is important to the Navajo, keep her close to you". Raul had no idea, once again, what that meant, and hell, he didn't know anything about this woman. Was she married? Where does she live? What about her family? All he knew for sure was that she was lovely, courageous, and didn't take shit from anyone. "God, what a woman!" Raul closed his eyes and drifted off into deep sleep.

When Raul awoke some five hours later, the first thing he did was gasp for air. The stench in the room, or wherever he was, was terrible. "Who shit here?" he thought, "and where the hell am I?" He looked down at his leg and the bone was back inside where it belonged, and there was a splint on the outside. Raul was quite impressed with the stitch job the vet had done as well. "Now", he thought, "why have I been dumped in a bucket of shit to recuperate?" He looked around as much as he could, to try and get some idea of where he was, and what it was going to take to get away from it. "God! This place stinks!" he thought. "It looks like some kind of stable or barn or something". Just at that moment, he felt very uneasy like- he was being watched. When he turned his head to see, he was startled to see an old woman standing in the stable just watching him. Raul, trying to be a gentleman, looked at her and smiled,"Hello, my name is Raul Lightfoot, and who might you be?"

The old woman said nothing, but just kept staring at him.

Raul looked back at her and said, "Excuse me ma'am, but I have to assume you speak Spanish because we are in Colombia. Therefore, by addressing you in Spanish, I have to think you understand me."

"You have brought trouble to our farm. Why did you come here?"

"Excuse me, ma'am, but I have no idea where 'here' is and would never want to bring trouble to you intentionally. Where is Angelita? Maybe she can shed some light on the situation."

"My granddaughter is young and foolish to bring you here. Now the guerillas will come and they will kill us for helping you."

"Ma'am, I can only assure you, that as long as I am alive, nothing will happen to anyone here."

"This is Colombia, in very bad times, and, 'as long as you live' may not be so long. My granddaughter tells me you are a Navajo Indian from New Mexico. We cannot find that country on the map. Where is it?"

Raul looked at the old woman and smiled, then commenced to explain the Navajos are American Indians and New Mexico is a state within the boundaries of the United States. That led to a barrage of questions that made Raul very uneasy. First of which was, why is an American Indian in the jungles of Columbia with a fancy rifle like the one he had next to him? While he was trying to answer the question without really answering it, Angelita came into the barn. A sigh of relief came over Raul.

"Grandma, why are you out here in the barn? Let this man rest. Yesterday was a very bad day for him, and he needs to rest."

Grandma gave her a rather indignant look and left the barn.

"Where am I?" Raul asked.

"You are in one of the barns on my grandmother's farm. I put you here last night because I knew the guerillas would be looking for you."

"They know I'm here?" he asked.

"Not specifically here, but in the area. It is all over that an American sharpshooter was lost in the jungle and that he was here to kill one of the drug lords."

Obviously, the kid who ran away knew more than he let on, and went right back to tell everything he knew to the boss, Raul surmised.

Angelita looked at him and said, "Yes, you are probably right, and maybe I should have killed him too, but he was just a boy."

Raul was stunned. He had not said anything, he just thought it. And she knew.

"How could that be? Did she read my mind?" he thought. Now for the test, he pondered. Raul looked directly into Angelita's eyes, and thought to himself, "my God, you're beautiful and I think I'm in love with you. "

Angelita smiled and looked back at him and said…"Mr. Navajo Indian, it doesn't take any special ability to know what you are thinking. You are an open book. Any questions, ask Grandpa."

Raul's mouth dropped open and he didn't know what to say at all. The one thing he did know was that he prided himself on what he called his "poker ability"; that was being able to hide exactly what he thought at any given time. But this didn't work with this woman. "Why?" he asked himself.

Angelita stood and said, "Rest up, Mr. Indian, because we are going to need your help when, as the Americans say,'the shit hits the fan'. And that should take maybe a day or two before the guerillas get around to coming out here."

"Just one question," he said. "I don't want to sound ungrateful about the living quarters, but why does this place smell so bad?"

Angelita laughed and said, "This is a pig farm and it's supposed to smell like this."

"But why am I out here in all this shit?" he asked.

"Two reasons, Mr. Navajo Indian. First, I don't think my grandmother likes you much."

"Yeah, I kind of got that idea," Raul said.

"And, secondly, when the guerillas do come looking, I'm betting they won't want to walk around in all this pig shit, even though they, for the most part, are pigs themselves".

"Add smart to the list", Raul said with a smile.

Angelita was leaving, she turned back with a puzzled look and said, "What's that supposed to mean?"

Raul laughed and said, "Guess you'll just have to read my mind won't you?"

Angelita returned about two hours later with some food and a drink called a "refajo" which was, in fact, a favorite of Raul's. Refajo is a mixture of a beverage called Colombiana, a type of soda, and beer. Very simple and very good. Angelita looked a little worried and Raul spotted it right away.

"What's wrong?" he asked, very pointedly.

"They are coming sooner than I thought," she said, "they will be here by morning and rumor is that they know you're here."

The first thing that needed to be done was to get Angelita's grandmother out of harm's way and as far from the farm as they could. When Raul told Angelita that, she responded agitated, "Don't you think I have thought of that"? "I have begged her to go to the village and stay with some friends, but she won't leave."

Grandma's mind was made up and there was no changing it. This was her farm, it had been her father's, her grandfather's and in her family as far back as anyone could remember. She wasn't running away from anyone, and she had made that quite clear.

"Well, she's got balls," Raul said. "Will she at least stay out of the way so she doesn't get shot by accident?"

Angelita had convinced her to stay in the kitchen when the troops arrived and she was really hoping Grandma would do it; only time would tell for sure.

"Do we have a plan of action yet, or do we need to make one now?" asked Raul.

Angelita picked up a sledge hammer that was on the floor in the barn and knocked one of the slats, that was very close to Raul's head, off the side of the barn. He could now see outside for the first time since arriving at the farm. Examining the outside area, he estimated the house at about 200 yards away and he noticed that he had a clear shot at anyone on the front porch or in the front area of the house.

"What's behind the house?" he asked.

Angelita then began to explain the entire layout of the farm in great detail. She explained that behind the house was a small field area with a stream and behind that was the foothills to the mountains he could see just past the house. She also explained that the area to his right was a soft sand pit that was very dangerous because it had some type of "quick sand" in it. She said that they lost two or three pigs a year that wandered under the fence she had made around it, to keep people out.

"Is there anyone else here with you who can help?"

She told him that except for Jose and his wife they were alone.

"Jose and his wife?" Raul asked.

"Yes, they work here for Grandma and me. Jose helps with the pigs and Maria helps Grandma in the house. During harvest time I have two cousins who live in the village and come out here to help."

"How old are the cousins, and can you get them here quickly?"

"Pedro is about seventeen and Tito is in his thirties. I'll send Jose for them now."

"I'm going to need a carpenter. Do you know one?" Raul asked.

"Jose does all the carpenter work here. He's pretty good at it."

"Great, when everyone is here, join me in my office here at the barn and bring some Lysol back with you."

"What is Lysol?" she asked.

Raul laughed and said, "Not important, my sweet little angel, just hurry. I miss you when you're not here."

Forty-five minutes later everyone except Grandma was in the barn and the plans were being made. Raul had told Pedro to move the fence that was around the sand pit to the other side of the roadway, making the obvious access to the barn through the pit. Pedro looked a little confused, but said he had some friends and the job would be done in two hours.

"Tito, on the other side of that access, do you see a great place for a trench?"

"A trench sir? I don't understand."

Angelita had already told Raul that there was a working backhoe on the farm and that Tito knew how to run it, so the rest was easy.

"Dig a trench on the other side of the new walkway we are making, and fill it with brush, wood, anything that will burn. Then, soak it in gas or diesel fuel, whichever you can find, understand?"

"Yes sir, but if we set that on fire anybody close would have to run toward the sand pit and would die anyway."

"Yep, life's a bitch and if those assholes come here to dance, let's give them a prom to remember."

"Sir, excuse me, but what is a prom?" Tito asked quite innocently.

"Not important, my friend, but what is important is that when you finish the trench, you look directly at the barn and spot the plank that is missing on the wall. After you find it, set a pole into the ground and tie this detonator to it. Make sure it is facing the barn. Got it?"

"Yes sir, I will do that exactly as you say, and quickly, too." Raul looked into this man's eyes and knew he was afraid for all of them. "Good man, I know you will".

"Sir", said Jose, "What can I do to help?"

"Glad you asked," Raul responded. "I'm going to need you to get your saw, some nails, a hammer and whatever else you have and get back here, pronto."

"Maria," he said. "All you have to do is go into the house, and keep Grandma in the kitchen. Keep her from getting shot."

"With bullets?" she asked, wide-eyed.

"Well, I see nothing gets past you," Raul said sarcastically, although really not wanting to and sorry that he did.

Before he could say anything else, Angelita interrupted by saying, "Nobody here is used to what's going on right now and for sure what is going to happen, so try your best not to sound like a jerk. Or is that how Navajo Indians talk to old women?"

Raul really did feel like a jerk, a complete jerk. These people were doing everything they could possibly do to help him, a stranger who meant nothing to them. Raul thought to himself, "Raul, next time you're going to be an asshole, try to do it when no one is around, ok?"

Before anything else could be said, Jose was back with his tools and some wood and was ready for some plans. An hour or so later, they, Angelita, and Jose, under the direction of Raul, had constructed a tripod-type holder for his rifle and a ramp device he could lay on so he could get off clear shots. They had replaced the board on the barn wall and cut a series of small ports in the wall, one for the rifle and one that they fixed to hold Raul's binoculars so he could do his own spotting. The port for the rifle was made in the shape of a cross, which gave Raul maneuverability for shots in all directions, along with an unobstructed view for his scope.

By six o'clock in the evening everything was in place and they were as ready as they could possibly be. Raul checked his weapons and put the silencer on his rifle because he needed all the edge he could get. If the bad guys didn't know they were being shot, it would take them that much longer to find him. "Good plan," he thought.

Raul had given his Glock to Angelita and had shown her exactly how to use it, along with two extra full clips. They had no idea how many guerillas would show up in the morning, but they wanted to be as ready as they could for whatever happened.

The plan called for Jose and Angelita to protect the house and keep everyone safe on that end. Jose was equipped with a machete and a revolver that looked like Jesse James may have used it, but he was comfortable with it, so what else mattered?

He would watch the back of the house, Angelita would watch the front, and Raul was going to try to protect everyone, bad leg and all. They had sent Pedro and Tito back to the village thanking them and assuring them they would be okay, and not to worry. Well, it sounded good anyway, even though everyone had their doubts.

Darkness came and left while Raul struggled with pain in his leg, not wanting to take any pain killers, because he needed a clear, straight head for today's work. Angelita had spent the night going back and forth between the house and the barn.

She had been so wired in anticipation that sleep had been impossible for her as well. About 6am, to everyone's surprise, Pedro and Tito entered the barn. But what was more surprising was that Pedro had an AK-47 and 10 full clips. Tito was equipped with two Smith and Wesson 9mm automatics. When Raul looked closer, he saw Tito was carrying a box of something, and in a minute he was about to find out what. Tito said, "I must first tell you that everyone in the village supports you. These bandits have terrorized us for years and we are so happy to see that maybe there is help for us. We are all sorry about what happened to your leg, but we also cannot help but think maybe God sent you to us and we all thank him for that. Pedro has a book about the Indians in your country and last night we looked and found the tribe called Navajo. You are from a tribe that was known as great fighters, with some of the wisest of 'how do you call them'?"

"Medicine Men," Pedro responded...

"Yes, medicine men" replied Tito. "Anyway, we found this picture of a Navajo Indian, and we thought you might want it."

It was a good thing that Raul was lying down already, because when he saw the picture you could have knocked him over with a feather. The picture was of a Navajo War Chief in full dress, sitting on a war horse. Under the picture was printed the name "Lightfoot", War Chief of the Navajo, 1868. Raul was speechless; all he could think of was what Grandpa had told him in his vision and the actual vision he had seen of the War Chief. All Raul could say was, "thank you, this means a lot to me". Raul had heard Grandpa speak of this chief in the past, but had never seen a picture of him. Up until this point, he really had no interest in history, so had never really researched it. "Quite impressive", he thought. "I came all the way to Colombia to find my roots. How ironic."

"If you like that, then you're really going to like this," Pedro said.

Tito and Pedro then opened the box, which contained a pair of two-way radios, plastic explosives, and about a dozen or so sticks of dynamite.

Raul smiled from ear to ear and asked, "Do you by chance have the detonators that go with the plastics you brought?"

"Yes, sir," Pedro said very proudly. "Tito works in the emerald mines to the North of here and he knows all about how to make this plastic stuff explode and everything!"

Angelita then said quite excitedly, "you know the old truck that is sitting behind the house?" Everyone looked at her in anticipation as she smiled and said, "Tito, get the tractor and pull it around front, you know, where they will enter."

"Yes, yes I see. We will do it right now, quickly."

Raul interrupted, "Good idea. Take one of the radios with you and enough plastics with a detonator to make the bad guys wish they hadn't shown up for this dance."

"Pedro, go with him and help him with the truck then come back here."

"Tito, set the explosives, then hide with the detonator and let me know when they're coming. Hurry, there isn't much time. I can feel it."

As they were hurrying off, Raul chuckled when he heard Pedro say to Tito, "Tito, what is this dance thing he keeps talking about?"

It was eleven thirty when the two way radio announced that the troops were approaching and Tito could see what looked like seventy-five to one hundred men walking, preceded by two Jeeps. It looked as though the leader was in the first Jeep, along with a driver. In the second Jeep there appeared to be a driver, one bandit, and a young kid that looked like he had been beaten up.

Raul told Pedro to run to the house and let them know what was going on, and to get ready.

"You want me to return here, right?" Pedro asked as he was leaving.

"Correct, and make it quick. I don't want them to see you yet".

"Yet?", he repeated. "But I thought we were snipers and supposed to be hiding here?"

"No, I'm a sniper and you are a target, so hurry up and get back here".

"Yes, sir, I will be back very quickly and start being a target, and a good one. I won't let you down, I promise".

Raul started preparing for the inevitable battle that was going to occur. "God, I hope these people don't get hurt here", he thought. "This is not really their fight, it's mine, and they are stuck right in the middle just for helping me. Sometimes life really sucks."

Pedro was back in what seemed to be five minutes. "OK, I'm ready to do this target thing, let's kill bad guys."

Raul looked at him, shook his head and said, "Fine, try to control yourself. There's plenty of time to get shot at. For now, come over here and help me get on the ramp so I can see what's going on."

Pedro helped him with the logistics and lay down in front of the binoculars. Raul was watching through the scope on his rifle. After five minutes of Pedro's continuous chatter, Raul stopped what he was doing, turned to Pedro and said very calmly, "Listen to me very carefully. If you are talking, you can't be paying attention to what you are doing, and that's going to get us killed. Therefore, if you don't shut up, I'm going to be totally justified in slitting your throat to shut you up. That's sniper rules. Do you totally understand what I'm saying?"

"Yes, sir, I do, but I can't control myself. When I'm scared, I can't stop talking. A doctor once told me it was reflective action. Raul looked at the boy and said "reflexive, not reflective". Raul then commenced to explain to the boy that all normal people were afraid before a battle for lots of different reasons, and not to let it consume him. He told him about how all the great Navajo Chiefs would tell the warriors that any day you die in battle was a good day to die.

"This is what I do," he said. "Any time I have to wait before battle I remember my favorite song and I play it over and over in my head while I watch everything around me. Can you do that?"

"Well, I really like…

"Stop" Raul ordered. "Don't tell anyone your thoughts; it's bad medicine." This seemed to work quite well. The boy shut up. Life was good. Five minutes before noon, the radio sounded, but this time very softly.

"Sir, they are here, they are in front of the farm. They have stopped and are just looking. The man in the first Jeep is standing up and has binoculars like yours."

Raul thought to himself, "at least the guy leading the group has a little bit of brains, he's not just rushing in blindly. "

"A formidable foe", he thought, "now lets see how smart he really is". Less than a minute later, Tito was again talking very quietly, obviously way too close to the enemy and Raul hoped he had enough sense to retreat far enough so he wouldn't be killed by his own blast.

"Sir, he is dividing up the men. It looks like a little less than half are staying out on the road and he is coming in with the other group."

"Good work, Tito, now back away from them and get the detonator ready and wait for my signal. No matter what happens, wait for my signal. Got it?"

"Yes sir, no matter what, I'll be waiting. You can count on me."

"These people really wanted you to know you could count on them", Raul thought. "But, that was a good thing, not like a lot of people he had met who would tell you anything and then did whatever they felt like. This is kind of refreshing."

Now Raul could see the lead Jeep approaching the house. He was watching through his scope and could make out every detail of the man standing in the Jeep. This was the man he had been sent here to kill. The description was perfect. Approximately 5'9" tall, 200 to 210 pounds, ruddy complexion, black bushy hair and about 45 years old. "A short, fat, ugly fuck with an attitude. Yep, that was him." All Raul needed to confirm his soon-to-be- kill, was for this guy to announce his presence like all really obnoxious people had to do. The Jeep pulled up to the front of the house and honked the horn. When nobody responded to this action, this jerk pulled out a bullhorn. He actually carried a bullhorn to announce his presence. "Was he full of himself, or what?" Raul thought.

"This is General Miguel Santiago. Open the door and come out here right now or I will set your house on fire." Angelita came out of the house and was standing by the door, acting like the scared Colombian she was supposed to be. Santiago then demanded, "Who is in the house with you? And don't lie, like all you stupid farmers do so well." Angelita was pissed, and Raul could see it, but she handled it quite well, he thought.

"My grandmother and the lady that takes care of her."

"That's it; you don't have a Gringo pig hiding here with you?"

"No sir, why would you think that?"

The General then held up Raul's satchel that he had brought with him, the one he obviously lost in the jungle. "Because, my sweet little thing, in this bag is my picture and a bunch of stuff about me. We found it in the jungle where you helped him."

"Where I helped him?" she asked innocently.

The man in the second Jeep then, upon receiving a signal, brought a boy, who had been beaten badly, to the first Jeep.

The boy had a rope around his neck and his hands had been bound behind him. "Go into the house." Santiago ordered Angelita. "And get your grandmother. Bring her out here; I want her to see how you lie."

Angelita responded by telling him that her grandmother was very old and sick and could not walk, and that she spent her days in bed.

The General then leaned over to his driver and said something to him that Angelita could not hear.

The driver jumped out of the Jeep and ran to the house, pushed past Angelita and entered. A couple of minutes later he reappeared with Maria and confirmed, "Sir, the old woman is in the bed and she looks dead. This is the woman taking care of her."

Angelita thought, "What an actress Grandma is."

The general pounded his fist on the top of the Jeep's windshield and got out of the Jeep. "This man, one of my soldiers, saw you in the jungle with this gringo and told me you helped him. Is that true?"

The boy was crying and had his head hung so no one would see it, but Angelita knew that he was scared to death of this man.

"Sir first of all, that is not a man. He is just a boy, and who beat him up like that?"

"I did, but you don't ask General Miguel Sanchez questions. Who do you think you are?"

"Sir, all I see is what is right and what is not, and I don't think beating up a boy to get him to confess anything is right."

"Maybe I'll beat you up", he replied, laughing. "I run this area and nobody questions *me*, do you understand?"

"You beat up women, too?" she inquired, defiantly.

Raul could not quite make out what was being said, but he heard the General screaming at Angelita and figured she was probably getting to him. The General then jumped out of the Jeep and grabbed the boy by the hair screaming, "Is this the woman with the gringo you told me about?"

The boy, with tears streaming down his face, didn't want to say it and Angelita knew it by the look on his face. "Yes sir, that is the woman."

The General then exclaimed. "Good, now I don't need a coward like you anymore!" He then took out his pistol and shot the boy in the back of the head. The boy's lifeless body fell to the ground, and the general laughed and spit on the corpse. "Now you see what I do to people who piss me off? So tell me where the Gringo is so I don't get pissed at you."

Angelita was staring at the boy's body on the ground, unable to speak, and Maria was making the sign of the cross on her chest, praying for the boy this pig just murdered.

"Hey, lady, I'm talking to you!", the General growled, "Now you have forced me to have to kill the fat lady next to you, and then the old lady in the house, and soon everybody here will be dead and I will take this farm. Won't that be nice?"

Raul was so focused on what was happening that he didn't see how the boy next to him was shaking, sweat pouring down his face. There was a good possibility that he wouldn't be any help at all; only time would tell.

Raul was watching, and as soon as the general turned to the man who had been holding the rope with the boy attached to it, he raised his gun in the direction of the women on the porch. Raul took the first shot. Raul was using copper tipped .223's and the high speed bullet pierced the throat of the man so quickly that he just stood there.

"Shoot the fat lady!" the General yelled, "do it now!" In response the man fell over dead. Raul was using the silencer, and even though it cut down on distance travel for the bullet, 200 yards didn't really make that much difference.

No one heard the shot, and the General had no idea why this man fell over, until he saw the stream of blood coming from his throat. "What the fuck is going on here?" he screamed, "Who shot him?"

Everyone in his group was looking at each other in confusion, unable to figure out what had happened. This allowed Angelita to get herself and Maria back in the house and safe for the moment. The General glanced around wildly, trying to figure out what- or who-was shooting at them. Every time the general looked away from the barn, Raul took another shot and soldiers were dropping like flies. In total frustration, the General ordered his men to open fire on the house and kill everyone inside. The men started shooting at the house and the General, the brave hero that he was, was hiding under the Jeep.

"What a warrior," Raul thought sarcastically, and started taking out all the soldiers around him. Raul had shot about twelve of them before it dawned on them that everyone close to the General was getting killed, so they all began quickly retreating away from him. Raul needed to draw them away from the house and toward the barn so he said, "Pedro, it's time to be a target, are you ready?"

Pedro looked and him with terror in his eyes, and after collecting himself said "yes sir, what do I do now?"

What Raul wanted was for Pedro to run to the door of the barn where they could see him, and fire his rifle into the air. Then retreat back into the barn, quickly.

"Yes sir, I can do that with no problem."

Raul got ready, and Pedro went to the door and fired off two rounds at the soldiers. The General then withdrew from under the Jeep and yelled, "In the barn, he's in the barn, get him and bring him to me now!"

Raul wanted very much to take this man out right then and there, but very cautiously the General would not leave the cover of the Jeep. Besides, there were about thirty armed men running toward him so he was pretty preoccupied anyway. The General would have to wait. But his time would come, and that was a promise Raul made to himself. The men started running toward the barn and about half were stuck in the quicksand before they even realized it. They started screaming for help, and the others just ignored them and started to run around them, right toward the trench. Raul waited patiently until most of them were right next to the trench, and one shot later the trench exploded in flames.

"That was a very good shot sir; you are very skilled with the rifle, I noticed."

When the trench erupted into flames, about two thirds of the men in the area also burst into flames. Thus, the General had a problem. He rectified it by calling for the rest of the men waiting by the road and they began obediently running along the farm entrance.

"Tito, are you there?" Raul asked.

"Yes sir, I'm waiting like you said."

"Good. When the biggest part of this group gets by the truck, blow it up. Got it?"

"I'm ready sir."

"Perfect, after it blows stay hidden. I don't want you to get shot by accident, understand?" Pedro looked at Raul and said, "Excuse me, sir, but I don't think you ever do anything by accident."

Raul didn't have any idea how many explosives were in that old truck, so he told Pedro to get under something and hide as well. Pedro did what he was told and the stage was set, as they say. About three or four minutes passed, and then the explosion.

The truck went about 20 feet in the air along with a whole lot of bodies and their respective parts. Raul eyed the results of the explosion and knew they, or someone, would be cleaning up this mess for quite some time. The General was furious. He ordered a soldier, with what looked like a hand-held rocket launcher, to shoot at the barn. Raul knew this was a major problem, and as soon as the man shouldered the launcher, Raul shot him right between the eyes.

The man dropped the launcher and fell dead. The General yelled for another man to grab the launcher, and once again, as soon as he picked it up he fell over dead. The General's army had dwindled to about 15 or 20 men, and he truly looked a little concerned for his own safety, if not for his soldiers'. The General had ordered a total of five men to pick up the launcher, and all five lay dead next to each other. When the General ordered the sixth man to pick up the launcher, this man ran in the opposite direction and the General shot him in the back.

The General now had approximately 9 men left in his army and was out of options. He wanted to retreat, but he had been blocked by the old truck, and a whole lot of dead bodies.

"So, now what?" Raul wondered.

The General called for his driver, and then realized that he, too, had been shot when the men started shooting at the house. The General then turned to his remaining nine-man army, and ordered them to go into the house and bring him any one that was still alive.

"I'm going to need some sort of shield from the crazy man shooting at us from the barn." he grumbled. Raul normally could have never heard that remark, but this moron was talking to the last of his army through the bullhorn.

Angelita had also heard the General, and to the surprise of every single person there, she opened the door, walked out on the front porch, and raised the Glock pistol that was in her right hand. She pointed it directly at the General, who was frozen in astonishment, and announced, "The world will be such a better place with out the likes of you."

She then commenced to put three bullets directly in his chest. The General was so shocked at this, that he stood by the Jeep and proclaimed, "You can't shoot me. I'm the General."

Angelita's reply was classic. "No.... you're the Dead General", and put the fourth bullet right in his head.

Raul watched as the General's head exploded like a grapefruit in a vice, just as he fell to the ground. The rest of his army stood there, not knowing what to do, and with no leader, what better time to leave than now? And that they did quickly.

It was over. The farm was safe and so was his little angel, he thought. "This was a good day." Raul said to himself.

Now for the clean up. Angelita came running into the barn, right to where Raul was lying on the ramp, and kissed him over and over.

"Thank you for helping us rid ourselves of that garbage! You have made our lives so much better. We all owe you so much."

"If I'm not mistaken, I was the guy with all the problems when you found me. So it's you who has helped me. Oh, and by the way, keep the Glock. You certainly earned it." Angelita lay down next to Raul and was holding him so tightly that he actually forgot about how much his leg hurt.

Pedro appeared from wherever he was hiding in the barn and asked, "It is safe to come out now?"

"It certainly is, partner; go and find Tito and see about getting the clean up started."

"Yes sir!" he responded, and he was off.

Raul and Angelita lay in the straw together for quite some time, not saying a word, just enjoying the moment.

Finally Angelita said, "Your leg will take quite some time to heal and I would like very much for you to stay here with us. Who knows? After today maybe Grandma will even come to like you!"

"Under one condition…..before I can even think about staying here for any length of time….."

"And that would be?" she asked with a smile.

"Not another night in this barn, the smell is killing me."

Angelita smiled from ear to ear and said, "I've already prepared your room in the house. In fact, your new bedroom looks very much like my room" she said coyly. "There is only one slight problem, though; the house will be under going some renovation, to patch up all the bullet holes. I hope you won't mind the noise and dust."

"Let me think, pig shit or dust? When do I move?"

Just then Jose came running into the barn all excited. "Angelita, there are at least fifty people on the road from the village, they have tools and food and are here to help us fix everything!"

The towns' people were so delighted to be out from under the oppression of the drug lord that they all stayed and helped repair, and made the farm even better than it was.

Word spread like wildfire about what had happened at the farm, and many stories started circulating about the Indian Chief from a place called New Mexico, and how he had battled the drug lords and won.

Raul was as happy as he had been in years, and felt that this could, in fact, be a great place to recuperate. Except for Hector, he didn't really care if anybody ever knew for sure what had happened to him. When the time was right he would contact Hector, and he knew that one day Hector would meet his Guardian Angel.

CHAPTER II

'RICKY'

In this moment of time I have lost you, my brother, but I will search for you forever, as I would search for myself. To be connected in spirit is to be one with another, and to find that being you need only to look deep within yourself.

Ricky had been working with the heavy bag about an hour and a half when the telephone rang. "Oh for crying out loud!" he shouted in utter disgust. "Doesn't anyone realize this is Sunday morning, for Christ's sake?" Ricky, in real life, is Richard Armstrong Nelson, an avid kick-boxing addict, who is presently employed by the CIA. He also works for one of his best friends in the world, Hector Lightfoot. Ricky's story is quite simple; he lost his father to a ground-to-air missile that struck his F-4C jet somewhere north of the DMZ in a little country called Vietnam. Ricky's father, although it is really unclear why to this day, was on some sort of secret mission during the Vietnam War that took him way north of the Demilitarized Zone into "the Badlands", as it was called, all alone. Whatever he had been doing cost Major Richard Nelson his life, but had also won him the Congressional Medal of Honor. Ricky's mother had been told some story about how her husband had done this and that and whatever else that was above and beyond the line of duty and hence the medal, a flag, a spot in Arlington cemetery , and his name on the Vietnam Memorial. The real truth, Ricky was sure, was stuffed in a secret compartment somewhere in the White House basement, along with who really killed Kennedy and a lot of other things that we, the taxpayers, weren't supposed to know about. Ricky's mother picked up the pieces quite well and continued on with her life. She was a beautiful, petite Brazilian lady who was a master in the art of Capoeira, the well know Brazilian art of dance and fighting mixed with beautiful choreography .

Juanita, Ricky's mother, had, by the time Ricky was 12, taught him to be almost as proficient as she. She would tell him, "you are my home-grown natural and you will go far in life." By this time, Ricky also spoke, understood and wrote English, Portuguese, and Spanish flawlessly. Ricky had always been a very quick learner and these languages came easy to him. Maybe that was why at thirty five he was a linguist for the CIA and had mastered approximately 9 others, along with a high proficiency in lip reading.

Ricky had acquired many skills from his mother and was very close to her up to the day she died from ovarian cancer. This had been two years ago, at the young age of 58. He had not thought life had been very fair to her, and he developed quite a disdain for powers way beyond his control. His mother would tell him not to be so bitter because, as she put it, "if God wants me now, then it's time, and I need to go. You'll be alright." Ricky buried his mother shortly after that, and was not really sure if he was alright or not.

He had become very quiet and withdrawn, and that had prompted the request to transfer to Hector's branch of the CIA.

Ricky's mother had always told him that he had received his good looks from his father. Richard Sr. had been a tall, blonde hair, blue eyed looker, with a perfect physique. Ricky was fortunate enough to obtain these genetic qualities, making him a perfect catch. The problem was that Ricky had no desire to be caught. He was a player, and had been completely content with his life as it was. Now at thirty five he was beginning to wonder if life was slipping away too quickly, and quite possibly he would die a lonely old man, with no one around him.

Ricky snapped out of his trip down memory lane, one of many he had taken lately, and realized the phone was still ringing. He picked it up and very rudely inquired, "What the hell do you want? At this hour on a Sunday morning, why aren't you in church or something?"

"First of all, I only go to church when my wife drags me and secondly, is this a bad time?"

Ricky rolled his eyes back. "Hector, how are you this morning? What is it already six a.m.? Why wouldn't you be calling me?"

Hector realized that early in the morning is when Ricky took out all of his aggressions on the heavy bag, and that he really didn't like to be disturbed. But this was important and Ricky would be glad he had called.

Ricky held the phone next to his ear and watched the bag swinging left to right. For some reason, he got a flashback of the last kick boxing tournament he had been in and why he left the sport. After mastering Capoeira, he had gotten into kick boxing and loved the sport every bit as much as Capoeira. He did very well at it, probably because of the Capoeira, or possibly just because he was a natural. He didn't know, and at this point in his life it really didn't matter much. He knew only one thing for sure, that he would never compete in tournaments again. At the age of 18 Ricky had killed another boy in the ring. It had been an unfortunate accident, and the county medical examiner had said so. There had been no blame put on Ricky, except for that which he had placed on himself. As a result, the kick boxing champion of Bridgeport, Connecticut, would enter the ring no more. Ricky knew that because of his father's Medal of Honor he could receive an automatic appointment to West Point if his grades warranted it. His scholastic abilities had never been an issue, and after the all-important acceptance of the idea by his mother, off he went to be a soldier, like his father.

Ricky had met Hector through his acquaintance of Raul in Granada some years back. Ricky was a Captain, assigned to intelligence, and had been introduced to Raul under quite extraordinary circumstances. Ricky had been in a place called "the Ridge", and by information from his own intelligence network, should not have had safety concerns in this area.

For some unknown reason, or factor, as they called it, two or three enemy snipers were making their lives hell, not to mention the dead bodies they were responsible for. Ricky had come to terms with the fact that he probably wouldn't be coming home in an upright position, when a voice came over his radio ordering him to get as far in the hole as he possibly could, and not come out until he was told to. Ricky had no idea who had given him that order, and when he tried to look around the first bullet whizzed past his head, nailing an enemy sniper who screamed and fell out of a tree. The next thing Ricky heard was from the radio once again.

"Listen, you stupid shit, get in the hole like I told you, I don't want to have to explain to my boss how I shot my save by accident. Do you hear me?"

Ricky was ecstatic over the fact that he might just go home on his feet and definitely decided to stay down as far as he could. It took Raul about an hour of patience and perfect marksmanship to take out a total of three additional snipers. Ricky looked up, and there was this guy he swore looked like an Indian, headband and all, standing over him.

All he could manage to say was, "and are you here to scalp me?"

With absolutely no facial expression, Raul said "Maybe. Get out of the hole, you have been saved."

Ricky climbed out and introduced himself, and thanked Raul for what he had done. That was how they met, and because Raul refused to wear any insignias of any type, no one ever knew what his rank or anything else about him was. This was perfect, because he blended in the officer's club well with Ricky, and probably because Raul looked so scary they could sit at the bar and drink as long as they wanted, undisturbed.

As the friendship grew, Raul introduced him to Hector, and when the time came, they both left the military together and joined the CIA. Raul had gone off to work directly for Hector while, until recently, Ricky had been working in European intelligence.

As far as Ricky knew, Raul had been killed on a mission in Colombia and no one had been able to recover his body. This really bothered Ricky, but he knew Hector was, with good reason, more bothered. So like all good CIA agents, nobody said anything.

"Ricky, I know it's Sunday and all that, but I have just received some top secret intelligence that has made reference to an injured man in Colombia. The information came off the top shelf in Russian. The Coast Guard intercepted some messages making these references, but the dialect is really strange and nobody could really figure out what exactly they are saying."

Ricky assured Hector that he could, and would be in his office in an hour and a half. He felt confident he could decipher the message. If this had anything to do with Raul, Ricky wanted to be right in the middle of it. After all, he owed Raul. And he would never forget it.

Exactly one hour and twenty minutes later, Ricky's red Corvette convertible drove into the underground parking facility at the offices of the CIA. After showing his credentials to security, he was granted access to the parking area and was soon on the elevator to the fourth floor, and Hector's office. To the surprise of absolutely no one, Hector was already at his desk shuffling through papers, acting as nervous as a turkey on Thanksgiving Day.

"You have the correspondence?" Ricky inquired.

"Right here. Take all the time you need, but do it quickly. I'm anxious to see what it says."

Ricky started reading the message, trying to get a clear understanding of what it said.

"Hector", Ricky said, "this is one weird message."

Hector leaned over Ricky and looked at the paper, not knowing why he did, because he had no idea what all that gibberish was, but felt he needed to do something.

"What do you mean, 'weird'?"

Ricky then commenced to explain that the message was talking about an Indian battle that occurred somewhere north of an area called Lake Guatavita, which was located about an hour north of Bogota, up in the mountains. He continued to decipher, and disclosed that the message was very unclear about the actual location of this battle, except that it was not far from a large wooded area, and was fought amongst the pigs. Ricky stopped and looked at the message again.

"That's exactly was it says, boss, I'm sure of it. 'Amongst the pigs.' Yep, that's it, that's what it says." As Ricky read on his face went very somber and had a pained look about it.

"What is it?" Hector asked, wide-eyed. " Tell me whatever it says. I want to know."

"I understand", Ricky said, "give me a minute to figure this out. This part is very interesting."

After about five minutes of forced silence, Hector looked at him pleadingly, and gestured with his hands to get on with it.

The part that Ricky found so very interesting was that this battle occurred some six to eight months ago, and if the message was correct, it was talking about a battle with some self-proclaimed drug lord, who called himself General Santiago. The message went on to describe how over a hundred people were killed and that a "Navajo War Chief" had been in the battle. Ricky and Hector looked at each other and simultaneously exclaimed, "They are talking about Raul!"

"Anything else?" Hector asked, anxiously.

"They are talking about some veterinarian who claims to have seen this War Chief, and that he knows the Navajo man fought the battle with serious injuries."

"Why?"

"Because he had helped him in the forest where he was hurt."

"Anything else there that we can try to figure out?"

"Yes" Ricky said, "the part that bothers me most".

With a concerned look, Hector asked him what that was, and told him not to spare him any detail.

"The last line says the War Chief is a ghost, and none of the other drug lords believe he is alive or even existed."

Hector picked up the phone and after a minute asked, "What's our latest intel on a Gen. Miguel Santiago?"

The note had not made reference to a first name for this general, and Ricky wondered how Hector knew this guy's first name so quickly. Hector saw the question on Ricky's face, and motioned for him to hold on one minute.

"Thanks, "Hector said into the phone, and hung up.

"Before you ask me," Hector said, "this Santiago jerk was the reason Raul was in Colombia."

Ricky's expression said it all. "He was a hit?"

"That's what he was." Hector replied, "However, intelligence has just informed me that he is either dead or underground, because there has been no activity from his group in at least eight months."

Ricky wondered if Raul had killed him. But how? None of this was making a whole lot of sense, but he did know one thing for sure. He was on the next jet to Bogota to investigate.

Hector told Ricky to go home and pack, and gave him the rest of the day to make some kind of arrangements. He was going to need someone who really knew the area to meet him in Bogota. This was definitely a job where the best of help would be needed; after all, Raul may still be alive and they needed to bring him home.

Monday morning, at seven sharp, the phone rang.

"What do you have for me? " Ricky inquired.

Hector wasted no time explaining that he had set up a meeting at El Dorado Airport in Bogota with a Colombian agent who was very familiar with the area.

"Ricky," Hector instructed, "Get over to the hanger at Dulles. They are waiting for you, and call me when you get to Bogota."

By 9 am Ricky was in the air on his way to Colombia. The Lear Jet they had procured for him was fast and comfortable, and it allowed for plenty of time for planning. The only problem Ricky could see was that he had no plan, and had no idea where to begin. He was really hoping the agent who was going to meet him had some sort of idea where to start. He was as anxious as a race horse at the gate, but had no idea where the track was.

Seven and one half hours later the plane touched down in Bogota and pulled into a secluded hanger, away from the main terminal. This allowed for entry into the country without all of the customs and immigration hoopla, and afforded Ricky some of the secrecy that was very much needed. He called Hector and told him he had arrived, and asked if he had any new information for him. He also wanted to know where the Colombian agent might be, as he had not yet arrived. As Ricky finished talking with Hector and was putting his cell phone away, a woman approached him. The woman was about 25 years old, he figured, slender with short dark hair. All of her features, like the olive skin and dark eyes, told him she was definitely a native of the area, but what he didn't know was why she was in this hanger. As she approached, Ricky eyed the beauty, and said, "I'm sorry lady, but I don't need a tour guide, {even though he really did,) and I'm not looking for company (even though he thought her company would be just perfect). How did you get in here, anyway?"

The beauty looked and him and smiled, obviously not offended by anything Ricky had said.

"First of all, you do need a tour guide. Secondly, how do you know my company would be that bad?" And lastly she announced," I'm here because this is my hanger and you are my guest." "Hello, my name is Esperanza Marcos, and I am the agent assigned to help you."

Ricky, not knowing quite what to say, looked at this beautiful woman and said the first thing that popped into his head. "I'm confused; I thought I was going to Bogota when I got into the plane. I had no idea I was going to land in heaven."

"That's sweet" she said, "but I am a professional. Keep that in mind, and, by the way, my friends call me Epi."

"Does that mean I can call you Epi?" he asked.

"Sure. Where we are going, all you are going to have is friends, or the people who want to kill you. Where's your bag?" she asked.

Ricky produced a carry-on type satchel and said," I'm all set, let's go!"

Epi looked at his bag and started laughing.

"Do you have any idea where we are going?"

"Looking for Raul, north of here", he said.

"Indeed we are... and the light jacket you have on will do you absolutely no good. And I don't see any other warm clothes in that bag."

Ricky looked a little puzzled because this was Colombia. How cold could it be in July?

"Agent Nelson," she said, "by the way, what is your first name anyway?"

"Richard, but my friends call me Ricky."

She continued to explain about the mesetas, or the mountainous plateaus around Bogota, as they are. The higher or further north you got into these mountains the colder it was. Temperatures in the thirty's and forty's would be normal in some of these areas.

"OK, then, where now?" he asked

"You know, I just thought of something" Epi said as they were walking out of the hanger.

"And that would be?" he asked, inquisitively.

"Your name, it's the same as the singer Ricky Nelson "she said with a smile.

As they walked, Ricky explained how his mother had always been a fan of Ricky Nelson's and when he was born they had named him after his father the fighter pilot. But his mother had admitted to him years later that deep down, she called him Ricky instead of Richard, because of her love for the singer.

"And as the years passed it just stuck, right?" Epi asked.

"You got it, and I'll bet that is why you are Epi, because over the years it just stuck."

They both climbed into Epi's Jeep Wrangler and off they went to buy Ricky a coat, long underwear, and whatever else he may need.

In the car, Epi handed Ricky a 14-shot S&W 9 mm. pistol and said, "I didn't know if you were going to bring one with you, so I took the liberty of getting you one. Hope you like it."

"Actually," he offered, "if I were to go into a store to buy a pistol, it would be this one exactly."

"You're not just saying that, are you? Because I don't need you to try to make me feel good about anything," Epi replied.

Ricky laughed and lifted his shirt revealing a S&W 14 shot 9 mm pistol. "Nope, I wasn't trying to make you feel good. I actually meant it."

"That's two things in common," Epi laughed.

Ricky, looking a little puzzled asked, "Two things in common?"

"Yep, we both go by nicknames and our weapons of choice are the same."

"You know what they say, 'three things make a match'."

"I guess I'll have to be looking out for number three", Ricky said as he handed the 9 mm back to Epi.

"Keep it" she offered," it may come in quite handy where we're going, and besides, you look like a two-gun kind of guy."

As Epi and Ricky were leaving the clothing store and heading toward her Jeep, Ricky spotted two men sitting in an old Ford pickup truck watching them. Epi told him to act as nonchalant as he could and just get in the Jeep. She would explain after. As they pulled away, the old pickup was right behind them. About two miles down the road, Epi, watching her rear view mirror, told him that the two men in the truck were police detectives from Bogota, and that she had first noticed them tailing them somewhere around the airport.

"So, what's up with them?" Ricky asked, trying not to look suspicious.

"Would you believe me if I told you they were on the take, and that they knew somehow that you were coming here? Their job is to report anything they find out to some drug lord."

"I have no problem believing that", Ricky responded.

Epi went on to further explain that some of the Cartels believed Raul was still alive, and had put a bounty on him. Therefore, dirty cops like the ones behind them came out of the woodwork in hopes to score big.

"Score big?" Ricky asked.

"Yes, if any of these cops could confirm Raul is still alive and where he is, it would be worth a lot of money to them."

"The cops are going to try to kill Raul if he is, in fact, still alive?" Ricky asked.

Epi observed him for a minute and answered, "No way the cops will try; none of them have the ability or the balls to go after the Navajo War Chief. But they will run to the Dons and tell them what they know, in hopes of clinching a big reward."

Ricky then told Epi that he had read something about this Navajo War Chief in the encrypted message they had uncovered, and wondered what she knew about the story.

Epi thought for a little while, and then began telling him a story about a man who had been found by a village girl up in the mountains some time ago.

"This man was a Navajo Indian from New Mexico."

"My God, that's Raul they're talking about! Please go on", Ricky begged, anxiously.

Epi continued, telling him that the Indian, according to the story, had seriously injured one of his legs.

"I really don't know what the injury was, possibly a broken leg or something similar. Anyway, when the girl found him, this Indian was starting to suffer from hypothermia and she dug a hole and put him in it."

"She put him in a hole?"

"Actually, that was very smart .She could put warm stones wrapped in cloth around him and kill two birds with one stone", she explained.

"Two birds with one stone?"

"Absolutely. The hole would trap the heat and she could cover him up because, you know, the guerillas knew he had landed in the woods for some reason. Maybe someone saw him parachute in, and word of anything out of the ordinary spreads like wildfire up in the mountains."

Ricky really wanted to know more, but was almost afraid to ask. Afraid of what he might hear. "Is there more about the story you can tell me?"

"Well what happened next is kind of sketchy at best, but I'll tell you what I know." Epi went on to explain how a doctor of some sort returned with the girl and he supposedly did whatever was necessary to stabilize this man enough to move him.

"Could this doctor have been a veterinarian?"

"Actually that was what I heard, but I wasn't sure how it would sound, and I really don't know if that is true or not."

"You know what? I think it is."

"Why do you think that?"

"The message we decoded made reference to a veterinarian. I don't see these people lying about that. How many vets can there be up in these mountains?"

"Are you kidding me? These mountains are loaded with farms. What kind of doctors do you think are up there?"

"What about the people up there, don't they have doctors for them?"

"Yes, I'm sure there are, but trust me when I tell you these people think more about their animals than they do about most people."

"Well, that certainly doesn't make them bad people in my book. There are a whole bunch of people in this world I would put animals in front of."

"Amen to that," Epi muttered.

As they drove, Epi told him that there wasn't anymore, other than there had been some sort of battle that had ensued as a result of this rescue, and the only other thing she did know for sure was that one of the prevalent drug lords of the area had been very quiet since that time.

"How quiet?" Ricky asked.

"No one has heard anything about him, and the other Dons are starting to move into the area a little at a time. I think the man's name was Santiago, if I'm not mistaken."

Ricky's face lit up. "Why do I feel that Raul is alive up in those mountains, and that he took out this Santiago character?"

Epi asked Ricky if he had anything that he could add that might give them a direction in which to start looking.

"The only other thing that really jumped out at me in this transmission was a reference to the battle with the pigs, or in the pigs, or something like that. Make any sense to you?"

"Actually it does. There is an area up there that has a lot of pig farms in it and that just might be a good place to start."

"I have to tell you, I really can't see Raul Lightfoot as a pig farmer."

"Stranger things have happened, or so I've been told."

As they continued driving north away from Bogota, Ricky couldn't help but notice the compact disc Epi was playing.

"This music is beautiful. Anybody I might know?"

"Marco Antonio Solis and the name of the CD is 'Primavera'. Do you know it?"

"Sorry, I don't, but I think I'm going to", he replied, smiling.

Another thing that Ricky couldn't help but notice was the old Ford pickup truck that was still following them.

"You know those two cops are still behind us, right?"

"Absolutely, I'm just waiting for the right time to get rid of them."

"Get rid of them?"

"Right, we have options. First, we can take them up in the mountains where we are going, and, with the lack of witnesses, kill them and leave their dirty, corrupt bodies for the buzzards. Or we could create a diversion of sorts."

"Diversion of sorts? What would that mean in real life?"

"Fucking around, trying to lose these assholes, and wasting time we don't have. Is that real enough for you?"

Ricky didn't even have a response for that. Probably because he was so shocked at her bluntness. But he kind of liked that. No-bullshit-just–the-facts kind of approach. Yeah, he did like it a lot!

Epi reached under the seat and pulled out a two-way radio.

"Big Brother, you there?"

"Go ahead, Little Sister, I'm all ears."

"I need some interference run on an old white Ford pickup, just south of the dirt road turn-off to Guatavita."

"Are you talking about the taco stand road?"

"Yep"

"Give me a minute."

Epi tuned to Ricky. "You know, he's not kidding, when he says he's all ears."

"What are you talking about?" Ricky asked.

"What big brother said about being all ears. He's got the biggest ears I've ever seen on a person. They remind me of radar dishes. He has tried to hit on me a couple of times, but every time I look at him face to face, I see these two radar dishes and start to laugh."

"Don't you think he may be a little insulted by your reaction to him?"

"Oh, he doesn't know I'm laughing at his ears. He thinks because his family has a lot of money, that I'm just excited about the prospects of dating him."

Just as Ricky was trying to think of something cute to say in response to this, the radio chirped in.

"Little Sister, you there?" asked the ears, as he would affectionately be known to them from now on...

"And where else might I be?"

"Right, go to the taco stand, pull in and park."

"Got it; I'm kind of hungry anyway."

"By the way, Little Sister, what's the status on the interference?"

"Two dirty cops. Need I say more?"

"Aren't you concerned that someone is monitoring your transmissions?" Ricky inquired.

"Actually I'm kind of hoping they are. Maybe they'll get scared and leave."

They drove a bit further, and Ricky saw this nasty looking taco stand with two or three tables in the front, outside. As they drove in and parked, Ricky muttered, "I was afraid this might be the place."

"What's the matter, no taste for adventure?"

The old truck parked across the street on the side of the roadway and the two Cops sat inside watching them.

"They are so predictable, so stupid," she observed.

Ricky and Epi sat at an outside table eating tacos and making small talk, mostly about how surprised Ricky was at how good the food was.

About thirty minutes later Ricky noticed a semi-truck traveling at a high rate of speed and heading directly at the taco stand.

"Epi, we need to move, right now! There's a big truck bearing down on us!"

Epi continued enjoying her food, looked at Ricky with a sly expression and remarked, "That's what I like about you Gringos, no trust, always in a hurry, ready to jump at a minutes notice. Patience, my love."

Ricky looked at her in shock and exclaimed, "What are you talking about?"

Before she could answer him, the truck swerved away from them and hit the Ford truck at about 45 to 50 miles an hour.

"Holy shit, did you see that?!" Ricky yelped.

"Yep, I certainly did. That was to the point, wasn't it?"

"Ok, let me ask the obvious. What about the two cops inside?"

"You mean the two dirty cops inside the truck? Who cares? You finished? It's time to get moving."

"I'm ready, when you are," Ricky responded, still not sure he really digested what just went on.

"Good let's go find a pig farm."

As they drove off towards the mountains, Ricky could feel the temperature starting to drop and was really glad Epi had suggested the coat. It was about 6 pm when they pulled into some little town named San-something- or -other. It seemed to Ricky that 90 percent of the towns in this country were named after Saints for some unknown reason.

"This town has a hotel, so lets stop here, get some dinner and start fresh in the morning," Epi said.

Ricky had that hopeful look in his eyes and she read him like a book.

"Forget it, mister, I don't even know you."

"And your point being?" he replied, sarcastically.

"Tell you what, trooper. You can buy dinner and pay for the rooms, both of them. How's that for a date?"

"Obviously you're on a limited expense account," he laughed.

In the morning they would set out to find the truth about the Navajo War Chief, and all the stories that surrounded the ominous battle in the mountains. But for now, it was starting to get colder by the minute, and a Vodka by the fireplace in the company of this beautiful Colombian agent sounded just right.

Morning came quickly, and Epi and Ricky were sitting in the hotel café having coffee when a rather distinguished- looking gentleman approached them.

"Sir," he asked very slowly in broken English. "Might I be of assistance with your tour plans today?"

"No thank you, sir, we are not tourists and we are just passing through," Epi replied in Spanish.

The man then said something in Spanish which they both felt was rather strange.

"I see, but just because one is not a tourist, does not necessarily preclude them from wanting information on the possible sights in the area, now does it?"

Not wanting to play more games with this man, Ricky spoke in Spanish so there would not be any doubt as to where this conversation was headed.

"If you are, in some round-about way, trying to sell us information about something we may, or may not be interested in, then stop screwing around and tell me how much you want, for whatever you think may interest us."

"Two hundred American dollars," the man said without hesitation.

"Bullshit," Ricky replied. "I can't think of anything you could tell me that would be worth that much money."

"I can tell you the name of the animal doctor that set your friend's leg, and where to find him."

"Will you take a check?"

The man just stood there and looked at Ricky; it was obvious he hadn't understood Ricky's humor.

"OK, OK," Ricky said. "But I want you to know that I think the humor level around here sucks."

"Duly noted. Now pay the man, and let's get moving before it's dark again," Epi snapped, obviously anxious to get going.

Ricky peeled off two one hundred dollar bills from his money clip and said, "Before I just hand you this, and you ride off into the sunset, what is it that you have to tell me?"

The man looked around a bit and said nervously, "You can't tell anyone I helped you. There are people here that would kill me for that."

"Check." Ricky replied. "I don't suppose the fact I don't even know your name would even come into play here, would it? So tell me what I want to know or get out of here. I'm losing patience with all the bullshit!"

"Yes sir, right now", the man said quickly. "The name of the animal doctor is Sanchez, and he has a house in the next pueblo about 7 kilometers north of here."

Epi asked the man for a description of the house, and more importantly, of Sanchez himself.

"The house is blue with a sign that says 'vetra'..... , I don't really know what the sign says, to be honest, I can't read. It probably tells what he does."

"And what about Sanchez, what does he look like?" she inquired.

"Very old, ma'am, that's what he looks like. Sanchez is in his eighties and has had a very hard life, like the rest of us. And it shows on his face and in his eyes."

"Thank you." Epi responded. "We do really appreciate your help, whether my friend here shows it or not."

Ricky handed him the money and added, "Like she said, thanks."

"I will tell you one other thing for free," he said, as he was leaving.

"And that would be?" Ricky sighed.

"Everyone up here knows you are here and that you are looking for the Navajo War Chief. That for some people is a good thing. For others it is not. And for you, it makes danger a big part of your future. Trust no one; that is important."

"What about you?" Ricky relied.

"I have not asked you for your trust, only for your money." And the old man was gone.

Epi reached in her pocket, pulled out some change, and put it on the table. Then she turned to Ricky.

"Go get our things and put them in the car, and I'll pay the bill and meet you there."

"Aye, Aye," he said, snapping a salute.

As she was leaving the room, Epi turned with a smile, grabbed her crotch, and exclaimed, "Salute *this*, soldier, and when you're done with that, bite me."

This Colombian girl impressed him to no end. "Where did she learn this stuff? One day I'll have to ask her", he thought, smiling to himself.

By 8 am Ricky and Epi were on their way to Dr. Sanchez's house, in the next pueblo. They found the house quite easily. After all, a dark blue house with a veterinary sign hanging out front, how hard could that be? Ricky and Epi walked onto the porch and knocked on the door. After about three minutes they heard noises coming from inside.

"Dr. Sanchez," Epi called. "I need to speak with you, it is important."

An elderly woman then appeared at the door and asked what they wanted.

"We need to speak with the doctor about a friend of mine," Ricky answered. "Please ma'am, it's very important."

"You want to speak with the doctor, maybe, like the other three did this morning?"

"What other three?" they chimed together.

"This morning, about two hours ago, three men in their twenties came to the office and wanted to talk to the doctor. They said they were paramilitary and it was official business. We, like everyone else here, don't want trouble so we do as we are told."

The old woman then led Epi and Ricky into a small bedroom in the back of the house. There they saw an old man lying in bed, holding a towel on his face. The old man did not look well at all, and they, Ricky and Epi, hoped he was going to be able to help them.

"Sir." Epi said. "May we talk to you for a moment, please?"

"Come over here closer, so I can see you my dear, my eyes are not what they used to be."

Epi and Ricky moved closer to the old man and then they saw why he was in bed, and it had nothing to do with his aging years.

The old man was holding the towel to stop the bleeding under his left eye and his face was swollen and distorted. Ricky was pissed and when Ricky was pissed, look out! The good, easy going guy in him left and the want- to- kick- the-shit- out- of -somebody guy entered.

"Sir, "those three assholes that were here this morning did this to you?" Ricky asked, quite abruptly.

Epi could see very quickly the change in Ricky.

"Please, Ricky, wait in the other room, and let me talk to the doctor."

"But I want to know about……"

"I know you do, and I'll find out everything I can, but whether you know it or not, you are scaring this old guy, and the last thing any of us needs, him included, is more trauma. Got it?"

Ricky knew she was right, and even though he wanted to talk to the doctor, he relinquished the space and waited in the other room.

While he was standing in the office area, or what he thought was the office area, waiting, the old woman reappeared.

"Those three young men, it was terrible what they did to Dr. Sanchez, and for no reason."

"What did they want to know, exactly?" inquired Ricky in his most charming manner.

"They said they knew he had helped the Indian assassin, and they wanted to know where he had taken him."

"What did the doctor tell him?"

"Very simple," she said. "He told them the truth. That the man had been injured in a fall and that he had helped him at the request of a young girl from the country."

"Do you know how badly the man was injured, and where he was taken?"

"You speak very good Spanish for a Gringo, how did you come to learn it?"

"My mother was from Brazil. But what about my question?"

"Brazil, that would mean you speak Portuguese, not Spanish."

"Can I ask you why you are avoiding my questions? I'm one of the good guys. This man who was injured is a Gringo like myself, and he is like a brother to me. So if you could help me out a little here, I would really appreciate it."

"From what I understand, the man we are talking about is not a Gringo. So maybe we are talking about different people?"

"What do you mean not a Gringo? Of course he is. And we are talking about the same man, I know we are. So please, lady, help me out here, I'm getting desperate. "

"The man I am talking about is not a Gringo, he is a Navajo Warrior Chief and he saved the people of San Remo from a very bad and evil man."

"Raul killed General Sanchez?"

"You know his name? Maybe you are what you say, and so I will help you."

"Thank you, thank you very much." Ricky smiled.

The old woman commenced to tell him that Angelita Marques, a girl from the San Remo area, had come to the office some eight months ago and asked the doctor to go into the forest with her and help a man she had found. She had told them he was a Navajo Indian from the country of New Mexico. The man, Angelita said, had fallen from a tree and broke his left leg. The bone was sticking through his pants. Dr. Sanchez, although he is a veterinarian by profession, has helped many people with their problems in this area. So fixing a broken leg was something he felt he could do. The doctor returned alone later that night, and told her about this Indian man, and that he, the Indian, had shot a para-military soldier and killed him. She went on to tell Ricky about Raul being in a covered up hole and how Angelita had told him about the three soldiers that had tried to rape her. She had killed one of them, and Raul had shot another in the head while lying on his back in the hole.

"Sounds exactly like Raul," Ricky responded. "What else can you tell me about that day?"

"Nothing more about that day, but within one week of the Indian's arrival there was a big battle at the Marques pig farm, and the terrorist pig named General Sanchez and all of his men were killed."

"And....what about Raul?" Ricky asked, very hesitantly.

"Oh, your friend, he is fine. Two days after the battle, Dr. Sanchez went back to the farm and made a cast for the Indian's leg. Now he walks perfectly, because Dr. Sanchez is a very good doctor."

"Raul is still in San Remo?"

"Of course, and on occasion we get information that new drug dealers have gone to San Remo. Either to collect the bounty the other Cartels have set on your friend, or just to try and set up their businesses in the area."

"What do you hear about that?" Epi asked as she entered the room. The old woman looked at her and smiled. "We hear that the ghost of San Remo has made them disappear."

Epi, with a grin on her face said, "Sounds good to me. Looks like, with all your charm, you and I have gotten about the same information.'

"How is the doctor doing?" Ricky asked.

"Not too well. He is pretty old, and those bastards beat him up pretty good. I have called big brother and a team will be here shortly to take the doctor and this woman... I'm sorry, what is your name, ma'am?"

"Lupricia Benitez-Sanchez."

"You are the doctor's wife?" Epi inquired,

"Heavens no, she died many years ago. I am Franco's sister."

"Oh, OK. Anyway, like I was saying, there is a heliport over by Lake Guatavita, so it shouldn't take more than a few hours for them to get here, and take both of them to the hospital in Bogota. Besides I'll feel better getting them out of harm's way until we wrap this up.

"Did the doctor give you anything on the three that beat him up?" Ricky asked.

"He thinks they are locals who are working with, or for, some drug scumbag in the area. Not a problem, I have their descriptions. I'm sure we will meet them one day soon."

Epi and Ricky thanked the old woman as they were leaving, and suddenly the old woman stopped and said, "Young man."

Ricky turned to her. "Yes ma'am?"

"For the record, the three that came here were not told everything that you were."

"Thank you again, I am indebted to you."

Ricky and Epi walked to where they had parked the Jeep, which was quite a ways from the doctor's office, as they did not want to draw suspicion toward the doctor. When they rounded the corner to where the Jeep was parked, there they were. The three thugs that had beaten up the doctor. One was sitting on the Jeep's hood and the other two were standing next to it.

Ricky looked at Epi and asked, "Are these the assholes that beat up the doctor?"

Epi responded. "They sure fit the descriptions the doctor gave me."

Ricky put his hands together in praying fashion and said. "Thank you God, I don't even have to waste time looking for these shit bags. They came to me, thank you again."

Epi just looked at Ricky, but she knew the three men by the Jeep had a serious problem coming their way.

"Get off my Jeep, you piece of shit!" Ricky yelled.

"Great introduction." Epi said as they walked toward the men.

The three men stood together. The one in the center had a switchblade knife in his right hand. The one to the right of him had a billy-club in one hand and what looked like an ice pick in the other. The one on the left, directly in front of Epi, was holding a machete. The man in the center said, "You are a very nosey gringo, and we are here to teach you a lesson." Ricky held out his left arm to stop Epi from advancing any further and said. "And you are a dead piece of shit, so let's get school started."

The first kick from Ricky hit the man in the center so hard in the face that it broke his nose, knocked out at least three teeth, and more importantly, broke his neck. The man fell dead on the ground with his eyes still open. The second kick was a spinning back kick, which caught the man with the machete right in the throat. He immediately dropped the weapon and grabbed his throat with both hands. Blood was coming out of his mouth, and he was turning blue. Epi knew questioning this one about anything was also out of the question. Epi yelled to Ricky just before the final kick was launched.

"We need one alive for questioning!"

The next kick was delivered, and Epi heard the loud crack when the man with the ice pick and club fell to the ground. The kick had been sent to this man's right knee. The knee was forced inward with such impact that it was completely distorted and obviously shattered. The man was lying on the ground in great pain, when Ricky leaned down to the man and said, "Listen sport, I have a couple of questions for you. Feel like talking to me? Because if you don't, I really don't need you, and you can join your dirt bag friends wherever shit-bags go after they die."

"Please sir, I need a doctor, help me."

"No can do, Pancho, you beat him up remember?"

"What do you want to know? Please don't kill me, I want to live."

"How about we start with, who do you work for?"

"But sir, I can't tell you that. If I do, he will kill me in a horrible way."

"You're sitting here with a smashed knee and worried about some guy that may kill you? What about your friends here? They look dead enough to me."

"Sir, pardon me, but you are a Gringo, and you have no idea the means of torture that are used here in Colombia."

"OK, tell me what you told this tyrant boss of yours."

"Only that there was a Gringo from the United States looking for the Navajo War Chief, and that we thought he was with a Colombian woman."

"And this information would do what good?"

"Don Carlos wants to kill the War Chief and collect the bounty the Cartels are offering."

Ricky was sure the man had not realized he had just given him the name he wanted, so he continued.

"So tell me, how much is my friend worth to this scumbag?"

"A lot sir, more than a life's worth of money."

"How much?"

"Twenty thousand American dollars."

"If he is worth so much why don't they just go up in the forest and get him?"

"Many soldiers have wanted this money and they have gone to the forest to do that, but none of them have returned."

Ricky looked over to Epi and asked. "Anything else we need to know from this guy, or should I just kill him now?"

The man had a terrified look on his face, and Epi watched cautiously. Ricky laughed and looked back at the whimpering man on the ground. "Just kidding! Crawl away from the Jeep, I need to leave."

Ricky and Epi drove off in the direction of San Remo. It was about a two-hour trip; not because of distance, but because of the very poor condition of the dirt road they had to travel.

Much of the distance was hampered by 'washouts' in the road; those being spots where heavy rains had created large holes and mud slides, washing away large sections of the roadway. Thus anything short of a four wheel drive vehicle would never be able to traverse the terrain. They arrived in San Remo about midday and decided to stop at a little café for lunch before going on. They needed good directions to the Marques' farm before leaving San Remo. Getting lost in these mountains would definitely not be conducive to good health. The problem lay in the fact that the temperature after midday dropped drastically, the area was filled with people that would cut your throat in a heartbeat, and strangers were not accepted nor wanted. Not to mention the wildlife in the area; little things like mountain lions, different breeds of wildcats, poisonous snakes of all sorts and sizes, etc. After discussing what lay ahead, over a delicious meal of beans and rice, the possibility of a guide came up. Ricky was trying to figure out who in the café might be able to suggest a guide, or point them in the right direction, when the waitress returned to see if they wanted anything else.

Epi then spoke to the waitress. "We are looking for a place up in the mountains. Could you suggest a guide or help us with directions?"

"Depends..." she replied.

Ricky, being up to his ass in the games people played here, said, "Are you talking about geriatric diapers, or what?"

Epi was the only other one at the table that had a clue as to what he was referring, and she smiled as she asked the waitress, "We want to go to the Marques' farm, can you help us?"

"No ma'am, I can't help you. I'm a good catholic, and sending you there would get you killed. I don't want to have to tell the priest at confession that I did that."

Ricky had an idea. "Listen, what if I told you that the Navajo War Chief was my brother? And I'm just trying to find him. "

The waitress looked at Ricky in total defiance and said, "The Navajo War Chief is a ghost, and just a story people tell up here. And besides, you, sir, are a Gringo. If the Chief did exist, how could you possibly be his brother?"

Epi looked at Ricky and started to laugh, then said in English, "Your Spanish is very good, I'll give you that; but that was one of the lamest stories I've heard in a long time. Did you really think she would buy that?"

"Well, I'm sure that out here, in the middle of 'Bumfuck, Egypt', you have a better idea?" he laughed.

Epi turned and looked around the café for a minute and stopped suddenly. She fixed on a table with a single person at it. It was a boy, maybe 18 or 19 years old, eating lunch, not looking at anyone and totally minding his own business. Epi got up, walked over to the table and sat down with the boy. She returned about 10 minutes later and said, 'Paco will guide us most of the way. There is, however, a slight problem.'

"And that would be?"

"The road, or what there was of it, is completely gone in sections, and we can't drive more than maybe two or three miles north of town. The rest is on foot."

"This 'on foot' part, constitutes how much of the trip?"

"It's only about, maybe five miles, give or take. No problem for a stud such as yourself."

Ricky looked directly into her gorgeous eyes, and said, "I can't go another step until I ask you something. Where did you learn your English? I know it wasn't in school; you had to have learned it on the street long before school. Were you born in the States or something?"

"No, I was born in Barranquilla. You know the town where Shakira is from?"

"Shaka…..who?"

"Oh man, you need to get out more."

"Get out more?"

"Never mind. To answer your other question, I graduated from the University of Miami, and yes, I am a Canes, Marlin, and Dolphin fan. I lived in Miami 7 years, therefore, my handle on the English language and American men.

"So tell me, how did you get Paco to want to take us to the farm?"

"Very easy. I told him you would give him three hundred dollars to guide us."

"No wheeling or dealing, just give him the money, that's it?"
Wheeling and dealing?…. I'm not sure if I understand that."

"Bullshit! You understand everything. Who are you trying to kid?"

"That being the case, lets go meet Paco outside and you can give him the money. We need to get going before it gets too late and starts to get way too cold to be trouncing through the woods. Besides, we don't know how many 'big bad wolves' we will meet on the way to Grandma's house, do we?"

It was about one o'clock when they finally got going. Ricky had called Hector once again and given him the latest update.

"Don't forget, as soon as you find Raul, you call me. I want to talk to him as soon as I can. If I sound anxious, it's because I am."

"I understand, Hector, you will be the first one on my list to call. In fact, the only one on my list to call."

After about an hour and a half of some of the worst roadways you could possibly imagine, they came to the part where there was no longer any road.

"One thing is for sure," Ricky said. "I've been cured about bad-mouthing the roads in the Northeastern part of the United States."

They were all on foot now, walking through all the mud and slop not far from the farm, but having no idea when they would arrive.

Paco saw it first, and stopped dead in his tracks. He held up his left hand and whispered loudly, "Quiet please! I don't think it saw us, and it will keep moving, hopefully."

'It', was a huge mountain lion, looking for something to eat. All three of them were frozen in position. Nobody wanted the lion's attention. All of a sudden it turned, looked at them and growled. There it was, three hundred pounds of pure horror, looking right at them. It started to charge them. Paco yelled, "Go for a tree, anything, but run!"

The mountain lion was bearing down on them rapidly. Were the S&W's going to do the trick?

They didn't know, but they were out, and ready to shoot. When all of a sudden there was a loud cracking sound in the woods. The lion stopped immediately turned to his right, the direction the shot came from, and fell over dead.

The three of them were momentarily frozen in shock, and then started looking around, to see if they could tell where, and from whom the shot had come. Ricky had an idea, but saw no one.

In what seemed to be only a couple of minutes after the lion kill, they started to hear voices and the sound of footsteps running in their direction. They had just a few seconds to hide. The voices did not sound friendly and Ricky and Epi were ready for trouble. Paco, on the other hand, had found a hole, gotten in it and was shaking uncontrollably. He was scared. This fortified their thoughts that trouble was headed their way. Ricky saw a good-sized hole, large enough for two. A very large tree had fallen over, stump and all, creating a fairly good hiding place. He grabbed Epi and they both jumped in. It was about another minute before they saw a group of para-military troops come into sight. They started looking around wildly, obviously trying to find the three of them. A man, apparently the leader, immerged from the group and yelled, "We know the three of you are up here. Come out now, and we will show mercy and kill you quickly. No torture, I promise."

"There's a deal." Ricky whispered sarcastically to Epi, and before he could say what he was thinking, 'Who put these assholes on us?' the leader pulled a man from the group and demanded, "Tell me again how many there are. And get it right!"

"That's him - the man from the doctor's office - smashed knee and all", Ricky whispered. "I should have killed him too, I knew it."

"There are two for sure, Don Carlos, and the waitress told us some idiot from the town was guiding them."

"For your sake you had better be right. If this is a trap set by the Navajo Ghost, I will cut your throat before we leave here. Do you understand?"

He then threw the man down to the ground and planted one foot on his poorly splinted knee. The man was crying in pain, and for that, this Don

Carlos fellow kicked him right in the face, and told him to shut up. An act very easily accomplished, as the man passed out from all the pain.

The leader then ordered his group, comprised of about 15 soldiers, to start searching the area and then bring each person they found to him, alive.

Paco was in his hole shaking and whimpering so loudly that they found him very quickly. They took him to the leader and threw him down in front of Don Carlos.

"Why didn't you surrender like I told you, you stupid boy?" Ricky and Epi were able to see what was happening from their position, but just couldn't do anything about it. Don Carlos had the boy searched and they recovered the three hundred dollars that Ricky had paid him. "Where did you get this?" Don Carlos demanded as he was putting a rubber glove on his right hand.

The boy said nothing, just stood there while this son of a bitch started punching Paco in the face. After about three minutes of that, Don Carlos nodded to the man behind the boy, who grabbed him by the hair and pulled his head back with his left hand. With his right hand he slit the boy's throat. While the boy was bleeding to death, Don Carlos reached into the opening with his gloved hand and withdrew the boys tongue. As the boy was falling to the ground, dying, Don Carlos proclaimed laughingly, "There's a necktie for you, a Colombian necktie. Probably the only necktie you have ever had." Don Carlos was laughing loudly as the boy's legs jerked uncontrollably. His body went lifeless, surrendering to death.

Epi had her hand over her mouth and tears in her eyes; not because she feared for herself or Ricky, but because she had brought this boy into the woods, and for that he had suffered a horrible death.

"This was just a boy, no chance to live, no chance to do anything", she thought to herself. This affected Epi deeply, and would take a long time to heal, if in fact they had any time left themselves.

Ricky's reaction was of a different nature; in a word, rage. "I am personally going to kill this sadistic fuck, and make him suffer when I do," he promised himself.

Now they had serious problems to plan for, and they needed to concentrate on them now. Them, being the 15 troops in front of them with the crazy man in the lead.

"Epi, something is not right here. Who shot the mountain lion? It sure wasn't one of them. Someone else is out there."

Before Epi could even respond, they heard another crack, and the man that had slit the boy's throat screamed and threw his hands over his eyes. Blood started oozing from between his fingers and he dropped to his knees. Within seconds he was dead. There was four more shots in succession, and four more of the soldiers fell dead. The leader was totally stunned and yelled at the man on the ground with the smashed knee.

"You lied to me. This is a trap!"

The last thing the injured man heard was the shot from the 45 cal. automatic the leader had in his hand. The shot took off the top of the man's head at that close range.

"Raul is out there", Ricky offered excitedly. "That's who shot the lion, and he's shooting the soldiers. Here I am in a hole, pinned down, and there he is rescuing me. Talk about 'Déjà vu'!"

By the time the leader of the group had finished killing one of his own men; Raul had dropped three more soldiers. This sadistic, crazy man's army was dwindling rapidly. The soldiers were now scattering and running for cover .They were firing their automatic weapons recklessly in all directions, making it almost impossible for Epi and Ricky to get out of the hole and shoot back.

"Please don't kill the leader, I want him!" Ricky cried out loud, knowing that with all the shooting going on nobody could possibly hear him, but he so needed to kill the crazy bastard.

The wild shooting soon faded out and the troops were now shooting randomly at locations in the wooded area where they thought the 'Ghost Warrior' might be hiding.

This was a break for Ricky and Epi, because now the troops were distracted by Raul and had, for the most part, forgotten about them. They were now able to raise their heads over the edge of the hole and they were, for the first time, able to see where the troops were hiding.

"If I only had a radio I could spot for Raul. I have the perfect vantage spot and no way to tell him," Ricky told Epi.

Epi's response just blew him away; he never expected such brilliance, nor thought of the idea himself at all. But what a great idea if it worked. Epi had told him to try calling Raul on the phone. "Maybe he has it with him? And if luck is with us, the call will go through."

Ricky dialed Raul's cell and held his breath. After four rings he heard, "I'm getting really tired of saving your ass while you sit in a hole."

Ricky's grin could not have been any bigger. Raul was alive.

"Man, is it good to hear your voice again! You have no idea. Listen, first things first. I can see where these idiots are hiding from where I am. How is your view?"

"My view is about seventy five yards away in the trees. All I'm doing is waiting for one of them to stick their heads up so I can blow it off."

"Do you see the big tree stump behind the boy's body?"

"Yes, I do."

"The piece of shit hiding behind that is the leader. Could you save him for me?"

"Not a problem, my blue coat brother, but only if you promise to hurt him before you kill him. I tried to get a shot at him before they killed the boy but from where I was, it wasn't possible."

"I promise, my red skinned brother. I will hurt him. You going to scalp him?"

"Maybe."

"Look to the right of that stump, there are two soldiers hiding behind that tree."

"Think they are afraid of bees?"

"What did you say?"

Just then there was a loud crack. The shot was not at the base of the tree, but about thirty feet up in the tree. With one shot, Raul sent a gigantic bee's nest sailing downward toward the ground. The nest bounced off one soldier and smashed of the ground at his feet. Bees were now swarming and stinging all of the soldiers.

They came out from behind rocks, trees and holes in the ground. In response to the bees, the soldiers were again firing in all directions recklessly. However, because the bee problem had hindered their vision, the soldiers were now using the automatic weapons to shoot each other.

Epi and Ricky could hear Raul laughing over the phone. "Boy, are they stupid, or what? Looks like they're doing my job for me."

After about five minutes, the soldiers that were left decided to throw down their guns and run off, swatting at the bees as they escaped.

"They should be pretty easy to find later on, if we even care." Raul said into the phone.

"Can you see if that crazy son of a bitch is still there?"

"You are not going to believe this, but he is standing on the other side of that cluster of trees with a machete in one hand and a pistol in the other. It looks like he is calling one of us out."

"Good, I was hoping, no, praying, that he was stupid enough not to run. Now I don't have to chase him. See, good things come to those who wait."

Ricky got out of the hole and started towards the man. He most definitely had a crazy look in his eyes. He was like a rabid dog that needed to be put to sleep. Ricky was walking directly towards the man, with his S&W automatic extended out in front of him, pointed at his target.

In his clearest Spanish, Ricky ordered, "Put the gun down, you psychopathic fuck, and fight like a man!"

To everyone's total surprise, if not shock, the man threw the gun down, and raised the machete, charging Ricky. The first spinning back kick sent the machete sailing through the air, plunging it into a nearby tree. The second kick landed just above the man's right knee. The break was so loud that Raul, who had walked over to Epi, who was standing about forty feet from Ricky and his opponent, said, "Ouch, I know for a fact that hurt."

"Yeah, I suppose so, but what goes around comes around, or so they say."

At just that moment, Ricky hit him with another spinning back kick and broke his other leg. Ricky then punched the man in the chest so hard he spat blood. The final kick to the head probably broke every bone in his face and sent blood spraying in all directions. Before the man could fall to the ground, Ricky grabbed his chin and the back of his head and snapped his neck. The world was minus one sick psychopath.

Ricky, after completing his self assigned task, turned and saw Raul for the first time in about a year. They both smiled and hugged each other.

"Man, is it good to see you, I thought they had finally killed your Indian ass!" Ricky exclaimed.

"Contrary to what you may think, 'Blue Coat', you're not in my will!"

"Like you have a will."

Epi broke into the conversation and said, "For the record, I can put in my report that we recovered agent Lightfoot and he is in good condition."

"And you are?" Raul asked.

"Oh, I'm sorry, how rude of me! My name is agent Esperanza Marcos, and I work for the same company that you do."

"Well, that's nice. But let me set the record straight right now. I am living up here because I want to. If I wanted to be 'recovered' I would have done it myself."

"So, where do you live? What's going on in your life, and can we go get a drink and catch up?" Ricky interrupted, in an obvious attempt to change the direction of the new conversation.

Raul smiled and said, "We most certainly can. Come with me to the farm and spend the night. See why I love it here. There is someone very special to me whom I want you to meet."

"You're not going to tell me this farm is a pig farm, are you?"

"I most certainly am. How did you know that, Bluecoat?"

Epi interjected. "It was just something we heard along the way. But more importantly, what's with this 'Redskin and Blue coat' thing? It sounds like the Wild West and cowboys and Indians! Wait…! I get it. It *is* Cowboys and Indians, right, boys?!"

They both smiled and Ricky answered, "No, that's not it. What they are, are code names we used in the military when we served together in Granada.

"Come on back to the farm with me. I want to introduce you to my Guardian Angel."

"Guardian Angel? Sounds serious." Ricky teased.

"She's very special to me. In fact, so special, I've decided to stay right here."

"For good, like you're not ever leaving here?" Ricky inquired.

"I suppose it's time to call Hector and fill him in, but believe it or not, today was the first time my phone actually worked in eight months. I know that's hard to believe, but it is a fact."

Within an hour they were all sitting together in the living room at the farm talking; catching up on old times. Ricky and Epi had been introduced to Angelita, and immediately knew why Raul was happy.

Ricky, in his conversations with Raul, had noticed that Raul seemed to be a much happier person than he had been in the past, or in a long, long time.

"Maybe Raul is right about wanting to stay here?" Ricky thought to himself.

Ricky charged the battery on his cell phone and then called Hector. Raul and Hector talked for a long time, and Ricky knew that Hector wasn't happy about Raul's decision to stay. This was evident by Raul's constant diversion of language to Navajo while talking to his brother.

When Raul got off the phone, he told Ricky to call Hector in the morning, to go over some further details. Hector didn't want to talk to anyone right now, he had told him. Raul also told all of them that Hector would be coming to the farm within a week or two to meet Angelita, and probably try to convince all of them to return to the States with him.

Ricky knew Raul, and he knew that if Raul didn't want to go back to the States there was no one who was going to change his mind. Raul had told Ricky that Hector, after talking to Raul, told him that he was going to put him on medical leave and they would decide together what to do next.

"Hector is sharp and has a lot of resources at his disposal. You know he is going to come up with a plan, don't you?" he asked Raul.

"I suppose he will. We will have to see what comes our way. But for now, have another drink and try to get Angelita's grandmother to smile. I've been trying for eight months, with no success."

"She looks like a hard case. Maybe she used to be a sniper, or something?"

"Raul laughed and said "Now, that wouldn't surprise me at all. By the way, what's up with the cute Colombian agent you have with you? You move on her yet?"

"Not yet, but one never knows, does one?" Ricky responded, with a twinkle in his eye. "I'm going to talk Hector into approving her ride back to D.C. with me, so he can get the complete report. She will be able to fill in all the blanks which I can't."

"I've never known you to forget anything. But it's a great plan. Good luck trying to convince Hector."

The two couples talked nearly all night, about everything under the sun. By morning the four had bonded very well.

The next day, Angelita and Raul went with Ricky and Epi to San Remo, to send them off. As they were loading Epi's Jeep for the trip home, Ricky spoke. "I can't wait to see what happens next."

Raul smiled. "Knowing my brother, I'm sure it will be interesting."

CHAPTER III
THE THREE JUDGES

Evil, touch not the world of my angel, as the wrath of my staff shall be cast upon you with the mighty force of all that is good. Is vengeance in the name of good still vengeance?

Raul was sitting in a rocker on the front porch of the farm house, enjoying a Cuban cigar and the music of Pepe Aguilar on the compact disc player Ricky had sent them.

Ricky had sent the player with a note telling them that it was a housewarming present from the boys at the company. No one on the farm, except for Raul, had an idea what that meant. But as far as Raul was concerned, the less they new about the company, the better.

Hector had visited Raul on the farm about two weeks after Ricky and Epi had left. The two of them talked for two straight days while Hector tried to convince Raul not to throw his career away by not returning to the CIA. After the lengthy conversation, they came to an understanding that Raul would, in fact, remain an agent for the CIA and could work out of the farm. Where an agent lived was not really a concern of the agency as long as the accountability was in place. Hector told him that because of the highly specialized type of work that Raul did, there was a lot of flexibility for life style. Hector had also given Raul a hefty pile of American Express traveler's checks to compensate him for back pay and earned bonuses. A system of direct deposit would be put in place and a checking account was arranged for at a leading bank in Bogota. All the details of daily life had been made. Now, to get Angelita to accept what he did for a living. This was very hard for her to do, but she was trying. Angelita, after meeting Hector, had commented, "He looks very much like you, but is so very different from you. I would wonder if you were from the same family, if I didn't know better."

They were quite cordial to one another and both had said separately how much they liked each other. With Hector he felt the feelings were accurate. Angelita was a different story, however. It seemed she could read Raul perfectly, but Raul, for the most part, hardly ever had an idea about what she was truly thinking. Except when they were alone, no guessing there. He knew that her feelings for him were every bit as strong as his for her.

After Hector had left, Raul and Angelita had gotten a ride to Bogota from a neighbor who had a car. There they shopped for three days, for what Raul called 'creature comforts'. The first thing they purchased was a brand new Jeep Wrangler, which he promised to teach Angelita how to drive as soon as they returned. They also purchased a trailer that he had hitched to the back of the Jeep. Not a tremendously large trailer, about an eight to ten footer, he had told the sales person. He just wanted to be able to purchase what ever they needed, or more importantly, whatever Angelita wanted.

The problem here was that Angelita didn't ask for anything. She was always more concerned about Grandma or Raul. As a result, Raul continually bought what he thought she might want, and she continually stood there shaking her head and smiling. Raul loved it when she smiled. She was truly his angel, and God help the person who ever tried to harm her.

While they were in Bogota, Raul met Angelita's brother, a defense attorney whose eyes never left Raul, making him a little uncomfortable. As they were leaving his office, Jorge put his hand on Raul's shoulder and asked, "May I speak with you a moment, sir?"

"Absolutely, I want you to say what ever you're thinking." Raul replied.

"Well sir," he said. "Angelita is my little sister and I have always looked out for her. Grandma has told me of things since your arrival at the farm that have concerned me, to say the least. Everyone knows of the battle at the farm some time ago, and I know you looked out for everyone there. I thank you for that. I also know what you do for your government. That troubles me somewhat, but I also know that sometimes the system I work in fails us, and we need different measures. Is it true you are known as the Navajo Ghost in the San Remo area?"

"I suppose it is, but lately the amount of 'narco terrorists 'in the area have thinned out considerably, and we feel relatively safe on the farm now. I have taken security measures, however, to maintain that feeling of security. As a result, I would ask that you let us know if you are coming to visit."

"How would I do that? The phone system is not good in that area, and cellular phones seldom work."

"Write down these numbers. They are the cell numbers for me and Angelita. Within a week or two a new tower will be constructed close to the farm, compliments of my government. The phones will work perfectly, I assure you. Give the numbers to any family members that may want to talk to Angelita or Grandma."

Jorge hugged Raul and said, "Welcome to our family, you will be good for Angelita. I can feel it. Now I know why Grandma likes you so much."

"She does? I had no idea." Raul raised an eyebrow.

"She told me that from the first time she talked to you in the barn, - you remember the barn, I'm sure, - she liked you. She said if Angelita was going to bring home a strange man, a Navajo Indian from New Mexico was a perfect choice."

"Thank you, Jorge, you have made my day. If there is anything I can do in the future, don't hesitate to call."

"Thank you, sir, just take care of my little sister, as, after meeting you, I know you will."

Raul liked Jorge; he was a genuine person. "That was a rare thing these days", he thought to himself. "Such a good person; how could he be an attorney?" he asked himself with a chuckle.

Angelita had no idea why he was laughing. She just looked at him, slapped him on the shoulder and said, "Come, lets get going. I want you to meet my cousin, she is a Superior Court Justice, and her office is just down the street. Her name is Maria, and I know you will like her as well."

When they arrived at Maria's office, they discovered she was not there. The secretary, who knew Angelita well, told her that Maria and two other lady judges had gone to a conference in an undisclosed location and would not be back for four more days. She would, however, tell the Judge about the visit, and she knew the Judge would be sad to have missed her.

Angelita smiled, hugged the secretary and turned to Raul, remarking, "Too bad she is not here now, but you will meet her soon and I know you will like her."

With that they left and headed off to do some more shopping. Angelita wanted to buy Grandma something special. Now that Raul knew how the old woman really felt about him, he was ready to buy her something special as well.

"By the way, what is your cousin's last name? So when I do one day meet her, I'll know."

"Very simple, it is the same as mine, Marques. Her family is that of my father's brother. They came to this country together, long before I, or my brother, was born. They came from the South of Spain."

Raul had yet to ask or trade information about parentage or events in the past which had left them both orphans at young ages. They were sitting at an outdoor café in the Rose District of Bogota having a drink when Angelita opened up about her past.

"Shortly after I was born, my mother was working on the farm when she was bitten by a Bush Master snake. They mainly live in the coffee plants, but can be found in other places as well. Because the farm is so remote and my father couldn't get to Dr. Sanchez in time, my mother died. Grandma is the mother of my mother, and the farm is actually hers even though it is known as the Marques farm. My father was wrought with guilt over my mother's death, or at least that is what Grandma has told me. I was way too young to know about anything. I think I was one or two years old. Jorge was about 9 at the time, and remembers both mother and father very well."

Raul could see this conversation was troubling her, but she looked as though she wanted very much to talk, so he didn't interrupt or say anything.

"Anyway, Grandma told me that my father and my uncle, Ramon, were returning from a trip to Bogota when, for some reason, they went off the road and over the side of the mountain. Both men were killed in the accident. Grandma said it was just a tragic accident, but Jorge has told me that he had seen our father and uncle drunk many times together. My uncle was also grieving because his wife, Maria's mother, had died from cancer when she was five. Jorge believes to this day that both of them were drunk and could not take the pain of their losses any longer. It is very difficult to know the truth, but if you love someone that much, is it not very believable that a person might kill him or herself to stop the pain? Maria, Jorge, and I were all orphans at the same time. All three of us had, or for that matter have, for a parent is Grandma. Maria came to live with us and she is to me more my sister than cousin. We all grew up together at the farm under the watchful eye of Grandma. In our family Jorge is the oldest, Maria is in the middle and I am the baby. Both my brother and my sister are so smart they went to college because of grants given to them from the government and extra money Grandma could make from the farm. We are very proud of them both."

Now it was Raul's turn. He had never opened up to any one in the past and didn't know if he could do it now. But he loved this woman and he would try his best. An hour later he had told her everything; about his and Hector's lives, about Grandpa, and even about killing Billy Dirtyface, the reservation cop who had murdered his grandfather.

This was the first time either of them had shared their pasts with any living person, and now they felt closer than ever. They returned to the farm later that evening and found dinner waiting. Grandma and the house keeper was anxious to hear all about the trip, and she and Angelita were like a couple of kids opening Christmas presents as they went through the boxes Raul retrieved from the trailer. Grandma had told Angelita that she could see new shining stars in her eyes, and knew she was in love. She also told Angelita how happy she was about that. This was a real shocker to Raul because Grandma was still not making a whole lot of friendly gestures in his direction. But she did smile and thank him for the sweater he had brought her. That was a start, in his book. Neither Raul nor Angelita had ever been happier in their lives, and their lovemaking that night showed it. They exhausted themselves and fell into blissful sleep, wrapped tightly in each other's arms.

Everything looked like it might just be that "get married, live happily and raise kids life" which Raul had dreamed about. Then his cell phone rang. He looked at the caller I.D. display, and it was Hector. Before he could even answer his phone, he heard Angelita's phone start to ring. "What the hell is going on here today?" he asked as he answered.

As he was answering his phone and greeting Hector, he heard Angelita say, "Hello, Oh, hi, Jorge. I didn't expect to hear from you so soon".

"What's up Hector? I thought you were going to give me another month or so before I had to start back to work."

"And, little brother, I wish I could, but we have a big problem in your neck of the woods."

Just then he heard Angelita cry out. "Oh, God, no! This can't be! Not Maria! Please God, not Maria!"

"Hector, Angelita just got some really bad news. Is it related to your call?"

"I'm sure it is," Hector answered.

Raul could hear Grandma and Angelita crying in the other room and wanted, no *needed* to know right now what was going on. "Hector, what the fuck is going on? Hurry up, tell me!"

"Three superior court judges were in s seminar out side of Medellin last week"

"Yes, I know. I didn't know where, but I knew about the seminar."

"Why would you even know about the seminar?"

"One of the judges is Angelita's cousin. They are like sisters, raised together. More like sisters than cousins. What happened?"

"Some bandit group has kidnapped them. They killed seven bodyguards and twelve soldiers. These judges were targeted. There were fifty- two judges of all types, from all over Colombia at this so-called secret meeting. These three were the only women judges, and the only ones taken. One other male judge was shot when he tried to intervene. His wound was critical and it doesn't look like he'll make it."

"What kind of intel do you have so far? Give me everything you got."

"First reports had them heading northeast toward Cucuta. But that didn't make a whole lot of sense, because the area is too populated for a kidnap hideout.

"What else do you have that you know for sure?"

"Estimates put this group at about twenty-five with some guy named, 'Panama Pete' leading the group. Another classic asshole, running loose in the jungles of Colombia.

"You get any ransom demands yet?"

"Not formally, but this 'Panama Pete' fellow told the other judges he could take anybody, anytime, from anywhere, because he had connections in high places. He said he knows everything about everybody and if the government wanted these three judges back alive, they would cost one million each."

"This guy is headed for Panama; he is not even a Colombian bad guy. I would bet anything on that", Raul was pondering.

"He has only given the Colombian government two weeks to pay, or he promises to deliver them back in pieces. The Colombian President asked us, via the White House, for help. Needless to say, whatever you want, you got."

"You know where my cross bow is?"

"I brought everything from your apartment to my house when I closed it up. I'm sure it's here somewhere. I'll find it."

"Get me a dozen exploding arrows for it, along with another dozen razor- tipped arrows. Send them to me with the helicopter that meets me at the heliport, at Guatavita tomorrow at noon. I need a ride to Medellin. Have a four - wheel drive vehicle waiting for me there, full of gas with at least two extra cans on board."

"Where are you headed to exactly?"

"I really feel this guy is headed toward the jungle at the Panama boarder. That's where you hide kidnap victims. Not in Cucuta."

"I will keep you updated with everything I know, just as soon as we get it."

"Spread some money around Medellin and get me some good intel before I get there."

"Will do." Hector assured him.

Raul hung up. Now for the really hard part. He went into the house and saw Angelita on the sofa with Grandma. They were both crying and it hurt him to see that. Somebody was going to pay and pay dearly for what they had done to his Angelita.

Raul went to Angelita and held her. Grandma looked at him with the saddest eyes he had ever seen and pleaded, "Please, Raul, bring my baby back to me, these children are all I have in the world."

"I am leaving in the morning, and my intention is to bring her home with me."

"Thank you, Raul. God bless you and be with you on your journey."

Angelita cried most of the night and that pained Raul. He comforted her as best he could, but he really wasn't good at that kind of thing. All he could do was promise her he would return, and that he would bring Maria with him.

Come morning, after the goodbyes, Raul loaded his gear and headed for Guatavita and the helicopter. A man named Red Tucker was the pilot and Raul knew him well. They had worked together before, dating clear back to the army days. Raul trusted this man and knew he could count on him.

When Raul approached the chopper, Red handed him an envelope with all the latest intelligence obtained by the Company, and, to his surprise, a photograph of this Panama Pete fellow. Raul loaded his gear and got on board the chopper.

Lying on the floor next to the seat was his cross bow and a box, obviously containing the requested arrows. Red looked at him and asked, "What, the fancy rifle isn't good enough anymore? Now the Navajo in you is coming out?"

"This mission is kind of personal and I may take a scalp or two."

"Way to go, Geronimo."

"So much for your history, White Eyes. He was an Apache not a Navajo. But you have the right idea. How long before we land in Medellin?"

"With the wind pushing us, a few hours, give or take."

"Give or take?"

"This is a Black Hawk helicopter, not a Black Hawk jet. We'll get there as fast as we can. I promise. I've never seen you this anxious to start killing people. What's up?"

"These shit bags kidnapped a relative of someone very close to me."

"A relative of Angelita's?"

"You know about Angelita?"

"Like you think there are secrets here, and the whole world doesn't know. Wake up, Lightfoot, the whole Company knows what happened. Actually, I have to tell you, I wouldn't want to be the guys you're chasing. Think they have any idea how stupid they really are?"

"No, they probably don't, but they are about to find out."

"I know I wouldn't want to be the guy you're chasing. Everybody knows you're unstable", he laughed.

When they landed, a courier brought Raul the most recent intelligence report.

"You were right, sir", the man said. "They headed toward Panama, into the jungle. Your Jeep and supplies you requested are over there and ready to go."

As Raul was getting into the Jeep his phone rang. Hector told him that these bandits had bombed a police station in San Luis. They had taken the district police chief and two of his officers hostage. Witnesses had confirmed there were three women with the group. They had been tied together with a rope attached to each of their necks, along with their hands being bound behind their backs.

"Now they have six hostages? This is out of control. How long ago did this happen?"

"About two hours, as close as we can tell."

Raul turned to the agent that had brought him the package and questioned, "How far is San Luis from here, and is the road good?"

"About three hours, and yes, the road is good."

"I'm about five hours behind them. I'll call you after I have killed a couple of those bastards."

"Raul", Hector said. "Do you want some help? There is a team on standby ready to go. Just say the word."

Raul hung up the phone.

Hector looked at his phone and said. "I guess that means no."

By three o'clock, Raul was approaching San Luis, a sleepy little pueblo that meant nothing in the "big picture". He stood in front of the charred, smoky ruins of what was once the police station. The blast had killed five other officers. Young men, who were in the prime of life, had their lives snuffed out. Their widows were also at the building, crying and praying for their souls. This was an act of, Raul didn't know exactly what, but he was disgusted by what had happened here. He returned to his Jeep and set out for the jungle and the confrontation he knew would ensue. He was ready; in fact, he was not only ready, but was anxious.

Ghost Warrior

It was nightfall when he entered the jungle area near the border. He was on foot because the roadway had ended and the jungle had begun. Raul felt at home; so at home in the jungle.

Raul spent the night searching and making ready for the hunt to come. Raul tracked as well as he could, but the trees and thick brush in the jungle allowed for no light, so he could only make his way as best as he could under the circumstances. He needed to make up precious time. He knew he was close, so it was just a matter of finding the right clearance or break in the jungle where a camp could have been established by the enemy.

It was almost dawn and Raul was beginning to wonder if he was even in the right part of the jungle. He came upon a river and decided to follow that to see if it would bring him closer. He was moving through the jungle like a ghost - swiftly, without making any sounds. His grandfather had taught him these skills, and Raul was very proficient at them.

"Just make yourself one with the forest. If you think you are a tree, you will be one."

Raul was so good at this that he had actually walked up on sleeping animals in the forest. The only thing close to this discipline was what he had learned from the Orientals in Thailand. Raul had stopped and was just listening to the jungle. It was amazing what it could tell you.

He heard an animal splashing in the river. He was standing by; he heard monkeys waking from the night, and most important of all, he heard a man yawn, and blow a horrendous fart. The man then complimented himself on his great effort. This would be the last thing this man would hear. Raul now knew he was very close to where he wanted to be. Ever so slowly he moved toward the sound and the man from where it emanated. The man was a sentry who had been posted. "And what was he guarding? Where was the camp?"

Raul looked around for a little longer and found an old miner's cabin. He remembered that years ago there had been emeralds in this area and the mining had flourished during these times. The mines had played out and everything had been abandoned. What a perfect location to bring hostages. Raul listened and watched. No sounds from the cabin.

"Was it occupied, or were they somewhere else?" he thought.

Then he heard, "Wake up you sluts, and cook us breakfast!" a man yelled from inside the cabin.

"Perfect, now I know exactly where you are."

The door opened and a woman in her mid-fifties came out of the cabin. She had a rope around her neck and was carrying a bucket. The woman was followed by a guard who had hold of the rope and was continually pushing, knocking her down, and generally being an asshole. Raul needed to return to the first guard and take him out. He also wanted to send a message of his own to these scumbags.

Raul moved swiftly through the jungle, back to the location of the first guard.

He was looking at his watch and then at the cabin. He was waiting to be relieved. Raul had to move fast. Raul raised the crossbow with a razor arrow in it. He took the steadiest of aim and then....... Thump! The arrow struck the man in the neck, passing through the opposite side. The man was on his knees when Raul got to him, trying to pull the arrow out, with no obvious success. He was dying; he just didn't know it yet. The arrow had passed through his larynx making speech impossible. In fact, making any sound impossible. Raul approached the man and he was trying to yell or speak but instead of sound, blood was squirting from his mouth. In this condition the man would drown in his own blood. But that was not the message Raul wanted to send. He wanted these people to know, or at least to think that the baddest, craziest motherfucker they could have ever imagined had just entered their lives, and it was going to be hell. Raul dragged the wounded man over to a tree and threw a rope around the top. He made a noose and commenced to pull the dying man up in the air. The man was about two feet off the ground, kicking and strangling, when Raul took out his hunting knife and gutted the man. The man was now lifeless. Raul wrote a note, smeared it with the man's blood, and took a small, sharpened branch and plunged it along with the note into the man's chest.

It was about thirty minutes later when the man's relief showed up. As soon as he entered the clearing he saw the dead man swinging in the breeze. The new guard looked horrified, and started talking to himself so fast that Raul, who was watching from the thicket, couldn't discern anything he was saying. The only thing he knew for certain was that the man was truly scared shitless. The man approached the body cautiously and read the note.

"Oh my God!" he yelled, and ran off, not looking back.

"That was effective", thought Raul. "Maybe I'll scalp the next one."

About five minutes later the man returned with six other men, including one who Raul thought was this 'Panama Pete' clown. The man was pointing at the body, yelling.

"It's the Navajo Ghost Warrior! He said he will kill us all for taking the judges!"

"Shut up!" ordered this Pete fellow. "You are a fucking idiot. This is one man and there are over twenty of us. Shut up or I will kill and gut *you*!"

Panama Pete was a short, fat, burly fellow, about fifty years old with sweat stains all over his shirt. He had black curly hair and a black bushy beard, and wore the same kind of hat Castro wears. In fact, to Raul, this was a short, fat version of Fidel Castro. He would enjoy killing this tub of shit.

One of the bandits ripped the note from the body and handed it to Panama Pete. He read the note out loud, trying to show no signs of fear, but Raul could smell fear in this group.
He read, "You have kidnapped the wrong people. Now you will force me to kill one of you each hour, in a terrible fashion, until you release these people. Don't even think about harming them. Because if you do, I will scalp you and burn you alive. This is a promise. Signed… the Navajo Ghost Warrior."

"This man doesn't scare me; he hides in the bushes like a coward. Come out and fight like a man. I'm waiting for you."

Raul let a few minutes pass without answering.

"See, he won't do anything. He's just a Gringo shit."

With that, Raul fired an arrow with an exploding tip. The arrow struck a man to the far left of Panama Pete. It hit him dead center in the chest. The man stood for a minute, unable to speak or move. Everybody looked at him in shock, and a moment later he actually exploded. Body parts flew in every direction. Brains and bone matter flew everywhere. The explosion was just enough to cover all of them with the man's blood. It also severed the left arm of the man standing next to him. This man was running around screaming, also spraying blood in every direction. After this, all of the men, including Panama Pete, ran for the shack. The man with the severed arm also ran, but fell short of his destination.

He lay about twenty feet from the front door; on the ground, moaning and shaking uncontrollably. He bled out and died with his comrades watching from a safe distance, not wanting to or being able to help.

An hour or so passed, and Raul lay covered up in a hole, drenched with sweat. It was at least ninety degrees and it wasn't yet high noon. But the winner of this battle would be the one with the most patience. And he was going to win. Raul had noticed that the shack did not have a bathroom and that meant there would be an outhouse. Raul was positioned with an optimum view of both the house and the outhouse.

As Raul had expected, the front door of the shack opened slightly and there were two men standing in the doorway. The first, however, was in a police uniform and had his hands bound behind his back. The second was a bandit who was holding onto the end of a rope that was tied around the first man's neck. They edged out onto the porch of the shack. Raul could have shot the man at the end of the rope, but he decided to wait and see what he was up to. Following that man were two other bandits, all crouched closely behind the policemen. The first man yelled out to Raul.

"If you shoot at us we will kill this pig. I will slit his throat, I promise."

Not answering, Raul just watched.

"Indian, do you hear what I am saying? I will kill him!"

Still, no answer. Raul had put the silencer on his rifle and was using the 220 cal. copper jacketed, high velocity bullets. And at two hundred and fifty feet he could shoot a gnat off a cat's ass.

Ghost Warrior

The four men moved slowly off the porch toward the latrine. The man behind the cop had a knife to the cop's throat and was watching very warily, from all sides. The three appeared terrified. Sweat was running into the first bandit's eyes, and he was constantly moving his right arm to wipe the sweat from his face. Raul watched this carefully, because every time he moved his arm to wipe his face, he took the knife he was holding in his right hand away from the cop's throat. Raul thought for a moment.

"The idiot is holding the rope with his left hand, the knife with the right hand, and trying to walk and wipe sweat at the same time. He goes first, but I have to knock the cop down without giving away my position."

As the four approached the latrine, Raul changed weapons. He picked up the cross bow, inserted an exploding arrow and aimed at the side of the building. The four were about twenty-five feet from it when he fired. The arrow struck the side of the building and exploded.

To say that shit flew everywhere would not be an exaggeration. The policeman took the brunt of the force, knocking him flat on his back. He was covered in shit and debris from the building. More importantly, by this time Raul had switched weapons and had his rifle in hand. The three bandits were trying to wipe the excrement from their faces and eyes when the first bandit's head exploded. Raul had capped him right between the eyes. The bandit behind him was holding his left eye and screaming. The bullet had passed through the skull of the first man and come to rest in the eye socket of the second. The man started running in circles, blindly screaming in pain. The third man was trying to wipe his face and grab for his automatic weapon at the same time.

"Christ." Raul thought, "Does every bad guy in Colombia have a machine gun? The kidnapping business must be booming."

Raul watched this clown as he grabbed the gun and in his excitement fired the weapon at the ground, destroying his right foot. The man fell to the ground, crying out in pain.

Raul was chuckling to himself, thinking about the cliché referring to a person shooting themselves in the foot when failing to correctly execute a speech or presentation. "I wonder if this qualifies?" he laughed.

Just then the policeman jumped, his hands still bound, and kicked the wounded man in the face, knocking him unconscious. He fell down next to the wounded soldier and grabbed the knife from the sheath on his belt. He stayed low, as he expected shots from the house in his direction. He then cut his hands free and grabbing the machine gun, he opened up on the man running around with his hand covering his eye. The man flew off his feet and fell dead instantly. The policeman, clutching the weapon, ran into the jungle.

"Hopefully he will keep on running right out of the jungle," Raul thought to himself. "That cop was just a kid, but he had balls, I'll give him that. Now if he just gets out of here before he gets killed, maybe one day he will have kids of his own."

For the next two hours there was nothing from the shack. No voices, no commotion, nothing. This was supposed to be the old, "make me think they got out somehow and were gone" trick, Raul pondered. He had calculated that if all the intelligence was correct, and that if what the Panama dipshit had said was true, there were still approximately twenty bandits, plus hostages, in that two- room shack. He needed a look inside.

Raul inched his way through the jungle and got within fifty feet of the shack, still camouflaged by the jungle. He peered into his scope, looking down the side of the building. The building was very old and had not been constructed very well. The slats on the side walls were placed loosely when nailed on. In spots, you could actually see into the building, through the walls. With his sophisticated, high- powered scope, Raul was actually able to see quite clearly through them. He waited.

About twenty minutes had passed when he saw the first bandit walk up to the targeted spot on the wall and stop. Raul fired through the wall of the building and caught the man just below the left ear. No one noticed at first, because he was using his silencer and the thump of the weapon went totally unnoticed. The shot entered into soft tissue and passed through the man's neck so swiftly that it left only a small spot of blood under his left ear and little more on the exit side. When he fell, the others in the room started laughing because they had thought that he had drunk way too much and had passed out. Raul froze in his position, waiting for the next shot. A short time later, one of the bandits went over to the man to wake him and move him. Before the man could yell that he had been shot and was not passed out drunk, Raul fired again. This shot hit its target in the forehead. Raul saw the back of the man's head explode as the bullet exited.

The force of the shot knocked him back and sent him sailing across the room. For some unknown reason, a third man ran over to the first dead body, stopped and turned to the wall. Raul had a shot, but then noticed that the man walked in Raul's direction and put an eye to the wall as if to look to see from where the shots were coming. Raul obliged him, firing one shot into the man's right eye. Just like the second target, this one flew back across the room with a large portion of his head now missing. Raul then heard Panama Pete start to yell.

"Stop shooting my men in the house! You are a cheater and you do not fight fair!"

"What, this moron thinks we are playing soccer, or what?" Raul thought. "I'm not fighting fair? This guy is really a total asshole. He is going to need a reality check. And I see one coming his way soon", Raul said to himself.

"If you want to see people dead, I will show you dead people!" Panama Pete cried. "Just to show you I can do it, and you can't stop me, I'm going to kill someone. What do you think of that, you Gringo Indian pig?"

Raul was a little concerned. Had he pushed this wacko too far? Was he stupid enough to start randomly killing people? Unfortunately, the answers to all his questions were yes. And he needed to put an end to this game now.

About ten minutes passed and all was silent. No noise from inside the shack. Raul was just quietly biding time, waiting for the right opportunity.

The cabin door swung open with a bang. There was another policeman, in uniform, with his hands bound behind his back and a rope around his neck. The other end of the rope was held by a short little skinny bandit, with bad teeth and a ruddy complexion. The short man was pushing the policeman, who was about six feet tall and towered over him, forward. The two moved to the edge of the front porch and stopped.

H. Richard Slichter

Raul could not get a clear shot at the little guy, because the policeman was so much taller. So he waited. The two men stood on the porch, the bandit, huddled behind the policeman. And the policeman, who was about mid forties, gazing out into the jungle with a look of desperation, mixed with hope in his eyes.

Raul thought to himself. "What is this crazy son of a bitch going to do now?"

And then he, the crazy son of a bitch, yelled out. "I told you I can do anything I want, and no one can stop me, or do anything about it. If I want to kill this pig, I can and you can't stop me. I'm Panama Pete and I am king here. You hear me you Gringo, Indian, faggot?!"

This great warrior was behind the door yelling at the top of his voice. He has a midget, out on the porch, with the cop. And Mr. 'I have no balls' is hiding. "What now?" Raul said out loud in a low voice.

Just then the door swung open again and Panama Pete stuck a .45 cal. automatic out of the door and shot the policeman in the back of the head. The door then slammed shut.

The policeman fell, lying lifelessly at the end of the rope, the little bandit was still holding the end of the rope looking into the jungle. When he realized that his boss had just left him on the porch to die, he started banging on the door of the cabin.

"Let me in, please boss let me in. This crazy Indian will scalp me. You have to let me in. I don't want to die out here."

Raul knew why Pete had left the little guy on the porch. He figured that if I shot him, he could then get a fix on me, and open with everything he had. What Raul needed was a distraction. "Let me see, the midget is banging on the door. Where is Mr. No-balls? There he is, on the other side of the cabin, looking through binoculars. What's that next to him? What a surprise, a man with a rifle. Here is a little surprise of my own."

Just then, instead of shooting the open target, he fired on the man with the rifle in the window. Raul preferred head shots but he needed affect. And a shot to the heart would do it. The shot hit the bandit dead center in the sternum, piercing the bone and exploding his heart.

The bandit dropped the gun, but remained standing momentarily. Raul grabbed his cross bow, jumped out of the hole and brush he was under, and fired one exploding arrow into the midget, at the front door. As soon as he jumped up Pete grabbed the man next to him, not realizing he was dead, and yelled excitedly.

"Shoot him, here he is, shoot him!"

The man fell over and landed in a sitting position against another wall. There was blood running from his mouth, nose, and ears. He was so dead.

"Pete stared at him and said." What the fuck, when did you die?"

Just then the midget and the front door exploded. The door, mixed with body parts from the little bandit, blew into the shack.

Raul heard at least two other people cry out in pain at the time of the explosion. He hoped he had not harmed a hostage. Especially the cousin he had not even met yet.

"Gringo, Indian, you are really starting to piss me off. You have killed too many of my men. Now I am going to do something to really piss you off. Let me see, yes, I think I will rape one of these bitches, slit her throat, and throw out for the wild dogs to eat. Doesn't that sound like a fun idea? It does to me."

Raul was running out of time and options with this crazy man. He needed to end this, and soon. Then, for the first time, he heard the female judges screaming and yelling at this bastard...

"Get away from us. Stop that! Leave her alone!"

From Raul's position he could see the front of the shack, the right side and the back door. The cabin was relatively small, maybe, twenty feet by twenty feet square. From what Raul had been able to determine, the cabin had two rooms. One in the front, which was probably used as a bedroom, living room, originally. In the back of the building was a smaller area which had been used as a kitchen and eating area. Most of the men that were left were hiding in the back area of the shack. Raul knew that because most of the talking was coming from that area. It almost sounded like they were making plans or taking a vote. Meanwhile Mr. No Balls was in the front of the cabin harassing the judges and screaming at the remaining cop. Raul could hear Panama Pete yelling at the police and telling him how he would die like the other pig and very soon. On and on he went, non stop. Then Raul heard someone get hit. Panama Pete was laughing and beating up somebody, probably the police chief. There were only a couple of men with him in the front part of the shack. Raul estimated that there were maybe ten or eleven bandits remaining in the group. Just as Raul was contemplating his next move, the rear door opened. Raul counted seven bandits exiting the shack. It looked like they were sneaking out.

The man in the front was carrying a white tee shirt in his hands, and none of the seven men looked to be armed. Once they cleared the shack they began running, and all of them disappeared into the jungle.

Raul smiled and said. "Well that's that, seven less to kill. Just the moron and his one or two friends with him inside. Truth be known, they probably would have run too, given the opportunity. Boy is that fat piece of shit going to be mad when he looks for his troops."

Raul was just getting ready to leave his position, and sneak up on the shack, when automatic weapon fire erupted in the jungle. It came from the direction the seven deserters had fled to.

"Don't tell me that kid policeman stayed, and was waiting for an opportunity. I wonder if he realizes that he just gunned down seven unarmed men. Maybe he saw the other cop be assassinated and really doesn't care? In any case, I need to stop this now." Raul thought to himself.

As soon as the shooting started, Panama Pete and his two 'associates' ran to the back of the cabin. He could hear the fat man shouting into the jungle.

"I hope they killed all of you cowards. How dare you run from Panama Pete! If I see you ever again, I will kill you myself if they haven't."

Raul then heard one of the remaining men say. "But Panama, who are they? I think it is just the Indian Ghost out there."

"Shut up stupid, I know what I am saying." Panama Pete said as he punched the man that had questioned him.

Raul heard the second man then say, in an almost panic stricken voice, "Panama, he has killed everybody but us. Now it is just the three of us, and we can't fight him. Maybe we should give him the hostages and he will leave us alive?"

Panama Pete looked at the man for a moment and said. "That won't work for you."

"Why not Panama, why do you say that?"

"Because, my cowardly little shit, you are going to be dead already."

Panama Pete then took out his .45 caliber automatic pistol and shot the man three times. This in fact, was overkill, as the man took the first 45 slug directly in the face; the mouth, to be specific. With the back of his head no longer attached, the other two shots were totally unnecessary. But being the certifiable psycho he was, he thought two more 45 caliber slugs might just do the trick, and dispatched two more rounds into the already lifeless, destroyed body that lay on the floor in front of him.

Needless to say, the remaining man was more than hesitant about staying on with Panama Pete. Before Pete could shoot him, or holster the weapon, this man thought it was anybody's guess. He picked up a board which was lying on the floor, and struck Pete from behind landing the blow across Pete's fat neck and head. Pete fell to the floor and before he could get up, the man was out the door, running for the woods. Raul saw the man exit the shack and run in the same direction the other seven had. Raul figured this man's day trip to the jungle was about to be cut short. Didn't he remember the automatic weapons fire? How about the pissed off cop in the woods? Nothing rung any bells with these idiots. Just then, two short bursts from the machine gun.

Raul was about twenty feet from the shack and was looking into it via the missing front door. The short fat man was coming into the front room from the kitchen. He had the pistol in his right hand and was holding it outward. The man was mumbling something to himself. Raul had no idea what he was saying, but figured whatever it was had to be bad.

He could see the three judges huddled together in a corner with the police chief standing between them and Panama Pete. Raul moved cautiously toward the house, and onto the front porch. He was standing in the doorway, watching the fat man as he spoke to the police chief. "Well, my pig friend, today will be the day you get to meet Jesus. I think I will start by shooting you in the knees, one at a time. And then all over until you die. How does that sound to you?"

The Chief shook his head slowly and said. "Sounds like a lot of shit from a crazy man, to me. Why don't you ask him what he thinks?"

"What are you talking ab……?"

The round house kick from Raul sent the pistol flying into the other room. The Karate chop to the neck caused Panama Pete to choke for air and his eyes to bulge. The four finger jab to the solar plexus made him start spitting blood. Things were not going well for the fat man, but they would get worse. It appeared as though Raul had spun and struck the fat man in the throat with his fist, but closer examination revealed that Raul had a small knife in his hand and he had just cut the fat man's throat from ear to ear. Panama Pete fell to his knees and then forward on his fat stomach. The fat man was dead and the Judges, not to mention the policemen's ordeal, was ended. The Chief turned toward Raul and Raul saw for the first time how badly they had beaten this man.

His left eye was swelled shut. His lip had been cut several times and it looked like his nose was broken. This man was in a lot of pain and didn't show one sign of it. "Sir", the police chief said through his swollen mouth and cheeks. "We all owe you our lives and a deep debt of gratitude. I don't know who sent you or why you picked us to rescue but thank you very much for killing this man. The police officer he murdered was my brother in law and a dear friend of mine. It will be a sad day when I have to tell my sister of his death. My other officer - is he alive, do you know?"

"Did you hear all that automatic weapons fire? That was him. I think he was getting a little pay-back."

Just then one of the judges turned to him and Raul got chills down his back. At first glance he thought it was Angelita.

"Sorry, your Honor", he said." You have no idea how much you look like some one very dear to me."

"How is Angelita? I am Maria Marques, Angelita's cousin. And it is a great pleasure to finally meet you."

"Same here." Raul smiled. "I want you to know that I came to your office with Angelita last week in an effort to meet you under less strenuous circumstances."

She smiled and laughed a little. After what had happened to all of them it was good to see some smiles. When she smiled she glowed just like Angelita, Raul couldn't help but notice.

Raul dialed the home number, but no luck. "Angelita and Grandma are really anxious to talk to you. As soon as we can get in range I'll try again."

Just then his phone rang and Raul just looked at it.

Maria smiled again and said, "That would be Angelita; she has always been a little different. You know, she does a lot of things everybody whishes they do, but can't."

"You are one scary chick." Raul said as he answered the phone. "Here's Maria all safe and sound. We will be home as soon as I hook up with Tucker and get the chopper out of Medellin." The other two judges were thanking Raul when the young policeman walked into the cabin. He walked over to Raul and embraced him.

"Thank you so very much sir. You are a Godsend" the young man said.

Raul looked at him and smiled. "No, I'm a government-send. But listen, you can do something for us."

"Anything sir, name it!"

"Go down river about five miles and get my Jeep and figure out how to bring it here. Can you do that?"

"Yes sir, I saw the Jeep; in fact, I was going to use it to go get help, but I decided to stay and help you, instead."

"And help me you did."

"There is an old mine road that swings around the marshy area and ends up right over there in that clearing," the young police officer pointed.

As the young man walked away from the group, Raul called out to him. "By the way, what's your name?"

"Raul Montoya Garcia" the officer responded as he turned, still walking.

"Well, from one professional to another, you did one hell of a good job today. I know your Chief, and I'm going to put in a good word for you."

"The Chief smiled through his totally messed up face and said, "Raul has always been a good boy, and he has proven to be a good police officer. I am very proud of him. He will be a lot of help to me rebuilding the station and getting more officers."

"Raul studied the Chief for a minute or two and said, "I have to tell you, chief, you look to be what, 60 years old?"

"To be exact sir, I'm going to be 63 tomorrow. Why do you ask?"

"No special reason, I just admire how tough you are."

"Well, I appreciate that, however toughness is a way of life in Colombia these days. I'm sorry, sir, what is your name?" the Chief asked, almost apologetically.

"Raul Lightfoot, an honor to meet you."

"No sir!" the Chief said. "The honor is all mine. It is truly an honor to meet the Navajo Ghost Warrior, in person! Judge Marques said that shortly after we arrived here that the Navajo Ghost Warrior would rescue us. We all just looked at her, and asked her how she knew that. She just said Angelita told her you were coming"

"The Marques' definitely have some kind of mind thing going on." Raul laughed.

Within forty five minutes, Officer Raul Montoya Garcia was back at the shack with the Jeep. "Your limo is here, folks. Lets go home."

Raul dropped the Chief and Officer Garcia in San Luis, to a jubilant reception. That is, except for one young lady who just stood waiting. The Chief looked back at Raul with tears in his eyes. The young lady was his sister, and her husband was in a body bag, waiting to be picked up.

"Strange how a single moment in time can be happy and sad at the same time", Raul thought to himself.

Raul and the three judges arrived to a waiting Red Tucker at the heliport.

Red looked at them, smiled and said, "Ladies, ready to go back to Bogota, courtesy of the Navajo Ghost Warrior and his pilot?"

"Shut up, you bozo", Raul laughed. "Get in the chopper, crank it up and take us home; it's almost dinner time and Judge Marques will be joining me, Angelita, Jorge, and Grandma at the farm. Who knows, maybe we'll get a smile out of Grandma?"

They were all laughing as the chopper lifted off.

CHAPTER IV
THE SCARRED MAN

To look upon a badly scarred man is to feel sadness. To see that the scars the man bears are but a mere reflection of the ugliness and hate harbored within his spirit brings even a greater sadness to a world plagued by the face of evil.

Ghost Warrior

The funeral was nice; sad, but nice. Grandma had been 93 years old when she passed away, in her sleep. Calmly and quietly, she went to sleep and didn't wake in the morning. She had had a good life. Her grandchildren had been near to her and she had been a happy woman. No pain, no suffering, just a quiet stillness as she moved on to the next life. The old people prayed for Grandma's soul. The rest stood around the freshly dug grave, staring at the coffin resting so peacefully in the hole. They stared, reminisced and thought deeply about life, and the void left in many lives without Grandma's presence. None more than Angelita. Raul was holding her tightly as she wept. She, probably more than anyone else on this earth, would miss Grandma. She cried for the loss of this woman, but was comforted inside knowing she had not suffered, and had had many good years on this earth.

The farm was now Angelita's. Jorge and her cousin, the judge, had both agreed that the farm should be Angelita's. And both of them being lawyers, they had written documents proving it. Raul and Angelita would return to the farm together, and life would go on.

They, the Marques family and Raul, were leaving the cemetery after the graveside service, when a black limousine pulled up to them and stopped. Raul had instinctively pulled Angelita behind him and had his hand on his Glock automatic. The passenger door opened and Epi stepped out.

"What the hell are you doing? You gave us all a jolt we weren't expecting. What could you possibly want today, at the graveyard?" Raul asked.

"Time to go to work, Ghost Warrior" Epi said. Making a fist and lightly tapping Raul in the stomach. "There are fish to fry and dirtbags to kill, and I'm looking for the cook."

"Ricky teach you that stupid expression?" Raul responded.

"What do you mean?"

"I mean, it sounded stupid enough to have been something Ricky came up with. Do yourself a big favor. Sleep with him, but don't listen or repeat his expressions. They, for the most part, all suck, big time."

"Who told you we were sleeping together? You don't know that, big fellow."

"You see I do know that, because I know Ricky only uses that 'big fellow' line when he is in bed."

"Really!" Epi said, making a fist and holding it against her mouth.

"So tell me, why are you here, and what is it that you need from me?"

Before Epi said anything else, she looked at Angelita, went to her and hugged her. "I'm really sorry about Grandma, and if there is anything, anything at all I can do to help you, you know I'm there for you."

Angelita smiled at Epi. She liked Epi a lot, and knew she meant what she said. "Thank you, Epi, I really appreciate that. And I promise, if I need you I will call."

"Good, it's settled. Now for the reason I am here."

Epi started by asking Raul if it were true that he had spent quite a bit of time teaching Angelita how to fire his rifle, and basically be a sniper.

"We do a little target practice. Why, what does that matter to the Company?"

"Angelita, could you kill somebody if you had to?"

Before Angelita could answer, Raul put his hand over her mouth, and responded. "Tell me, right now, what's with the questions?" Raul knew there were stories circulating about Angelita having killed a man who was trying to rape her. Raul didn't want this verified, because he didn't want any friends of this guy looking for Angelita when he wasn't around. And he just didn't think their lives were anybody else's business.

Angelita very gently moved Raul's hand and said, "Simply put, I can take care of myself." Then she walked over to where Jorge and Maria were waiting.

Epi looked at Raul. "I know she has got to be tough to be with you, and I think that is fantastic. Would you consider taking her on a mission with you?"

Oddly enough, Raul had thought just that. If she was with him he could protect her.

He really didn't like going off on jobs and leaving her alone. And now with Grandma gone it would be even worse. He stared into Epi's beautiful eyes and said "Maybe, what do you have in mind?"

"We have a terrorist group moving along the western edge of Colombia. The last report put them southwest of Cali in that mountainous jungle area, you know, that area with all the rivers and water falls."

"Yes, I know it. Go on."

"Anyway, the group is robbing banks and government facilities and taking the gold. No paper money, just the gold. Reports indicate that this group has stashed away somewhere around forty million dollars in gold bullion."

"What is the exact mission?"

The government wants its gold, back. And would like very much if the Carranza brothers fell to an ill fate.

"The Carranza brothers. What's the story with them? You know, descriptions, how many, the basics. What is it about them, besides being thieves, that makes them worth the hunt? And why does the Company care about these thieves?

"There are three of them. Santiago, the oldest; Pepe, the next in line, and Rafael, the youngest, about twenty or so. Pepe is a follow-the-leader type guy, but this Rafael is a loose cannon, mostly because he is trying to prove himself."

"What is this group? One of those 'put all their brains together, turn it into dynamite and you still wouldn't have enough to blow your nose'?"

"On the contrary. Watch out for these guys. They may be bad, but they're not stupid. Especially watch out for the leader, Santiago. You will know him by the gigantic scar on the right side of his face. The scar is a result of a machete accident when he was a boy. Probably about twelve or so. From what we know he was playing in a field with a neighbor boy and they were swinging this machete. As a result, the boy struck him accidentally on the side of the face. This Santiago nearly died from blood loss before they could get any type of medical help. His father, if I have my facts correct, seared the wound shut with an iron to stop the bleeding and save the boy's life. So, what he was left with was a very ugly burn type scar that runs from just above the right eye along the side of his face to just below the chin." Epi moved her right index finger along Raul's face as she was explaining.

"OK, he sounds ugly enough. What else?"

"Remember the kid that hit him with the machete?"

"Ya."

"Four years later, this Santiago cut both of his arms off with a machete, and threw him, still alive, into a truck and drove to a park at the center of the closest town, Santa Teresa. Then the young man was thrown from the back of the pickup truck in broad daylight onto the ground. The place, I hear, was loaded with people, because it was Sunday or something like that. This Santiago fellow made no bones about what he had done, and in fact, stood in the back of the truck, while the horrified crowd watched this young man, with blood gushing from both sides of his body, die in front of them."

Raul stood looking at Epi and after a minute or two said, 'Well, if you were to ask me what I thought of that story, I would have to say it sounds like it came from a Garcia Marquez book. But who knows, or cares?"

"Well, just for what it is worth, Intelligence also has informed us that this Santiago's criminal career started at age sixteen. And by the way, before he left home at age sixteen, he slit his father's throat and hung him by his feet on the sign post of Santa Teresa.

"So, what we have here," Raul said, "Is an ugly, scarred, sadistic guy, who gets off on revenge. Stop me if I'm wrong. But what makes this guy so smart?"

"The Colombian government has been chasing this man and his group for quite some time, and can't even get close to him. He has some type of fortress in the jungle area that we talked about, and when they get close he disappears."

"He disappears? Just him, or who, disappears?"

"They all disappear; the entire group. There are, at last report, approximately seventy in his group. The police, the army and even our intelligence groups track this guy to the same area. And consistently he and his group have disappeared."

"Interesting, that he can make an entire group disappear. Any idea where his base is? I mean, to store forty million in gold bars is going to take some space, don't you think?"

"There are a lot of people at their wit's end about this. This guy steals whatever or whomever he wants, and to date, no one has been able to do a damn thing about it."

"Whomever he wants?"

"What we are being told is that this guy steals young women and any males he feels are old enough to be in his army, and they disappear also."

"What about prisoners? Hasn't anyone captured at least a single soldier of his?"

"Not alive. He either has them so scared or so brainwashed that before one soldier will be taken captive he or she will kill themselves."

"He or she? He has woman fighting with him also?"

"Absolutely; there are no innocents running with this wacko, so be very careful. He is very smart and very, very dangerous."

"And you want me to take Angelita on this mission with me?"

"The company thinks you are going to need help with this job. Trust me Raul; this is not a one-man kill. They are organized and well equipped. They don't appear to be into drugs or kidnapping. They just steal gold. And they are very good at it. This Santiago runs a tight ship, and his entire army fears him."

"Is Ricky in Colombia? I could make this work with him along, also."

"Sorry, he is in Washington. But you need a third sniper, not Ricky."

"I don't have a third sniper and I don't know any army people well enough to work with them. So what's plan B?"

"It just so happens I brought someone with me."

"I told you……"

"Giles, could you step out of the car?" Epi asked.

Raul's look of surprise was a classic. "That's not the Giles I know, is it? Because he got killed in Turkey last year; it was confirmed."

"Not quite confirmed, old chap!" Giles chirped in. "You see, old man, the idea was to make it appear that I was dead, without actually having to go through, well all of that, you know."

Raul grabbed his friend and hugged him. "You are such an asshole, Giles; I can't believe some of the things you do."

"Yes, well my heart is in the right place, and all of that, you know."

Raul looked at both of them a little puzzled and asked, "Why is the Queen's private agent in Colombia? You here for the festival of flowers, or what?"

"That would be because I asked Washington to make that happen", Epi replied. "Ricky told me that you would say exactly what you did, and that if we were going to pull this off I would have to get Giles to work with you."

"You're telling me that Ricky knew Giles was alive?"

"No, not at all. None of us knew, until I went to the White House with Ricky for the briefing on this mission. That's when Ricky told them that you would need one more really good cover guy, and it was really a shame that Giles wasn't around, because he would have been perfect for this. The Chief of Staff said he would make some calls and see who he could find. To all of our surprise, Giles showed up.

"Glad to be of service, old chap. I'm ready for the hunt as soon as you are. Let me get my gear and we will be off."

Epi stopped Raul as he was turning to leave. "There is one more thing I wanted to ask you to consider. Hector told me I should ask you this and that he wants you to consider it, so don't answer now. OK?"

"I'm not leaving here, so ask whatever you want. If it involves leaving Colombia, I won't need time to think. The answer is no."

"Believe me when I tell you that everybody, including your brother, knows that's not even an option. What they want to ask you is to consider letting the Company use the farm as a Colombian base for operations. They feel it's secluded enough and would make the perfect location to set up shop. With the mountains behind you and the woods in front, how much better could it get?"

"That's an interesting proposal. The mountains have some nice large caves in them and it would be a textbook cover. You forgot one thing, however."

"What's that? Because if it's money, you know the Company will foot all the bills for the farm and any extra help to keep it operational. Anything it takes to keep the cover natural.

"It's not my farm, it's Angelita's and she says what happens there, not me."

"Absolutely, everybody knows that also. We just thought she might accept the idea quicker if it came from you. You might tell her that Ricky would be promoted and would run that branch."

Raul smiled and looked at Epi, who had the most girlish, 'please say yes' look on her face. She was a looker and he knew why Ricky had grown very fond of her. After all, hadn't he done the same with Angelita? "Let me guess, if Ricky runs this branch, correct me if I'm wrong, then you'll be transferred here also?"

She smiled. "Busted, but would that be so bad? I don't think so. There are many benefits to this, you know. Just think, the four of us could have drinks and dinner together whenever we wanted, and not have to leave the farm. "

"Well there you have it! I'll talk it over with Angelita while we are on our hunting trip, and we will let you know. How's that?"

"Perfect. I'm anxious, aren't you?"

Raul smiled and winked at her as he walked over to where Giles and Angelita were waiting. Everyone would meet at the farm for dinner and in the morning the three of them would head west.

Morning came and they were ready. The Jeep was all packed, including the new high-powered .223 cal. sniper rifle Raul had ordered from the States, especially for Angelita. He had used his to train her with, and she had become quite proficient with this type of rifle. Raul was very impressed with the natural ability she had shown during the learning process. This woman was a natural with this weapon. She had mastered, rapidly, the concept of being one with the rifle. And this, more than anything, was important.

Of all the backup shooters Raul could have asked for, Giles was the best. He was a tall, thin, and some thought, a little feminine looking, individual. He had shoulder length blonde hair and fair complexion. That, with his very English accent, and the fact he had his nails done regularly, made people wonder and even talk about the possibility of him being gay. To Raul it made absolutely no difference; Giles could be very obnoxious, and after a couple of drinks a total asshole, but he could shoot, and shoot very well. He was steady, hit his marks, and could tough out conditions with the best of them. What else mattered, in the middle of a desert or jungle, buried in a hole, waiting for six hours for just the right shot?

Giles used an English, modified .30 cal. rifle. He had started with a basic .30 cal. rifle and had completely built his own type of weapon. Raul thought the rifle was a little big and awkward, but if Giles was happy with it, what else counted? Not to mention, he had an accuracy level of 99.8% with this weapon. To Raul, this was the perfect backup.

Hector had sent, along with additional mission data, some new updated, state of the art equipment. This included compact headset-type radios, different types of battery operated lighting, compact, high powered cell phones, and assorted types of explosives and gas canisters.

Raul had taken the time to speak to Angelita about the Company's latest brain-child. She, to his surprise, was quite receptive to the idea. She, of course, had her own ideas about how the farm would continue working. She would decide on any and all future and existing employees. This would refer to type of jobs, etc., etc. She was going on and on and Raul and Giles were just looking at her in amazement. Giles started laughing and said "Well it would appear, the government will be towing the mark, on your, what is it again? A pig farm?"

Raul couldn't help but laugh at what was going on. Here they were, driving along the highway headed for Cali, and then on to some nasty business, in the jungles west of there. And just what was going on in the car at sixty miles an hour? They were analyzing the pig farm business, and listening to the suddenly emerging pig farm operational skills that Angelita was displaying. Raul was thinking to himself about what a hard business they were in. There was very little levity or joy in their chosen field. They had to grasp each laugh as if it was their last, and hold onto them through the hard times, which came so often.

They had driven all day and arrived in a small town west of Cali late that evening. They found a little hotel-café, and checked in for the night. They had unloaded the Jeep, and were sitting in the bar eating dinner, doing some last minute planning for the day to come, when they heard the men at the bar talking. These men were discussing a military band that was seen near a small village earlier in the day. The three of them strained to listen, trying to get the name of the village, but to no avail. They all knew very well that being outsiders, these men were not going to talk to them about anything more than the weather.

"We could save an awful lot of time if we knew what village they were talking about", Giles said. "Let's grab one and make him tell us, what do you say?"

Before either of them could make any kind of move, Angelita stood. She walked over to the men at the bar and smiled.

"Excuse me, I was hoping you might be able to help me?"

Two of them turned toward her. One of them answered. "Well, aren't you a sweet little thing. I think I have exactly what you need. Right here in my pants." They all started laughing, and Raul was ready to start hurting people.

Angelita, however, just smiled back at the man. "Well, maybe later you can help me, but for right now I'm trying to find my sister. You see, I'm from Bogota and my sister, Rosita, lives in a village west of here. But I don't know which one, and I hear there are guerillas all over the place around here, and frankly, I'm a little scared."

"You don't know the name of the village?" the man replied.

"No sir, but I think it's just before the jungle."

"Well, little sweet thing, you are right about the guerillas, and Emerald Village is the last one before the jungle. But you definitely can't go there now."

"But my friends are here to help me; we can find her."

"Sweetheart, there is a band of guerillas camped outside of Emerald Village. If you sister is smart, she will run before morning."

"Sir, please tell me, how far is Emerald Village from here?"

"It's only about seventy miles west. But travel by dark is impossible. The road is very bad; you will need a 4-wheel drive vehicle just to drive the road in daylight."

"What time does the sun rise around here?" she asked.

"It is daylight by 6:30am; you could drive then. You could make Emerald Village in three hours, maybe a little less. Maybe you can find your sister, and return back here tonight. You know, both of you. We can all party together."

"Thanks for the information, and no, I don't think so."

Angelita returned to the table and asked "Did you two, by chance, overhear exactly where we are going in the morning?"

Raul smiled at her and replied. "Yes, my love, we heard, and you did a better than excellent job. Let's get some sleep and get out of here early."

By daybreak the three of them were on the road to Emerald Village. The man at the bar had been right on the money about how bad the road was. Because of washouts and the poor condition of the road, they could only make about 25 to 30 miles an hour. After about two and a half hours, they approached a little village with a sign that read, Emerald Village Welcome. They all noticed it at the same time, but Giles was the first one to say it.

"This is a bloody ghost town. There is not a blooming soul about here. What do you suppose it means?"

Angelita was looking around the village and looked at Raul and spoke. "Raul, there is something terribly wrong here. Bad things have happened here, today."

Raul, knowing that Angelita could sense things, asked her, "Angelita, tell me, are we in danger at this moment?"

Angelita looked as though she was in a trance, speaking very slowly. "No, the soldiers have gone. They have taken girls with them, I can't tell how many, but they have also hurt a lot of people here."

Giles was also looking around in amazement. "My God, what do you suppose happened, and where are the people?"

"They are hiding. Some of them are watching us now. But they are all hiding", Angelita said.

Then Angelita got out of the Jeep, walked to the center of the street, and stood looking upward with her palms facing up.

Raul did a double take, because he could have sworn there was an aura of light radiating from her. After about three minutes of this, people started to come out of their hiding spots and approached Angelita. These people had been beaten and cut, with some severely injured. One man came running from an alley, and was screaming. His left arm had been severed at the elbow and he was bleeding profusely. Raul pulled a tourniquet from his pack, and rushed to the man. After Raul stopped the bleeding, he gave the man a very strong pain killer. With the help of Giles he was able to get an iron heated and sear the wound shut, before the man bled out and died.

As more people started returning to the village, they approached Angelita, and she was talking with them all. It appeared that this Carranza group had camped outside the village last night, and early this morning attacked the village, talking supplies and anything else they wanted. This anything else had included five girls from the village. These were young girls, between 14 and 17 years old. Anybody that showed any form of resistance was dealt with harshly, if not cruelly. Example being the man, minus his left arm.

Angelita came to Giles and Raul, and told them that there were people in holes, just outside the village, who had been shot and dumped. The parents of all the girls kidnapped had been assassinated along with the village officials. She also told them that it was definitely the Carranzas, by the descriptions she had been given. She had also found out that they, the Carranzas, had left approximately an hour before the three arrived, and had headed west into the Jungle. Angelita promised the people of the village that they would return at a later time and help any way they could.

As they were getting back in the Jeep, an old woman took Raul's arm and begged, "Please, sir, these evil people have taken my grandbaby, Angelita. They have killed my daughter and her husband as well as Angelita's older brother. There is no one left in my life, and I beg you, sir, please return my Angelita to me."

Just then Angelita reached out her hand and touched the old woman's cheek. Wiping the tears from it, she said, "Grandma, I promise you that the Warrior Chief will bring your granddaughter home safe." The old woman smiled, and took her hand.

"My sweet little angel", she said, unwavering. "I know that you are an angel, sent from God. I also know you can see things no other can. For this reason, I will light a candle for each of you, and wait by the door for your return."

"And return we will, in jolly good fashion, I might add." Giles chirped in. Giles continually spoke in English, make that the Queen's English. Raul, knowing full well that Giles was, in fact, quite proficient in Spanish, was constantly telling him, "Giles, you're in the jungles of Colombia, say it in Spanish so they have some clue as to what you're saying."

All Giles would do is laugh and say, "Yo quiero Taco Bell! How's that, bloke? Spanish enough for you?"

Raul just shook his head slowly, and they were off. They were able to drive another 15 or so miles before they came to a clearing, where there were three Jeeps and two troop trucks parked. Obviously, this was the 'start walking 'part of the trip. The question now was, which direction did they go? It took about 10 minutes of recon before Giles returned to the group. He advised them he had located a well- hidden swinging bridge, approximately one mile west of them. The three of them headed in the direction of the bridge, and started on the trail of the bandits. The bridge was scary but proved to be serviceable. It was about a hundred and fifty feet long, and spanned between two very high cliffs, overlooking a fast moving river. All they could see in front of them was a very thick jungle, and the afternoon thunderstorms were moving in rapidly. Raul knew they needed to find some cover, and fast. They all got across the bridge safely, and started into the jungle. It was more than thick, it was barely passable, and they all wondered how an army passed this way. After swinging the machetes another five minutes or so, they stopped.

"This is bullshit!" Giles stated. "Nobody has been this way today, there are no tracks, and there is no way a group of seventy people passed this way."

"Well, I have to agree with Giles on this one. I think we need to reassess this plan." Raul said.

They back-tracked to the bridge and started scanning the face of the jungle in front of them. The storms were still moving in rapidly, and cover was going to be a priority very soon.

Angelita looked worried. "Raul, the lighting is very dangerous in the jungle; the rain comes down very hard and disrupts everything. Maybe we should return to the Jeep and wait for the storms to pass."

Raul knew she was right, and they decided to head for the Jeep. As they reached the bridge they stopped suddenly. The bridge was swinging and whipping back and forth violently from the high wind that was blowing through the canyon. They all stopped, staring at their only way out. They all knew that anyone going out on this bridge would be lost to the raging river below. As they stood looking and wondering what plan 'B' was going to be, a crashing blow of lighting struck the face of the jungle, about forty feet to the left of where they had tried to enter. At that moment, trees appeared to open up, creating a passage way in the jungle. They just stared; they couldn't believe what they had just seen. It was impossible, but yet it had happened. After a moment they all ran to opening, and then they realized that the lighting had been a well-placed blast from the heavens that had moved and separated the brush that the bandits had used to hide the trail they had used. They started into the jungle, moving along the cut trail they had found.

Thunder was pounding in the sky and the lighting was putting on a spectacular light show. Soon the heavy rains would be on them, and they needed to find a cave for cover. Advancing along the pathway, they started to hear what sounded like voices. Although weather conditions were making hearing and seeing almost impossible, they stopped, cautiously waiting, trying to distinguish what it was they were hearing. The rain started with heavy drops hitting the ground, as well as them. The drops hit like gun fire, thumping on the ground, randomly bouncing off of each of them. It was a hard rain, and the drops hitting their bare arms hurt. They left the trail, searching for cover. As they moved upward along a hillside, they discovered a hole the size of possibly a bear, or large cat of some sort. Raul broke open a blue light stick and started into the hole. He knew bears weren't a threat in the jungle, but something very large could well be waiting for them inside. Cautiously they moved into the opening, Raul in front, Angelita in the center and Giles bringing up the rear. They had crawled on their hands and knees, about thirty feet, when they discovered that the cave opened into a larger chamber. This cave had not been made by an animal, but rather by humans; probably Indians, native to this region of the country. The cave was old, musty and damp. On the good side, however, it was dry, and provided good protection from the weather.

Wanting to be familiar with their immediate surroundings, the three started exploring their new-found shelter. After some thirty minutes of looking, it was discovered that the cave consisted of a center chamber approximately forty feet in diameter, and five shafts that led away from it. The shafts were all made large enough for a large man to crawl through, unencumbered. Two of the shafts were passage ways to the outside, and one went into a black hole that abruptly dropped off, into what looked liked nothing below.

One of these shafts contained the skeletal remains of what was probably one of the earlier inhabitants. From the two shafts that led outside, they could hear the rain was letting up a bit, and that it was for the most part over, leaving just a steady, light rainfall. Raul crawled to the opposite shaft from the one they had entered, and was looking through his scope, hoping to see anything. After about five minutes of scanning back and forth through the jungle, he thought he heard voices. He motioned to the other two, and they moved to the opening behind him and listened. After a few minutes they were sure of the voices and decided to investigate. Raul and Angelita would check the voices, and Giles would follow them with his scope and provide cover. Raul and Angelita had moved about thirty feet away from the cave opening, and decided it was time to check the new headset radios that Hector had sent them. These were the latest, light-weight, powerful little transmitters available, according to Hector.

Raul activated his radio and whispered. "Giles, can you hear me?"

"Like a bird", he whispered back.

"Angelita, you're hearing everything as well?"

"Perfectly, and do you see what I see beyond those trees?"

Raul moved closer to Angelita and saw what it was she was pointing at.

There were the five girls from the village. They were tied together with a rope around their necks and their hands were bound. They were huddled together under a canopy tree, trying to get away from the rain. Their clothes were torn and out of place, and they had obviously been sexually molested. They had been traumatized and looked to be in shock.

Angelita whispered to Raul. "They are all shaking, and I don't know if it's from being drenched by the rain or from being so scared."

Raul was just observing, scanning through his scope. "It looks like there are only two guards here. The rest of the camp must be further down the trail. Giles, can you see us?"

"No, I lost you in the trees and I can't see the girls, either."

Raul thought for a moment. "This can't be a trick or set up; there is no way they know we are here."

"Let's take out the guards, and get these girls out of harm's way", Angelita whispered.

"Giles," Raul said, "Come out of the hole and get us in your sights, kill anything that comes down the trail."

"That's a 'Roger' on that! I'll let you know when I'm ready."

"Angelita and I will wait for your signal."

Raul assembled his crossbow and Angelita took out her Glock pistol. They were ready.

"OK, I've got you covered" Giles advised. "I've put the silencer on the rifle just in case."

The rain was still coming down at a steady pace as Raul and Angelita moved toward the captives. The first thing they noticed when they got close to where the girls were tied up was that both of the guards were passed out in a drunken stupor. They were so sure no one would try to escape that they left the girls out in the rain, and they were passed out under a make-shift shelter. This was way too easy, but an easy one now and again was kind of nice, so they would take it. Raul watched the two guards while Angelita cut the ropes that bound the girls. She kept them quiet and motioned them to follow her. They were headed back to the cave as Raul watched the guards sleep. Angelita was crossing the trail with the girls when Raul spotted the soldier coming toward her. He had a machete in his right hand that he had raised, getting ready to strike Angelita. Raul's heart stopped for a second. Just as he started running toward the man, he froze. The soldier with the machete stopped in mid- swing, dropped the knife and grabbed his throat. He was trying to scream but nothing, except blood, was coming out of his mouth. His eyes were wide open in shock, and he stood silent momentarily, before falling, lifelessly to the ground.

"Raul, old mate! Did you see a ghost or what? I'll bet you forgot I was covering the trail, didn't you?" Giles booming voice came out of nowhere.

"Actually, Giles, I was just admiring that shot. Through the throat, in the rain, and where the hell are you anyway?"

"Look to your right, up in the trees. Yes, that's me shooting you the bird, mate!"

Raul took the body off of the pathway and hid it in the heavy brush. Maybe some animal would drag it off before the morning, he thought.

They all met back at the cave, where Angelita was helping the girls get themselves together. It was decided that the girls would wait in the cave until the soldiers had moved on and it was safe. The girls had assured Angelita that they knew how to get back to their village, and they would be safe doing so.

The rest of the night passed quietly; the rain finally stopped and the stars came out. The jungle was so tranquil at night. The birds sang and everyone and everything slept. Except Raul; he had taken the first watch and was guarding everyone. He looked around the cave; the girls were huddled together, but he knew they finally felt safe. Giles was snoring off in the corner by himself. There was Angelita, not far from him, sleeping peacefully. She was so beautiful, so perfect, and tough as nails. God had created a perfect woman; he was sure of it.

Giles, who had taken the second watch, woke Raul and Angelita and motioned not to talk. He signaled them to follow him to the cave opening.

When they got into positions where they could all see, what they saw was the two drunken guards standing at attention and another man yelling at them. A closer look revealed that this was their hit - the man with the nasty scar. He was flanked on either side but what looked to be his two brothers. All three targets right together, this could also be an easy hit. With silencers, if they each took one at the same time, no one would know where they were, and in the confusion they wouldn't be looking anyway.

"What do you say, Chief?" Giles whispered.

Raul looked at him, and before he could answer his cell phone started vibrating.

"Who the hell could be calling me here? Who is this?" he demanded.

"Raul, this is Epi. I know the three of them are great targets, but don't take them out right now. We need them alive for the time being, OK?"

"You're in the jungle right now, close to us?"

"Yes. Ricky and I are both here. Listen, I can see the soldiers from where I am, but I'm not sure where you guys are and I need you to do something."

"What would that be?" Raul asked.

"I'm going to approach this guy in a minute, and unless everything turns to shit, don't do anything. No matter what you see, no matter what you think. Unless this wacko looks like he is going to kill me, don't take any shots. OK?"

"I understand; we will be here watching."

They then turned their attentions back to the soldiers. The yelling was getting louder and the ugly guy in charge was really getting worked up.

"I want to know how the fuck those girls got away. Who has my answer?!" Santiago Carranza stood glaring at the two guards who were speechless, and obviously scared to death, with good reason.

"Where is your sergeant? We can't find him, either. Did he run off with the girls? Does he want them all for himself? Does he think he can fuck all of them himself? He doesn't want to share those cute little bodies? Well, answer me, you stupid morons!"

The two stood mute; they knew better than to antagonize the situation any further by saying anything.

Carranza was pacing back and forth, swinging the machete he was carrying. He was talking to himself. No, correct that, he was arguing with himself. This was a scary man, no doubt.

Finally he stopped, looked at the two men and said, "Tell me the truth, you were drunk and passed out and those little bitches just walked away. Isn't that right?"

"Well, sir." One of them spoke, almost inaudibly. "Maybe what you said about Rafael, I mean Sgt. Hernandez, is true. Maybe he took them somewhere and will be back."

Carranza glared at him and yelled in his face. "Everything is maybe with you; is that because you were asleep at your post?! I've decided you need to go to sleep for good, both of you." He then motioned to two other soldiers, who grabbed the man and threw him to his knees. The man, with terror in his eyes, started to plead for his life just as Carranza's machete came crashing down on his neck, decapitating him. He looked at the other soldier, and chuckling, said "Next."

Fear had already caused this man to lose all bodily control. He was shaking uncontrollably, smelled of feces, and was crying and babbling incoherently. When the other soldiers tried to grab his arms to put him on his knees, he broke free and started running at Carranza.

Carranza, without hesitating, started hacking the man to death with the machete. Decapitation would have been a welcome option to the torture this man suffered. Raul cringed at what he had just witnessed and thought to himself, "I should have killed him last night and saved them from this."

Angelita took his arm. "Then they would know we are here, and those five innocent girls wouldn't be out of danger, like they are now."

As always, Raul could only look at his angel in amazement. She not only read his mind, but she was absolutely correct in her assessment of the situation.

Just as Raul and the rest of them were wondering what was next, their question was answered. Epi came walking up the trail, dressed as a soldier. More surprisingly, Ricky was following her. His hands were bound, and she held the end of a rope that was tied around his neck. Epi walked right up to Santiago Carranza, who was covered in the soldier's blood, and spoke. "Excuse me; I'm looking for Capt. Santiago Carranza."

Raul looked at Giles, who was shaking his head, and asked, "You have any idea what is going on?"

Giles laughed. "None whatsoever, my good man, but you Yanks never cease to amaze me."

Angelita had a strange look on her face and offered, "It would really be nice if the right hand knew what the left hand was doing. Don't you think?"

Raul was busy setting up the portable voice transmitter. "Give me just a minute, and we'll all know what's going on."

Santiago looked and Epi and smiled. "Who, might I ask are you, my cute little soldier?"

"The name is Esperanza Marcos, and I'm not yours, or anyone else's, cute little soldier. I'm a mercenary soldier from Cuba. Are you Carranza or not?"

"Well aren't you the tough little thing? What do you want with Santiago Carranza?"

"Listen, Jack, I didn't come all this way to play twenty questions with some underling. If you know where Carranza is, tell me, or get the fuck out of my way."

"The name is not Jack! It is Capt. Santiago Carranza, and normally I would kill someone who talked to me like that. But you're tough, and I like that. What do you want with me, anyway?"

"Well sir, if you are in fact Capt. Carranza, then I have brought you a present."

"A present? This man is a present?"

"Not just a present, but the Ghost Warrior."

Raul started to laugh as he listened. "I don't know who wrote her script, but it is hilarious."

Capt. Santiago looked at Ricky and then back at Epi. "How long have you been in Colombia, my cute little butterfly?"

"I arrived two days ago, found him in the Guatavita area, and decided to find you. Why?"

"Why did you want to find me, might I ask?"

"I told you, I'm a mercenary from Cuba. I go where the money is."

"They know about Capt. Santiago Carranza in Cuba?"

"Why does that surprise you? Actually, you have quite a reputation, and that is why I wanted to look you up. Possibly you need another good soldier?"

"You are right about the good soldiers, but this man is not the 'Ghost Warrior'. I can assure you of that."

"How do you know that, if the guy is supposed to be a ghost?"

"Ghost or not, the Ghost Warrior is not a Gringo. He is some kind of Indian."

Rafael Santiago, the youngest of the three, stepped between Santiago and Epi. "He is a Navajo Indian, and I know all about him. That man is a Gringo and not the Ghost Warrior, you stupid bitch." Rafael grabbed Epi by the shirt and lifted a fist to punch her.

Epi's right foot came up and caught Rafael right in the crotch. Rafael doubled up, grabbed his crotch, and fell over, groaning.

"I'm not stupid, you little shit, and never put your hands on me again. The next time I won't ring your bell; I'll kill you."

Santiago and his other brother Pepe were laughing uncontrollably at what had just happened. Santiago bent over to help Rafael up. "Get up, tough guy, and go put ice on your balls. And don't fuck with girls tougher than you. You could get hurt."

Rafael hobbled off and the older Carranzas were still laughing at their little brother. Santiago stopped abruptly and asked, "So, who is this guy, anyway?"

Epi handed him a badge case. "I thought he was the one you wanted. He's CIA. How many CIA agents are running around in the jungle in this country, anyway?"

Santiago looked at her. "You would be surprised, my little butterfly, about just who is running around in the jungles of Colombia. But that doesn't matter now. What does matter now is what to do with this gringo CIA shit. I say let's cut him up and feed him to the crocodiles."

Ricky never stopped watching Santiago Carranza. "You're pretty tough with the machete in your hands and mine tied up, aren't you, Sport?"

Carranza got so angry that he actually began to growl. "I think I'll cut your hands off, you gringo pig!" Carranza started moving toward Ricky with the machete in the air.

Epi stepped between them. "Wait just a minute! If this is not the guy you wanted, then he is my prisoner and I get to kill him." As she was talking, she withdrew a S&W 9 mil. automatic from her belt and fired twice, hitting Ricky square in the chest. Blood shot from the wounds and Ricky flew back three feet and fell to the ground. Carranza, with a shocked look on his face, stared at Ricky lying on the ground with blood trickling out of his mouth.

"Holy shit! You are a pretty tough broad! I can use you in my army. Want to join?"

"Let's go back to camp and talk money", Epi said with a smile as they walked off towards the camp.

Raul and the other two were speechless. Raul had just witnessed Epi killing a good friend of his, not to mention hers as well. Something was definitely not kosher here.

The troops had all cleared out, leaving the bodies on the trail. Giles and Raul left the cave and Angelita stayed to watch over the girls. They approached Ricky's body on the ground, and he sure did look dead enough, but Raul thought, "That can't be, it just doesn't add up."

Giles was standing over Ricky and said, "I'm sorry mate, this one took two square in the chest, and there is an awful lot of blood hereabouts, now isn't there?"

Raul and Giles were staring at Ricky, when to both of their surprise, he suddenly opened his eyes and exclaimed, "Giles, I thought you were dead!"

Giles jumped back and yelped. "My God, man, you've given us a scare, now haven't you?!"

Raul didn't move; he just smiled and said, "Well I figured as much. There is no way Epi was gonna kill 'big fellow' now, was there?"

Ricky was smiling and replied sheepishly. "She told you about the 'big fellow' thing?"

"Every single detail, you Saxon Dog, you. Here, let me help you up."

"Help me out of this bullet proof vest. Epi insisted I put the armor piercing plate in, and it weighs a ton."

Giles looked at him and laughed. "Those two red welts on your chest have got to hurt. Not that you don't deserve it for the bloody scare you gave us."

The three of them headed back to the cave, and as they walked Raul radioed Angelita and told her about the acting job Epi and Ricky had done.

They had been in the cave approximately ten minutes, talking about everything from the five girls huddled in the corner to Grandma's funeral, when Giles finally asked what everyone was thinking. "So Ricky, would you care to enlighten us as to what the hell is going on, or shall we remain in the dark, flying by the seat of our trousers?"

Ricky smiled as he looked at everyone. "OK, here's the deal. We needed to find out exactly where Carranza's hiding place was. So we thought, what better way than if one of us was in his army. Epi came up with the little show you saw, and we thought it might just do the trick. And it did."

Raul stared at him with a concerned look. "Didn't you think for one minute how risky this plan was? You had absolutely no control over the situation, not to mention what an unstable character this Carranza is."

"Possibly", Ricky said. "But we knew you guys were here after we talked to you, and falling on *this* hurt as much as the two shots hitting the vest." Ricky pulled a S&W 9 mm that was stuck in his belt at the small of his back. "Besides, it's a dangerous job. We all know that."

"So, now what?" Angelita asked. "What's the plan to find the hide out?"

Ricky pulled a miniature tracking device out of his pocket, and explained. "Epi has the locator part of this GPS on her, so we will track her that way. I really don't think Carranza's hideout is far from here, - just hidden well."

Angelita smiled. "Good. Now we can track her, and we have one more shooter with us to help even the odds."

Ricky just looked at Angelita. "Actually, the tracking part is correct, but the shooting part is not. I'm an intelligence officer, not a sniper. I thought you knew that."

Giles abruptly jumped into the conversation. "What a riot! Ricky is a linguist, not a shooter. You didn't know that? What that means is while we are killing people with our rifles, Ricky is busy talking them to death. If I'm not mistaken, you also read lips or something of that sort."

Ricky stared at Giles. "That's right, asshole, and can you read this?" Ricky was holding up the middle finger of his left hand.

"Testy, testy. You Yanks take everything so seriously." Giles laughed.

"Yank this", Ricky muttered as he walked away.

Meanwhile the five girls, under the direction of Angelita, had prepared dinner from the rations they had brought with them. They called everyone to dine.

After they had eaten, Raul and Ricky were outside the cave enjoying the evening before the inevitable storms moved in. Raul was looking out toward the trail, and asked, "So, tell me Ricky, what's the real reason you and Epi got involved in this job? We both know this shoot was relatively cut and dry. You know, follow the bad guy, find out what you need to know, and take care of business."

"The President called us in for a meeting after you left. It seems this Carranza has some strong political ties to the government that everybody forgot to tell us about. He apparently has ties in the judicial system, and on and on. I personally think he's got stuff on a lot of people in high places, and it's scaring them. Oh, and by the way, it's not forty million in gold bars any longer."

"It's not. Why?"

"Because after the dust settled, the figure went to over one hundred million, plus he is supposed to have a lab out here somewhere for coke processing. I personally think that part is bullshit, and they threw it in to help us. You know, the United States wants to help get rid of him. Only time will tell us that for sure."

"So what is Epi going to do, now that she has infiltrated them?"

"She has the GPS I told you about, plus she has a voice transmitter. We should be hearing from her soon."

"So I guess we just sit tight until we do, right?"

Just as Ricky was getting ready to answer Raul, he stopped and put his right index finger on the device in his right ear. "Got it, you OK? Let me know if there are any problems, promise? Good, we'll wait for your call in the AM. You, too, and be careful!"

"Just a guess, but I'll bet that was Epi. What's up?"

"They are going to break camp at 6:00am sharp and head for the hideout. It is supposed to be about a day's walk from here, to the north."

"Looks like we'll be tracking come morning." Raul smiled.

Just then lightning flashed across the sky, followed by an ear-shattering crack of thunder. "Five o'clock." Raul said. "You could just about set your clock by the weather out here in this jungle."

"I guess it's time to rendezvous with the troops in the cave and start making some plans?" Ricky asked.

"Not much to plan until we know where this Carranza fellow hides, but I'm all for going inside the cave", Raul said with a grin.

By 5am everyone in the cave was ready to go. Angelita had taken the girls out the 'back way', and sent them back to their village. She had promised to come and visit them, after her work was done in the jungle.

The girls all hugged her and ran off in the direction of the village. Angelita felt good about saving them; she felt like she had actually done some good in a very nasty business.

By 6 AM they had received a call from Epi, and the troops were moving out. Raul and the rest of them waited about another 15 minutes to give them enough time to assure themselves they weren't being followed. Raul and Angelita tracked on the right side of the trail while Giles and Ricky stayed on the left. Carranza and his army were forced marching and didn't stop the entire day. They just walked and walked, never taking a break. It was about 2:30 pm when the troops came to a point in the trail where the trail narrowed from two lanes to a single path. The path stretched about a half mile and hugged the side of a steep mountain. On the left side was a three hundred foot drop, to a river below, and in front of them was a gigantic waterfall that cascaded from fifty feet above them, crashing into the river below.

Angelita marveled at the sight. "What a beautiful spot this is. It's probably as close to heaven as you can get on earth".

Raul was studying the area, watching the troops, wondering where the hell they were going. Then it dawned on him. He keyed his mike and asked, "Giles, Ricky, do you see where they are headed? No one has found them because their hideout is in a cave, behind that waterfall."

Ricky responded. "It must be one hell of a big cave to hold all those troops, the gold bars, and everything else that is supposed to be in there."

Giles broke in. "We don't know for sure that this is a cave. Maybe it's a pass-through to the other side of the mountain. We need to find a place to set up and do some recon before we start anything.

"I agree." Raul answered. "Hopefully, we will hear something from Epi about the inside of the cave."

The group back-tracked and found a small plateau on the side of the mountain, with a clear view of the waterfall entrance. The four of them set up camp and waited for some word from Epi.

It was about 8pm. The storms had passed and the night was peaceful, as usual. Ricky's phone started to vibrate. "Hey, how are you doing? Good! What do you have for us?"

After about a five minute conversation, Ricky closed his cell phone and told the group that Epi was going to meet him on the trail in 15 minutes. She had drawn a map of the cave and detailed everything she could for them. She had also told him that the cave was gigantic, and that all the troops were inside. The cave contained four large chambers that she had seen, along with six or seven small rooms that were closed off with doors. This was not a nasty 'hole in the mountain cave', but rather a well fortified compound, complete with all the comforts of home. There was a radio room, armory, kitchen and dining facility. The troops were bunked in two chambers and she believed that the Carranza's had private rooms, but she didn't know exactly where, yet. The compound had six large air shafts and the top of the cave was guarded by three men at all times. There was a rear escape route that would be on the map, with directions on how to get there. The four of them looked at each other, knowing full well that everything they did would have to be from the inside. They were going to have to sneak into the cave to start their offensive.

Ricky returned with the map and a layout of the operation inside. Epi had told Ricky that she had not seen a laboratory in the cave, and did not think there was one in there. "Well, that's a plus", Giles told them. "At least we don't have to worry about blowing ourselves up, along with them. You know, all those chemicals and such. Definitely a nasty business when the shooting starts."

After thinking for a while, Raul responded, "Here's my idea. Ricky, you take these gas canisters, go to the top of the cave and drop them in at a set time. Giles, you work your way around back of the cave and set up just outside. You know, so you have as clear a view as possible for shots inside. Angelita, I'm going to need you to set up at the front of the cave, by the waterfall. If anyone besides Epi or me leaves the cave, shoot them."

"You?" they responded in unison.

"Yes, me. One of us has to go into the cave and start this job. It might as well be me. I will take a gas mask, sneak into the cave, and push them out. Once they are outside, you guys will take over. Angelita, you up for this?"

She looked at him, smiled, and answered, "Absolutely, but I would appreciate it if you would help me set up."

"That goes without saying. Giles, Ricky, what do you think?"

Giles laughed a little. "Jolly good plan; let's get on with this bunk."

Ricky just gave Raul a thumbs up, and asked, "When do you want to get started?"

"No time like the present, is there? Give those clowns in the cave about an hour and they should either be passed out drunk, or well on their way. That gives us surprise on our side.

Ricky got ready to go, and the group set their watches. At exactly eight o'clock Ricky would drop the gas into the cave. After that, he would join Raul in the cave to help him. Giles would be set up at the rear, and Angelita would be ready in the front. Angelita took out four red armbands and they each put one on. This was especially important for Raul and Ricky. There was going to be a lot of shooting and confusion; identifying the targets was most important.

Ricky set out, carrying two bundles of gas canisters. He was approximately two hundred feet down the path when Giles keyed his mike and his voice sounded very anxious. "Raul, look down the path, there are three soldiers walking toward Ricky. I think we have a problem. Do you want me to assist him?"

"No, stand down, wait to see what happens. I don't want to give anything away. Besides, it's only three troops. What are you getting excited about? Ricky can take care of himself."

"Well, I don't know all that much about Ricky, but I bloody well think he has a problem. I mean, he doesn't look all that tough to me, and there are three of them."

Angelita laughed and keyed her mike. "Well, Sport, as they say in this country, maybe you had better look again." Angelita looked at Raul, who was intently watching the path. "Your friend Giles, he's from England, right? Is it just me, or is he really kind of an obnoxious fellow? Doesn't he know Ricky could tear him apart without even thinking about it?"

Boy, has this Colombian girl really done well learning English, he thought. "Yes to your first question; Giles is obnoxious at times, and no to your second question; he has no idea what Ricky can or can't do. But I think he's about to find out, isn't he?" Raul set up his crossbow and got ready.

Raul and Giles had good vantage points on the pathway. Although they were in different locations, neither one could hear what was being said by the soldiers. The rush of the waterfall was overpowering every sound in the jungle.

The three soldiers approached Ricky with their rifles raised. The soldier on the far left pointed to Ricky and yelled, "Gringo, what are you doing in my jungle, and what are you carrying?"

Ricky waited until they were in range - close contact kicking range. The first kick was a spinning back-kick that caught the man on the left in the throat. The kick sent the man over the edge of the cliff into the river below. The second kick, which was part of the same smooth action, was a reverse spinning back-kick that landed square in the face of the man on the right. He dropped his rifle and grabbed his face. Blood was pouring from his mouth and nose, and running through his fingers.

The man in the center was completely startled and just stood there, waiting for the inevitable. His demise came in the form of a low sweeping kick that broke his right knee on contact. The man dropped to his other knee and started to scream in pain. Before the scream could come out of his mouth, the second kick hit him on the side of the head. His head spun around abruptly snapping his neck. The man stayed kneeling momentarily, and then fell to the ground, dead. The soldier with the broken face turned and started to run back toward the waterfall. Just as he turned, an arrow from Raul's crossbow struck him in the base of the skull. It was an instant kill. Ricky looked back toward Raul, keyed his mike and asked, "You thought for some particular reason I might need help?"

"No, I knew you didn't need help. I just didn't want you to drop the gas canisters. They're all that we have."

Ghost Warrior

Ricky smiled, set the bags of gas down gently, and threw the two bodies over the edge of the cliff. That done, he continued down the trail towards the cave and the air shafts.

Giles was a sight to see. He was watching the entire fight through his scope, with his mouth hanging open. "Raul, did you see what I just saw? He took out the three of them without dropping the gas cans or using his hands. That bloke can certainly fight with his feet, can't he?"

Ricky keyed his mike and broke into the conversation. "Giles, give it a rest, you are starting to annoy me. I hope you shoot as good as you run your mouth!"

"Quite actually, I shoot better." Giles replied matter-of-factly.

Ricky, as well as everyone else, just ignored him. "Giles is Giles, and he is a hell of a shooter", Ricky thought as he walked along toward the top of the cave.

Giles studied the map Epi had given them and found the best area to set up in behind the cave's back exit. He tied the map to a rock and threw it to where Raul and Angelita stood. He waved to them and was off.

It was a quarter to 8 and Raul was getting ready to go into the cave. Angelita kissed him and made him promise to be careful. "That's kind of an oxy-moron in our line of work, isn't it?"

He knew that Angelita didn't understand what he had just said, so he just laughed to himself, and helped her get set up. "Remember, anybody except Epi or myself trying to leave the cave are your targets. You up for this, right?"

Angelita looked at him, smiled and said, "What is it you Americans say; 'does a bear shit in the woods, or what'?"

"That's my girl, you sexy thing, you!"

"Another gringo expression?"

Raul laughed, put on his armband, took his crossbow with both exploding and regular arrows, and put them in their case. He took his rifle, stuck his Glock automatic in his belt and started off. He went about 15 feet, snapped his fingers and turned. As he turned Angelita threw him his gas mask. "Now don't forget to come back; Navajo Ghost Warriors are hard to find around here."

"Keep it hot, honey." Raul said as he walked away.

"Keep what hot?" Angelita said to herself. "Another American expression. I wonder what he means by that?"

Five minutes to eight and Raul was under the waterfall. He had just killed the single guard that was posted outside the cave. He had used his knife to cut the man's throat, and he figured Ricky had done the same with the other three guards at the top of the cave. He had seen one body go over the waterfall, the same as he had done with his kill. Raul slipped into the cave unnoticed. The first thing he saw was a large chamber, which looked like a dining or meeting room. Off to the right was a radio room with a single operator at the desk. To the left of that was a door marked 'armory'. Epi had done a great job laying out the cave's interior for them, he thought to himself. Behind the meeting room was a kitchen. There were two men inside who he pegged as cooks, cleaning up the kitchen after dinner. He was totally surprised to find no one else in sight. Once again he wondered if it was a trap, but then no one knew they were here. He deduced rapidly that they just felt very secure in their hide out. 'Well, that will change soon", he said to himself with a chuckle. Raul withdrew his crossbow, put a standard arrow in it, and aimed at the man sitting at the desk in the communications room. The man's back was to Raul and he had no idea death was coming his way. The arrow hit with a thump. Raul had fired at the man's back, through the chair. The arrow had pierced the chair's back and stuck in the man's heart. When it hit the man, he was so surprised that he put his right hand on the protruding arrow tip that was sticking out from the center of his chest. He looked down at the tip and died. He was stuck to the chair, just as Raul wanted, and everything looked normal. Raul put on his mask as he looked at his watch. Eight o'clock; time to play.

The first gas canister landed in the kitchen; in fact, it hit one of the cooks standing under the air shaft. When it exploded it caught his hat on fire. Before the man could yell out, a little black spot appeared in his forehead with a trickle of blood. The back of his head exploded as the 22 round exited his skull. The other cook stood looking at the man in total disbelief. The second round caught this man just above the right ear, sending him crashing into the stove and setting his left arm sleeve on fire. The kitchen was now burning.

As the canisters fell, Raul could hear the troops scurrying about further into the cave. The cave was now engulfed in smoke from the gas canisters, and there was yelling and confusion throughout. Just the way Raul wanted it. Raul started down the tunnel next to the radio room. As he was moving, he saw a group of five or six soldiers coming at him. They were huddled together, unable to see clearly from the smoke. Raul quickly loaded an exploding arrow into the crossbow. He fired into the group and the arrow exploded, sending body parts in different directions. He continued down the corridor, He saw a group of about fifteen soldiers advancing toward him. Raul noticed that the younger Carranza brother was leading this group. He had his pistol out but was busy wiping tears from his eyes as he ran. Raul couldn't believe that there were no gas masks in this cave. For sure they weren't boy scouts, because they sure were not prepared. Raul let them run past him as they headed for the exit. He radioed Angelita and told her they were coming, and the lead runner was one of the Carranza brothers.

Angelita radioed back. "Got the little maggot in my sights. OK, he just went swimming without part of his head. What about the rest of them?"

"What are they doing now?" Raul asked.

"They threw their weapons over the cliff and are lined up with their hands in the air."

"Don't give your position away. Fire one shot over their heads and see if they sit down."

"They did, they are just sitting along the path, waiting."

"Good, just keep your eye on the waterfall and see who comes out and what they do."

Just as Raul rounded a turn in the corridor, he saw Ricky coming into the cave from the rear. He waited for him and they began searching together. They still had two Carranza brothers and about fifty or so troops to deal with. Neither one of them could figure out why they hadn't emerged with all the gas that had exploded in the cave. So far Ricky and Raul were the only ones wearing masks. This was not right, and needed further investigation. Ricky was carrying a sawed-off shotgun in one hand, and had his other hand on the S&W 9mm in his belt. They approached a door and tried to open it. "Locked", Ricky observed out loud as he stepped back from it. He fired one blast from the shotgun at the door's handle. The door swung open slowly. Ricky covered Raul as he entered the room. In the room they found fifteen partially clothed women, who were obviously prisoners of this perverse, fucked up group of guerillas. The women looked as if they had been sexually molested, beaten up and just plain abused in general. They were grouped together and scared to death. They were being guarded by three soldiers who had thrown their weapons down when the door blew open.

The soldiers were standing together on the opposite side of the room with their hands in the air. "Please don't kill us, we are just guards!" they pleaded. Ricky saw what looked like riot batons standing in the corner. There were about six of them; night sticks that were larger than the normal 24". These were about 40 inches long. He looked at Raul, smiled and walking over to them, picked up three and took them to the women huddled together.

"Here, take these, and watch the guards for us. Don't leave this room until we come to get you. Consider yourselves free as of this moment, and, oh, don't let the guards escape, either. OK?!"

The women grabbed the batons from Ricky, and as they stared at the guards, one of them said, "You don't have to worry at all about the guards leaving here; we will take care of them." Ricky glanced towards the guards and saw that they were terrified, as they should have been. They were about to get a dose of their own medicine, with the same sticks they had been using on these women.

As Ricky and Raul were leaving the room, Raul smiled and asked, "Don't you just love it when people get what they deserve?" They could hear the guards yelling and crying as the batons bounced off them.

"Good to see there is some fight left in these women!" Ricky said.

"Raul looked at him, paused for a moment and added, "There is a lesson to learn here, you know."

"And that would be?" Ricky responded.

"Never piss off a woman with a stick in her hand, let alone, fifteen of them."

They both smiled as they exited the room, knowing justice was being served.

They rounded another corner in the corridor and discovered that the passageway split, with one corridor emptying into a large chamber; one of the two sleeping quarters Epi had put on the map. The other was the passage that Rick had used to enter from the rear.

Raul had asked Ricky if he had passed any other rooms or doorways as he entered. Ricky had seen two doors, both locked, and he had not tried to open them.

Raul and Ricky were standing right at the dividing point for the two passageways when one of the doors Ricky had passed flew open. Leading a group of about ten troops was the second Carranza brother. But still, brother number three, the scar-faced ugly bastard, was nowhere to be found, Raul thought. Just as they were getting ready to start shooting at the approaching group, they saw another group of about ten soldiers coming from the large chamber. They were caught in the middle. They also noticed that most of these men were wearing gas masks, so their vision wasn't as impaired as the first group.

Quickly, they decided that Ricky would take the chamber side and Raul the passageway side. The only problem was that these men were carrying Russian-made AK 47 machine guns. Ricky and Raul stepped back from the division of the passageways behind some cover, ready to make a stance, when they saw men from the group coming down the corridor start to fall. In less then twenty seconds, nine of the ten men lay dead on the ground, all from well-placed head shots. 'Instant kills', as they were known in the Company. Ricky was shooting at the approaching soldiers from the chamber when he noticed the only one standing in the corridor was Pepe Carranza. Pepe lifted his machine gun and pointed it directly at Raul and Ricky. He was about to start yelling and charging them when his forehead exploded, sending blood gushing down over his face. Pepe Carranza stood in the hallway for a few seconds with that 'what just happened?' look in his eyes. He fell forward, not having fired one shot from his gun. His face hit the dirt floor of the cave and bounced once. There, Pepe Carranza lay lifeless, in the blood-soaked dirt. Ricky had either killed or wounded four of the approaching troops. There were six left that entered the corridor. They stopped when they saw Carranza's body. The lead man turned, eyes searching down the corridor, trying to see who was shooting at them. This was the last thing he did before he died. As the soldier stood with his right palm facing out staring looking down the hall, a fast moving rifle slug pierced his hand and struck him directly between the eyes. The impact from the shot threw him back a couple of feet, and he struck the side of the passageway. As he slid down the wall, he stopped in a sitting position, lifeless, not knowing who or what had done this to him. The other five soldiers were deciding between fighting or retreating. The question was solved when Raul asked them if they were ready to die for these crazy leaders. They threw down their weapons and surrendered. Ricky told them to sit in the corridor and not to move, because if they did, they would suffer the same fate as the others. They all sat perfectly still, just looking down at the dirt floor.

"Giles is one hell of a shot!" Ricky exclaimed. "He made some fantastic shots down this corridor, didn't he?"

"No doubt about it, he's a great shooter. If his sense of humor didn't suck, he could be fun to be around. But, a spotted pony will always be a spotted pony."

"Indian philosophy, right?" Ricky asked.

"Nope, just an observation, Blue Coat.", Raul chuckled.

Raul and Ricky were starting to get concerned. They had not heard from Epi nor had they seen any sign of her. "Time to start looking for Epi." Ricky announced.

"I agree. You want to split up or stay together?" Raul asked.

While they were deciding, their radios keyed and Epi asked, "Have you boys cleaned up the cave yet?"

"Pretty much so.", Ricky answered. "We were just looking for you. Can you give us an idea where you are?"

"Look on my map; you will see a second chamber."

"We are standing in front of it.", Raul responded.

"Good. Go through the chamber, down a little hall off to the left, and you will see a door. I'm in that room.

Ricky asked, "Do you have any idea where Carranza is, or the so-called gold vault is?"

"Yep, I sure do", she said flatly.

Ricky looked at Raul with concern. "That did not sound good at all, did it? Do you think it's a set up, and Epi is the bait?"

"I think something is definitely not right, but I don't think Epi would let them use her to lead us into a trap. I think she is telling us something. I just don't know what yet."

Ricky looked at him. "OK.... Let's go find out."

Very cautiously they moved through the chamber. They discovered eight more dead soldiers. Each one had been shot at close range and left sitting at tables or on the floor, against the walls. "She must have killed them earlier and set them up like this, not to draw suspicion." Raul said. "You've got a pretty smart girl there, big fellow."

"Cute. Pay attention to our work and less to my sex life, OK?" Ricky added.

Raul was laughing as they passed through the chamber and up to the door. There were no sounds at all on the other side. After listening a few seconds, quite unexpectedly Ricky kicked the door open. That startled Raul, but what they saw in the room startled them both more. Epi was standing in front of them with one foot on Santiago Carranza's face. Carranza was dead on the floor, with his throat cut from ear to ear, and a serrated hunting knife stuck in his forehead, between his eyes. Epi's clothes were in shambles; her blouse was torn and her bra had been torn open, revealing one of her breasts. Ricky took off his vest and went to her, covering her up. The three of them were standing in the gold vault, with over one hundred million dollars in gold bullion staring at them. "If you don't mind me asking", Raul said cautiously, "What happened? And I would add, you have done a fine job handling the situation."

Epi looked at Raul very seriously. "This pig son of a bitch asked me if I wanted to see the gold vault, just before the shooting started. I figured it would be nice to know where the vault was so we wouldn't have to look for it later. Two guards came with us into the vault, and I figured, OK, this is business, no problem. We were in here for maybe five minutes and the guards slipped out, closing the door behind them. This piece of shit says to me 'time to show me your tits'. I laughed at him and said, 'not a chance', and started for the door. He grabbed me, ripped my blouse and said, 'I inspect the tits of all the cute little things I fuck, so show them to me'. He then proceeded to tear my bra. 'Nice tits' is what he said, just before I slit his throat. I guess I was really pissed at him, and that's why I stuck the knife in his head."

Raul and Ricky looked at each other, shaking their heads in unison. "Nice touch, very clean; you handled it perfectly."

"You clowns want to get out of here and let me fix my shirt before we do a cleanup sweep?"

"Absolutely." Ricky said smiling.

Epi smiled at him, winked, and pointed her finger at the door. "Out, Bozo!"

Both men left the room, and Raul keyed his mike. "Angelita, do you copy?"

"I do. What's going on with Epi? Is she alright?"

Raul answered her. "All is well; we will be coming out soon. What's going on with your prisoners?"

"Seven more came out of the cave, surrendered, and sat down with the others. Everything is fine. I'm still in position, waiting for you."

Epi came out of the room, clothes repaired and talking on her cell phone. She handed Ricky his vest and said to both of them, "I have notified headquarters, and troops and helicopters are on the way. On the way here we asked the people of the little village, just the other side of the swing bridge, to make a clearing on this side for the choppers. They said they would, and we should have government troops here in about twenty minutes."

Raul told Angelita to meet them at the waterfall in five minutes, and the three of them left the cave. Raul called to Giles and told him to meet at the waterfall. Giles told him all was well with him, but he had to leave, and he would see them on another mission sometime in the future.

"What the hell is he talking about?" Ricky asked. "He doesn't have a ride out of here, does he?"

Raul smiled. "Nothing Giles does would surprise me."

At that moment, the three of them saw a very British helicopter approach the cave, hover at the top and throw a rope ladder out. Giles climbed into the chopper and keyed his mike. "Talley ho, I must say, this was a bloody riot. See you again; don't hesitate to call!"

Giles waved to them as they flew off. They all waved back and Angelita turned to Ricky and Epi. "When the government troops get here, Raul and I are going back to Emerald village to meet with a little old grandmother and help out if we can.

Ricky looked at Raul, smiling. "Boy, that doesn't sound like CIA assassin's day, now does it? Why do I keep hearing Celine Dion singing 'The Power of Love'?"

Epi eyed Ricky with a blank expression. "I'm going with them. Weren't you planning on going?"

"Absolutely, sweetheart; wouldn't miss it for the world."

Laughing, Raul addressed Ricky. "Let's go, tough guy; you and Big Fellow can lead the way."

Ricky feigned annoyance. "Can't I get a little slack here? Some things are supposed to be personal."

The three were laughing at him and Epi grabbed Ricky's arm and hugged it. "I personally think I hear the government helicopters headed this way, so after we help the people of Emerald Village, we can once again 'personally' discuss whatever you would like."

As the government troops loaded the gold and assembled the prisoners, they saw the women who had been held captive coming from the front of the cave. The women were splattered with blood, obviously from the guards they had beaten with the batons. They looked exhausted and a little in shock, but when they saw Ricky and Raul, they started waving and yelling to them. "Thank you, thank you. God bless you for helping us!"

Ricky and Raul waved back and smiled at them, as Raul looked at Angelita and Epi. "There are a few more people whose lives will be a bit better from today on. The women were getting into a government helicopter as Ricky, Raul and their women slipped away, headed for Emerald Village and a night of peace and quiet.

CHAPTER V
THE PHANTOM WITH THE CLAWS
PART I

Is the face of evil truly real, or is it a ghost that jumps from place to place? Are there spirits amongst us that attract evil, and render a comfortable home wherein it may dwell? Can one man nurture an evil seed and cause it to bloom into a garden?
I think maybe so.....

Raul and Angelita were sitting in the airport in San Jose, Costa Rica, waiting for their flight back to El Dorado Airport in Bogota. Raul was listening to the music coming from his MP3 player. "There is nothing more difficult than living without you...." Marco Antonio Solis was singing. What a great line that was, Raul was thinking. Solis was one of Raul's favorite Spanish singers. "Mexico certainly has produced some great singers over the years", he thought to himself.

Raul and Angelita had taken a well-deserved vacation, while Epi and Ricky were supervising the construction of a South American base camp on the farm. The two had always wanted to spend some time in Costa Rica, and that they had done. Los Suenos Resort had been home for three weeks, while they toured the parks and beach cities in the area. They had seen every tourist spot in San Jose, including the museums and cultural centers. Raul had watched the glow in Angelita's face as they shopped in the stores and even visited the large mercado downtown. She was happy, and that made him happy.

Ninety days had passed so quickly, and they had seen every square mile of Costa Rica together, just like tourists. Raul thought each day had been better than the day before. He could get used to this; maybe they should take a cruise somewhere.

"Raul, wake up! Stop day dreaming! I think they are calling our seats. Could you check the tickets?" Angelita asked.

"Yep, that's us, let's go. You got your stuff?" he asked as they were headed for the jetway.

"What are you thinking about?" she asked as they were settling into their seats.

"I was thinking that these first class seats are really the way to fly. What do you think?"

"I think that is a big fat lie, that's what I think."

"OK, maybe I was thinking....wait, you know exactly what I was thinking, you always know."

"Just relax my love; we have plenty of time for a cruise. In fact maybe we could take one with Ricky and Epi. I like them; they are good people."

"How about I ask you that, after you see what they did or didn't do to your farm?"

Raul and Angelita were shocked to find the farm looking the same as it did when they left, with the exception of an extra closet in the bedroom Grandma had used.

"Do you think they changed their minds, and didn't do anything?" Angelita asked.

Raul laughed and said, "Sweetheart, they did everything they said they would do, they just did a good job of it. If I remember correctly, Epi promised you she wouldn't change the farm, right?

"But look, Grandma's closet looks the same; it even has some of her clothes in it, like we left it. The other closet just looks like a closet. I don't think they did anything."

As they were unpacking, Epi and Ricky arrived carrying some supplies they had purchased in Bogota. Epi ran to them, hugged them both and welcomed them home. Ricky kissed Angelita on the cheek, gave her a hug, and held up a bottle of Colombiana Soda and some beer. "Refajos anyone? Just what I thought. All the way around." The four were catching up on passed time, talking about the vacation, and the four of them taking a cruise soon, when Angelita asked Epi if plans had changed and they decided not to do anything to the farm.

"All done." Epi smiled. "Come, let me show you your 'state of the art' farm."

They all walked to Grandma's room and Epi open the old closet door. "See this shelf here?" As she raised it, a panel at the rear of the closet slid open, exposing a tunnel. "This is an escape tunnel; it goes underground and comes up by the pond out back. You know, where you two skinny dip! Yes, we found some personal clothing items out there." She laughed, "That is all this closet is for, just an escape from the house." They all moved to the new closet. Ricky opened the door and moved a necktie holder to the left. As did the other closet, a panel in the rear slid open, revealing a tunnel. They all entered the tunnel and walked about twenty feet and discovered the tunnel split, going in two separate directions. Ricky pointed straight ahead. "Don't concern yourself with that tunnel, it goes to underground storage; you can check it out whenever you have the time." They all went to the right and down a tunnel about one hundred yards from the house. The tunnel came to a dead end. Epi walked up to the stone wall in front of them and moved a small stone that looked like part of the wall. It revealed a small hole with a red light.

"Is that a retina scanner?" Raul asked, with admiration and surprise.

"It sure is, and this week we will get you both programmed for it."

Epi looked into the hole and part of the stone wall opened, allowing them access.

"Wow, I can't believe what you've done here in just a few months. How is it possible?" Angelita asked Epi.

"Epi smiled and told her. "Money, girlfriend. With money everything is possible.

This operation is a joint effort of the United States and the Colombian governments.

Besides, they were so happy to retrieve the 100 million in gold we got for them that they couldn't do enough for us."

"This cave is so big, I had no idea it was back here." Angelita remarked, looking around in amazement.

Ricky smiled. "Well, we can't take total credit for this idea. Remember the cave behind the waterfall? We started thinking and planning, and when we discovered a smaller cave back here we just made it a lot bigger, complete with chambers and different rooms. Everybody working here is either a Colombian National, fluent in English and Spanish, or an American who has been schooled in Spanish. Ironically, the company uses the language schools in your vacation spot, Costa Rica. These people working here are the best in Latin American affairs; you can have confidence in them."

They walked into the cave and in the first chamber was a young, blonde woman named Sarah. She was the communications expert, and would be there to assist the agents with any type of communications equipment they needed. Sarah introduced herself and welcomed them home. She was a woman of about thirty years old, approximately 5'6" tall, thin with very white skin and deep blue eyes. She spoke with a New England accent.

Next, Epi introduced them to Ed. Ed was a 6' tall, thin, balding man about 45 years old. Ed was all North Carolina and all business. He adjusted his silver rimmed glasses and introduced himself. Ed was their lab and inventing person. He explained how he spent his days inventing things and ways to make their job easier. Ricky and Raul just looked at each other; obviously this guy had never been in the field, because nothing made what they did easy. They both smiled at Ed and followed Epi. There were assorted guards and computer personnel, and they would be met as time went on. The cave contained a dining area, complete with a kitchen. There were also individual rooms for agents, dormitories for guards and support personnel, and a lounge area. That is where Raul met the two new field agents for the first time.

Epi introduced the two as Gabriela and Jess. Gabriela was about 25 years old, medium height, very thin, with shoulder length black hair and coal black eyes.

Raul figured that with her olive skin, she was of Hispanic background, but he couldn't quite place her. It turned out she was from Spanish Harlem, in New York, and the background was Puerto Rican. Jess was all Texas, from Fort Worth. Somewhere around thirty years of age, with brown hair, green eyes and a baby face. This was offset by his 5'10", 200lb, muscular build. Both agents were anxious to meet Raul and Angelita, and showed it. Gabriella smiled and extended her hand to Raul. "This is quite an honor, to finally meet the Navajo Ghost Warrior in person. You're quite an item in Washington. For that matter, they even talk about you at the academy."

"They talk about me at the academy? Why?"

Jess jumped into the conversation and added, "They talk about survival, you know, how you cut ropes knowing you would fall and get hurt."

"And the battle here at the farm", Gabriela chimed in. "You're like, a legend."

Angelita asked Epi what their job classification was, and was dumbfounded when she answered. Epi told her that Jess is a marine-trained sniper, and that Gabriella is a marine-trained spotter. The two had worked together in the Gulf War for three years before they were recruited.

"But they look so young!" she exclaimed.

Raul and Ricky both laughed and Ricky answered, "That's how you start this job, young, and you get old fast or die."

They continued the tour for another ten or fifteen minutes, and then returned to the farmhouse. During dinner, Raul asked Ricky what was next on the job planning board.

Ricky told him they had nothing for the moment, and in fact, he had to go to Washington for a briefing. Raul was welcome to come with him if he would like. Raul graciously turned him down, and told him that Angelita wanted to go to Bogota, to visit her brother and her cousin, and he should probably stay and keep an eye on the farm.

Ricky laughed. "There are twelve men working on the farm now, what are you going to keep an eye on?"

"I don't want to go. Is that better?" Raul responded curtly.

"Got it. See you when I get back", Ricky replied.

After about six days of doing nothing, Raul wished he had either gone to Bogotá with Angelita or had broken down and gone to Washington with Ricky. He had become totally familiar with every new addition to the farm, and believed he had met every single person there, at least twice. Raul was sitting on the front porch listening to music when his cell phone started to vibrate. He looked at the ID and saw that it was Epi calling him.

"What's up?" he responded.

"Could you come back to the cave? I have a bit of a problem and I may need your help", Epi said.

About five minutes later Raul was walking into the cave. Epi was standing next to Sarah, and she looked troubled.

Raul, seeing the trouble in both of their eyes asked, "What happened? Something is wrong…. I can see it in your eyes. Is Angelita alright?"

"Of course, it's nothing like that. The problem is, well, we……"

Sarah interrupted. "We have lost the two new agents. They were supposed to check in yesterday, and we still haven't heard from them."

"Do you have a general area to start looking?" Raul asked.

Sarah pointed to a glass board behind her, containing a map of Colombia. "They went south towards the Amazonas. The last time we heard from them, they were headed for Leticia. They have been gone four days, and the last time we heard from them was two days ago. Something is wrong; I feel it."

Raul looked at Epi. "These two, Jess and Gabriela, isn't this their first time out alone?"

"Well, they have to start sometime, and they only went on an intelligence gathering mission. It's not like they are on a shoot or anything."

"Epi, did they take their rifles with them?"

Sarah replied. "What difference would that make?"

"The difference is that if they were spotted as snipers they are fair game in these jungles. Two gringos walking around in Colombia with rifles are asking to be shot or kidnapped. Did you send them to Leticia, or was that their idea?"

Epi sighed. "We are trying to gather intel on some drug lord in the Amazonas. He is supposed to be in tight with police officials in Leticia."

"The Amazonas are full of drug lords, corrupt police and drug laboratories. I can't believe you sent two beginners right into the fire, right off the bat. I need to go and get them, *if* they are still alive."

"Raul, you have no idea how much I was hoping you would say that", Epi replied.

"Let me get some stuff together and I'll be out of here by morning."

Sarah smiled at him and said, "By this evening I will have communications and strategies worked out for you. I know you're not used to all this but please, come and see me before you leave. Promise?"

Epi took Raul's arm and begged, "Please, let's go see Ed. I think he has some things that can help you."

"What's he going to show me, all the James Bond toys? This is a little out of control, don't you think?"

"What I think is that he has a brand new Hummer with your name on it. And don't pretend you don't want one, because I know you do. Angelita told me."

"Is nothing sacred between you women? What color is it?"

Walking into the laboratory, Epi called out, "Ed, I told Raul you had some things that might help him. What have you got?"

"Well, as you know, I'm an inventor by nature and so working in a cave in South America has inspired me to come up with some very interesting inventions. I think you might enjoy them. Bear with me while I show you. First, any questions before we get started?"

Raul was staring at Ed. He wasn't sure if he liked him, or if he wanted to knock him unconscious. "Let me tell you what I told Epi. I'm not much into this James Bond stuff. I kill people for a living, that's my job, and I'm quite good at it. Secondly, what color is my Hummer?"

"Black, with chrome wheels. I do realize your job description and its difficulties. What I would like to do for you is make your equipment more efficient. I understand that you are partial to the .223 cal. That is a fine rifle, and with a couple of changes it could be an even more efficient weapon."

"Modifications? What kind of modifications?" Raul was beginning to get interested...

Ed commenced to show Raul a fully automatic .223 cal. rifle mounted on a tripod. This rifle was complete with a silencer, laser-activated scope, and a rocket launcher attachment. The rifle had long- range accuracy and more importantly, it was operated by remote control. The operator had a screen no bigger than an MP3 player, and the scope visually set the target. The weapon could be operated at a distance of up to a quarter mile away.

Raul thought this was really a neat invention, and he thought he was beginning to like Ed. "I like this weapon; put one in the Hummer."

"Why just one? This pad will operate up to three, or they can be operated individually."

"No shit! I've got to hand it to you, this is quite the weapon. Anything else?"

Ed motioned to Raul to follow him. "Follow me; I want you to meet your new partner."

"Who?"

"Raul, I want you to meet King. King is your new dog, and you're going to love him."

"I don't need a German Shepherd, or any other dog, but thanks anyway. Besides, that dog has got to weigh a hundred and forty pounds. Where did you find such a big Shepherd?"

"Be careful, you don't want to hurt his feelings", Ed said.

"Hurt his feelings? You act like he understands us or something."

"You never know, maybe he does", laughed Ed.

"Yeah, right, and pigs can fly", Raul sneered.

"Hum, now that's an idea. King, what do you think of pigs flying?"

King stood up, looked at Ed, and in a human voice answered, "Stupid idea."

"Raul stepped back two or three paces and stared at the dog. "That dog just spoke to you! That's impossible."

"First of all, in my world nothing is impossible; and secondly, yes, he did. Would you like to get to know King now?"

"Absolutely. What else can he do?"

Ed began explaining how King was voice activated and computer programmed to a specific person. King was also equipped with cameras in his eyes and was totally operational using the same keypad as the weapon.

"So, let me get this straight. This dog can walk into anywhere I want him to, on my voice command, and after he is inside, I can see everything on my pad?" Raul asked.

"Oh, it gets better. Trust me". Ed smiled. "Let's say you wanted to enter an area that was guarded and you knew there would be trouble doing so. Well, all you need to do is send King in, a lovable German Shepherd, and he will, on your command, fart, spraying knock-out gas in a fifty foot circle. Be very careful with THIS program, however, because if you tell him to take a dump, that gas is totally different. That gas is toxic and will kill everything within a fifty foot radius."

"You're serious? This dog farts knock-out gas and shits toxic waste?!"

"Toxic waste...that's great! I hadn't thought to call it that. I like that!", beamed Ed.

"Is that it, or do I need to know more?"

"Two more things. First, his urinary tract is really an acid dispenser. The acid is strong enough to melt locks, metal, etc.... you get the idea. Secondly, and most importantly of all, King is a walking bomb - in case of dire emergency and only as a last resort. If you need to, you can enter your pin number and say, "explode", and King will do just that. In fact he has enough explosives in his cute little body to level an entire city block. Please, this is a last resort. Life or death thing, OK?"

Next they went to the garage area where Raul saw his new gloss-black Hummer. Behind it was a trailer with an air boat.

"The air boat has secret compartments with extra weapons - such as a fifty caliber automatic weapon that lifts out of the hull on a power device. There is a grenade launcher, rocket launcher and a nice stash of plastic explosives. The Hummer does some neat things also. Here, read the book."

"The boat looks a little bulky, how does it run?"

"It is super-charged and if it had wings it would, in fact, fly. Maybe my next one will.

I need you to sign for the equipment, the car and the dog. And that's all I have for now. See you next trip."

Raul left Ed and went to see Sarah. She explained that the last information they had obtained put the two agents in the Leticia area, but that she had no contacts there for him and that he was pretty much on his own, except for the communication devices she handed him. She gave him a small radio transmitter and a new, more powerful cell phone. The Amazonas were a difficult area; they were very swampy, full of waterways and jungles. The swamps were loaded with drug labs and fields, and the jungle was loaded with deadly snakes and crocodiles; not to mention a few dozen other dangerous animals. Sarah assured him that these radios and phones had strong enough signals to reach base anywhere in Colombia. She also handed him a watch and said, "Please wear this all the time. It's a navigator system as well as a tracker. We don't want to lose you, too! Please find Jess and Gabriella. I went to the academy with them, as well as to school in Costa Rica. We are close, and I know in my heart, if anyone can find them, it will be you." She leaned over and kissed Raul on the cheek. "Thank you and God speed."

Raul loaded his equipment and his new friend King into the Hummer and started it up. As he was getting ready to put it in gear and drive out the back of the cave, he saw Ed running toward the truck.

"Oh, I'm so glad I caught you before you left!"

"Why, you have this strong urge to go with me?"

"Oh, heavens no. I just wanted to tell you that I loaded the secret compartments in the boat with extra ammunition, and I stuck a third remote control rifle in there also, for good measure."

"Thanks, I appreciate everything you've done." Raul said.

"Oh! And before I forget, here is a cassette on the operations of the devices I've installed. I was talking to Epi, and when I told her I gave you a book to read about them, she started laughing. I took that as a, 'not going to read it' sign, and so I transcribed the book last night onto a cassette for you. Please listen to it on the way to the barge."

Raul stuck the cassette into the radio, smiled at Ed and drove off. He had a good twenty hour drive to the river's port, where he was going to load the Hummer and boat onto the barge and paddle down the river to Leticia. The big paddlewheel barges they used on the river were old, but dependable. Raul's cover was simple. He was a hunter going to the Amazonas on a hunting trip. This had been Sarah's idea, and they had supplied him with camouflage pants and jacket, along with a soft jungle hat. He had stashed his .223 rifle with the sniper scope and had a 30.06 hunting rifle. He drove and listened to the tape. "God", he thought after two hours of listening to Ed on the tape, "what is this, a Stephen King novel? It just goes on forever". He looked at King, his dog who was sitting on the other bucket seat looking as bored as he was. "Enough of this shit, I can't take anymore. How about I put in a Shakira CD?" King turned his head and looked at Raul. He looked like he was smiling at Raul's suggestion.

Raul was having a hard time believing this was a robot. This was the most real looking dog he had ever seen.

"So, King, tell me, do you know how to do all that dog shit? You know, like bark, growl, shake hands, rollover? You know, all the stuff dogs do."

King started panting and slobbering all over the front seat. He topped it off by shaking his head and throwing saliva all over Raul.

"What the fuck are you doing?! Stop that! Jesus Christ, you got my new 'handy dandy' camouflage hunting suit all wet!"

King was staring at Raul. "How's that for dog stuff? Want me to fart now?"

Raul was shaking his head. "I can't get over the talking part, and for God's sake, don't fart. You put new meaning to the term 'killer farts'."

"That's not my farts, that's my shit. My farts knock you out. My shit kills."

"So, tell me, why are you talking so much right now?"

"I'm responding to suggestion. Mr. Ed told me to keep you company, and respond to your questions. If you want me silent, you must give me the command 'stand down' and I will remain silent until you activate that part of me by voice command."

"Well, alright then. I find you great company, so tell the secrets of life."

"There are no secrets of life. It's just a matter of what you know, and what you don't know."

They talked and listened to every different CD Raul had with him. At one point while he was playing some Motown music, he swore King was keeping the beat with his head and feet. It was about 8pm when they pulled into Boca Rio, the town on the river's bank where Raul would catch the barge to the Amazonas. Raul locked the Hummer and set the alarm to gas. He liked this feature; it had been one Ed put on the tape. If a burglar tried to break into the Hummer while this was set, it would automatically spray knock-out gas from whatever location the person was attempting to enter. It would render the person unconscious for about 45 minutes to an hour. So while the alarm siren sounded and the police arrived, the burglar would be waiting for them. "How convenient", he thought. He told King to lie down in the boat and protect everything. "Just act like the baddest German Shepherd these people have ever seen. But stand down, and don't talk to them. Bark, growl, fart on them if you want, but just be a dog. OK?"

Raul went into the café-hotel and ate dinner. He was having a drink, looking out the window at the river, when he caught a glimpse of someone walking past him. When he turned, he saw a young man in his early twenties standing at the bar, with his back to him. Raul watched him for a while, and then as he was turning away, the young man turned around and looked directly at him. The young man definitely had a very familiar look to him. Raul didn't think he knew him; he could not place the face, but his expressive, clear blue eyes gave him a strange feeling. The young man said nothing, turned back to the bar, paid his tab and left. Raul didn't think anymore about it, paid his bill and went to his room. The morning would be here soon, and he needed to be rested for the twelve hour boat trip to the Amazonas.

Morning came and Raul loaded up the Hummer and drove to the boat launch. There weren't many people traveling on this day, so loading went very quickly and smoothly. There were, of course, the routine inspections by the Federal police, including the basic questions of "what is your final destination", "why are you traveling", etcetera. Raul had told them he was on a hunting trip, and would be in the jungle area around Leticia. They wanted to search his vehicle and he, of course, cooperated. They checked the Hummer, commented on what a nice vehicle it was and how they wished they could afford one. After a few minutes of this rhetoric, Raul asked if they were finished, as he wanted to board. Either because he didn't want to placate them or offer them money - he wasn't sure which, but was leaning toward the latter- they decided further searching was necessary. The highest ranking of the four asked Raul "What's in the boat, drugs, guns, some type of contraband? Maybe you're a smuggler or something like that?" Raul was now sure it was about a bribe. "Christ almighty", he thought to himself. "Is there a fucking honest cop in this country?"

The cop glared at Raul. "What kind of name is Lightfoot? That's not a gringo name."

"It's a last-kind-of-name, and you know what? You can kiss my ass with this 'gringo' shit. How much of a bribe are you looking for, anyway?"

The cop continued glaring at Raul. "You know what, Gringo? I think we will tear your boat apart, just to see what could be in there."

Three of the four cops went to the boat while the other was watching Raul. One of them jumped up on the trailer and King came out of the bottom of the boat. The cop saw King and had an instant look of terror on his face at the sight of the growling dog staring right at him. The cop was so startled that he fell off the trailer. The ranking cop, the one that had been the real pain in the ass, pulled his gun and pointed it at King. Raul yelled to him. "Just know that if you shoot my dog I will shoot you!"

For some reason the cop lowered his gun and turned to Raul. "That sounds like a threat; maybe I should shoot you instead?"

Raul was starting to get really pissed at this piece-of-shit cop. Just as the confrontation was about to start, Raul noticed the young man from the café leaving the police shack. Following him was a high-ranking police official. When the four cops saw this man, they put their guns away and came to attention. The piece-of-shit cop told Raul to get moving and stop holding up the line. There were exactly two other cars in line, so that was stupid, Raul thought. "What's going on here?" he pondered. "Something is definitely not right".

As Raul was moving toward the Hummer, the high-ranking official announced, "Hold on there, sir; I would like a word with you."

The young man had disappeared, and the chief, or whatever he was, walked over to him and asked, "Mr. Lightfoot, is there a problem with your boarding?"

Before Raul could answer, the cop that had given him all the trouble chimed in. "No sir, no problem at all. We were just admiring his truck and boat."

The chief glared at the cop. "I wasn't talking to you now, was I? But now that I think of it, why would an admirer of a truck pull his gun out?"

"Just a reaction sir, the dog startled me."

Ghost Warrior

"Do you think I'm stupid, or what?" The chief glared at him with a disgusted look. "The officer with the shit stains on his trousers is the one the dog startled, you idiot!"

Raul kind of liked this; he didn't say anything, but just watched.

The chief looked sternly at the officers. "If you clowns were trying to heist Mr. Lightfoot for a bribe, I *will* find out and investigate all of you. And trust me, you won't like it."

Raul was getting in his Hummer as the chief turned to him. "Sir, please accept my apology for these disgraces of the uniform. Believe me when I say, I will correct this."

Raul just smiled, looked at the problem cop, who didn't look so tough now, and said, "Who knows, maybe you'll get a raise and solve all your problems."

As Raul was driving onto the boat he could hear the chief yelling at the officers about what they had done. The cop who had fallen from the trailer was pointing at the lead officer and saying something that the other two were agreeing to. Well, the rock was lifted, and the snakes were turning on each other. It won't take long for the honest cop to get to the bottom of this. Raul couldn't help but wonder what the young man had said to the chief. He could only imagine.

As the horn on the barge sounded and the boat pulled away, Raul was standing on the barge looking back at the dock. It was really pretty nice to see some justice without anyone dying; "not the norm in my life", thought Raul. Kind of a nice change. He had also wondered where that kid had gone. Who was he, and why did he look so familiar? The dock was fading and Raul could no longer see anybody or anything on it. He hadn't eaten breakfast, so he thought he would go to the boat's bar and see if he could get a plate of calentado. He liked that; a very simple dish of rice and beans with a sunny side egg on top of it. Nothing fancy, just good. How much better could it get? Raul was sitting at his table thinking about Angelita and her reunion with her cousin, the judge. He hoped they were out doing girl things, and just plain having a good time. While he was day dreaming about Angelita, he thought he caught another glimpse of that same kid he had seen in Boca Rio. The young man was standing out on the deck by his Hummer. Raul paid his bill and went out to talk to the man. He was more than curious about what had transpired between him and the police official at the loading area. By the time Raul got to the Hummer the young man was gone. "Am I seeing things, or what?" he thought. "I could have sworn he was on this boat." Raul was starting to wonder more about the kid. Not only that he looked so familiar, but he had to have told the police official Raul's name. "How did he even know that? What else did he know about Raul and why did it appear that he was following him? Who was this kid?"

Raul sat with King for a while as King was busy guarding the equipment. He turned to the dog. "I don't suppose you know who that kid was who was standing here a minute or two ago, do you?"

"No, but he liked your car and the boat too! He has a boat and a Jeep on this barge. He also said he wished his government would spring for some equipment like this."

"He was talking to you?"

"No; he thinks I'm a dog, like everyone else is supposed to. He was talking to himself."

"Did he say where his government was, by chance?"

"No, he didn't tell himself that, but he does have a slight accent. I would speculate maybe from the Netherlands."

"Well, that would explain the white complexion and the blonde hair now wouldn't it?" Raul asked.

Raul pulled out his MP3 player and sat back in the boat with King and relaxed. He must have dozed off because he jumped when his cell phone started vibrating. He answered, and it was Sarah. She was doing a progress check and making sure everything was alright so far. Raul didn't bother to tell her about the jerk cops at Boca Rio, but did ask her if she had heard anything about any other Governmental agencies besides the US or Colombia working in Colombia.

"Funny you would mention that", she answered. "We have had some unofficial intelligence about the Swiss Intelligence Network being in

Colombia for some reason, but as of yet I can't confirm it. I also can't imagine what they would be doing in Colombia, anyway, unless maybe they were on vacation or something. Why, have you met an agent or something?"

"No, not yet. I was just wondering. Nothing important."

"Oh, by the way, Angelita called home for you, and Epi talked to her. She told her you had gone on a job, but didn't talk about it. Angelita sends her love and will see you when you get back. Epi told her not to hurry home, if she wanted to spend more time with her brother or cousin. Angelita told her that she would stay a few extra days, being as you're not home. That's the news update at the boring cave headquarters. Talk to you soon, bye."

"Thanks, talk to you later." Raul hung up and turned to King. "Well, what do you think? Is it possible that kid is with S.I.N., and if he is, what or whom is he looking for?"

King just looked at Raul; he had no answers for these questions. Only time would reveal these answers. The hours passed and finally they were at the river's southern port. Leticia was just a few miles away and he would be there soon. Raul and King pulled into Leticia around nine o clock in the evening and Raul drove straight to the hotel Sarah told him about in a briefing. Just as in Boca Rio, Raul set the alarm in the Hummer and told King to be a guard dog. Raul went into the hotel and registered. After putting his overnight bag in the room, he went to the café which was in the hotel. Raul ordered a drink and a sandwich, and just observed his surroundings. He needed to ask questions, but he didn t want to raise a lot of suspicions, either. There were two plain-clothed policemen sitting at a table in the cafe with an officer in uniform.

Raul watched them for a moment or two, and finally the uniformed officer got up. Raul thought he was leaving, but instead one of the other policemen stood as well and said something to him. Raul couldn't make out what he had said, but it didn't take long at all until the uniformed officer turned around and looked at Raul. "This is just peachy", Raul thought, "Here comes more shit from the cops".

"Sir", the policeman said, "You are not from here. Might I ask, what is your business in Leticia?"

Raul looked at the policeman for a moment, thinking, "why do these jerks always start conversations telling you what you already know?"

"I have no business in Leticia, I'm on a hunting trip, and I'm in your lovely city just for the night." "There", he thought, "I did that quite graciously".

The policeman looked over at the other two, as if to ask, "What do I do now?"

Raul sensed this cop had no idea what he was doing; after all, the cop was maybe 21 years old. So Raul took out a picture of Gabriela and asked, "Excuse me officer, maybe you could help me. My sister and her husband live somewhere around here, but I'm not really sure where. Possibly you know them, and could point me in the right direction?"

The policeman stared at the picture of Gabriela and said nothing. He didn't have to; his facial expression said it all, thought Raul. Raul shook the picture to get the officer's attention and said, "From the look on your face I can see you recognize her, so how about you tell me where she is?!"

The policeman said nothing; he did an about-face and returned to the other two cops. They whispered amongst themselves for a moment, and the uniformed officer left the café without saying another word. As Raul sat staring at the other two officers he thought, "These bastards know exactly where these two agents are, and exactly what happened here." He knew the difficult part lie ahead. How to get them to tell him? The two officers pretended not to notice that Raul was staring at them, but they were uncomfortable and Raul knew it. They wanted to leave, but for some reason had to stay put. Were they assigned to follow him? If so, how did the bad guys already know he was here? Maybe whatever the kid had told that police chief in Boca Rio had already gotten to Leticia? "If that's the case, I guess that says it all about finding an honest cop in Colombia", he thought. Raul had decided to approach these two cops and ask them point-blank if they had seen Gabriela and Jess. He was getting up when he noticed the kid outside by his Hummer. Raul lifted his watch, which was also a transmitter for King (this he had discovered by listening to Ed's cassette), to his mouth and said to King, "Get a picture of the blonde guy by the Hummer".

King stood up immediately and walked to the bow of the airboat. He looked directly at the kid and barked twice. The kid, who was not expecting this, jumped. When he did, he looked directly at King who commenced to take a series of pictures of him.

The young man said nothing, looked back at the café, and saw Raul watching him.

He turned and walked away. When Raul looked back to where the two officers had been sitting, he discovered they had left. Raul pulled out his computer pad and with the little pen, punched 'E-mail'. He instantly was connected to Sarah's computer. His screen lit up and the words "Hi, been waiting to hear from you" rolled across the screen. "Damn, this thing is pretty neat!" he thought. He then told Sarah that King had just taken a series of pictures of the young man he had told her about and he was e-mailing them to her. He wanted her to find out everything she could about the kid and let him know right away.

"Got it, Ghost Warrior, I'm on it."

Raul looked at the screen, smiled and wrote back. "Don't start with me, young lady, I've been known to turn kids like you over my knee and spank them." He laughed to himself and put the pad away. He walked out to the Hummer and when he looked at King he saw that the dog was staring at something on the other side of the truck. Raul reached under his jacket and took out his Glock automatic and held it by his side. He cautiously walked past the front of the truck and discovered the two policemen from inside the bar standing by the airboat.

"Well, let's see…. two of Leticia's finest. What are you looking for? A bribe? Donuts? Why are two cops standing by my airboat looking like beggars?"

The taller of the two looked at Raul and quietly said, "First of all, let me put your mind at ease by assuring you that neither of us are looking for donuts or bribes. You will probably be very surprised to hear that we are here to help you, not harm you, or heist you for money. You can also relax, and put the 40 cal. automatic away. That won't be necessary in your dealings with us. Let me introduce myself, as well as my partner, to you. I am Carlos Mendez and this Arturo Urbine. We are narcotics officers with the Federal task force, assigned to Leticia." Raul studied the two men;

both in their mid to late twenties and both of very Latin ancestry; black hair, dark brown eyes and dark complexion. Generic looking cops. The difference between the two was Carlos' tall, slender build and his well-trimmed mustache.

"Federal task force narcotics officers, assigned to this shit hole. Who did you piss off? Besides, working narcotics in the swampy jungle is kind of like digging a basement with a teaspoon, isn't it?"

Arturo spoke up and answered, "Yes sir, you are absolutely correct. The narcotics are out of control in these parts, and we, as well as you, need help to try to make a dent in the problem here."

"So why are you following me?" Raul asked.

Carlos smiled. "Let's not try to kid anybody here. We both know you are a CIA agent and that your name is Raul Lightfoot. Also known to many as the Navajo Ghost Warrior. I am from the Amazonas, but Arturo happens to be from Guatavita, and it seems your reputation precedes you."

"That's special," Raul said, staring at the two. "So tell me, where are my two agents?"

"We think we know where at least the girl is, and we are ready to help you rescue her." Carlos said.

"What do you want from me? And please don't say something stupid, like 'just to help you' or some bullshit like that. OK?"

"Once again, you are correct, sir, it's not just to help you. We are looking for a drug lord who has terrorized the Amazonas for the last two years. He kidnaps women to work on his farm and in his clubs. He addicts children and makes prostitutes out of them. He does just whatever he wants to because he owns the police here, along with the city officials. Anybody he doesn't own he either kills or terrorizes so they won't bother him or his operation. His name is Juan Carlos Zalazar, and his trademark is a nasty set of gloves with tiger claws on them, which he uses to inflict pain and death on anyone who doesn't agree with him," Carlos responded.

Raul looked at the two, still unsure. "Well, he certainly sounds like one of life's total shit bags, now doesn't he? Do you two, by chance, have a plan or know anything that would help?"

Carlos seemed to be doing most of the talking and replied. "About a week ago, your agents, the young woman, Gabriela, along with her friend...." He turned to Arturo.

"Jess, his name is Jess. They both seemed to be such nice kids."

"Yes, anyway," Carlos continued. "We had met them right in this café and had introduced ourselves. At the time there were three of us, however, Juan Carlos had our friend, Hector, killed. The four of us, the two Americans and us, were trying to gather intelligence on Zalazar's operation, when somehow he got word and had Hector killed and kidnapped your two agents."

Raul thought for a minute and asked, "Your friend Hector; was he a federal agent as well?"

"No, he was an officer with the Leticia police force. He worked narcotics for years, and we trusted him. We don't believe he leaked anything to the bad guys."

"No, but it is surely possible that his boss or bosses did," Raul answered. "Do either of you know who his bosses were, or anything about them?"

"No, sorry we don't." Carlos replied. "Hector never talked much about his department. Only that he was one of ten narcotics officers and that he worked for a Major named Ramirez. I sometimes got the feeling that he didn't trust any of them, especially this Ramirez guy."

"What about the other narcs, ever meet them?" Raul asked.

Arturo answered; telling Raul that the only narcotics agent they had been introduced to was the uniform cop he had seen in the café. That man had been Hector's partner, and after Hector was killed they transferred him back to uniform and gave him a foot beat.

Raul thought for a moment and asked, "What do you guys know about where this Don Carlos stays when he is here in Leticia?"

Carlos then told him about the club. It seemed that this man had a night club in downtown Leticia and this is where he frequented. The club was the usual 'have a drink, dance and buy a girl for the night' type of club. Both of them had been in the club, but knew very little about it other than it was a two-story building that probably had a basement, because it sat high off the street. Access to the main floor, or club area, was up about ten steps from the sidewalk. He further explained that because of the swampy, soft nature of the ground in the Amazonas, they used what was called a 'shallow basement'. This provided a structure with basement facilities; however they were usually only six and a half to seven feet high. They believed this existed because there was a guarded door off to the left of the entrance. The upper floor they knew very little about, only that there was an apartment and some offices up there. Carlos had wandered up there, supposedly by accident, and had seen as much.

"Will that uniform cop help us with something and are you sure we can trust him?" Raul asked.

Carlos and Arturo looked at each other for a moment and Arturo replied. "Yes to both questions. What do you have in mind?"

"We definitely need an inside look at this place before we do any kind of rescue mission, and I'm going to need a city gas uniform and a uniformed cop to escort me. Not to help or get in the way; just be there. Got it?"

The next morning at about seven thirty, Raul, King and his uniformed escort, one Armando Cristal, or Glass, for short, were standing in front of Zalazar's night club. For a young man, Glass looked very confident and dominating in uniform. He was about six feet tall; thin, with a bushy black mustache that matched his curly black hair. His very dark, nearly coal-black eyes carried an unmistakable air of determination.

Raul looked up at the flashing neon sign and couldn't help but laugh. The sign was written in English and looked like it was about forty years old. It had a laughing black cat on it, and in red and yellow letters was the name of the club, 'The Happy Pussy'. Raul knew that ninety percent of the clientele in this area had no idea what the sign said, just knew that it had been shipped here from the states. To be more exact, Miami, because under the cat, that's what was blinking, in hot yellow.

Raul, dressed as a city gas inspector, started banging on the door. He had tried opening it, but it had been locked with no one around. After about five minutes of banging on the door and calling out to anyone inside, a speaker box sounded.

"Who is it, and what do you want at this hour?" a male voice growled.

Raul looked at Glass and whispered. "I can't believe they don't have a camera hidden out here somewhere, you know, for advance warning on raids and such."

Glass smiled and said, "Sir, there are no raids at this club, and yes, they do have a camera. It has been broken for two years that I know of, and no one is equipped to fix it around here."

"City gas inspector." Raul announced. "We need to enter the premises to check a possible gas leak."

"You have got to be fucking kidding me. Come back at a decent hour, like when we open, and maybe you can check then. Get out of here before I come out there and kick your stupid ass all the way down the street."

"I'm really sorry to disturb you, but we have a serious problem that needs immediate attention. There has been a rupture in the city gas line somewhere in this area, and we need to find it before there is an explosion. The leak could well be in this building, and we need to know. Due to the serious nature of the problem, I have a police officer with me and we are authorized to break down doors to check if necessary."

"Why didn't you say so before? Just a minute, I'll be there in a minute," the man replied.

Raul looked at Glass and reminded him to not say anything and stay behind him. A middle-aged man in a robe and slippers answered the door. He looked something like a beach-ball in the red robe which he wore tied loosely under his expansive belly. He was rather short and sported a bad toupee which looked like an extension of his bushy mustache. He jumped back and yelped when he saw King. The toupee then fell to the floor, leaving a fat little bald-headed man with a stupid look on his face.

"That's the biggest fucking German Shepherd I've ever seen! What's he for? I mean, why do you have him with you?"

"Newest addition to the city's public service force. He sniffs gas leaks. Don't worry, just gas, nothing else." Raul replied.

"Where do you want to look?" the man asked, as he started to light a cigarette.

Raul reached over and grabbed the cigarette from the man's mouth. "Sir, do you understand 'gas leak'?" Raul glared at him and thought to himself, "What a fucking moron, if this was a real gas leak nobody would have to kill him, he'd do it himself."

"Oh! I forgot," the moron replied.

Raul and Glass just looked at the idiot for a moment, and Raul spoke. "Well, no harm done, let's start upstairs."

As the three started up the staircase toward the apartment, Raul checked his watch and at the same time programmed King to look like he was searching, while all the time taking photographs of the entire interior of the building. They moved through the apartment checking things and looking official. Raul had noticed a large skylight window in the apartment, which was a lavish two bedroom suite with a large bath, complete with Jacuzzi tub and shower. In the main room of the apartment there were four more guards sitting at a table, playing dominoes. All of the men were smoking cigars and the moron yelled to them to put them out, there was a gas leak. All of the men complied, never saying a word as they continued playing. Raul was mentally counting guards and taking notes while King continued to take pictures. The three moved down a narrow hallway to a small office, which served as a reception area for the larger office beyond it. The larger office had a balcony with a fire escape ladder attached. The doors leading to the balcony were glass panel, covered by wooden louvered doors.

"Well everything looks fine up here, let's check the bar and kitchen area," Raul said as he walked toward the stairs. "Oh, by the way, I wanted to ask Mr. Zalazar something. Is he available?" Raul asked as he turned toward the guard.

Instantly the man responded, "No, he's not here. He went to his farm for a few days." Just as soon as he said what he did, a terrified look came over his face. "I wasn't supposed to tell anybody that, please don't tell him I slipped! He would be very angry with me, and he is not very nice when he is angry."

Glass jumped into the conversation quite unexpectedly and said, "I hear he can be very nasty with those claws of his, and I've seen some of his work."

"You know about the gloves with the tigers claws on them?" the man asked.

Glass looked at Raul and then to the guard. "I saw the agent, you know, the cop that betrayed him."

"Oh, that man. Poor fellow, I kind of felt bad for him, Don Carlos can make death's door very slow to open. That is why you must not tell him anything about today, promise?!"

Raul looked at him for a moment or two, and replied, "Don't worry, my friend, your secret is safe with us."

They continued searching the dance club area and the bar area. In the kitchen Raul found two more guards frying eggs.

"So far I've got seven to deal with", he thought. As they were leaving, Raul pointed to the door behind the reception podium and asked what that was. The guard told him it was where the girls stayed and that they were all sleeping. He stated further that there were no gas lines in that area, just bedrooms with little lamps. Raul needed to see in this area, so he thought for a moment and said to the man, "Tell you what. I have bosses too, and they said all areas of buildings have to be checked. I don't need to personally go in and disturb these girls. What do you say about the dog just walking through quietly and sniffing the air, so I can put in my report that all areas were checked?"

The man looked at Raul and started laughing. "Sure, send the dog in there to smell the air, but all he is going to smell are 'happy pussies'."

King entered the dark area and Raul watched him descend about six steps and he was gone. The dog had been in there about five minutes when another guard came running up the stairs and out the door. He was yelling at the first guard, and cursing him for sending in the big dog to scare him. The moron told him the dog was harmless and was just smelling the air for gas leaks. The second guard started to laugh and said, "We ain't got no gas down there, just ass down there." The two guards started to laugh loudly.

King returned a few minutes later and Raul told them everything checked out ok. He thanked them for their cooperation, and as they were leaving, the moron yelled to them to stop. "Hey, wait a minute, you forgot something!" Raul and Glass turned to each other, not knowing what to expect. Both of them turned slowly, Raul with one hand on his Glock pistol that was concealed under is shirt.

"Forgot something?" Raul asked as he turned.

"Yes indeed" the moron replied as he handed them two free passes to the club as well as a Cuban Cigar for each of them. "Got to maintain our bribe level for our public servants, you know," the moron said, still laughing.

Raul and Glass thanked him, and as they walked down the steps to the sidewalk they heard the door close behind them.

They returned to the hotel and met Carlos and Arturo in the café. After retrieving the photos from King they studied the entire layout of the club. They discovered that the basement quarters were actually small one-man or woman jail cells and that there were, in fact, two guards down there at a table in the entrance way to the cells. There were ten cells on either side of the entrance way and an open large shower and bathroom facility at the end of the passageway. King had not been able to get photos of the girls inside, as all of the doors were closed, but he had gotten enough photos that Raul knew exactly what to expect and what he needed to do.

They spent the rest of the day formulating a plan of attack. After dinner, they agreed that Raul would meet the three of them by the Hummer, at 5:45 am for a 6:00 am assault.

The sun was just breaking the skyline and the morning was still damp from the rain that night. Carlos, Arturo and Glass were already waiting by the Hummer when Raul arrived at approximately twenty minutes to six the next morning. The three policemen were dressed in black jump suits, complete with combat boots and flack jackets. Raul was dressed in black fatigues, black shirt and a jungle vest. He liked the vest and this type of pants, because they had large pockets and were easily accessible for ammo or explosives.

He handed Carlos and Arturo satchel charges and some gas grenades. The four of them checked their individual handguns and made sure they had sufficient ammunition. Raul looked over at Glass' gun and saw he was using a departmental issue Colt .38 cal. revolver. Carlos and Arturo were both using S&W 9mm. automatics. Standard government issue. They were also carrying pump shot guns, riot style with the 18" barrels. Raul handed them some exploding shells to assist their entry through the roof's skylight. He also provided assault ropes, knives and some additional plastic explosives.

Glass stood by quietly as Carlos and Arturo were being outfitted for the assault, and when they were as ready as they were going to be, Raul turned to Glass and shook his head. "You, on the other hand, are going to need some work. Can you shoot an automatic weapon? I guess what I mean is, have you ever qualified with an automatic? Do you know how to operate one?"

"I carry this old weapon because that is what the department gave me, however, I do know how to shoot an automatic and I am familiar with them, I just don't have one. They cost way more than I could afford to spend," Glass told him.

"That being the case, if you promise not to get hurt or shot on this mission, my uncle will give you an automatic Glock pistol."

"I will do my best sir, but why would your uncle want to give me a weapon?"

"What Sam don't know won't hurt him." Raul said with a wink as he handed him a new, Glock .40 cal. automatic pistol, complete with a shoulder holster and three spare clips.

"Wow!" Glass exclaimed. "This is very nice; you must thank your uncle for me. What was his name? Sam?"

"Every April 15th I send him a thank you," Raul said with a chuckle, knowing full well that Glass had no idea who Uncle Sam was.

The plan they had devised was fairly simple. Raul and King would be at the front door and make their assault from there. Glass would place an explosive device on the rear door and enter that way. Carlos and Arturo would go to the roof, blow a hole in the skylight and enter from above.

Glass was responsible for any guards at the rear of the building; Carlos and Arturo would take care of the upstairs apartment and offices. Raul and King would come in the front, make that safe, and enter the basement. The team would assemble there after the assault. They set their watches at the same exact time and decided on a six fifteen assault. Everybody would be sleeping and entrance would be much safer. As they were leaving the Hummer for the assault, Raul stopped and looked at the three. "Something just hit me, and I need to ask all of you. Have any of you ever been in a gunfight or killed anyone?"

Carlos and Arturo looked at each other, obviously not having been in a situation like that before. Glass, on the other hand, surprised Raul by stating that he had killed two men in the past, and had been shot at on numerous occasions. "Bank robberies are quite frequent here, as well as armed confrontations." Glass then pulled up his shirt and exposed a four-inch scar where he had been shot in the side just below his rib cage. "Present from a bank robber two years ago. You don't have to be concerned about my performance sir. As you gringos say, I'm here for the whole show."

"One thing I'm not is concerned about how you will perform, and it's the whole dance, not the whole show."

Six-fifteen and everyone was in place. The first explosion took out the skylight, just as planned. As Carlos was dropping tear gas into the building through the roof's new opening, the front door, as well as the rear door, was blown off their hinges by the plastic explosives planted on them. Raul could hear gun shots coming from the upper level and just as he was headed for the stairs he heard foot steps running toward him. He turned, facing the club room area just as a guard was exiting the kitchen. The guard was carrying a machine gun, and was trying the put in the clip as he was running toward Raul. Raul raised his Glock and was ready to shoot when the man stopped suddenly, dropped his gun and stared at Raul.

The guard stood motionless for about ten seconds then fell forward onto the floor. That was when Raul saw the 12" butcher knife protruding from the man's back. The man had been stabbed between the shoulder blades, just below the neck. The knife had been stuck in him with such force it was half buried in his back and obviously had severed his heart. Glass followed the man from the kitchen, and when he saw Raul, told him the back of the building was clear. He had left one dead in the kitchen, and this one had run after he stabbed him. Raul turned the dead man over, and saw that it was the guard they had spoken with the day before.

He looked at Glass and then back at the body on the floor. "One in the kitchen and this one make two, for sure. You ok? We need to get to the basement and see what's there."

"I'm fine sir, and I hope Hector feels a little better where he is, knowing I got at least two of the bastards that killed him."

Raul smiled at Glass and asked, "Ever thought of a career in the CIA? Something tells me you could blend quite well."

As Raul and Glass were headed for the door to the basement they saw Carlos, followed by Arturo, coming down the stairs. They were both still wearing gas masks, and when they got to the bottom of the stairs they took them off. Carlos looked at Raul and told him that between them they had killed five guards on the upper level, and there was no one else up there.

"That leaves two, if my calculations are correct. They are the two guards in the basement with the girls", surmised Raul as the four of them headed for the basement door.

Raul had left King by the door to prevent anyone from escaping, and the door was still closed. When Raul tried to open the door he noticed that it had been locked from the inside. Carlos placed a small charge on the door and it flew off the hinges into the basement with a loud crashing sound. Raul and his three assistants followed right behind it. They had expected to meet resistance, but there was none. All of the doors to the cells were closed and because they were rooms, not cells with bars, they couldn't see into them.

"This is a trap. We can't be sure how many guards are down here; be careful", Raul told them.

The only light in the entire basement was that which was coming from three cellar half- windows that faced the street side of the building. They didn't really want an all-out gunfight with however many guards were down in the basement, because they had the girls to think about. Raul and Glass took one side and Carlos and Arturo took the other. One by one they moved along the walls of the cells. Raul reached the first one on the right and took the door handle. He pushed down firmly and the door opened. He waited a second, dropped to his knees, and Glass took a position behind him at shoulder height. Raul swung into the room with his Glock extended in front of him. What he found in the room was a petite girl, about 16 or 17 years old, huddled in the corner on a mat, shaking with fear. Raul spoke to her softly, and assured her she was safe and that they were here to rescue her. He was speaking to her in Spanish, figuring that she was a native of Colombia. The girl looked at Raul and said nothing. The girl was pretty with dark eyes and hair and Raul started to speak to her again. The girl held up her hand and asked timidly, "Do you by chance speak English? I haven't been here very long and I really don't understand what you are saying. Is there anyone in your group that speaks English?

Raul smiled at her and said in English, "Well, I have been here a long time, and I really don't speak Spanish very well, either. I'm Raul Lightfoot, a Navajo Indian from New Mexico."

The girl started crying, then jumped up and hugged Raul. "I'm Sissy Barcetti from Queens, New York. I was in Bogota visiting a college friend of mine, and we were kidnapped and brought here."

"Your friend is here also? Do you know which room she is in?"

"She is across the way from me, right where those other soldiers are", she responded as she looked outside her room. "Her name is Florence Alba. Please help her, too!"

"We will, I promise. First tell me, are there more than two guards down here, and do you know where they are; which rooms they went into?"

"There are two guards, at least that's all I've ever seen, and they ran past my room when we started hearing gun shots and explosions. I don't know where they are for sure, but it sounded like they were down by the bathroom."

"Are you strong enough to help me do something?" Raul asked.

"Whatever you need, just tell me. Can I ask you a favor, also?"

"Sure, what?" Raul asked.

"I want you to promise me that you will kill the guards down here. Not just kill them, but make them suffer."

"I'm afraid to ask why a girl from New York wants that favor…"

"These guards made us work in the club and then they used us in bad ways. They abused all of us, and hurt us. There are girls, merely children, down here who are 13 and 14 years old. These guards raped all of us, continually, whenever they felt like it. Yes, this Italian girl from New York wants those fuckers to suffer."

"Got it, I do understand" Raul said as he beckoned Carlos and the other two into the room with him and the girl. "These guys work with me, they don't speak English, but trust me, they're here to help you. Glass is going to stay with you .As we clear these rooms, you know, make sure there are no bad guys in them, I want you to tell the girls everything is alright, Most importantly, all of you need to stay together with Glass. OK?"

"Mr. Lightfoot", the girl called as Raul was leaving the room.

"What is it?" Raul asked.

She smiled as she at looked at Raul. "I am really a nice girl, I'm not a whore. These bastards did this to me. Don't forget our deal."

"I know that, Sissy, as well as I know these kinds of people. I will set things right, I promise. Do you know if there are any more Americans down here?"

"There is the new girl. I don't know her name yet. She is a pretty little brunette. I don't know where she is from exactly, but I think around the DC area."

"Why do you think that?" Raul asked.

"The two pig guards were in her room raping her, and we could all hear them laughing and yelling at her. One of them was saying things like, 'Is this how they do it in the capital?', and stuff like that."

"You understood him?" Raul looked confused.

"One of the guards is not Spanish; he is Russian or something like that. He speaks Spanish to people but he also speaks English, with a funny accent. Like maybe a Russian."

"Thank you, you have been very helpful. Now stay with Glass and we will get all of you out of here" Raul told her as he was looking at his watch. "King, come here!"

Within a minute King stuck his head around the corner of the doorway, and walked in. The girl didn't jump or looked scared at all. She ran to King and hugged his neck.

"Oh! You are gorgeous! What a pretty dog! I just love German Shepherds; they are the best dogs. I have one back home in Queens. Her name is Sassy."

Raul smiled at Sissy. "This is King. He is my partner and if you let him go he's going to help us. King, kiss the pretty girl and let's get to work."

King licked Sissy's face and put out his paw to shake. He looked at Raul and Raul swore the dog was saying something like, "How's this boss? Am I doing good? How about I hump her leg or something?"

Raul looked at King and said, "Perfect, now I want you to open the door of these rooms for us, one at a time. Got it?"

Everyone in the room appeared startled when King shook his head yes, and turned to leave.

As they were leaving the rooms, Sissy said to Glass, "You see how smart that dog is? He is probably smarter than most humans". Raul chuckled to himself and Glass just smiled at the girl, not having any idea what she had just said.

Ghost Warrior

King started down the corridor, with Carlos and Arturo across from him and Raul behind him. Glass and the girl waited by the door of her cell. When King got to the first door, he reached up with his right paw and pushed the handle down. As the door opened they all heard a scream from inside.

"It's alright, Casey, don't worry! The dog won't hurt you", Sissy yelled out from her cell.

Raul looked back at Sissy's cell. "I thought you said there was only one other American here?"

"Yes, that's right', she replied. "Casey is from Australia."

Raul rolled his eyes up and said, "Ok, now tell me how many *English speaking* girls are here."

"Oh! In that case, of the seventeen girls down here, at least half speak English. I'm sure of that."

King left the doorway he was at and moved across the hallway to the opposite door. Raul motioned for the girl to come out and she did. She went directly to Sissy and hugged her. "Only fifteen more", Raul thought, "and those two guards are in here somewhere. Like the prize in a Cracker Jack box, you just have to keep looking".

On command, King pushed this handle down and they discovered the room was empty. Raul motioned to King to move to the right and he moved to that door. When the door opened, the smell startled the three of them and they gasped. There was a young girl, in her late teens, lying on the floor with her head propped against the wall. She looked like a rag doll with her eyes open. There was a lot of blood around her, and at closer examination they discovered that the girl had cut her wrists some time ago and had bled out.

"Is Carine alright?" Sissy asked. "She is from Argentina, and she only speaks Spanish."

Carlos closed the door, as Raul told the girls what Carine had done. They took each other's hands and clenched them tightly, tears welling up in their eyes. "Oh, my God", whispered Sissy. The men moved on down the corridor. They had opened twelve of the twenty little rooms and had ten girls, of all different origins, huddled in Sissy's room with Glass watching the door.

Door number thirteen opened and Raul heard the Russian yell. "I'm going to kill this little bitch whore!", and he fired two shots at King. Both rounds went over the dog's head and struck the door of the opposite cell. King didn't run at the man; he just stood in the doorway awaiting orders from Raul. Raul could see, with the help of King's eyes, that the Russian had a young girl, holding by her hair with his left hand. She was half sitting and half standing. Her clothes had been ripped off her body and she looked as though she had been beaten. In his right hand the Russian had an automatic pistol, which looked like an old .45 cal. army issue. The Russian was lowering the gun, pointing it directly at King when Raul told the dog to attack the man. The weapon sounded once and then the Russian let out a horrible scream. King dragged the man out of the cell by his right shoulder. The shoulder looked to have been crushed by the pressure of the dogs bite, and the man, in obvious agony, was yelling and swearing at the dog. Just as Raul was calling the dog off, Sissy ran past him into the room. She emerged with the Russians .45 cal pistol, that he had dropped when the dog attacked him.

She walked over to the Russian and demanded with a cold stare, "Remember me, motherfucker?" She then shot the Russian in the right knee. The bone exploded from the force of the .45 cal slug. The Russian cried out in pain.

Arturo started to take the weapon from Sissy, and Carlos put up his hand to stop him.

"Let her give this piece of shit what he deserves."

King had let go of the Russian's shoulder and was standing next to him, motionless.

The next shot from the .45 Sissy was holding struck the opposite knee of the Russian, and as Sissy was aiming for the man's crotch, she exclaimed, "That was from Carine, and this is from all of us, you shit bag!" She fired three more rounds in the man's mid-section and crotch. The Russian jumped from the impact and then lay lifeless on the floor.

"You have quite a temper", Raul observed.

"It's not temper", Sissy said. "I told you, I'm an Italian girl from New York, and *that*, sir, was justice." She handed the gun to Arturo and walked back to the rest of the girls.

Glass returned to guard the girls, and Raul, King, Carlos and Arturo continued searching. They had cleared all but two of the rooms, and had counted a total of sixteen girls. Gabriela was not amongst them. "Two rooms left and one guard", Raul thought to himself. "Gabriela has got to be in one of them". They opened the next door and found the guard huddled in the corner behind the little brunette. "Please don't kill me! I give up, don't kill me! I'll tell you everything you want to know!" The guard was crying as he held onto the girl.

Raul went to the girl and picked her up. He had only seen Gabriela once, and the lighting was really bad in this cell. "Gabriela, are you alright? Are you hurt?"

"Who is Gabriela? I'm Samantha Peterson", the girl told him. Then she began babbling on. "I don't know any Gabriela, but I haven't been here long. I was on a cruise with my boyfriend and we got off the boat in Barranquilla. We were at a restaurant and some man said he had jewelry cheap if we were interested. I didn't want to go but Hal, my boyfriend, wanted to buy me something really nice, he said. Some other men attacked us outside the restaurant, and I think they killed Hal and I wound up here. I'm from Arlington, Virginia. Can you get me back home? I really want to go home now." She was crying, holding onto Raul very tightly.

Raul looked at her and smiled sadly. "I promise you that you will get home, and very soon."

She kissed him on the cheek and was crying. "Thank you, thank you. I know God sent you."

Glass was staring at the guard as if he knew him, and the guard was doing his best to try not to be noticed. "Victor, I can't believe you are involved with these people! I have worked with you for how long now, and you are doing this?!"

"Victor is a Leticia policeman", Glass told the others.

"I really needed the money, so I took this part time job working for Don Carlos. Am I so different than one third of the department that is working or being paid by Don Carlos?" Victor asked sheepishly.

"Don Carlos is a slave trader, kidnapper, gun runner and drug lord. And you find nothing wrong with taking his money? Not to mention, that he personally killed Hector, my partner. You are a police officer working both sides of the fence. I'm all for killing you right now, and leaving your worthless body here with these shit bags, for all of Leticia to know." Glass turned and walked back to where he had been standing.

Raul grabbed the guard and threw him against the wall. "I don't like cops much, but I detest corrupt cops, so if you can't help us I don't need you. Keep this in mind, you piece of shit. I am a full- blooded Navajo Indian, so when I tell you I am seriously considering skinning you alive and hanging your body on a hook down in this basement for the rats to eat, I do mean it."

"Please, oh please, don't hurt me! I will tell you anything you want to know. Just please don't hurt me." Victor was crying and had pissed all over the front of his trousers.

Raul could see to his right, and all sixteen of the girls who had been captives were staring at Victor. Raul knew they wanted revenge, but he needed this guard for the moment. "Let's start with, where is Don Carlos right now?" Raul began with a question he already knew the answer to, as a test.

"He left with six of his body guards three days ago. He went to his farm in the swamps. I heard you call that girl 'Gabriela'. Don Carlos had an American woman with him named Gabriela. He also has her friend. Some guy, I don't know his name."

Raul thought, "I must have really scared this guy; he's answering questions before I ask them!" Raul could see the girls were starting to get restless and he needed to get them out of there, quickly.

Carlos looked directly into the eyes of the guard and said, "You have one chance to tell me where the farm is, and remember, I'm from this area so you had better be right."

"I have never been to the farm", Victor replied. "But I have heard the other guards talking about it and I know for sure that it is close to the swamps and very near to the thick jungle south of San Marco de Las Rosas."

Carlos turned to Raul. "The village he is talking about is about a day south of here, but it is only accessible by boat. There is a series of tributary rivers that come from the main river and they flow into this area. It is kind of difficult navigating those waters without a map or a guide."

As Raul and his crew were debating their next move, a young woman of about twenty or so stepped from the group of girls at the end of the corridor. The girl was Latina, but looked very much like one of the Indians, native to the area. The girl spoke to the group in Portuguese and told them she had been kidnapped from a village along the border between Colombia and Brazil, and she knew the jungles and the area very well. The girl's name was Maquita and she told them that she could guide them to the village very easily.

It was time to leave the club and get the girls to safety. Raul really didn't want to kill Victor in cold blood. He was torn, because he feared if he let him walk out of there, either this Zalazar would get a message they were coming after him, or even worse, every bad cop in Leticia would be looking for them before he could get the girls to safety.

As he was debating his options, Sissy walked down the corridor. Immediately Raul thought, "Here comes trouble".

Sissy looked at Victor and turned to Raul. "None of us girls know this guy. He must be new or something. He never did anything to any of us, so we don't care what you do with him."

"Great", Raul thought to himself, "another female that reads minds." He looked at Sissy for a minute, smiled and said, "I have got to ask you something, do you mind?"

"Not at all, what do you want to know?" she asked.

"You are what, maybe 17 years old? You handled a .45 cal. automatic like a natural. Pretty, young ladies don't, for the most part, know how to do that."

"First of all, I'm 18 and will be 19 years old in a month. To answer your second question, I have been handling weapons since I was fourteen, and I'm on the pistol team at my dad's club. A .45's no problem if you expect the recoil and brace for it".

"Hmm...I'm impressed!", Raul answered, guessing that maybe Dad was a New York cop who believed in making sure his daughter would always be able to have "one-up" on the bad guys.

Glass looked back at Victor and asked, "How long have you been working here?"

"This is my second day, but I swear I never touched these girls, I'm not like that. I just needed the money. My daughter is sick and I couldn't afford the medicine. I just wanted to help her, nothing else."

Raul, as well as everyone else, was staring at Victor. Raul broke the silence by telling Arturo that he and Glass would take the girls and Victor to his farm and wait for the helicopters he was going to call. After the girls were gone, they could let Victor go. He also told them that he and Carlos, along with Maquita, were taking the airboat south and they would all meet up in a few days, probably at Arturo's farm.

They got the girls back to the hotel, and Glass and Arturo used the two vans they had borrowed to take the girls and Victor on to the farm to await the choppers. Raul got on his phone and called Epi to let her know the status, and advise her that he had not found Gabriela or Jess yet, but was headed into the jungle with Carlos and one of the girls from the club.

He also talked with Sarah and arranged for transport helicopters to pick up the girls from the farm and return them to Bogota. Sarah got the names of the girls and contact numbers for as many as they could, and assured Raul she would contact families and let them know their daughters were safe and would be home soon. She promised him that transports would be arriving as soon as possible, probably by evening.

Within an hour, Raul and King, along with Carlos and 'the Mezcla', as they called them, [them being the Colombians that were mixed Spanish and Native Indian], were in the airboat headed to one of the waterways that led South. Raul knew that a chopper would be much faster, but the airboat was definitely much less obvious, and inconspicuous was better of the two choices. Drugs lords were famous for their farms in the swampy area around Leticia. Processing plants for narcotics were buried deep in the swampy jungles of Southern Colombia. "What a way to go", he thought. These guys are supposed to be in the boondocks on the outer edge of civilization, but these farms had everything you could imagine, from heliports to satellite tracking devices. They all had self-contained power plants, computers, big screen televisions and swimming pools. They, for the most part, had cutting edge everything. Who says crime doesn't pay? That person obviously hadn't seen one of these resort farms. What the good guys had on their side was greed. The track record of the drug trade was also famous for its propinquity to piranhas. Greed, and the desire to have it all, made these people like a pool of piranhas eating away at each other. If it wasn't for all the innocent people who would get hurt, it might be just as well to let them feed off each other, and just go after the winner.

Carlos discovered that Maquita , if pushed, also spoke Spanish, though she was more comfortable speaking Portuguese. Being as Carlos was also from the area, he spoke some Portuguese, so they went back and forth between languages in their conversations. Maquita had drawn out a pretty detailed map for Raul and Carlos, and after about an hour's worth of geography about the area, Carlos felt he had a good understanding of the rivers and the proximity of the farm to them. They traveled for most of the day in the airboat, and late in the afternoon Maquita started to get very excited. They were nearing her village and her family. This would be a happy reunion, as she had been a captive for nearly two years and she was sure everyone here thought she had been killed. Maquita showed Carlos on her map where to dock safely near the farm to avoid detection, and which way to travel once they got on land. As Raul pulled into the waterway which led to Maquita's village, it looked like they had stepped back in time to a different century. Maquita was calling out from the boat to Indians standing on the shore. Some had spears and some were carrying bows. They were dressed scantily in loin clothes and moccasins.

None of the people looked very happy to see Carlos or Raul, but they recognized Maquita from a distance. They jumped in the water and swam to meet the airboat. To both Raul's and Carlos's surprise, Maquita jumped out of the airboat and swam to people in the water. As Raul was shutting down the engine on the airboat, he and Carlos looked at each other and simultaneously asked each other if they had heard another airboat nearby. They both listened more intently but heard nothing, just the sounds of the jungle and the happy sounds of the reunion in front of them. Raul's airboat had drifted to the shore and some of the Indians were helping to secure it. As Carlos and Raul were exiting the boat, Raul's cell phone rang. The Indians closest to him jumped and stepped back, obviously not accustomed to the sound of progress. Raul answered and discovered it was Sarah calling him.

"Hey, what's up Sarah, got any news for me?" Raul asked.

"Sure do!" she replied. "I just got a confirmation that the picture you sent me is that of a Swiss S.I.N. agent named Jonas Borge. Want the data on him?"

"Did you say BORGE? Are you sure of the name?" Raul asked, appearing quite concerned.

"That's what the data sheet says. Jonas Borge, twenty three years old, mother was a S.I.N. agent, and no information on a father. It appears his mother was killed in an explosion somewhere near the West Bank, about fifteen years ago. Her name was Mandolin, you know, like the instrument. Not much else on him and the Swiss won't say why he is in Colombia. I spoke with a senior agent named Wilhart Bletcaf and he said if you want to know why this Jonas is in Colombia, you should ask him. He said you and his agent would probably bond quickly. I have no idea what he is talking about, do you? Last but not least, this Bletcaf fellow sends his regards to you, and said dinner in Zurich is on him. Any idea what he is talking about?" she asked.

Raul never answered Sarah as he closed the receiver on his phone. Carlos noticed that he had a very strange look on his face and asked, "Are you alright? Did you get bad news or something? You look like you just saw a ghost."

"Maybe I did" Raul answered. "I'm not really sure yet, but I think we are going to find out in the very near future."

Maquita had told the entire tribe how Carlos and Raul had rescued her from the drug lord, and how she owed her life to them. The tribe was very hospitable, and Raul and Carlos stayed with the tribe the night. After dinner and a welcome home party for Maquita, they made their last minute plans for the journey ahead.

The morning came all too quickly and it was time to go. The airboat was repacked and Carlos and Raul were in the launch, ready to go, when they noticed Maquita running to the boat along with two tribe members. The two young men with her looked to be in their late teens. "Mr. Lightfoot" she said, "These are my brothers and they want to show you where the Don's farm is. I told them how dangerous it was, but they insisted."

Before Raul could say anything, the boys were in his boat and pushing it off with the spears they were carrying. "These are kids!" Raul yelled to Maquita, "I can't take them where I'm going!"

"They are sixteen and in the jungle they are men. They are twins, and think as one. Neither of them can speak, but they hear better than anyone can. They will be of great help to you and will not be in your way, I can promise that." Maquita held her right hand over her heart and yelled to them, "You are in my heart forever! God be with you!"

Raul looked at the boys and chuckled, "Together what do you weigh? About hundred and fifty pounds, I suspect. And when is the last time someone shot at you?" He looked over at Carlos who was staring down river. "Well, don't you have an opinion about this or is driving a fucking school bus up river alright with you?!"

"I think you are truly underestimating these Indians, that's my opinion. They grow up very quickly out here. I have heard stories about some of the wars in the jungles and different things that have happened in the past, and some of it is really scary."

Before Raul could respond to this, one of the Indian boys ran past the driver's seat where Raul was sitting, and stood on the platform at the rear of the boat. He was staring down river behind them, very intently. After a few minutes he went to his brother and made a fast motion of signs with his hands. The brother motioned to Raul to shut off the engine of the boat. Raul did so, wondering what it was they had seen or heard. After a few seconds they could all hear another airboat traveling at a very slow speed.

Carlos stood and went to the rear of the boat. He was looking through field glasses, trying to see who was following them. Meanwhile, Raul had restarted the boat and was traveling at a very slow coast toward the shore. He banked the boat in the grassy area, which provided good cover. The boat had no sooner landed and the two Indian boys were out of the boat and had disappeared into the jungle.

"Well at least they had enough sense to get out of here", Raul said.

Carlos was still looking toward the sound of the motor, which had, by this time, stopped as well. "No, I don't think they were running away, I think they went after whoever is following us. I just hope they are not in over their heads."

King was standing at the front of the boat when Raul's watch started beeping. It was King's way of telling him someone was approaching them. "Carlos, someone is coming this way. Get behind those bushes and cover me."

Before Carlos could turn and head for the bushes, he and Raul were surrounded by gun -wielding soldiers. Raul counted seven, maybe eight, all dressed in camouflage fatigues. Raul and Carlos were surrounded on three sides, with the river to their backs. There was no escaping, and as Raul was counting the steps to the boat, and contemplating their chances, a man stepped from the bushes. This man was also dressed in fatigues, but he was displaying American Colonel eagles on his collar. Obviously stolen from the U.S. for a self-appointed colonel, in a home-made army.

"I am Colonel Pablo Picasso and you two are my prisoners of war."

Raul looked at this idiot and thought to himself, "Great, another power hungry moron, in a country full of these kinds of dangerous fucks." Raul decided to placate this guy, as he obviously had the upper hand for the moment. "Colonel Picasso", Raul said, trying his best not to laugh at this stupid son-of-a-bitch. "My friend and I are mere hunters, looking for crocodiles and large snakes. We know nothing of a war, and we are certainly not your enemy. What have we done to offend you?"

"You are on private property. This is the land of Don Carlos Zalazar and you are trespassing. The law here says it is alright to shoot you for that. If you are wondering who makes these laws, it's me." And at that moment he started laughing like a crazy man, while he motioned to one of his men.

Three soldiers moved toward Raul and Carlos, knocking them to their knees. One of the soldiers told them to put their hands on top of their heads. King sat quietly, awaiting instructions. The two soldiers searched the pockets of Raul and Carlos, and one yelled out upon retrieving a badge case and badge from Carlos's shirt pocket.

Raul looked at Carlos, totally disgusted. "You brought your badge with you to the jungle. What a totally stupid, fucking move. There aren't any donut shops out here, no discounts; what the fuck were you thinking?!"

"I'm sorry; I forgot it was in my pocket. I'm an idiot, I know it."

"The problem is, if we don't do something quick, you're going to be a dead idiot."

"Shut up!" yelled Colonel Picasso. "You two are liars. You are not hunters, you are both policemen. Pig shit policeman, and I hate policemen. Somebody get my machete. I'll teach you to come to my jungle."

Raul was ready to command King to attack this dip-shit, self appointed colonel, as he advanced toward them with the machete held over his head, when an arrow struck the guy right in the side of the neck. The arrow was shot with such force that it penetrated the left side of his neck and emerged on the other side. Colonel Picasso stopped suddenly and spit a mouthful of dark red blood onto the ground. He dropped the machete and stared at Raul and Carlos trying to speak. No words came out, just dark red blood from his nose and mouth. He fell over dead on the ground, with his eyes still open.

Raul told King to attack the man closest to them as he and Carlos jumped for cover and grabbed their weapons. King grabbed the next soldier by the face and brought him to the ground. Once on the ground, he tightened his jaws, smashing the man's face under the force. The man's legs were jumping, from a nerve reaction even after he was dead.

Raul and Carlos were taking aim when a shot from a high powered rifle rang out. The left arm of the soldier next to the one under King was blown from his shoulder.

Before the soldiers, who were in total shock, could react, a spear landed in the chest of one, followed by two more arrows in others. Carlos was about to stand when Raul grabbed him, pulling him down.

"Just stay put. Someone is out there with one fucking high powered rifle, and you don't want to be in his sights."

Carlos looked around and said, "The Indians are the ones with the arrows and spears and shit like that. Any idea who's popping the caps?"

Before Raul could answer, another shot rang out and the bullet hit one of the soldiers directly in the face. Raul had no idea what part of the face, because the man's entire head exploded. The next shot sent one of the two remaining soldiers slamming up against a tree. He had been shot in the chest, and the impact sent him backward about fifteen feet. The remaining soldier turned to run away, and when he did, he saw the two Indian boys standing behind him. He immediately threw his gun down and put his hands up in a sign of surrender. Raul yelled to the Indians not to kill him and at the same yelled out to whoever was shooting to stop. "I need this one alive; he needs to tell me some things!" He had yelled that in Spanish, but the stranger replied in English.

"That's cool, not a problem. If he won't talk to you, maybe he'll talk to me."

Carlos then yelled to the stranger. "Thank you for your help, it was greatly appreciated! Please join us, you are most welcome!"

Raul was smiling at Carlos, and said in Spanish, "Carlos, you just said all that in Spanish because you don't understand English. When I spoke to the man in Spanish, he answered me in English. Have any idea what he said?"

"Well, no I don't. Is he a friend of ours?"

"I think he wants to meet your sister." Raul said laughing.

As a blonde-haired man about twenty or so years old approached them, Carlos was looking at Raul and said, "I don't have a sister". Raul nodded to Carlos indicating that the man was approaching.

Carlos turned to the man and his mouth dropped open. "My God, this man looks like a young blonde version of you. Do you know him, is he family? My God, he looks like you!"

The man in question was the S.I.N. agent Sarah had told Raul about. The young man had shoulder- length blonde hair with deep blue eyes and strong facial features. He was about six feet tall, probably 210 pounds, Raul figured, and built like the proverbial brick shit- house. He was fair skinned and was wearing a headband that Raul recognized right away. The young man was a blonde version of a Navajo Indian.

Just for the hell of it, Raul greeted the young man in Navajo and without hesitation the man replied in Navajo.

"So, you are Mandy's son?" Raul asked next.

"Jonas Borge. Nice to finally meet you. You know you were the only person in the world that ever called her Mandy. She told me that you told her once; Elton John wrote a song about her. I like to think it's true, even though it probably isn't."

"It was Barry Manilow, and one never knows, do they? " Raul answered. "That is one hell of a rifle you are using. What is it? It doesn't look familiar at all."

"It's a Borge .50 cal. Not much good for long distance but it really rocks up to 2,000 feet. Great for jungles and places like this, without distance shots. The projectiles are kind of heavy but they kick ass on impact, don't they?" he said with a grin.

"You said Borge .50 cal... Did your grandfather make this weapon for you?"

"Actually, we made it together. After my mother died I went to live with Heidrick and during my boyhood days and before the military I trained as an arms maker with him. While I was in the military my love for weapons, along with my natural shooting ability, landed me a spot in the intelligence branch."

"So you're a sniper for the Swiss government?" Raul asked.

"Kind of a family thing, what with my mother and all being in the service."

"Your mother was an intelligence hunter, not a sniper."

"From what I hear she was quite close to some snipers.... American as well as Swiss."

"Are you talking about me in particular?" Raul asked.

"I really don't know. Am I?" Jonas replied with a grin.

Raul didn't answer him; instead he turned to Carlos and returned to the Spanish language. "Let's get this bozo soldier over here and find out where this Zalazar's farm, or fort, or whatever the hell he has, is."

The two Indians were guarding the soldier, and when Carlos motioned to them they brought the soldier over to where Carlos, Raul and Jonas were standing. "Look," Raul said. "I'm tired and not in a very good mood after you assholes tried to kill us. So, now you are going to tell me where this farm of Don Carlos is, aren't you?"

The man stood silent for a moment and then with a smug look said, "There is nothing you can do to make me tell you anything. I am a soldier in General Zalazar's army and I am a prisoner of war. You are an American and Americans don't hurt prisoners. Take me to your jail. I am hungry and I hear the food is pretty good there".

"Boy, is this guy fucked up." Raul said in English. "Somebody filled his head with so much shit it turned his eyes brown."

Jonas walked over to the soldier and in perfect Colombian dialect told him he was not an American and that if he didn't start talking really fast he would fuck him up big time, and not think twice about it. Jonas then took out a hunting knife from a sheath in his boot, and plunged it into the left leg of the soldier. He stuck the man in the center of his thigh about four inches deep. The soldier let out a scream that Raul was sure they heard in Leticia. Carlos looked stunned, but said nothing. The soldier turned his head away from Jonas and spit on the ground. "I'm still not telling you anything, little boy. I think your mother is calling you."

Ghost Warrior

Definitely not the thing to say to this young man. He was a bit sensitive about his mother, and Raul could see it. Jonas looked at the soldier and without saying a word, reached down and grabbed the knife sticking in the soldier's leg. He twisted it and then pulled it out. The soldier let out another scream and Jonas showed him the bloody knife.

"You know what, you piece of shit? I decided I'll find the farm myself. I don't need help from a shit bag like you, anyway." He then turned to Raul and asked, "Do we need this cocksucker anymore? Because if we don't, I'm going to cut his balls off and shove them down his throat and let him suffocate on them."

This got the soldier's attention. "Get this crazy man away from me! I'll tell you whatever you want to know. Just get him away from me!"

The soldier explained in detail how to find the farm, and gave them a brief layout of the property. When Raul asked him about Gabriela and Jess, the soldier got a very scared look on his face. After a minute or two he told them that the girl was in the compound and working in the lab. He also told them that all the girls were made into drugs addicts and all the soldiers used them whenever they wanted. He looked like he didn't want to talk about Jess, but finally he said, "I think Don Carlos killed him with his claws. He knew he was a CIA agent and he tortured him. That's what I heard."

Raul looked at the soldier when he had finished talking and told him if he went anywhere near the farm he would have to deal with Jonas. The soldier tied a rope around his leg and hobbled into the jungle as quickly as he could. A couple of minutes later, Raul noticed the Indians were gone as well, once again. He turned to Carlos and asked, "Any idea where the Indians are now?" Carlos just shook his head, but Raul, for some strange reason, thought he wasn't telling all he knew. He didn't push it; there were much bigger things to think about.

"By the way," Raul asked Jonas, "How did you know we were in trouble?"

"The two Indians. They popped out of the water, one on each side of my boat. I know they had every intention of killing me, until they realized I was an Anglo and after a couple of minutes we could all hear those clowns acting like class-one assholes. So we formulated a plan of attack. I will tell you one thing for sure."

"What's that?" Raul asked.

"I really wouldn't want to fight these Indians here in their jungle. They are scary."

Carlos had been over by the airboat with King and returned, with the dog following.

"You want to make camp here tonight. If what that soldier said was true, we are about five miles from the farm. We are at a good distance away to rest, and we can check it out in the morning, first thing."

Raul nodded in agreement. "Let's get these bodies out of here before they start to stink and attract every animal in this jungle."

Carlos grabbed his badge case from Colonel Pablo and started dragging his body toward the water. "We can throw all the bodies into the river and the crocodiles will take them away during the night."

"Why, is tonight trash pick-up?" Jonas asked with a smile.

They all settled in for the night with Raul taking first watch. As he stared into the jungle he couldn't help but wonder, once again. Where had the Indian boys gone to, and why did they leave?

As the sunlight peered through the canopy of the trees, Jonas, who had taken third watch, woke Raul and Carlos. They had agreed that Carlos would stay and watch the equipment, while Raul and Jonas checked out the farm. Raul and Jonas drank coffee and made last minute checks on equipment. By the time the sun had completely cleared the horizon they were on the trail through the jungle, towards the farm. As they moved through the thick brush, cutting it away with their machetes, the temperature was already climbing. Within a half hour they were soaked with sweat and decided to take a break.

They noticed a little clearing through some trees and headed toward it. As they emerged from the thick brush and entered the clearing, they stopped suddenly, surprised to see what was in front of them. The soldier they had let go the night before was hanging by his feet from a tree branch. Someone had tied his feet with a rope and hung him upside-down and left him swinging. The soldier's eyes were open wide and he had a look of terror on his face. Beneath him was a large puddle of dark red blood. His throat had been cut from ear to ear and he had been left to hang, bleeding out like a hog.

"Well, I guess this answers my question about where the Indian boys went last night."

Jonas looked at Raul and shook his head back and forth slowly. "My guess is they thought we made a mistake letting him go last night. They know this area; this is their home and maybe they felt they needed to correct our mistake. Tough little bastards, aren't they?"

"Indeed they are. I'm inclined to agree with your analogy about how tough it would be to hunt these people. In a way, they kind of remind me of my ancestry. But then again, look what happened to the American Indian. Hell, if it wasn't for casinos where would we be today?" Raul replied laughing.

After a short rest they continued towards the farm, and in less than an hour they cut a pathway through the heavy jungle growth and were staring at the farm through binoculars and taking notes. They noticed a large, three story house in the center of a walled compound. The compound had one entrance, a double wooden gate with a guard house on each side, with two guards each. Inside the compound they could only see three other buildings. One had six garage doors in a row, all of which were closed. The one next to it looked like a dormitory of sorts. Probably big enough for seventy five to one hundred troops. Off to the left and closer to the wall was a large storehouse facility. The door to this building was open and troops were loading drums of something. "Probably cocaine", Raul thought. The warehouse was also decorated with 'no-smoking' and 'high explosive' signs. This was a combination drug and weapon storehouse, they both agreed.

"The lab must be in the large building in the center. Maybe there is a basement under it, or something. The building is just too big to be just a house", Raul stated.

Lastly, they noticed a fenced compound not far from the dormitory building. It was empty, but guarded. The area was about forty square feet in size, surrounded by a combination of chain link and barbed wire fencing. There was a roofed structure similar to a pole building with open sides. "That looks like a detention area of some type", Jonas observed. "Do you think that's where the drug addicted sex toys live?"

"What I think, is when I catch this Don Carlos mother- fucker, I'm going to shove his claws up his ass and scalp him. That's what I think!"

Raul also noticed a small helicopter on what appeared to be a helipad on the top of the house. "Copy these numbers - JO77468, we made need them later."

When they returned to camp they found another surprise. Carlos was by the airboat, checking things, and King was being petted by a young girl.

When the girl saw Raul and Jonas she let out a yelp. Carlos turned around and looked at her, telling her everything was alright. The girl sat on the ground and acted very strange. Jonas was staring at the girl, and Raul asked Carlos who the obviously mentally challenged girl was, and why was she in the camp.

"First of all, if you think she's "mentally challenged", she's got a good act. I thought it was just me she fooled. Secondly, she has a sister at the farm and goes there every day." He turned to the girl. "Sally, these are my friends. Cut the act and talk to them."

Like day and night, the girl changed into a young woman. Raul could have sworn she was about thirteen when he saw her, but when she turned to speak to him, he realized she was probably between eighteen and twenty years old. More surprising, she spoke English.

"How did you do that?" Jonas blurted out. He had obviously noticed the same thing Raul had.

"Let me introduce myself, I am Sally Fields Montoya"

"Raul started laughing. "What is with the people in this area, and their names? First we have a Colonel Pablo Picasso now Sally Fields. I give up, is that your real name, and why the retarded act?"

"Well sir, I don't know any Pablo Picasso other than the Mexican artist, and my name really is Sally Fields Montoya. My sister and I are from Barranquilla. We were kidnapped by soldiers of Don Carlos a year ago while visiting our aunt in Leticia. We were taken to the farm to work in the labs and to be abused by those pigs. From the first day I acted like a little girl who was mentally ill, and my sister Doris Day went along with my act. After about two days, the guards told Don Carlos they had picked up a 'rotten egg', as they put it, by accident, and they needed to get rid of me. Don Carlos told them to let me go, that the jungle would take of me and they wouldn't have to. My mother loves old movies and she watched them in English. She didn't know everything they were saying, but she especially liked Sally Fields and Doris Day. When my sister was born, she got Doris Day and I got Sally Fields. My mother loved our names, as well as us, until the day she died, so I wear my name proudly just like my sister."

Sally continued on talking and telling them about the farm and her daily visits. Raul couldn't help but admire this girl's wisdom and guts. She told them that she lives with the Indians and every day she goes to the farm and takes rolls and cakes to the girls. The guards always take some from me, but they leave me alone and there is always some for the girls.

"The guards just let you walk in every day?" Raul asked.

"Because they think I'm a retarded little girl, all they do is take some of the food, pat me on the ass, squeeze my tits and tell me what they would do for me if I was older and not stupid. There is the pot calling the kettle black. I think if you took all their brains, and turned them into dynamite you still wouldn't have enough to blow your nose."

"Where did you learn to speak such good English?" Jonas asked.

"El Paso, Texas, that's where my father is from. He was an officer in the US Coast Guard and that is how he met my mother. When my mother died, he couldn't take it. She died young from diabetes and it crushed him. He is still in El Paso. We keep in touch, but he has no idea what is going on right now. If he isn't over the edge already, this would do it."

"You are one brave young woman", Raul told her. "Are you up to helping us get your sister and the other girls out of that place?"

"Absolutely! What do I need to do? Just point the way."

Raul commenced to lay out a plan that included Sally returning to the compound with King. He needed pictures from the inside of the compound and King was the way to get them. He also needed to get the girls out of the farm before the shooting started.

"Is there any other way into the compound besides the front gate that you know of?"

"Actually, there is an opening to the left of the barracks. It's small, but I can get through it."

"How long would it take you to get the girls out of their cage and through the hole, if the guards were asleep?"

"Maybe ten minutes or less."

"Make it less, and I'll tell you my plan."

Raul told them that Sally was going to go to the compound with King so he could take pictures and knock the guards out so she could free the girls. Everybody in the camp was looking at Raul like he was crazy, but said nothing as he continued. He told her that she would go to the farm with a basket of rolls, and under the rolls would be a gas mask. The dog was going to emit knock-out gas on her command, and King would then pee on the lock and open it. After it was open and while she was escaping with the girls, King could take the pictures he needed.

Sally looked at Raul with a sad look of compassion. "Sir, I don't know you very well at all, but I should tell you these men are very dangerous and your plan sounds very strange, to say the least."

"No shit, they're dangerous! If they weren't, we could negotiate with them instead of killing them. And as far as my plan goes, you think it's strange because you don't know King." Raul lifted his arm and pushed a button on the watch. "King, stand up, smile and tell the girl how cute she is."

They were all looking at Raul like he had totally lost it when King stood up and smiled from ear to ear and spoke. "I think you're just too cute."

"King" Raul said, "Will you protect this cute little girl?"

King turned his head to Sally. "I will protect this cute little girl."

Needless to say, you could have dropped a pin in the camp and heard it hit the dirt. Carlos and Sally were staring at King with their mouths hanging open.

Jonas looked at Raul. "Your fucking dog talks? How did you teach him to do that?"

"This demonstration was to make all of you aware that King, although he looks like a dog, is really a robot. So much for your ideas that I'm a total wacko. King's eyes are cameras and I will be watching everything that is going on while you are in there, so don't worry. As for knocking out the guards, the dog farts knock-out gas and pisses acid. So, does everything I told you make sense now?"

Jonas had a bigger smile than King. "That dog is just too cool. I want one like that. Can you get me one?"

Sally looked sad. "He is such a sweet dog, how can he not be a dog?"

"Sally, it is important that you convince those guards *he is* a real dog, and your newest best friend in the world. Can you do that?" Raul asked.

Without turning away from King she told Raul not to worry; she could be very convincing. Raul handed her a small flask with whiskey in it and told her to pour it on the guards after they passed out. "If the boss thinks these guards got drunk and passed out, they won't be looking for us and we will still have an advantage. After you have the girls, bring them back here. Carlos is going back to the village and get some Indians with boats to meet you here. Take the girls with Carlos to the village and wait for us. When clear, stay there so I know everyone of you girls are safe. Promise?"

"I promise, right back here and then to the village. I will meet you later. Got it."

Raul, Carlos and Jonas started taking weapons and supplies out of the airboat, and when they were finished Carlos left to get the Indians and additional boats. Raul gave Jonas an extra control pad he had and explained how the remote control rifles worked on automatic as well as semi. They reviewed the plans they had drawn, and made last minute plans. Raul would be in the compound with explosives, and Jonas would set up the rifles and work from the front of the compound. King would be with Raul on the inside and Jonas would join them later for the clean up.

Darkness was settling in on the jungle and Sally, King and Raul set out for the farm. Jonas was staying behind with the equipment and radio, in case they needed support of some type.

Raul was well hidden with the computer pad, watching everything. The front gate had been reduced to one guard and three more watching the girls. The house was dark and the dormitory building was only partially lit by individual lamps. The compound was totally quiet. Sally skipped to the front gate with King

"Come on, good little doggie, let's skip!" Sally was speaking a low intellectual level of Spanish, and sounded just like the mentally ill little girl she was supposed to be. She had put her hair in pigtails and put a different colored bow on each one. She intentionally had different colored socks on, with mismatched shoes. She was carrying the wicker basket containing the rolls, flask and gas mask.

"Hi! Mister man, it's Sally! I have bolls now in my ...what do you call this again?"

The guard at the gate started laughing at Sally. "They're ROLLS stupid, not BOLLS, and you are carrying a BASKET. It's called a BASKET. Whose dog is that?"

"His name is.....uh, I forget. No, his name is King. He is my new best friend in the whole world. He talks to me and tells me he loves me."

"The dog talks to you, is that right?"

"Everyday, he says 'I'm too cute'."

"Does he also tell you that you are a fucking idiot? Because you are. Dogs can't talk, you stupid girl. What's in the basket?"

Raul was so tempted to have King speak to this moron guard just to see the look on his face. But then he would have to kill him and he needed to stay with the plan. Besides, Sally was doing her job perfectly.

"I told you bolls, don't you remember? Do you want one?"

"Come on in, stupid, and we will get the other three guards. We can all eat your rolls, and feel your tits to see if they got bigger." He started laughing again.

"Oh! That's fun, we can see if I grew up, right?"

"Right, maybe we will pat your ass too, if you're lucky. Come on, let's go."

"Little pats, little spanks, little pats, little spanks." Sally was looking directly into King's eyes and smiling, as she skipped along.

Raul watched and thought to himself, "This is one tough girl, smart and tough. She reminded him a little of Angelita. He hadn't spoken with her in some time now, and he was starting to miss her. Raul went back to the computer pad. Sally was standing in the middle of four guards and they were taking the rolls she handed them and all but the first guard was busy eating. Raul could see the girls in the cages. For the first time he saw Gabriela. She was sitting in a corner, not moving, just staring at the dog and smiling.

Raul knew she was aware of King's existence and he was sure she had recognized him. The guard who was not eating was the original guard from the entrance shack. He was groping Sally, and the girls in the cages started hissing at him, telling him to leave the little girl alone. Sally was pretending to cry a little. "Not fun, you hurt me, with your hands. Don't touch Sally more." One of the other guards walked over to them and pushed the other man down.

The guards started arguing with the man on the ground, telling him to leave the little girl alone. If he needed some, get in the cage and get it. Meanwhile they stopped paying attention to Sally. She was busy putting her gas mask on and King was starting to fart knock-out gas. "Jesus Christ!" one of the guards yelled, "get that nasty fucking dog out of here!" Then they started dropping to the ground.

King ran over to the lock, pissed on it, and it also fell to the ground. Sally was telling the girls to cover their mouths and noses and come with her. She started pouring the whiskey on the passed-out guards as the girls were all heading for the exit in the wall. As Sally and the girls were leaving the compound, they passed Raul, who was entering through the same hole. He glanced at Gabriela and noticed she was totally wiped out on some sort of narcotic. About half of the twenty-some girls leaving the compound had obvious narcotics problems. They were going to need help, and he knew Epi would see to that. As Raul entered the compound, he saw King moving about, photographing key areas. King disappeared into the house as Raul planted plastic explosives throughout the compound. After approximately twenty minutes, Raul was ready. Before he left, he went to the cage and replaced the lock on the door. He threw the destroyed lock under the dormitory. The four guards would be out for a little while longer, but to make sure it lasted the night, Raul gave each of the sleeping men an additional injection of a mixture of valium and assorted sleeping agents. "That should keep them until morning", he told himself. Raul headed for the hole in the wall and told King to meet him. King emerged from the house and met Raul at the hole. They left the compound and headed for the camp.

By the time Raul got back to the camp with King, Carlos had returned with eight Indians, each with a canoe of their own. Raul opened his cell phone and rang Sarah.

"Hey, how would you like to hear some good news?" he asked.

"Please, I've been on pins and needles. Did you fine Jess and Gabriela?"

"I don't know the exact status on Jess just yet, but Gabriela is here with us now. She is pretty messed- up, along with about nineteen other girls, so this is what I need you to do." Raul explained the plan to get the girls to the safety of the Indian village, and that he needed a handful of American Rangers to help him take a walled compound. He told her that he had met up with the S.I.N. agent and that he was helping him. He further explained that they were once again going to need transports to get these girls out of the jungle. She advised him that she would handle it all and not to worry. She copied down coordinates and all the data she needed. "There are some Rangers helping the Colombian Army with some exercises in the Cauca area. I'm sure they would love some real action. I'll call their commander."

"When you get them, tell them this guy has some heavy-duty armament, including a tank. When I was in the compound setting explosives I went into the garage facility. He has rocket launchers, and.... you name it; this guy has one or two. He also has a helicopter, and if he makes a break for it before I can blow it up, we're going to need an Apache Longbow or something like it, to blow this son-of-a bitch out of the sky. Got it?"

"Copy, I will advise them, and Epi is here with me now and copied your transmission," Sarah told him. "Someone else wants to say hi. Got time?"

"Only if it's Angelita!" Raul replied.

Angelita came on the phone and after a couple of minutes of telling him to be careful and how much she loved him, he responded with a few words in Navajo that he had taught her and she smiled. Raul felt safe that no one understood what he had told her, until he turned towards Jonas, who was helping the girls in the boat. He had forgotten that Jonas had studied the Navajo language. Jonas pretended not to hear what Raul had told Angelita. Then he turned to Raul, winked and smiled.

"Got to go now," Raul said into the phone as he stared at Jonas, who had turned away and was acting like nothing had happened. "Just what the world needs, another smart ass", Raul said to Jonas, whose smile got even bigger as he continued helping the girls.

By six am that morning the girls had been tucked safely away at the Indian village, with Carlos watching over them. Raul and Jonas were set up outside the compound. The computerized rifles were in place at strategic locations, and Jonas was operating the computer pad. Raul and King had gone back into the compound, through the hole in the wall, and were hiding on the roof of the dormitory, waiting. The plan was to fire one shot into the compound to wake everyone up at six- fifteen. They had hoped to draw this Don Carlos out into the open as soon as possible.

Raul looked at his watch and at the quiet compound. Four guards were sleeping in front of the empty, locked cage. There was a large bell hanging in the front of the compound, next to the dormitory. At six- fifteen sharp, Jonas fired one shot from his fifty caliber rifle. The target was the bell, and he hit it dead center. The bell rang as it was torn from the cast iron hanger that had secured it to the post. It struck the side of the building with a crashing thud.

Six men, half -dressed, with rifles in hand, came running from the dormitory. The front door of the house opened and a skinny little man, with a gigantic handle bar mustache, came running out onto the porch. He was followed by a taller man with a large afro-style hair-do. Even larger was this man's stomach.

Raul thoght he had to weigh at least three hundred, maybe three hundred and fifty pounds. This man was about 5'11" tall with a tremendously fat face that almost concealed a tiny black mustache. His eyes were small and very dark, and also almost hidden by the fat face. This man wasn't running, but waddling behind the little man. The fat man was wearing only his trousers and the fat belly he sported was shifting from side to side as he waddled. He and the little man walked over to where the bell had been hanging. Without inspecting the bell, which was lying on the small porch against the wall, they didn't observe the large dent the .50 cal. had made in it. The fat man made some sort of undistinguishable noise and the little man agreed. They apparently thought the bell had simply fallen from the hanger. The fat man then turned to the entranceway and shouted, "Where are the fucking guards?"

As the two of them left the porch they noticed the four guards on the ground, still sleeping. The fat man waddled over to them and kicked one of them in the back of the head. The man groaned and started to come to. The little man commenced kicking the other four guards until they also started to wake up.

"You assholes were so drunk, I can still smell you! Did you have a nice party with the girls?" He then turned to the cage and noticed for the first time that it was empty. Still locked but empty. "What did you stupid fucks do with the girls?" He motioned to the little man to hand him something. The little man reached in a bag he was carrying and took out a black leather glove with a full set of tiger claws mounted on the fingers. Raul watched as the guards started to tremble with fear.

"So this fat fuck is the famous Don Carlos with the claws. I am going to have to shoot him two or three time just to sink one bullet in all that fat," Raul was thinking to himself.

"What the hell were you dumb shits doing last night and why were you drinking on duty? I want answers and I want them now!" the fat man bellowed.

The guard he had kicked in the head said very meekly, "Sir, we were not drinking, and we don't know how the girls escaped. The cage is still locked."

"That is why you smell like whiskey and the girls are gone. I don't need you." The fat man then withdrew a pistol from his pants. Raul had not noticed the gun as it was hidden under all the fat. He shot the guard in the face twice and the guard fell motionless on the ground in front of him. "Which one of you stupid idiots is next?" the fat man asked.

Nobody spoke, and they all stood motionless. The skinny little man walked over to one of the remaining guards and put his left arm around the man's shoulders. "Now tell me what happened. How did the girls escape? Can you can tell me?" The man stood mute. He had no answer because he honestly didn't have any idea. The skinny little man had a 6" Stiletto concealed in his right hand. When the man didn't answer, he stuck the man in the center of his throat with the knife. The man grabbed his throat and tried to scream, but nothing came out. He was bleeding from the throat and mouth. He started running in circles trying to get the knife out of his throat but looked more like a chicken with no head, because he had lost his hand coordination and couldn't get a grasp on the knife.

The fat man, as well as the skinny man, was laughing at him. After a minute or two, the fat man looked at the other two guards and said, "Look at him, you shit heads, because if I don't get a good answer from one of you before he dies, you two are next."

The two guards looked at each other in terror and one of them said, "Sir, the retarded girl came here last night to bring the girls some rolls. She had a new dog with her. Maybe there was something in the rolls we ate that made us pass out."

"Yeah, like whiskey, you fucking moron!" The fat man shot the guard in the right knee. The guard fell to the ground, screaming in pain. "You got anything else to tell me?" He then shot the man in the left knee. The man was screaming in pain when the fat man put the glove with the claws on his right hand. He then swiped the man's throat, tearing open the front. The guard was flopping around on the ground, trying to breath. Blood was squirting from his throat, nose and mouth; he was not long for this world. Raul actually felt sorry for the guards. This fat pig was one of the most sadistic pieces of shit he had seen in a long time. The last guard was on his knees crying and pleading for his life. Both the fat man and his skinny friend were once again laughing.

Raul decided to send King down to the cage area to distract the two and give this guard some chance to run. King went into the yard and was walking toward the skinny man, growling. The skinny little man looked at King, surprised. "Boss, look out, there is the wild dog!", and the skinny man ran off.

The fat man started yelling at the skinny man, "You cowardly little bastard, get back here and fight!" The fat man started shooting at his skinny little friend. When the fat man failed to hit him, he looked back at King and fired the two remaining bullets in his gun. Raul commanded King to lie down and play dead. Raul needed the camera view, through King's eyes. King lay down and played dead, with his eyes open. The fat man had been joined by at least seventy- five troops, which had exited the dormitory.

Raul keyed his mike. "Jonas, do you have a clear shot at the fat guy?"

"Not really, but maybe." Jonas replied.

"When I blow up the garage, take the shot."

"Got it."

Raul set the detonator on the garage explosives and the left side of the building exploded, tearing off three of the six doors and the end of the building. Within three seconds of the explosion, a shot hit one of the soldiers next to the fat man. The shot tore the man's shoulder apart and knocked him to the ground. The entire group separated and spread out. The fat man was looking around trying to see where the shot came from. Meanwhile, the little skinny man returned to the yard, bringing a machine gun with him. He handed it to the fat man and took the claws from him, putting them back in the bag he was carrying. King was slowly moving his head, providing an excellent view of the yard to Jonas and Raul. The next explosion took out the front gate, along with the guard shack. The shack and the gates blew about twenty feet in the air, crashing down in the yard, striking at least five of the soldiers running around inside the compound. The fat man and the skinny man were now both running towards the house. The next shot Jonas fired struck the skinny little man, who was trying to hide in the shadow of the fat man. The skinny little man screamed as the .50 cal. round tore through the man's left hip and lower back. The little man left the ground on impact and fell in front of the fat man. The fat man tripped over the body, falling on top of it.

Raul keyed his mike. "Jonas, the rounds are dropping, you're too far away for that rifle. There are about twenty troops headed for the front gate. Are the others rifles set up and ready to go?"

"They are all ready to go." And as the troops headed for the front gate, Jonas opened up with the first rifle which he had placed directly in line with the gates. The soldiers reacted by firing their automatic weapons at the rifle mounted on the tripod. The explosion that followed this computerized gun battle rocked the entire compound. Raul had detonated the arms warehouse. When it exploded, the force from the explosives contained in it, along with the four Raul had placed, took the roof off the building and forced two walls completely off of the foundation. The explosion had also destroyed an entire room within the structure. This was a room approximately twenty-feet square in size, and contained a minimum of two hundred yellow plastic barrels, full of processed cocaine. To say the compound was snowing cocaine would have been an understatement. The force from the explosion had actually sent some of the barrels out of the compound, intact. The fat man had gotten to his feet and had, with great effort, reached the porch of the house. He was breathing heavily and was almost totally out of breath. Raul watched as he disappeared through the door into the house. The battle raged on. Jonas was busy operating the three strategically located automatic rifles, and Raul continued setting off the explosive devices he had placed earlier during the night. Next to explode was a large area connected to the left side of the house.

With this explosion, part of the roof and the room's front wall collapsed. A laboratory was exposed, along with some technicians who had been killed in the blast. It had been a two-level laboratory, and appeared to have been quite sophisticated, prior to this morning's explosion. Raul was just about to detonate the explosives he had placed on the front porch when he noticed the helicopter's propeller starting to rotate. He was ready to explode the helipad when bullets started striking the building all around him. He had been detected by some of the troops, and now had to concentrate on fighting back.

Raul was busy now fending off advancing troops, and it was going to get worse. He was watching the troops, taking shots and just trying to survive when he noticed two of the remaining three doors on the garage were open. From one garage emerged a tank, and from the other, there came a half-track vehicle with a .50 cal. machine gun attached, as well as a rocket launcher. Raul brought the detonator for the garage area on the screen and exploded the remaining charges. The third door was opening when the building exploded. Whatever that vehicle was, it never got out. The building crashed down on top of it, along with the troops inside. Raul, however, still had a problem and it looked like a tank and a half track. The tank was moving across the yard toward Raul's hiding spot.

The half track followed behind it, keeping pace. Raul and Jonas were both taking heavy fire and it was about to get heavier. The helicopter was lifting off and there was nothing Raul could do about it. The only option he could think of was to explode the remaining two or three charges, and if that wasn't enough, he could blow up the dog. King was still on the ground moving his head, serving as a camera for both Jonas and Raul. Raul brought up the remaining charges on the screen. There were two. One of which was very close to the house, and the other on the dormitory, right under him. The tank was in position now and its cannon was turning toward the roof where Raul was hiding. Raul exploded the charge near the house as he was watching the helicopter start ascending out of reach. Raul remembered the third charge. The one on the roof, by the helipad. It had been on a manual detonator. He pulled that detonator from his bag, lifted the cover and flipped the switch. The explosion rocked the chopper as it started flying away, but it was able to stay aloft.

The chopper had been airborne about two minutes when Raul saw the flash and the chopper exploded. "What the fu... Jonas did you do something?"

"Not me, look to your left!" Jonas yelled. Coming towards them were three Apache Longbows and two Huey transport choppers. All three with US markings. The transports landed, and Colombian and American troops poured out of them. They covered the ground like ants moving toward the compound.

The next flash Raul saw was a rocket hitting the half track, sending it into the air. The tank fired at the dormitory striking it just below Raul. The roof of the building collapsed and Raul fell into the dormitory, landing on the floor. Two bandit soldiers came running into the building with their machine guns raised. Raul was ready for them, and had his Glock pointed in their direction when they entered. Two shots, two hits and Raul rolled out of the way, seeking cover. Raul could now hear the army and the Colombian soldiers moving into the compound. The tank had changed direction and was now headed for the front gates, firing as it moved. After a couple of minutes of the tank's aggression there was another flash from one of the Apache helicopters and the tank exploded. There were about twenty bandit troops left alive in the compound when the Rangers entered, and they threw down their weapons and surrendered. Raul withdrew from the dormitory and walked toward the yard where he saw Jonas, Carlos, Arturo and even Epi. "What is this, old home week or something?" he asked, grinning.

Epi ran over to Raul, hugged him and gave him a kiss on the cheek. "Boy is it good to see you in one piece! And I've already met your new friends Carlos and Arturo, you know, the two guys from DAS. I had no idea that the Department of Administrative Services was working in Leticia at this time. But apparently you were a big help to them. General Camacho called me personally to thank us."

"Did you get the girls from the farm and the village picked up alright?", Raul asked without showing any signs of emotion whatsoever.

"As a matter of fact, we did. It seems you were quite a hit with some of them. Some girl named Sissy from Queens, New sends her love and wants you to come and visit back in the states."

Raul smiled at that comment. "Do you think I should bring Angelita with me or not?"

"Probably", she offered quickly. Then she did a double-take and fired back, "you're not serious about going to visit her, are you?"

Raul started to laugh and ignored her. "King, get up and go into the house and make a sweep. Chase any bad guys out." King stood up; shook off the dust just like a real dog would have, and ran into the house.

Raul turned to Carlos and the rest of the group and said, "Well, I think the Apache Helicopter took care of the fat piece of shit with the claws." Carlos and Arturo looked at each other puzzled, but said nothing.

Epi turned to Raul with a smile and commented, "I met Jonas, the S.I.N. agent. What a handsome devil he is. I couldn't help but notice that he has a strong resemblance to a Navajo Indian I know. Didn't you know his mother or something like that?"

"Yes, I knew his mother, but she's dead now. And no, I don't see a resemblance, other than he has long hair with a head band on it."

As luck would have it, Jonas picked that exact moment to walk over to Raul and Epi. He patted Raul on the shoulder and said something to him in Navajo, then walked away.

Epi winked at Raul. "Didn't he just say something to you in Navajo? No resemblance my ass. What did he say?"

"He said, roughly translated, we are a good team. Lots of people know sayings in Navajo and other Indian languages."

"Raul, you are so full of...." Just then she was interrupted by a loud scream. The fat man came running from the house with King chasing him.

"I give up! Get this fucking dog off my ass!"

Raul told King to stop, then asked this man, who he thought was Don Carlos Zalazar, who it was who tried to leave in the helicopter. The fat man told him it was the pilot who was trying to get the craft out of the compound before it got damaged. He was afraid Don Carlos would be furious with him if it were damaged or destroyed

"Don Carlos? What do you mean? Who the hell are you?" Raul asked, confused.

Before the fat man could answer, Carlos interceded. "That's not Don Carlos Zalazar. That fat piece of shit is Capt. Jose Ramirez, Chief of detectives for the Leticia police."

Carlos then drew back and round-housed the fat man. The punch looked like it possibly broke the fat man's nose. He fell to the ground, holding his face with his hands, crying.

"Can't say he didn't deserve that", Raul said. "Well, we need to sweep what's left of the house and see where this Tiger Claw shit bag is hiding."

Carlos was putting handcuffs on the fat man, telling him how many years he would be spending at hard labor in prison. "The real shame is that Colombia doesn't have the death penalty, because I would personally put your fat ass in the chair and flip the switch."

Raul and Jonas, along with Epi and two Rangers, left to do a sweep of the house. They searched every room and level still standing and found nothing. They were about to give up when one of the Rangers yelled. Everyone spun around and looked down the hallway they had just walked through. There was an old woman standing at the end. She was dressed all in black and looked every bit of ninety years old. The Ranger that yelled said, "She was not there a minute ago. Where did she come from?"

The old woman said something in Spanish and Raul and Epi just looked at each other. She was pointing to a picture on the wall of the hall. Before the five of them could get down the hall to where she was standing, she had disappeared. The Ranger turned to Raul. "Sir, did you understand what she said?"

Epi looked at the soldier and nodded, "Yes, Sergeant, we understood. She said 'the past'."

"What do you suppose she meant by that?" the sergeant asked.

Raul was busy trying to move the picture to see if it concealed something, and everyone else was watching him and nobody responded to the sergeant. The picture was secured solidly to the wall and didn't move at all. After about five minutes, Epi's arm lifted and she touched the picture with her right index finger. The picture was that of an old house sitting on a hill in the middle of a field. Epi's finger touched the front door and the wall in front of them opened. Raul stared at her in amazement. "How did you know to do that?"

"I didn't know and I didn't do it." Epi replied, as amazed as he.

Three out of the five people there looked at her like she was crazy. Raul wasn't one of them.

He had seen enough strange occurrences in this country that he had truly become a believer and he didn't think there was a strange phenomenon that would ever affect him. The wall opening revealed a staircase that dropped into a basement. The Rangers insisted on leading the way. Raul and Jonas had been shot at enough today, so that idea appealed to them. They all descended into the basement without resistance of any type.

What they found in the basement was another set of jail cells; along with the most disgusting odors any of them had ever smelled. The cells were empty, except for one that contained a skeleton of some poor soul and the dead decaying body of another. The only other thing in the entire ten-cell jail was a box that had been nailed shut. The box was about four feet square and three feet high. Jonas found a crow bar and hammer, and started to open the box. The first hit with the hammer evoked a moan from inside the box.

"Did you hear that?" Jonas asked, his blue eyes widening.

Everyone had heard it and one of the Rangers grabbed another bar and started to help. They got the top off and found a naked man inside. He had been severely beaten and had the addition of claw marks across his face, neck and chest. The light in the room was not good and they could not see who this poor guy was, but he was still alive.

One of the Rangers turned on a flashlight and the man in the box cried out covering his eyes. Epi and Raul stared at the young man in the box. They both knew him. It was Jess.

He was in bad shape, but alive. That sadistic son of a bitch put this kid in the box alive and left him to die. "He buried him alive", Raul thought to himself. Raul leaned into the box and whispered to Jess, who was trying to smile. "I am going to hunt this guy down and kill him, I promise you that. No matter where he goes, I'll find him."

The Rangers got help down to the basement and got Jess out and into the medevac chopper. The rest of them returned to the yard where Carlos and Arturo were questioning the fat man.

Epi took a look at the fat man and grabbed Carlos' arm. "Stop beating this man! I need to question him."

"We are Colombian agents and this is a Colombian suspect. This is not your business."

"Excuse me! I am a Colombian as well, and I want to talk to this man."

Arturo smiled at Epi and said very quietly, "It is true you are Colombian by birth, but you work for the American CIA and I'm sure with American citizenship. Secondly, this is not a man; he is a big fat sack of shit. He pretended to be a policeman while he was really a bad guy. No one here has any sympathy for him, and nobody is going to extend him any courtesies. Now, what did you want to know about?" he asked, still smiling.

Epi knew the two DAS agents were right and she didn't have any right to step in, so she smiled very diplomatically and asked, "Could you please ask this man where Don Carlos Zalazar is? I would really like to talk to him."

"So far he has told us that Zalazar left two days ago in a different helicopter and that he was headed for Miami to make some deals. He has also given us a list of cops in the area that work for this guy, along with lots of other helpful tips. I'm sure when he arrives at headquarters for another chat he will have much more to tell us."

"You saw what happened to our agents. I want to know if he did that to that young man or if it was Zalazar. And so help me God, I want the truth."

The fat man lowered his eyes and told her Zalazar had ordered him to make the girl a drug addicted whore and to hurt the other agent. Zalazar was responsible for burying him alive, he claimed.

"You sadistic son of a bitch, you did that to that man!" Epi stared at the fat man, and then in a move that surprised all of them, she took out a pistol from her belt and pointed it at him.

Carlos grabbed it from her and whispered in her ear, "If you want to kick this man in the face, be my guest, but you can't kill him here. We need to talk to him some more. One Colombian to another, I promise you this man will pay for what he has done. He will go to prison and I will personally let people inside know he helped us. His death won't be pretty, but it will be well-deserved."

Epi had tears in her eyes. Tears of rage for the fat man and tears of passion for Jess.

Carlos hugged her for a moment, then she turned without saying a word and walked to the waiting helicopter. The Colombian army and the Rangers stayed to clean up and retrieve the coke and weapons, and process the prisoners. Carlos and Arturo also stayed to supervise.

"Miami," Raul pondered. "I've been to Miami. It's nice." He turned to Jonas and asked, "Think you might like a trip to Miami?"

"I hear the girls are hot in Miami. I'm already packed! Let's go get our airboats and get out of here."

Raul and King left for the camp along with Jonas. Sarah had promised to have a cargo plane at Leticia large enough to carry the Hummer and Raul's boat. Jonas had rented his airboat so he would drop it in Leticia and fly to Bogota with Raul. Epi was going to fly in the medevac with Gabriela and Jess. She would meet them in Bogota.

When Raul and Jonas arrived in Leticia they found two Leticia police officers waiting for them by the Hummer. "This ought to be interesting", Raul told Jonas.

As the two of them approached the Hummer, one of the uniformed police officers spoke. "Good afternoon, sir, is this your Hummer?"

"Why, yes it is, as a matter of fact", Raul replied. "What seems to be the problem, officer?"

"Well, I'm not quite sure. It seems your car knocks out people that try to break into it. In the past two days we have arrested and jailed seven thieves who were found lying by the car, unconscious. All of them have had burglary tools in their hands and were passed out on the ground next to the car. Actually, there is something more strange than that which has occurred. It seems each time a burglar attempted to break in the car, the car called our office to report it. How can that be?"

Raul laughed and patted the top of the car. "Let me ask you this. Did the car say that its name was Ed, by chance?"

"As a matter of fact, that is the name we have for the caller. How did you know that?"

"American technology, my friend. American technology," Raul smiled.

"We have another question, sir," the policeman said.

"And that would be?" Raul asked.

"My partner and I have never seen a car like this before in our lives. We would like very much to see inside the car. You know, just to sit in it for a minute or two so we can tell the other guys we work with. I hope our request doesn't sound too stupid to you."

Raul looked at Jonas, who was smiling, and then to the police officers. "Not at all, help yourselves." Raul punched a five digit code on the door and it opened. The young policemen jumped back when the car began to speak to Raul.

"Welcome home, Raul, I hope your day went better than mine. There were a total of seven burglary attempts while you were gone. I disarmed them all, and called the police. Please park me in a safer location in the future. You know your uncle will not be happy with you, if you lose me. And Sam can be very nasty if he wants to be."

"Well, that's that," Raul said to Jonas. "Let's get the boat hooked up and get to the airport. Sarah just called me and the transport is waiting. Time to go home."

It was approximately one month later when Raul re-united with Carlos and Arturo. Raul and Epi returned to Leticia, by air this time, to attend a police ceremony. Jonas was not with them, as he had returned home after the 'incident' in Leticia, as it had been called. He had assured Raul that when it was time to go to Miami in search of Don Carlos Zalzar, he would return to the states to help him. Raul had been surprised that Jonas had never asked him questions about the relationship between him and Jonas' mother. Jonas, who looked like a blonde clone of Raul, never even asked him the obvious question regarding who his father may or may not be. On the other hand, Raul didn't offer any answers, either.

"You two were so cut from the same cloth," Angelita told them after she met Jonas. Angelita liked Jonas right off the bat. She had told Raul in private one night, "I was ready to tell you that American saying, about how after they made you they threw away the mold. Well, I look at Jonas and see they didn't. He not only looks like you but he even acts like you. How could he not be your son?" Raul had not answered her.

While Raul was in the jungle with Carlos, one of the many conversations had been about Carlos' desire to become the chief of detectives in Leticia. Leticia was Carlos' home town, and he was prepared to leave government service for this job. Raul had called Hector, who reached out to some other people, and made it happen. To Raul's surprise, he had learned from Arturo that Sally would be at the ceremony also. It seemed that Sally and Carlos had really hit it off well, and, according to Arturo, they were a couple now. After the ceremony a large group had gathered at Carlos' home for a party. Raul and Epi approached Carlos and Sally. Raul looked at Sally and smiled. "I brought you someone who wants to live with you."

Sally looked at him suspiciously with a smile. "I have absolutely no idea what to expect from you, so go ahead, I'm ready."

Raul reached into his jacket and pulled out a German Shepherd puppy.

"Say hi to Prince. He wants to be your new roommate."

Sally looked at Raul and laughed a little. "Is this dog real or is it a robot? It's probably a robot, knowing you." Sally held the dog and said to it, "Talk to me; tell me how much you love me."

Prince just looked at her, tilted his head to one side, barked like a puppy and licked her face.

Everyone laughed and Raul told her, "Sweetheart, I couldn't afford to buy you a robot. This one is real, so when he lifts his leg, watch out!"

CHAPTER VI
THE PHANTOM WITH THE CLAWS – PART II

To what lengths will evil go to seek what it considers a justifiable end to any situation?
If an evil man seeks to put terror in the hearts of innocent people, simply to satisfy his own whims,
then retribution should be hard, swift and meaningful. Don't you agree?

Raul couldn't help but regress into his past as the driver pulled into the CIA complex at Langley, Virginia. He had been picked up at the airport and driven straight to headquarters for a briefing. Hector had called him two days earlier and told him about some recent sightings and intelligence they had gathered on Don Carlos Zalazar. He had arranged a meeting to discuss going after him. When Raul entered Hector's office, Epi and Ricky were already waiting for him. They had been in Washington on prior business and had told him they would meet him. No surprises there. There was, however, a different surprise along with Epi and Ricky. Jonas Borge was also waiting in the office. Raul looked at him with no expression and asked, "I thought maybe you were kidding when you said you wanted to go to Miami to catch the shit-bag?"

"Nope, I wasn't kidding, and yes, I very much want to go to Miami", Jonas answered.

"So, you have been gone for what, two months now? And you still have an interest in this Don Carlos asshole. Let me ask you this. What is it you didn't tell me back in Colombia that maybe you should have?"

Jonas stared at Raul for a minute. "If I understand correctly, your brother plans on holding a briefing about that today, so maybe we should wait."

Raul stared right back and smiled a little. "Well, I'm not much on surprises, and even less on waiting. So how about you fill me in right now."

Ricky jumped up, deciding the timing was right to change the mood. "Hello to you, too! How was your flight and aren't you glad to see Epi and me?"

"Of course I am", he answered matter-of-factly, "and let me also ask you why you are staring back and forth at Jonas and me. Did you want to say something, or what?"

Jonas had walked over to Epi and was out of earshot. Ricky just stood there for a moment, shaking his head back and forth. "Incredible", he responded, "just incredible. This kid could be your clone and I also see he has your charming temperament as well. I wonder why Mandy never told you about him?"

"What was she going to tell me?' Raul shot back. "There was no reason for her to tell me anything."

"You mean you don't think this kid, who looks and acts just like you, is yours?"

"Maybe, I don't know for sure. We don't have any DNA tests or anything."

"DNA my ass. Next you're going to tell me you flew here from Colombia on the back of a cow."

Before Raul could respond to his mode of travel, Hector entered the room. "Good afternoon to all of you", he greeted the group. "Come into my office and let's get started." As they were entering his office, Hector was shaking hands and individually greeting them. When he got to Raul, he hugged him and kissed him on the cheek. "How are you, little brother? Your two little nieces miss you and can't wait to see you this evening. Not to mention Paula, who, by the way, wanted me to ask if Angelita came with you. She is so anxious to meet her."

"No, not this time. Ever since she returned from Bogota on her last visit, she has been ill with some sort of stomach flu or something. Next time for sure, I'll bring her and we will all spend time together."

Hector turned from Raul and greeted Jonas, who was following Raul. "Good afternoon to you. Your supervisor, Mr. Heidrick, briefed me a little on your purpose for being involved in this. Needless to say, I'm always interested in International Terrorists."

Raul looked at Hector and then Jonas. "What the hell are we talking about here, International Terrorists? I was under the impression that we were here about this Don Carlos asshole. Something change when I wasn't looking?"

Hector smiled at Raul. "In due time; let's get the meeting under way."

Raul turned to Jonas before they entered the room. "I don't like secrets, especially between people I'm supposed to trust. In fact, secrets really piss me off and you don't want to see me pissed off. Trust me on that."

Jonas had a very sheepish look and explained, "I was trying to tell you what was going on outside when your brother walked out. Things have happened that I have just recently been made aware of, and that's what this is about."

The four of them were in Hector's office and he closed the door. "Now, let me make sure I'm on the right track here. Jonas Borge is here representing the Swiss Intelligence Network, and it appears this Zalazar fellow has become quite the international terrorist. Last month while Raul and Jonas were in the Amazonas chasing this guy, he went to Zurich and blew up a bus station. He killed about seventy- five people and injured scores more."

Epi interjected. "Are they sure it was our guy who is responsible for that? I'm asking because he had just left his compound when Raul and Jonas got there and I'm not sure he had time to do that bombing. Besides, our detainee told us he had gone to Miami, not Switzerland."

"By the way, your 'detainee', as you put it, was found floating in a river near Espinal. Colombian Intelligence put out an alert that he had escaped, and the next thing you know, there he is floating in a river near some small little town. All three hundred fifty pounds of him. You gotta love those agents from D.A.S., don't you?"

Epi smiled. She did love those guys. Carlos had told her he would set things right for what had happened to Gabriela and Jess, and he had been true to his word. Besides, she couldn't think of a living soul who would miss that tub-of-shit corrupt cop, anyway.

Ricky stood up and asked Hector, "Do you think this informant lied to our guys as well as the agents from DAS? I ask because I wasn't there for this mission, so I have no idea what the credibility level of this detainee might be."

"It appears this bad cop worked for this Zalazar and was loyal to him to the end. Either out of fear or loyalty, the Colombian agents couldn't get a straight answer out of him about anything", Hector replied. "However, let me state emphatically that we now know he did the bus station bombing because a German tourist got a picture of him leaving the station just before the explosion. And to make matters worse, he sent the Director a letter that was received yesterday. Zalazar stated that he knew the American CIA was responsible for his recent setbacks in Leticia as well as damage to property at - as he called it - his 'private estate'. He claimed all these attacks were unprovoked and without reason."

Raul was studying Hector and asked, "Speaking of reason, what is the status on Gabriela and Jess?"

"Gabriela was in the primary stages of cocaine addiction and was suffering from gonorrhea. All other tests came back negative. She is in the rehab center, and of course her treatment is a top priority. She has indicated that she wants to stay with the CIA and after her full recovery I'll find a good, safe spot for her. Jess, on the other hand, is not in very good shape. He will undergo cosmetic surgery to correct the damage done by the claws, and physically he's coming along. He is young and that helps. Psychologically, however, he is a wreck, and I'm really not sure if he's going to come around or not. The doctors tell me that being left in a box to die left psychological scars that may never heal. Needless to say, he will be in the hospital a long time; maybe forever, who knows? We will, of course, not abandon him; he is still one of us."

Raul looked over at Epi, who was sitting next to Ricky on a sofa. Epi had tears in her eyes. She was not crying, but the tears were obvious. What had happened to Gabriela and Jess had affected her immensely, and she was going to need time to get over it. "Some things just take time", he thought to himself.

Hector interrupted his thinking, continuing with the letter. "Anyhow, this Zalazar told the director that as a result of our actions against him, he intended to get our attention. After the Zurich bombing I honestly believe that he had his picture taken on purpose. Take a look at this guy."

This was the first look any of them had really gotten at this man. It seemed that he was, up to this point, very camera shy. The four of them stared at the picture, which had been blown up to an 8x10 size. There he was, the Phantom With The Claws, as he was called. Don Carlos Zalazar. Actually, he was not a bad looking guy for being the crazy son-of-a-bitch that he was. Hector turned the photograph over and read the stats on Zalazar to the group. "Ok, we have here Don Carlos Zalazar, six feet one inch tall, 190lbs. He is thirty-one years old and was born in the Colombian State of Casanare, in a little village near Orocue. He was orphaned at the age of eleven and has no known family members. He is not married, and has no known children. As you can see by the picture, he has brown, shoulder-length hair with piercing dark eyes. Tall and skinny with crazy eyes, and has nothing but his money to live for. And folks, that makes him very dangerous. You will never take this man alive. It will only be a matter of how many others he will take with him." Hector provided copies of the photos to everyone in the room.

After studying the picture and data a few minutes, Hector continued. "Now, what we have here at present is another soon-to-be problem. This man was brazen enough to tell the director that he hoped the bus station incident had gotten our attention, and he was headed for Miami. The only other information at this time is that he told the director in the letter that he thought he would travel by tri-rail and see a ball game at Pro Player Stadium."

Ricky responded with his analysis. "I don't think he'll bomb the tri-rail, especially after warning us. It's too easily secured, compared to Pro Player Stadium. The problem, however, as I see it, is that the Marlins are in the baseball playoffs, and we are already into football. And if I'm not mistaken, the first home game for the Dolphins is in two weeks."

Epi then advised the group that she would return to their base, and together with Sarah they would coordinate the intelligence on this mission. Everyone agreed, and decided that right away Miami customs and immigration, as well as officials at Pro Player needed to be contacted to help get things on track. They would also alert Tri-Rail as to possible dangers so the three counties which the train covered could coordinate and beef-up security. Hector advised them that he would contact Homeland Security to assist Epi and Sarah.

Hector looked at Ricky, Raul and Jonas. "I will have contact names for you when you land in Miami. The three of you will take the company jet in the morning. We need to keep this as low-keyed as possible; we don't need a major panic in Miami."

As everyone was leaving, Hector turned to Raul. "Raul, stay for a minute. I have a couple of personal questions for you."

"What's up?" Raul asked. "I've got a lot of things to do, so I need to get started."

"Yeah, I know. But you *are* coming for dinner tonight, right?" Hector asked.

"Absolutely, wouldn't miss it for the world. In fact, I brought surprises for the girls."

"Your two nieces are looking forward to seeing you very much. They actually miss you, if you can believe that. Oh, and by the way, Jonas - you know, the kid who looks like a blonde haired clone of you? You know, the one you don't admit to fathering. I have pretty good information that he is Mandy's son, and you are the father. So why don't you just own up to it and treat him like your son?"

Raul appeared resigned to the facts at this point. "I don't really know, he hasn't brought it up, and I don't think he is here looking for a father."

"Next time you talk to Grandpa, ask him what he thinks. Yes, in case you're wondering; and from the stupid look on your face, I see you are. I see Grandpa too, and yes, we talk. If you feel like it, bring Jonas with you tonight. He is family and will always be, whether you admit it or not."

"You done?" Raul asked. "Call the hanger and see if the transport is here from Colombia with my Hummer and my equipment. Red Tucker flew it here for me."

"Yeah, I know Red. Hell of a pilot. Is he taking the stuff to Miami for you?"

"We will all fly down in the transport with him. You know, save Uncle Sam a buck or two."

Hector was on the phone as they were talking, and held up his hand to stop for a minute. "Hector Lightfoot here. Has the transport from Bogota arrived yet? That's right, Red Tucker. OK, copy this cell phone number, and have him call it when he arrives". Hector hung up and spoke to Raul. "Tower says he's forty minutes out, and when he gets here he'll call you. You are all booked at the Hilton out by the airport, so have the driver take you, get changed and we'll see you and maybe Jonas, about six thirty."

Raul left and met with Ricky and Jonas. Epi had already taken a car to the airport, and was probably on a jet back to Bogota by now, he figured. The three of them left for the hotel, and Raul filled them in about the transport.

By five thirty Red Tucker had arrived at the hotel, and they were all sitting at the bar, discussing strategy. Raul had asked Jonas if he wanted to come to Hector's home with him, but Jonas had declined and opted to sit in the bar with Ricky and Red.

Raul didn't much blame Jonas; after all, for Jonas to feel a little out of place would be very understandable. "Maybe one day we can all get together like a real family. Angelita, Jonas and me; at a picnic with my brother and his family. But somehow this picture is a little fuzzy", he thought. Raul returned to the hotel by ten thirty and found everyone had gone to their rooms, leaving him alone in the bar for one last drink before bed.

The four of them were up and on their way to the airport by six-thirty in the morning. At the airport Red filed his necessary paperwork while Raul checked his equipment. The Hummer was tied down in cargo, and everything he had wanted was on board. Jonas had left his .50 cal. Borge rifle at the farm when he returned to Switzerland, and it was also on board, packed with the equipment. There was one piece of equipment inside the Hummer Raul had become attached to, and it was waiting for him. Raul entered the sitting area of the craft as they were preparing for take off. He was being followed by King. Raul was smiling from ear to ear and Ricky and Jonas just watched him as he went to his seat. King sat in the seat next to him, looking and acting completely like a large German Shepherd dog, panting and all. Ed had added this feature, along with the customary drool, which was the nature of these types of dogs. Ed had added some other touches, and Raul was studying the paperwork Ed had generated to accompany the new and improved King. Raul was also sporting a new watch that Ed had made for him, and when Raul touched one of the buttons and a video of Ed appeared, telling Raul he knew that the notes regarding King's modifications would go unread. So he, Ed, had taken the liberty of providing this short video to explain them. "Please, Raul, take some time during the flight to acquaint yourself with the new options. Remember, be nice to King; he tells me everything. Be safe and bring everything back in one piece."

Raul looked up and Ricky was staring at King. "So this is the robot dog I've heard so much about. What special thing can it do besides farting tear gas or knock-out gas, or whatever it is?"

Raul smiled and looked at King. "Look at me and smile." King obliged. "Now respond to Ricky's comments, use track A-7."

King turned his head toward Ricky. Jonas was already laughing because he knew what was coming. "Fuck you very much for your comments. Were you born an asshole, or do you have to work at it.?"

Ricky's mouth was hanging wide open. He was speechless and showed it. King panted a little more then added, "Catching flies or what? Maybe I should fart right now."

Raul was snickering, but Jonas was at the point of hysteria, he was laughing so hard. "Jonas, calm down or you'll piss your pants and embarrass us all!", Raul teased.

Three hours and twenty two minutes later they touched down in Miami. "Welcome to Miami International. Home of the hottest Latin Chicks this side of Bogota, and the nastiest drug dealers this side of the Amazonas", Red Tucker announced into the P.A. system. The CIA transport was taxied into the special hanger on the West side of the field by Red Tucker and after the doors of the hanger were secured, they started unloading the craft. While the Hummer was being unloaded, an agent unknown to them drove up in a red Jeep Wrangler. "Hi, I'm George Backner, special agent from the Miami office. A woman named Sarah called the office and said agent Nelson preferred a Jeep and that agent Lightfoot ….excuse me for asking, but is that your real name?" Raul shot him a look that would have awakened a dead man. "No offense meant; I've just never met an Indian CIA agent before."

Raul smirked at the young agent and shot back, "Don't get to Washington much, do you?"

"No, sir, not at all since the Academy, but I am anxious to get started with the action part of my career. So far, all I've done is intelligence and office work here in Miami. I hope we didn't get off to a bad start, sir."

"No, trooper, we haven't started at all yet. I'll be in the Hummer, Agent Nelson is in the Jeep, and Jonas here is in what?"

"I don't have a car for him. He is not CIA and I didn't get an authorization for one."

Raul looked at George and said, "Two things; write them down if you need to. First, I want all the intelligence you have on Don Carlos Zalazar. And secondly, and this is important", Raul leaned over and whispered in George's right ear. "Don't fuck with me, and get agent Borge whatever car he needs and do it before you piss me off. Got it?!"

Jonas smiled at the agent who looked a little concerned, to say the least. "Get me a Ford F-250 four wheel drive, with a large V8 motor. And trust me, sport, you don't want to see this Indian pissed off. You do understand that he lives in a jungle, and kills people for a living?"

"Yes sir, I've been briefed somewhat about the assignment and will do everything I can do to help". George pulled out a cell phone and made a call. After about two minutes on the phone he turned to Jonas and asked, "Any particular color?"

"Nothing loud."

"Truck will be delivered in one hour to the hotel", George replied. "I have an intel package on everything we have to date right here." He handed it to Ricky and asked the group to follow him to the hotel where they would be staying.

They all drove to a hotel on the west side of Dade county, out by the Turnpike extension. George had told them they used this one because it was fairly secluded and would give them easy North-South as well as East-West access. He also told them Metro Police headquarters was in close proximity if they needed a lab or support of any type.

After everyone was settled into the hotel, they all met in a designated room on the third floor. The room was a banquet type with a sign indicating that the room was being used by the Zalazar family for the "Zalazar Reunion". There were two Latin men stationed at the outside of the door with the sole purpose of keeping unwanted guests out. Raul looked at the two of them and figured that together they could probably bench press his Hummer. The two were dressed informally in Guayabera shirts and slacks, and as the three of them approached, one of them greeted them and asked if they were with the Zalazar party. They showed their I.D.'s to a camera which had been installed above the doors. The doors clicked open and they entered. As they entered, George, the agent from the airport, approached them. George was about twenty-five, Raul figured. He had a baby face, complete with a black mustache which obviously was there to help him appear a little older. He had a slight build and stood about five feet ten inches. This kid was as anxious as they come, but totally clueless to the real dangers of the job.

"Everything OK with the rooms? All settled?" George asked with a smile.

Ricky, as cordial as always, smiled back and replied, "The accommodations are quite acceptable, thank you. I notice you have quite an array of equipment in here. What specific types are you using, if you don't mind me asking?"

"Not at all, sir. Most of the equipment is tracking and surveillance stuff mixed with a lot of communications gear. You know, personal and group types. Any other questions before I introduce the group?"

Raul looked at George and asked, "George, were you in the military? What exactly is your background?"

"I have a Master's Degree from Princeton and I majored in Linguistics. I speak nine languages, including Spanish, Portuguese, Russian and Chinese, not to mention German, French, and, of course, English."

"That's seven", Jonas responded.

"Right. Well, I also have learned the Seminole dialects and I can sign."

"Sign what?" Raul asked.

"No sir, not sign, but I can sign", George laughed.

"Sign is a type of silent language; you know, for the deaf", Ricky interjected.

"Right. Let me ask you, George. Do you have a gun?" Raul asked.

"Certainly, sir, a Smith and Wesson nine millimeter. Why do you ask?"

"No particular reason. Why did you decide to learn Seminole? Is an Indian language that important in Florida?" Raul asked.

"If they trust you they will help you. Besides, my wife happens to be a Seminole Indian. That was why I asked you about your last name earlier", George responded.

"He's a Navajo Indian from New Mexico.", Ricky replied. "So what else do you do?

We know nothing about South Florida so we will need your assistance. You up for that?"

"Absolutely, sir, I've been waiting for the chance", George replied quickly.

Raul looked at the two of them. Ricky and George were bonding. Two language specialists who carry the same type of weapon. Raul chuckled and asked, "George, you into karate or kick boxing?"

Ricky looked at Raul and shook his head slowly. "Fuck you, Raul."

Raul was laughing, Jonas was just looking at him and George said, "No karate, sir, but I do box. Funny you should ask. I'm lightweight champion at the 44th street gym. You know, Golden Gloves and all that."

It was Ricky's turn to laugh, and he did. "Birds of a feather stick together", Raul thought.

George introduced the three of them to two other men, both from Homeland Security.

"This is Tom and Frank. Bill, over there, is FBI and the other Bill talking on the phone is Secret Service. We have a cross section of security services in the room, so anything we need won't be a problem. This Zalazar is a top priority, so just tell us how we can help."

Raul thought for a moment. "This guy is Colombian, so if he hasn't surfaced yet, he's hiding and probably in a Spanish speaking area. We know he speaks English, but not very well and with a heavy accent, so he will try to go underground for a while."

"Little Havana, that's where he would be", George said. "We should start looking there."

"George, I need two Spanish-speaking agents to go with Ricky to Little Havana. Preferably Cubans, if they are available. You two guys from TSA, Tom and Frank, would you guys go with Jonas to the Tri-Rail center and start there, just in case? After you're sure that area is covered, go to the stadium. We are going to have to start sweeps there, so we will need bomb dogs from Miami-Dade. Can you guys cover that?"

"No problem, sir." Frank answered. "We are on it. Oh, and there is a new Blue Ford F-250 that was delivered here. Who gets that?" Jonas took the keys and Frank added, "It's a crew cab, should we ride together?"

"No problem." Said Jonas as the three of them left for the Tri-Rail station.

Everyone there had been set up, so communication would not be a problem.

"Ricky, I need you to cover Little Havana. I'm sure this guy has a base set up there somewhere, and we need to find it, as well as whoever is helping him." As Raul was talking to Ricky, two very Latin men walked into the room.

"Who is George?" one of the men asked.

George stepped from the group and introduced himself. The two men were from the Secret Service and were not only Cuban by descent, but both lived in Little Havana. They added that a check of Hialeah, another very Hispanic area, would also be warranted. The men had introduced themselves as Jorge and Renaldo. They both had very thick Cuban accents, and Raul knew they would blend perfectly.

Ricky and the two Cuban Secret Service agents left, and Raul turned to George and said, "Let's go talk to the Indians."

Raul and George walked down to Raul's Hummer, and as they approached it Raul touched his watch. King stood up in the back seat and filled most of the area with his massive body. George jumped. "My God, I had no idea you had a dog with you! And such a monstrous one! That has to be the biggest German Shepherd I've ever seen. You keep him in the car.... isn't that dangerous or unhealthy for him?"

"No, King is fine. I walk him whenever he needs it, and he stays in my room with me," Raul answered with a chuckle.

Raul and George drove to the Miccosukee casino on Krome Ave. "Let's go in here and see if my brother-in-law is working. He can help us, for sure," said George. As they entered the Casino, a very Italian-looking man, about thirty, approached them. He hugged George and asked how he was doing. After the warm greetings, George introduced the man as Tony Jr. "Tony," George asked, "Is Johnny here? We need to speak with him."

"Absolutely." And with that, Tony Jr. directed them to Johnny's office on the second floor. Looking a little confused, Raul asked George where the Indians were in this Indian Casino. He was then advised that the Indians hired firms from Chicago and New York to run the Casinos, and as a rule the Indians weren't permitted in the casinos. This had been a mandate passed to the tribe by the Tribal Council. Indians only came into the casino for special shows or functions, but not to gamble or run the operation.

There were Indians working in the offices as counters and accountants, but never on the floor.

Raul asked, "Your brother-in-law is the casino manager and isn't he an Indian?"

George chuckled. "Nope, his name is Johnny Castellano and he is married to Maya's sister, Rebecca. Maya is my wife."

"And Johnny 'the Italian' Castellano knows all about the Indians?" Raul asked with a skeptical tone.

"You would absolutely be surprised what he knows about" George replied, winking.

The two of them approached a closed door and knocked. A buzzer sounded and the door opened. A beautiful young Indian woman was seated at a desk in a reception area.

"Oh, hi George, you here to see the Big Chief?" she asked.

"Well, I could be here to take you out for a spin but that would probably get me scalped. So Johnny will have to do."

The young lady pushed a button and spoke into a box on her desk. "The non-Italian Gringo is here to see you."

The speaker box announced, "Rebecca, stop ragging on the Gringo. You know he's going home to tell your sister." The door to the office opened and there was Johnny. Thirty-something years old, handsome as they come and, as they say, a physique to die for, Mr. Perfect. Johnny came out of his office and hugged George. "How are you doing and when are you going to come work for me and make real money?" Johnny then turned to Raul and asked bluntly, "You're an Indian aren't you? You know, the Council has a rule against the Indians hanging out in the Casino. You're not from here. I don't recognize you."

Raul wondered how long this guy was going to babble. "Sad", he thought. "This guy presented a good image until he opened his mouth."

George interjected before Raul could tell Johnny to stick his casino up his ass. "Johnny, let me introduce Agent Raul Lightfoot from the CIA."

Before anyone in the room could move or say a thing, Rebecca jumped to her feet and ran over to Raul. "Oh my God, you are the Navajo Ghost Warrior! My friends from Colombia talk about you. They say the drug lords and terrorists in Colombia are scared to death of you. If half of what they say is true, you have got to be here in Florida to kill someone! I would definitely not want to be that guy. Johnny, remember the night the Gonzalez sisters were talking about the battle in the forest near Guatavita?" She turned to Johnny and turned her right hand up pointing it toward Raul.

Johnny had a bit of a sick look on his face and cleared his throat. "Pardon my comments, Mister Lightfoot, I had no idea who you were. I meant no disrespect. And of course, anything you want just tell us. We are very close to a lot of Colombians who live in the area and anything we can do to help. We are here for you."

George spoke before anyone. "Listen, you two, it is very… and I repeat…*very* important that Raul's presence here is not a newspaper issue. We are here on official business and do not want our presence made known to the public. We do need your help, but only if you can promise us it won't go any further than this office."

They both looked at George like scolded school children and agreed to cooperate any way they could. Raul had been standing there, just taking in this entire scene, slowly shaking his head.

"That Navajo Ghost Warrior stuff is a load of crap. I don't know who made that up. Probably someone really bored. I'm a CIA intelligence officer who happens to be assigned to Colombia. I am a Navajo Indian, but the rest is all someone's fantasy."

George was staring at Raul. He had also heard the rumors, but until now hadn't really put it together. He was just nodding in agreement. Rebecca and Johnny were focusing on Raul, also agreeing to whatever he was saying. They did, however, both have those 'now this is a load of crap' expressions on their faces. But they said nothing and let Raul continue to talk, uninterrupted. Raul and George were halfway convinced that Johnny and Rebecca would keep the secret, for at least a while, and they continued. "We are looking for information about a terrorist cell that may be working, or trying to set up in this area. The leader is Colombian and we think he's here to blow up something – something big." George told them. "We need you to get your ears to the ground and find out who's doing what and where. Can you help us?"

As Johnny and Rebecca were readily agreeing to George's request, Raul's cell phone sounded. Sarah was calling Raul to inform him that Carlos, the chief of detectives in Leticia, had called to advise her that his detectives, along with agents from DAS, had raided a house near the city last night. He wanted her to know and to pass on to Raul, that along with ten million dollars in American cash and a large stash of weapons and explosives, they had come across some very interesting notes. The notes had made reference to a training camp which was located in the swamps of Florida. It was located south of highway eighty and west of some fishing camp named Max's Swamp Safari. There had also been notes referring to 'the play-offs' and a Sunday game with some team called the Cubs. They had a map of Pro Player Stadium and a letter from a woman in a city named 'Weston'. Sarah told Raul she was going to fax him everything Carlos had sent her, including an address in some country club in this city called Weston.

Raul closed his phone and addressed the group. "Weston, what can you tell me about a city named Weston?"

Rebecca replied first. "Weston is in Broward County. It's north of here, but not far.

It has probably the largest population of Colombians in any particular area."

Raul looked at George. "You are familiar with this town and how to get there, right?"

Once again, before anyone could speak, Rebecca announced, "I know Weston like the back of my hand. I have a lot of friends who live there. I'll show you any thing you want to know. And in case you are wondering, I am fluent in Spanish."

Raul looked at Rebecca and smiled. "I wasn't wondering, and I'm not about to put a civilian at risk. Just tell me where the Country Club is and that will be enough."

Rebecca looked back at Raul and smiled. "That won't be enough, because most of Weston is made up of gated communities and without a reason or person to see inside, the guards won't let you in. And, before you say it, even if you push your way past the guard, whoever you are going after would know something is up when all the Deputies, who the guard calls, show up."

George looked at Raul for a moment then asked, "What could it hurt if she rides with us? She points out the house; we get a team and go in. Even if Zalazar is there she won't be in harm's way."

Johnny's mouth fell open and Rebecca looked like she had just swallowed a frog.

"You are not talking about Carlos Zalazar, are you?" Johnny asked.

Raul looked at them and responded. "No, we are talking about a man named Don Carlos Zalazar, and the name is not uncommon. So don't get excited."

Rebecca turned to Raul and George, and asked if they had a picture of the man they wanted. George obliged and showed them of a picture of Don Carlos Zalazar.

"Oh my God, that's Stacey's husband!" Rebecca gasped. "They come here all the time and gamble. He plays poker and she plays the machines. They are big spenders and they live in Weston in the Country Club. I have been there two or three times. She is a sweetheart and I can't believe she broke the law!"

Johnny was staring at the picture in disbelief. "He has dropped two hundred thousand easy, in this casino, just this year. They have been coming here at least, what, three years maybe four? She is as sweet as they come. Never gets mad or nasty, even if she loses. She never even asks for comps and is a big tipper. Everybody loves Stacey. Carlos is OK. He tips, but the girls complain that he gropes them a lot, and then tips them big to shut them up. He's not much different than twenty percent of the high rollers here. There was a time, I remember, about two years ago he got into a screaming match with another player about Stacey. If I remember correctly, Stacey had walked over to the table and Carlos was losing and not happy. She put her arm around him and tried to tell him not to worry, it was just a game. He had been drinking and pushed her away and told her to shut up and go back to the 'stupid machine', as he put it.

Stacey's feelings were hurt; she is sensitive and showed it. I remember he said the strangest thing to her. He told her to shut up again or he would take her to Leticia. I don't know what the hell a Leticia is, but it scared the shit, pardon my French, out of poor Stacey. She did an about-face and disappeared into the casino. She didn't return to the table at all that night, but another player made some crack about Carlos being an asshole and not knowing how to treat a lady. Carlos lost it, and started screaming in Spanish to the player who was as Anglo as they come. He just looked at him and told Carlos he was in America, try to learn the language. Carlos got up and left the table. I guessed he had found Stacy and went home. At least that is what I thought. It seems that he waited outside for the other player to leave, and got into a fight with him. He hurt the other player really bad. I mean to the tune of forty-two stitches in the face and I don't know how many in his shoulder and neck. I guess Randy, that's who the other player was, Randy Baker, had really provoked Carlos, and he cut him with something. Randy was rushed to Jackson Memorial Hospital and was in intensive care for a couple of days."

George looked at Johnny and said, "I remember that incident, at least I remember hearing about it. I know Randy Baker. He owns a roofing company and has been here all his life. He is definitely a 'Red Neck' local."

Johnny laughed. "Not anymore... he doesn't work at all and he drives an E class Mercedes."

"Why is that?" Raul asked. "Did he hit the lottery or something?"

"Just about. The cops came to the hospital to interview him. We have to report everything that happens here. Gaming laws, you know. Anyway, Randy pressed charges against Carlos for cutting him and Carlos was arrested by Miami-Dade. Randy told the strangest story about the fight. He said Carlos approached him and he had something in his right hand like an animal claw. Randy said he punched Carlos in the face once or twice but he was like a crazy man. He just kept coming at him. Randy told the police that Carlos swung this claw at him and hit him first in the shoulder. He said the claw was attached to his hand and was so sharp it cut right through his jacket and shirt like butter. He told the cops the pain shot right down his arm and almost paralyzed it. The second swipe from the claw cut his face. The scar starts at the top of his left eye and goes right down the side of his cheek and stops by his mouth. It is a nasty cut and it didn't heal very pretty. Randy said Carlos was going to kill him; he knew because he was getting ready to cut him again. Randy told the police that Carlos told him he was going to slash his throat so he could never speak again. He said Carlos raised his arm to swing when a group of six women walked by and saw what was going on. They screamed and Carlos ran off. That saved his life, according to Randy."

"What do you think?" Raul asked.

"Randy had been drinking; in fact I tried to comp him a room because I thought he had drunk too much. But he wouldn't take it. He said he was going to call his brother to come and get him. As a matter of fact, I remember him throwing me his car keys and telling us he was going into the parking lot to wait."

"So how did Randy get rich? You haven't told us." George asked, rolling his eyes.

"Oh, right. Well, it seems when the cops arrested Carlos and charged him with attempted murder, which was a second degree felony, Randy's wounds were definitely considered life-threatening. The cops never found the so-called claw, but it didn't matter, anyway. It seems Randy changed his mind and told the police he wouldn't testify or cooperate. The cops knew Carlos had gotten to Randy, but there wasn't much they could do about it so the State Attorney dropped the charge, and Carlos walked. About two months after that, Randy shows up at the casino and, as usual he gets drunk. This time he throws me his keys and they aren't for a Ford pickup, but rather a Mercedes E class. He tells me that his brother is coming to get him, but he is going to wait in the VIP lounge if that was alright with me. And I told him it was. He laughed as we went in and told me he had to protect his two million dollar scar. He has never said a word about it since. But I think Carlos paid him two million dollars to not press charges against him. Is that incredible or what?"

Raul smiled and agreed. He then made the observation that Stacey was not a Hispanic name, and he wondered if maybe Don Carlos' wife was Anglo. Rebecca smiled and told her that Stacey was as gringo as they get.

But she had lived in some small town in Southern Colombia for a while and that was how she learned Spanish. Rebecca told them that Stacey was really Stacey Princeton, like the college, she had told them. She also remembered that every time she had gone to Stacey's home she had to use Stacey's maiden name, because that was how the house was registered.

They also discovered that Don Carlos was here in South Florida for only about four months out of the year. He was supposedly an importer for South American goods and had offices in Colombia, where he spent a great deal of time. Stacey was at the home in Weston much of the time alone.

Raul was smiling. "South American goods", he thought. "All the cocaine and illegal arms he could smuggle in." He looked at Rebecca and asked hesitantly, "Do you know for sure that this Stacey is married to Carlos, or just living with him?"

"Well, she wears a ring, but now that you ask, she made a comment once when we were together that I thought was really strange. She was depressed one day and called me and asked me to go shopping at Sawgrass Mills with her. We went, and as you know it's a big place, so we walked a lot and talked a lot."

Raul leaned over to George and whispered, "I'm assuming Sawgrass Mills is a really big department store mall."

"Very big mall", he answered. "Many, many blocks of stores and shopping."

Rebecca continued. "Anyway, we were walking along, talking, and she said the funniest thing. Not funny ha-ha, but the other funny. She had this starry look and said she loved the malls in Vermont and used to go shopping all the time before she was kidnapped. Well I just looked at her, and she got this, 'I just let the cat out of the bag' look of terror on her face, and then she smiled and started laughing. She told me she meant that she was shopping in Bogota when Carlos swept her off her feet, and took her away with him. She said that was how they met, and that they were married in Colombia and she lived there with him until they decided to buy the house.

"Rebecca", Raul said, "Do you think she is happy with Don Carlos? You know, like the happily married couple. Don't just answer; think about it for a minute."

"I don't have to think about it. I think he gives her everything she wants, including a big house in a classy city. He isn't here very often; three or four months out of the year. What's not to be happy about? She jumps in the sack, makes him happy, and gets everything she wants. She sounds like a lot of wives I know. And a lot I know with much less."

George interjected. "Rebecca, we are trying to find out if she would be any help to us. We are trying to take Don Carlos back to Colombia for trial, and without killing him first. So, if she would help, maybe we could do this in a much more humane manner."

"I honestly don't know if she would help or not. I know she is scared to death of his temper and I don't think she will cross him. He is very intimidating, you know."

"Intimidating, in what way?" George asked.

"For Christ's sake, George, he's Latin, what do you mean 'in what way'?"

"I don't know, Rebecca; will you talk to her and see if we can set it up?" George asked.

While this conversation was going on, Raul was on his phone talking to Ricky and Jonas. He had set up a conference call with the three of them, and he was informing them of what was going on. He had told them about the phone call from Sarah, and the information he had obtained. Ricky and Jonas had both come up empty at their locations, but everyone was on their toes and ready for anything. They decided to re-group at the hotel in two hours and put together a plan of attack.

Raul closed his phone and turned to George and the rest of the group. "George, can I talk to you for a moment, outside?" They stepped outside the office, and Raul asked George what he thought the chances were that Rebecca would actually get this Stacey to cooperate with them. George felt confident that, given a little time, they could persuade her.

George asked Raul if he thought the Leticia that Johnny had mentioned earlier was the same Leticia that he had been briefed about earlier. Raul looked at him with a mixture of sadness and concern on his face. "It's the only Leticia I'm aware of in Colombia, and before you ask, yes, I do believe this Stacey was kidnapped by Zalazar and his shitbag friends. I also believe she was held captive in the compound we raided, and for some reason Zalazar took a special liking to her and decided to bring her here. Obviously he trusts her, to a degree. I think he wanted to set up a domicile here without drawing attention to himself, and she was a perfect cover. Don't think he wouldn't kill and replace her in a second if he gets wind of what we are doing. I'm telling you this so you know if you get your sister-in-law to persuade her friend to help us, you need to protect this woman and watch her closely. They don't come any more ruthless and dangerous than Don Carlos Zalazar. So….what do you think? Want to try, or should we leave well enough alone?"

George thought for a moment and then replied. "I'll talk to her and see what she thinks about helping us. I'll let you know soon."

"Ok, let's do this. I'll go back to the hotel and meet with Jonas and Ricky, and you stay here with those two. Talk to her and see what you can do. If she wants to help, go with her to this Weston and talk to that Stacey woman and see what you can find out. Anything will help. Remember, if she decides to help, get her out of the house and to a safe house right away. Got it?"

"Absolutely, and if she won't help, you just want me to catch a ride back to the hotel and meet you there?"

"George, you have a cell phone right?"

"Yes sir, I do." George responded.

"Good, call me when you know something", Raul said as he walked away. He raised his right hand and waved over his shoulder as he was walking to the stairs.

Forty-five minutes later Raul was in the parking lot of the hotel. He saw the Jeep Ricky was using and parked in the empty space next to it. He told King to de-activate and lie in the back seat of the Hummer, and to only activate if someone touched the car. King obeyed, and Raul looked at the animal robot and thought it was a little weird how dead the dog looked.

As Raul was walking into the hotel, Jonas pulled up to the front with the two agents who had been working with him. They left the truck in front of the hotel and walked in with Raul. There were about ten agents from different branches of government service in the room when Raul entered. Ricky walked over to him and immediately asked about the new information Sarah had sent.

He was holding some papers in his hand and asked Raul if he was aware of a woman living with Zalazar in the area. He told Raul that the woman's name was Stacey Cunningham, and that she had been reported abducted four years ago from in front of the Republic Bank in Bogota.

As Raul was opening his cellular phone to call George, it rang. "Hello, yes George. She will help? Listen, George, what we were talking about in Leticia… Right, that is correct. Well, Ricky has information proving our suspicions. I don't want you to go to the house alone with Rebecca. If this Stacey has been brain-washed, you could be in serious danger. Ricky is coming out to the casino and I want you to wait for him. He is going with you to the house. Good, I'll tell him." And Raul closed his phone.

Raul then told Ricky to take a couple of local agents, who knew where the casino was, and go there. Raul had decided that the best course of action was to first try to talk this woman into helping them, but if Ricky thought for a moment she would be a risk for any reason, Raul wanted the woman taken into protective custody. They were unsure if Don Carlos was at the home right at this time, but information Sarah had provided indicated he was probably at a camp in the Everglades.

Ricky left for the casino with the two Cuban agents, Jorge and Renaldo. Jonas and Raul were studying maps of the Everglades, trying to figure where, in this very large swamp, the camp might be. They needed to see it and find out what they were up against.

Raul thought for a moment, and then looked at Jonas. "We need to find a guide we can trust. One with an airboat. I think if Zalazar wanted to hide this camp, it's probably accessible by airboat only."

Jonas, studying the map, added, "That would make sense; that's what he did in the Amazonas. But who can we get here? We could lose two or three days out in that swamp trying to find this camp."

"Give me a minute", Raul asked. Opening his cell phone he dialed. "George, Ricky is on his way with two more agents for back up. Listen, I have a request I think you can help me with. Do you have anybody you really trust, who has an airboat and knows the Everglades like the back of his hand?"

George was looking at Rebecca while he was talking to Raul, and thought a minute. "Hold on just for a second; let me check something." George lowered the phone and spoke to Rebecca. "Does Johnny Deerchaser still have his airboat?"

Rebecca looked at him with a puzzled look. "Of course he does, but he can't use it; he's in the Dade County jail, for some bullshit assault charge."

George raised the phone and said, "Raul I have a friend, well, he's more like a friend of my wife's family, but anyhow, give me a minute and I'll get back to you with a guide and airboat."

Raul went back to his discussions with Jonas and the other agents and waited. About fifteen minutes passed and Raul's cell phone rang. George was on the other end.

"Raul, I've got a boat and driver for you. He is a tribe member and knows the swamp better than anyone I know. His name is Johnny Deerchaser, and he told me that he will help you any way he can. There are two things that need to be done before he can help you."

"And they would be what?" Raul asked.

"First I have to get him released from the Dade County jail. He is serving six months for assault. Not a problem, I have a judge friend who can make that happen. I'll get him released in your custody. Secondly, please don't let him drink. Sober, he is the nicest guy you would ever want to meet. Drunk, he's a problem. He really doesn't like the white man, and when he drinks he shows it. That is why he is in jail right now. Anyway, I told him you're a Navajo Indian, and he said anything for a brother. I hope you don't mind."

"George, do you have any idea why it takes the white man so long to get anything accomplished?" Raul asked.

"Well no, not really. If I had to guess, it would probably be red tape."

"They walk through way too much bull shit to get to the dance. How long before I get the airboat and guide?"

"A deputy should be bringing Johnny to the hotel within the hour", George responded. "Raul, if you don't mind my asking, what dance are you talking about?"

Raul didn't respond; he simply closed his phone and resumed his discussions with Jonas and the other agents.

Ricky arrived at the casino with the two Cuban agents in about thirty minutes. Jorge and Renaldo waited in the Jeep while Ricky met with George and Rebecca. He told them that he had two other agents with him as back-up, and that they would follow the two of them to Weston and Stacey's house. After Ricky filled George in as to Stacey's real name and what had transpired in Bogota four years earlier, he asked the most obvious. Did they know if Stacey was, in fact, at home, and was Zalazar with her? George advised Ricky that Rebecca had called the house about thirty minutes ago and Stacey had answered. She had asked Stacey if she wanted to go out for lunch and Stacey had agreed and said she would be waiting for her at the house. Don Carlos had left earlier in the morning, she told them. She had no idea where he had gone or when he would be back. Rebecca had asked Stacey if she could bring her brother-in-law who was visiting from California with them. He was visiting for the week and she didn't want to leave him alone. Stacey had told her that she didn't mind and that maybe they, Rebecca and Stacey, could show him the sights, starting with the Sawgrass Mall.

Ricky and George decided that the best course of action was to give Rebecca enough time to talk to Stacey before she was surrounded with agents and totally scared to death. Ricky and the two other agents would stay back and just follow the three of them until the woman was more comfortable with what was going on. They arrived at the Weston Hills

Country Club about noon. Jorge, Renaldo and Ricky waited in the Jeep outside the main entrance while George and Rebecca entered. The plan was for George to call Ricky and act like he was talking to a friend from California. This would be the signal that they had the woman with them and were leaving the Country Club area.

George and Rebecca pulled into the drive of the Zalazar house and got out of the car. As they walked up to the house they could hear a dog barking inside the house. It was a little dog, but nevertheless it was determined to bark, and bark it did. Rebecca rang the door bell and they waited. The dog continued barking and no one answered the door. Rebecca opened her cell phone and called Stacey. "No answer", she told George. "Something is wrong, I feel it. This is not right."

George decided that they would check the perimeter of the house, and see what they could inside the house; but other than that there wasn't a whole lot more they could do.

Rebecca had already told George that it was not like Stacey to stand her up and there had to be a good reason for her not being there. George looked through the window on the side of the garage. There was a new Volvo parked inside. It was a two-car garage and the other space was empty. "That's her car," Rebecca said. "Maybe she is in the shower or something and can't hear us or the phone?"

George just looked at her; he was beginning to worry because things definitely didn't feel right. He wanted to check a little further before he started making calls and possibly sounding really stupid. Rebecca was standing in the driveway by George's Ford Taurus, and George was standing by the side of the garage when the deputies showed up. Three cars came skidding into the drive, and four deputies jumped from the cars with their guns drawn. One of them had sergeant stripes and he was yelling at the top of his lungs at Rebecca.

"Get on the fucking ground and show me your hands! Do it now!"

Rebecca was in shock; she was frozen in an upright position and couldn't move.

"Do what I say or I'll shoot!" the sergeant demanded.

Rebecca was so scared, she started crying; still frozen, standing next to the car. George heard the commotion and started around the side of the garage. He could hear Rebecca crying and the police, all four of them, now yelling at her. As George came around the side of the house he had his badge case out and was holding it over his head with his right hand. "Federal agent!" he yelled as he rounded the corner of the garage.

The first shot went over his head and struck the fence behind him. The second shot struck the corner of the house. George was on the ground by the time the third shot struck the garage door. The Sergeant was yelling at the other Deputies to stop shooting and holster their weapons. Rebecca was still standing by the car, frozen in position, sobbing hysterically. George got to his feet and ran to Rebecca to comfort her. The Sgt. approached George and asked to see his I.D.

"We got a call that there was a murder in progress, that's why we acted like we did.

We thought you might be the killers, or something."

"Get a supervisor and a Crime Scene Unit on the way here....now!"

"You mean for the shots fired, or what?" the Sgt. asked.

"No, not for the impetuous actions of your subordinates; we will deal with that later. I want a crime scene unit for what I think we are going to find in the house, and if there is nothing there, they can always take pictures of where the shots that one of you idiots fired at me struck the wall."

The Sgt. and two of the Deputies all turned and looked at one young man who had been riding with one of the other two Deputies. The Deputy was looking at the ground, not making eye contact with anyone. The Sgt. cleared his throat and very patiently explained, "That is Deputy Cratz. He is a probationary employee of the Sheriff's office. He has been out of the Academy about three weeks and is riding with his Field Training Officer, Deputy Cooper. Deputy Cratz was responsible for firing all three shots at you, and he will have to go to the shooting review board; but that is for internal affairs to work out, not me."

George was on his cell phone while the Sgt. was trying to justify their very aggressive behavior, and he wasn't really paying a whole lot of attention to him. "Ricky, we have a bit of a problem here and it would be best, I think, if you came to the house. The address is 1521 Ja..... ." George stopped mid-sentence as he looked up and saw Ricky, Renaldo and Jorge walking up the driveway.

"We saw the cops come through the gate like bats out of hell and we figured something was wrong, so we followed. We had a bit of a problem at the front gate. The security officer with the General's stars on his uniform thought my I.D. was phony and refused to open the gate. Renaldo had to go into the shack and open the gate for us and disarm the General at the gate. He was calling the cops as we left him." Ricky turned to the Sgt. and handed him a Smith and Wesson .38 revolver. "Here, you can give this back to the General at the front gate later."

The Crime Scene unit, along with an unmarked cop car with two detectives, arrived as George, Ricky and Jorge were headed for the front door. Renaldo stayed behind in George's car with Rebecca, who was still overwhelmed with the day's activities.

"Hello, you must be the Federal agents. I'm Detective Lt. Jim Procter and this is Det. Larry Arntz. And you are....?" he asked.

"Yes, my name is Agent George Backner from the Miami office of the CIA." Ricky and Jorge continued walking toward the house with out saying anything.

"We were notified of a possible signal 7 at this address. Probably a signal 5. Also, while we were enroute, neighbors called saying that our Deputies had cornered suspects and were shooting at them."

Ricky and Jorge were just looking at the detectives. Finally Ricky spoke. "If your signals mean somebody may be dead in there, don't you think maybe we should get the door open and go look? We are starting to draw a crowd of onlookers in the street."

"In due time. And who are you?" the detective asked.

Ricky ignored him, trying the front door and it was locked. The detective grabbed Ricky's arm and demanded, "Maybe you didn't hear me. I said, and you are....?"

"Tired of fucking around with you people, that's who I am", Ricky shot back. And with that, Ricky kicked the front door open and entered the house. George and Jorge followed right behind him.

Ricky entered the bedroom and stopped in his tracks. The room was covered in blood and the decapitated body of Stacey Cunningham was laying half on the bed and half on the floor. Her head had been placed on the top of a corner post on the bed. The word 'TRAITOR' had been carved in her forehead. Her eyes were open and the face still had a look of pain and horror on it. The body was naked and had been mutilated with claw marks. Don Carlos Zalazar found out that the CIA was on his trail and didn't want to take a chance on Stacey Cunningham giving away any secrets. Stacey Cunningham had been tortured to death. And she didn't even know why. All she was doing was going shopping with a girlfriend.

Crime Scene Investigators had roped off the house to keep the curious cops out and to maintain the crime scene for processing. Ricky and George searched the rest of the house for anything they could possibly use while Jorge ran interference with the cops. Zalazar had wiped down everything and had emptied out any and all documents that might give his plan away.

The agents returned to George's car where Renaldo and Rebecca were now standing outside. Rebecca had regained her composure and was talking with another plain-clothed detective.

George looked at Renaldo, who just shrugged. "What can I tell you George; that guy is from the Sheriff's Office's Internal Affairs department. He wants statements about what happened when the Deputies showed up and he wants to know about the shooting incident. He's talking about criminal charges against the young Deputy for shooting at you. He said he will probably ask the State Attorney to file attempted murder of a Federal Agent charges against that kid."

Ricky looked at the young Deputy whose eyes were red. He looked like he had been crying, or was about to. The kid was definitely scared to death of what was going to happen to him. Ricky looked at George. "What the hell is wrong with these cops? Attempted murder? Give me a break. This is too fucked up."

George smiled a little. "You have to understand the mind-set here. These are not cops who you see; these are piranha, and the minute one of them looks vulnerable they move in for the kill. I believe they thrive on eating each other. It is really a sad situation. I'll do what I can for the kid. I know he was just scared and overreacted. First, I'll have to talk to Rebecca." George walked over to the Detective who was interviewing Rebecca.

"OK, ma'am, I'll expect you to come to the office tomorrow for a full statement. And you can rest assured this Deputy will not get away with scaring you like he did. We don't work that way."

"Thank you," Rebecca said. "This is my brother-in-law. He is a Federal Agent and that stupid cop shot at him and kept shooting at him. His name is George Brackner, and I'm sure he wants to talk to you."

"Agent Brackner, I'm Sgt. Robert Marlowe from Internal Affairs. If I could get a statement from you right now that would be great, OK?"

"Give me a minute with Rebecca, and then I'll talk to you."

"Well, it doesn't work that way. First *we* talk, and then *you* can talk to whomever you want. That's Sheriff's policy and the way we do it. So, let's get started."

George took Rebecca's arm and motioned her to follow him out of this cop's ear shot. He ignored the IA Sgt. completely as he was walking away.

The Sgt. became very excited. "Hey, get back here! We are not done talking; you can't just walk away from me! Get over here before I arrest you!" Sgt. Marlowe moved to grab George's arm, and when he did, Ricky stepped between them.

"Get your hand off Agent Brackner, and step over there and wait like he said. Let me assure you that if you make any move other than that, I will fuck you up right here in front of all your friends. You got that?!"

Sgt. Marlowe thought for a moment then looked into Ricky's eyes and felt fear. "Yes sir, I suppose I can do that; after all, inter-agency cooperation and all that."

Ricky was staring at Marlowe, making him very uneasy. "You are truly a first- class asshole."

Sgt. Marlowe did not reply, he just patiently waited for George and Rebecca to finish.

"Rebecca," George said softly, "Stacey is dead, and it looks like Carlos did it. What troubles me is that only you, I, Johnny and a couple of agents knew what we were doing and somehow Zalazar found out. What am I missing here? Are Johnny and Zalazar better friends than I thought?"

"No, not Johnny; he wouldn't do this. He doesn't particularly like Carlos, especially after what he did to Randy Baker. And besides, he used to tell me Carlos was 'Bad Medicine' because he was mean to Stacey. The only one I've ever seen talking to Carlos was Tony Jr. He would get his car for him and whatever else Carlos wanted. Carlos used to tip him pretty good, and frequently".

Ricky was on his cell phone, talking to Raul and bringing him up to date as to what had transpired. George walked over to Ricky and asked him to tell Raul that he believed that Tony Jr. was somehow mixed up with Zalazar and that they would look for him. Ricky relayed the message and talked a moment or two more, then closed his phone.

George returned to Rebecca and told her that he didn't want to press any charges against the young deputy and would like her to feel the same way. "We have much bigger fish to fry than this, and besides, that Deputy doesn't deserve what that Sgt. wants to do to him." She hugged him and told him he knew best and whatever he wanted to do was fine with her. She did, however, add that detective work was off her agenda for the future, and he needed a professional for any further adventures of this nature. She smiled and kissed him on the cheek.

George asked Jorge and Renaldo to take Rebecca back to the casino in his car. He also asked them to look for Tony Jr., and if they found him, bring him to the hotel. Ricky and George walked over to three waiting Deputies. Two other men from Internal Affairs had joined Sgt. Marlowe.

One introduced himself as a Lt. and the other as a Captain. Neither Ricky nor George heard or cared about their names. The Captain looked at Ricky and George and said, "Let me apologize for Sgt. Marlowe; he can be a bit pushy at times."

Ricky laughed and interrupted. "No, pushy is not how we would describe his behavior." He looked at George then turned back to the Captain. "Obnoxious asshole' fits his category much more closely. Don't you think, George?"

George smiled and looked at Marlowe. "To a T."

George and Ricky had the feeling the superiors knew about Marlowe's personality and this wasn't the first time someone from the outside had brought it to their attention.

The Captain turned back to Ricky and George. "So, what should we do? How do you think we should handle this? After all, the kid shot at you. How do you want us to deal with it?"

Ricky and George caught each other's eye and smiled. They finally met a local cop with common sense. Not that they weren't out there; they just hadn't met one yet. George turned to the Captain and said, "Look, this kid needs help. This was a tough situation for an experienced cop, let alone a new one. He needs to be in training, not in prison. I'm not pressing charges, and as far as Rebecca and I are concerned, the incident is over."

"Prison? Who said anything about prison?", the Captain asked with surprise.

Ricky and George both looked at Sgt. Marlowe, and pretty soon they were all looking at Marlowe. "What?" he asked. "I think the statutes are quite clear in this incident."

The Lieutenant spoke up. "Marlowe, these guys are right. You are a total first class asshole."

Ricky and George shook hands with the Captain and the Lieutenant, and walked to Ricky's Jeep.

"What now?" Ricky asked.

"Back to the hotel and see what they got going. We definitely have a dead end here."

Raul and Jonas looked up simultaneously when the Miami-Dade Detention Deputy walked into the room. Along with him was a giant sized Indian. Johnny Deerchaser was, without exaggeration, six feet six inches tall and probably went about two hundred and fifty pounds. He was, at best guess, in his early forties, but that was really tough to guess accurately because years of heavy drinking had played a toll on this man's face. He looked very weathered and just plain tired. "Strange", Raul thought. "This giant Indian has the saddest pale blue eyes I have ever seen, even in any white man; not to mention a Seminole Indian.

"I'm Deputy Cook from Miami-Dade Correctional, and the prisoner is in your custody just as soon as you sign here", the deputy said as he approached Raul.

Raul signed, but couldn't help but notice that something was wrong with Johnny Deerchaser. He acted very lethargic, as though he had been drugged. "What's wrong with him?" he asked the deputy.

"Oh, that. It's nothing. The jail doctor gave him a sedative before I transported him.

I didn't want to have to deal with this guy if he got mad about something and wanted to fight. You know he is a fighter, right?"

Johnny Deerchaser was standing quietly next to the deputy. He was dressed in jeans, a plaid shirt and had a red head band. He was also sporting wrist and leg shackles. Finally, after two or three minutes of listening to the deputy, he raised his head and spoke. "You're safe now; you can take the chains from my body. My wrath will not be inflicted upon you, even though you are the symbol of the White Eyes Oppression, not to mention the total sum of the information contained in a proctologist's report."

The deputy started laughing. Raul was smiling as well. This Giant Indian had just called the deputy an asshole and the deputy thought it was funny. Obviously the deputy's intellectual level had not surpassed three-syllable words. "Well, he does have kind of a shit job", Raul thought.

"Dealing with jail-element on a daily basis has got to suck, but someone has got to do it and this deputy would do just fine".

The deputy was taking off Johnny Deerchaser's chains and he looked up at Raul and Jonas. "Let me give you some advice. Don't listen to this guy. He is really a wacko. I personally think it's because he drinks like a fish and his brain is fried. He always says weird shit and nobody understands it."

Johnny Deerchaser stepped from the shackles and told the deputy, "So you think my sometimes well-aimed obstreperous behavior is a result of over-consumption of alcohol?"

"You see what I mean? Nobody understands what the hell he is saying. It don't make no kinda sense, if you know what I'm saying."

Raul and Jonas just looked at this deputy. Jonas turned to Raul and said, roughly translated, in Navajo, "This cop is a fucking moron. And in this country you allow this kind of person to carry a gun and enforce laws?"

Raul laughed and so did Johnny Deerchaser. Jonas looked at the giant Indian with a puzzled expression. Still in Navajo, Raul replied, "I've actually seen them worse than this stupid shit."

Both Raul and Jonas stared at Johnny Deerchaser when he said in perfect Navajo dialect, "Actually, this idiot is not all that bad. You stay here long enough and you are going to see some real morons with badges that need to be shoved up their collective asses. Florida State, class of 86. I Majored in Indian Culture and Political Science". The last part the Indian said was in English, and probably meant for the deputy to hear.

The deputy was just shaking his head, looking at the three of them. "Don't you guys realize you are in America? You should save that Mexican shit for some other country. When in America, speak American. Look how well it has done for me."

Jonas looked at him and commented, "Yeah, just look." Then he stuck out his hand for the deputy to shake. "Thanks for bringing this guy here to us; we really appreciate it, and don't worry, we'll make him behave and act

Ghost Warrior

like an American. Oh, that's right, he is an American Indian. Well, anyway, we will make him behave. Thanks again."

The deputy was smiling and told Jonas if there were any problems, just call the station and they would send someone right out to fix them. He turned to Johnny Deerchaser, held up his right hand like a pistol, pointed it at him and lowered his thumb. "I know I'll be seeing you again, in jail." The deputy then turned and walked out of the room.

"He's stupid but he is harmless," the Giant Indian said. "How can I be of service to my fellow brother Indians? Well, at least one Indian and one, let me see, you look either German or Swedish - I'm not quite placing you. However, you two are obviously related, just looking at you. What are you? A father and son team, or what?"

"I'm from the Swiss Intelligence Network, and what we need is an airboat and a guide. You ready to go to work?" Jonas asked.

"Life is way too short to be so sensitive about genetics, but I must say your knowledge of the Navajo language is very good. It's a tough language to master. Not as tough as Comanche, or some of the other plains Indians, but nonetheless difficult. To answer your question, I have a beautiful airboat docked at the reservation out by the fifty-two mile marker on Alligator Alley. If one of you two would be so kind as to drive us there, I will be more than happy to guide."

Raul, who had just been watching the rapport between Jonas and Johnny Deerchaser, just smiled and told them he was parked downstairs in the lot and he would be more than happy to drive. As they were walking towards the Hummer, Ricky's red Jeep pulled into the lot. George jumped from the Jeep and ran to Raul. "The Medical Examiner's Office in Broward County just called me and told me that the body at Stacey Cunningham's house was not Stacey Cunningham. It turns out, after they ran dentals and prints, that it was a woman named Gloria Palowitz."

"Well, let me ask the obvious. Didn't Rebecca make an identification at the scene?" Raul asked.

Ricky was now standing next to George and replied. "We never took her inside; the shock of the decapitated body would have been too much for her. Besides she was still in a bit of shock from the way the first deputies arrived on the scene."

"What happened when the deputies arrived, or should I not ask?"

Ricky and George looked at each other and George responded. "Probably better left unasked at this time."

"Anyway, Rebecca called us on the way over here and told us that Stacey is hiding in her office at the casino", Ricky said. "We were going to head over there and find out what, if anything, she could help us with, if you don't have anything for us right now."

Raul looked at both of them. "No, that's a good idea. Do you know if the two Cubans found that Tony Jr. fellow yet? We need to get him, before he gets to Zalazar or has an opportunity to kill the right woman. It's pretty obvious that Zalazar didn't kill this woman at the house. He probably gave the order, told them what to do, and sent some asshole to do it. The person who did the killing didn't know Stacey Cunningham; I'm sure of that. Now the question is, where is Zalazar and what is he up to?"

Jorge coincidentally called Ricky while Raul was talking. Ricky was listening and nodding his head in approval. "Great! Have Renaldo stay with Rebecca and make sure she is ok. In fact, better yet, have Renaldo bring Rebecca to the hotel and have him wait with her in the meeting room. I know she will be safe there. I want you to meet us at the Dade County Jail. We are on our way right now."

"What's up?" Raul asked.

"It seems a Miami-Dade Police motorman clocked Tony Jr. and some other idiot at about ninety five miles an hour on Krome Avenue. They were headed back to the casino. The problem was, both of them were covered with blood and had a glove with claws attached to it in the car with them. The fellow with this Tony Jr. is a Colombian and either won't, or can't speak English. The motorman got back-up and took both of them into custody on suspicion of murder. They are waiting for us at the Miami-Dade County Jail, before any Metro Detectives talk to them."

"Great, find out what you can and get back to us. We are on our way out to the Everglades to look for a training camp. I think Zalazar may well be out there right now, and with a little bit of luck we will run into him."

"I see you've met Johnny," George said. "If anyone can help you out in the swamps, it will be him. Good luck on your hunting trip."

"Thanks, White Eyes," Johnny Deerchaser replied. "It is always nice to hear a vote of confidence now and then."

George and Ricky left the lot and the three 'hunters' continued to the car. They were about three feet from the car when Raul touched his watch and King stood up, taking up a great deal of the back seat. The giant Indian never jumped or appeared startled at all. This was a man at peace with himself, Raul thought; it didn't matter what the rest of the world thought of him.

The giant Indian smiled and looked at King. "That is quite an elegant dog you have there; I commend you on your taste in animals."

As the three of them were opening the doors to the Hummer, Johnny Deerchaser looked into King's eyes. King was panting and doing all of his dog tricks, as Ed called them. After a couple of minutes, the Indian just grunted and smiled. "It's very sad that an operation as large as the CIA couldn't provide you with a dog that has a soul. The next time you build a robot dog you may want to consider personality in the eyes. Anyone can tell this dog is artificial."

"Actually, sir," Raul responded, "You are the first to detect that, and I commend you on your instincts. King, say hello to Mr. Deerchaser."

"Hello, Mr. Deerchaser. Care to enter the vehicle?" King replied.

"Don't mind if I do, and you can call me Johnny. Nice to meet you."

"As it is you, Johnny," King replied.

Raul turned on the ignition and a screen that was built into the dash lit up. Sarah was on the screen and advised them that a team from Homeland Security had just arrested two Colombians at the Tri Rail station in Ft. Lauderdale. It had appeared that they were looking suspicious and drew attention to themselves. Actually, she said, more nervous than suspicious. When they were approached, one of them tried to run but the other stayed put and started thanking them for catching them. He also started begging them profusely for help. The one who had tried to run had a detonator in his pocket and both of them had plastic explosives all over their bodies. When Raul asked her to explain the 'all over the body' part, she went on to tell him that the two men were wearing latex underwear that was covered in explosives. It seemed that the men had long underwear-type suits on under their clothing and the plan was for one of them to sit in the front of the train by the engine and the other to sit midway in one of the cars. The one with the detonator would then detonate both of them as they pulled into the Boca Raton station.

"And before you ask, yes, they both work directly for Zalazar. It appears that Zalazar put two hundred thousand dollars in bank accounts for each of the two men's families, and blowing themselves up, as well as whoever else was near them, was how they would earn their money."

"Great. The smarter these terrorist shitbags get, the more clothes we have to take off at the airport check points. Ask Ed if he can invent an exploding underwear detector, and we will patent it and all go on a cruise. Anything else before we head out to the Everglades to look for this crazy son-of-a-bitch and maybe get lucky and explode *him*?"

"As a matter of fact, Epi is here with me and wanted to tell you something."

"Hey, Ghost Warrior, how you doing? I spoke with Angelita yesterday and she wanted me to tell you that she still has the stomach condition, and she is going to stay with her cousin, Maria, a week or two more. She told me to tell you not to worry. She is perfectly fine and will be back home by the time you return. Maria sends her love and is happy for you. I have no idea what that means, but that is what she said. On another note, Ricky called me and told me about the murder of Zalazar's wife. Anything new on that in the past few hours?"

"Actually, there is. It wasn't Zalazar's wife. We don't know yet why this other woman was there, but Zalazar's wife, if that is what she really is, is in protective custody and the cops caught the guys who killed the other woman. Ricky is on his way to the correctional facility along with George right now. Listen, do me a favor and keep an eye on Angelita, and if the stomach flu or whatever she has gets worse, get on a transport and take her to Bethesda Hospital. Also, next time you talk to her, tell her I found a shopping mall for her here in Florida that would be just her style and I will bring her back here later on."

"I will. Keep me posted on your progress, and it goes without saying I will look out for Angelita. Talk to you later."

The screen went blank and Ed's voice came on. "That's all of your messages, Raul, nothing else to report."

Johnny Deerchaser was sitting in the back seat with King, taking this all in. "Your car talks too? What a noisy world you live in. I have also heard of the Navajo Ghost Warrior. I have some Colombian friends and they have spoken about this Ghost Warrior. Are you truly him, or is it just a legend, like so much of the Indian unknown?"

Raul didn't respond to the question and just continued driving west on Alligator Alley. Just before the fifty-two mile marker there was a dirt road which led off the alley to the north. They followed it and came to an Indian camp that consisted of three log buildings, probably houses, and a little restaurant-bar and a dock with about seven airboats tied to it. There were also four different large cages sitting on tables in front of the bait store, located next to the dock. One cage held a very large boa constrictor, another held a four to five-foot long Iguana, and a third cage housed a three-foot alligator. The fourth cage was full of rabbits and chickens, that all appeared scared death. Most likely they were lunch and dinner for the other captives. The snake curled up as they walked by and the alligator snapped at the side of the cage. The Iguana was staring at the three of them, hissing and shaking. These were not happy pets, by any means. Johnny Deerchaser walked to the cage containing the very unhappy iguana, placed his hand on the top of the cage and spoke very softly to the animal. Immediately the reptile stopped hissing and lay down, closing its eyes. He then looked at the alligator, who stopped snapping, and also laid down. After that, the snake wasn't even an issue. "They just missed me and were a bit unhappy about life in general. Cages do that", the giant Indian said as they continued walking to his airboat.

Raul knew this was no drunken Indian, as the cops would like you to believe, but more than that he was becoming more and more impressed with this man and this man's insight. No, this was no ordinary man; there was something special about him. As Grandpa would have put it, "This is a man of strong medicine with the strength of a warrior chief". The three of them climbed into Johnny Deerchaser's airboat and off they went into the Everglades.

Ricky and George pulled up in front of the Miami-Dade Jail, parked and went inside. After meeting with a couple of detectives they were taken to the interview rooms. Tony Jr. sat alone at a table in room number one; he was just staring at the two-way glass, almost like he knew he was being watched. The other man was sitting in room number two. He also was sitting at a table facing the two-way glass. Contrary to Tony Jr., this man was quite actively picking his nose and wiping it on the table, the chair or anything that was handy, including his own shirt. George and Ricky looked at the two suspects and decided to take the Colombian man first. As they walked in, Ricky threw a stack of napkins at the man and said to him in English, "Blow your nose, you piece of shit."

The Colombian responded in Spanish, telling Ricky to go fuck himself. It was about two seconds later that the man realized he had indirectly told them he spoke English, or at least understood it. Ricky looked at the man and shook his head. "You two clowns are so fucking stupid; you killed the wrong woman. You killed a neighbor, or housekeeper, or someone like that. I am personally going to put the word out to Don Carlos Zalazar that you fucked up. Then I'm going to see to it that you are put in with the general population down at the Krome detention center.

Oh, and did I mention that I am also going to let it out that you gave up Zalazar as the man who ordered the hit? Let's see, what do you think, George, maybe he will last a day before they get to him, as well as his family, back home?"

"Knowing Zalazar as I do, I believe he will have every living relative of this asshole killed before he does him in. You know, kind of, 'look what I can do and you get to see it!' ".

The Colombian man was very quietly shaking his head, slowly, left to right and back.

His head was bent over and he was looking at the table. "American police do not use such tactics; I know you cannot do these things you are saying. It is against the American law."

Ricky looked at the man and laughed. "I see you can now speak English. What a surprise. I have another surprise for you, you arrogant cocksucker. I am not an American cop. I am with the Federal Government, assigned to Colombia. The Department of Administrative Services is my right hand in Colombia. DAS.... does that ring a bell, you woman-killing-sack-of-shit? In fact, I don't even want to talk to you any more. I am going to have you extradited back to Colombia where they don't have capital punishment. And after you get there, I am going to turn you over to DAS intelligence and tell them what you and that other sorry, son-of-a-bitch did to that woman this morning". Ricky and George started to leave the room and the Colombian man started crying.

"I'm sorry, I'm sorry; don't let them hurt my mother and my family back in Medellin.

Don Carlos brought me here to kill his wife; he said she was a traitor to the cause, and he told us exactly what to do to her, and how to do it."

George turned to the man. "Can you write in English?" he asked. The man shook his head no. "OK, in your best Spanish I want you to write out exactly what you and that other man did this morning. Did he pick you up at Miami International this morning?" The man nodded his head yes. "Write your name and age at the top of the paper and today's date. Don't leave out anything, got it?" The man nodded his head yes again. George handed him a yellow legal pad and a ball point pen.

As they left the room to talk with Tony Jr., Ricky turned to the Colombian man asked, "What is your name? Where was Zalazar this morning? And lastly, what exactly did 'shit-for-brains' next door do to that woman this morning?"

"My name is Jose Pino. Don Carlos is in the, how do you say, you know, the 'pantano'; I don't know what that is in English. Tony Jr. gave me four thousand dollars when he picked me up this morning and took me to the house. He was supposed to take me right back to the airport but he wanted to stop at his casino to pick up something. That is how we got caught, because he speeds."

"You just answered two of my questions, what about the third? What was his involvement this morning?" Ricky demanded.

"He is not a normal person; he has problems. Perhaps you should ask him?"

"Oh! Make no mistake; I'm going to ask him. But he has no integrity such as a man like yourself. So I want to catch him in his lies. Give it up. What did he do?"

"When we went into the house, I thought it was the wife so I never asked her name or anything. I hit her and she fell to the floor. Don Carlos had provided the glove with the claws, and Tony Jr. had it. He handed it to me and told me to work her over. I wanted to kill her first and not torture her, but he insisted. He ripped her clothes off of her and when she regained consciousness he told me to knock her out again. So I did. Then he.... well, he started having sex with her in her ass. She woke up and started screaming, and he grabbed the glove and started cutting her. He was really hurting her and there was blood all over him as well as her. I really felt bad for the woman, so I shot her in the head with a little .22 cal. automatic, I found in the bedroom. I had to shoot her three times before she stopped screaming. After she fell dead he told me that Don Carlos wanted to have her head cut off and 'traitor' carved in her forehead. I went to the kitchen to get a big knife, and when I came back he was doing her again. He had turned her over and was on top of her fucking her and she was dead. This bothered me too much and I went outside. He cut her head off and carved on her face with the claw. He was bragging to me what a great job he did, writing on her forehead. He also started to laugh really hard and said she turned out to be a really dead fuck. I'm not sure I understand that part, you know the 'dead fuck' thing."

"Write it up and don't leave out a single detail." George told him with a disgusted tone, as he and Ricky left the room.

Ricky and George entered the room where Tony Jr. was sitting and staring at the window. Tony Jr. turned toward them and said, "You assholes are wasting your time, I don't got a fucking thing to say, and you can't prove nothing. Give me my lawyer, and get the fuck out of my face."

Ricky looked at this little weasel. "I was really hoping you would say that; God, I was hoping that. I'm going out to call your dirt-bag lawyer. Give me his name, because I want to call him and be the first one to tell him I have a real prize at the station for him. Do you think he'll even show when I tell him his client fucks dead and dying woman, and then brags about it? Then I'm going to tell him that his client is so stupid that he killed the wrong woman this morning and I'm sure Don Carlos Zalazar is going to be thrilled with you. You killed the maid, you stupid shit, and left your DNA in her ass. How many times did you see Stacey in the casino and you are so incompetent that you couldn't even remember what she looked like? Aren't you a prize for a criminal attorney! Give me the number because I want to tell him that while his prize of a client was having sex with a dying woman he cut her head off and carved on the face. Let me just ask a horny guy like yourself, did you do her again after you cut her head off, or had you had enough by then?"

"That wasn't the wrong woman; she was a blonde with a good body just like Stacey. Besides, what would another woman be in her house for? You are lying to me; shame on you. Yeah, I might have fucked her a couple of times but I didn't cut her head off... the spic did. They all lie; you can't trust any of them. That's why they cut grass, and shit like that".

A crowd of about six Miami-Dade detectives had gathered outside the interview room and had been watching the interrogation. Ricky had slapped Tony Jr. in the back of the head with the yellow legal pad, and told him to write the incident the way he says it happened, because the Colombian was writing his version as they spoke. When Tony Jr. hesitated, he simply leaned over and whispered in his ear, and Tony Jr. began writing.

When they left the interview room, both suspects were writing their confessions and the detectives were all smiling. Ricky and George had just done their jobs for them, and a good job they had done. Ricky stopped, snapped his finger and turned back toward the room. He opened the door to the room where Tony Jr. was writing intently. He pulled out another small pad and a pen and walked over to Tony Jr. After about five minutes he left the room with his cell phone open, talking to Raul. He gave Raul the exact directions to the training camp and told him that there were booby traps around a fenced-in area, and probably about fifty to sixty men training out there at any given time. When he got off the phone, George asked him what he had said to Tony Jr. to get him to write a confession. Ricky smiled and said that he told him that he was going to give both stories to Don Carlos, and did he want Tony Jr.'s story to be 'fuck you, Don Carlos, I'm not telling you anything?' Grinning, the two of them got in Ricky's Jeep and headed for the hotel to talk with Rebecca and Stacey and to find out why she wasn't at the house this morning.

With the directions Raul had been given and passed on to Johnny Deerchaser, finding the camp was fairly easy. They stopped the airboat a distance away because they didn't want to alert anyone at the camp. This was a reconnaissance mission, and the object was to get information and find weak spots. The three of them, along with King, walked on the dirt trails and in mushy sawgrass for about twenty minutes. Finally they came to a clearing and a fenced compound. Ricky had warned them about the booby traps along the fence line and the camp had only one access road leading into it. It was a hard-packed dirt road, large enough for a pickup truck to travel on. They shot photos from the outside, but they needed a way in and eyes on the inside. Jonas was looking through his field glasses when he spotted a helicopter landing pad to the right of the compound. They decided that entrance to the camp would best be on the opposite side. The helipad side was probably patrolled, but they would feel confident that the traps would warn them about oncoming danger from the other two sides. It was time for King to go to work. Raul set King to detect explosive devices and urinate on them with his contained acid system. This would destroy the devices and not set them off alerting anyone. Jonas had brought a .220 sniper rifle with him as well as a pistol.

Raul had his Glock pistol as well as his crossbow. Raul and Jonas had decided that Jonas would cover Raul and King with the rifle, and Raul would follow behind King, using orange paint to mark a safe path for later. Johnny Deerchaser would be standing look-out on the roadway. They needed to find out what was going on inside the camp and if Zalazar was, in fact, there. And they needed to do all this without being noticed. The plan was set into motion, and Raul and King left. Jonas dug a hole and covered himself up. He had become invisible. Johnny Deerchaser had also slipped into the thicket and blended with the landscape. King stopped, lifted his leg and began to trickle acid on a Vietnam-era land mine. The mine sizzled and went dead. Raul followed, marking the trail. He was crawling in order to avoid detection, and the two hundred yards or so was going to take some time. About forty-five minutes later, Raul and King arrived at the fence. They were behind a metal Quonset hut, also Vietnam War era, undetected. Raul threw a soggy clump of dirt on the fence, and sure enough, it sizzled. The entire fence was electrified.

The problem was, if he shorted the fence, would it set off an alarm and alert everyone to his presence? Were they that clever? Electrical fencing is done in sections to maintain a constant level of power. Raul figured probably one hundred foot lengths. He crawled along the fence line looking for a terminal junction. Sure enough, there it was, and it had a red and green light blinking alternately. "Damn," he thought, "it's wired for an alarm. These Rednecks are a tad smarter that I gave them credit for", he said to himself. He had King spray the box with acid and the door fell open. It was a basic system. Two wires went one way and two the other, with a trip in the middle. Simple enough, he thought. He jumped the two terminals, keeping constant power to the alarm mechanism. He and King returned to their spot by the fence and King obligingly sprayed the fence, creating an opening for himself as well as Raul. They entered the compound. King's job was to photograph everything while Raul left some well-placed hidden explosives inside the camp. Raul observed, from a distance, the terrorist soldiers Zalazar was training in this Florida camp. "Colombian-Spanish terrorists, or South Florida Redneck terrorists, not much different from each other," he thought to himself. "They walk around with machine guns, play soldier, and are, for the most part, clueless as to what the cause is or what they are doing or why they are doing it. Some of them get talked into it by their friends, and some of them just want a little excitement in their lives. Either way, a lot of them die and never know why, or what they were fighting for. It is really sad", he thought to himself. "I see kids here that will probably end up dying for nothing more than a lunatic's cause of vengeance, because his drug and 'human slave' business had been interrupted by the CIA."

Raul placed his explosives and King took pictures. Raul was amazed how King walked all around the camp and didn't even raise one spark of interest from anyone. King had walked into every building in the camp, as well as the front gate and guard stations. Nobody seemed to be bothered by a stray German Shepherd dog running loose in the camp. Raul, after seeing that King didn't attract any attention from the soldiers, told King to leave through the front gate and return to the boat. King responded, took one last look around the camp, and walked to the front gate. One of the guards opened the chain link gate and let King out. King wagged his tail, barked and left down the road. Raul couldn't believe how strange that was and then he saw why. A German Shepherd, almost the size of King, exited one of the buildings and was followed by a tall, thin Hispanic-looking fellow, dressed in designer jeans and a two hundred dollar silk shirt. This was not one of the soldiers. It was, in fact, Don Carlos Zalazar himself. He was followed by two men; both looked like Colombians and both wearing uniforms. Raul heard a helicopter coming towards the camp. It was obviously there to pick up Don Carlos. It was a small chopper, civilian-style Bell, four-seater. It was white with green trim, much like the ones the Sheriff's Departments in the area used. Raul got the tail number and programmed it into his watch and sent it to Sarah. Don Carlos boarded the chopper with the dog and left the camp, flying east towards the city. Raul knew he must have heard about the incident at his home in Weston earlier this morning, but there was no way this man was stupid or ballsy enough to go there now. "Damn, I wish I had a tracker on that chopper", then he thought, "maybe I do." He pushed the screen button on his watch and Sarah appeared. He had his ear piece in to eliminate detection. "Sarah", he whispered, "did you get the tail number I just sent you? Good. Track it for me, if you can, and send me a print-out to the Hummer. Thanks"

Raul decided it was time to leave the compound. He was going to have to crawl, unlike King, who had been mistaken for Don Carlos' dog. Raul returned to where Jonas and Johnny Deerchaser were waiting and they all headed for the airboat. When they got to the airboat, King was standing on the bow of the boat waiting for them. Johnny Deerchaser's airboat pulled into the fishing camp. Parked next to Raul's Hummer was a Florida Fish and Game Commission vehicle. As they exited the airboat, a uniformed police officer approached them. He was dressed in a gray uniform, had on black cowboy boots and a baseball hat. The cop was every bit of six feet tall and weighed, Raul thought, about two hundred and thirty pounds. He looked maybe forty years old, but the tattoos on his arms made him closer to fifty. His arms were covered with tattoos that indicated he was a Vietnam veteran. He had been a marine; this indicated by 'sempre fi', and the classic tattoo of all, 'Kill 'em all and let God sort them out'. Raul and Jonas looked at each other laughing. Jonas then said, "Now here is a classic Florida Cracker if I have ever seen one."

Johnny Deerchaser interrupted them with, "No, this is a classic Florida asshole. I know him and he's here to give us shit. I guarantee it."

"How you boys doin'? I'm Corporal Billy Gator. You know, like the reptile. What you boys doin' in my swamp today?"

Johnny Deerchaser spoke. "Well, Officer, we were just out for a little airboat tour. No hunting or anything like that. We were just touring the swamp."

"First of all, it's Corporal, not officer; and if I wanted shit from a drunken Indian, I would squeeze his head. So, you shut up unless I talk to you. Got it?"

Raul stared at the obnoxious jerk and smiled. "Well, Corporal, it is like our guide said, we are touring the swamp, nothing more."

"What's your names, both of you? I want to see identification - right now. And what are you?" he asked, looking strangely at Raul. "Are you an Injun, Spic or A-rab? I really can't tell."

Raul was getting pissed and Jonas could see it. Putting this Wildlife Officer in the hospital right now wouldn't be good timing. "He's an American Indian; a Navajo, to be exact", Jonas said, before Raul could tell this guy to go fuck himself. "Is there some kind of problem here?" Jonas inquired.

"Fuckin' right there is! These Injuns are all poachers, and it's my job to arrest them."

"Well we 'Injuns', as you put it, are not poaching, and I, in particular, find your behavior rude and obnoxious." Raul was staring right into this guy's eyes.

Billy Gator put his hands on his hips and shouted at Raul. "I don't give a fat flying fuck what you think. I'll act however I want to. This is my swamp and you are trespassing. So, I think I'll search your boat and then arrest all of you, just because I fuckin' feel like it. So, Injun, what do you think of that shit, you red-skinned motherfucker?"

Raul was surprisingly very calm, and that, to say the least, had Jonas' attention. Neither one of them wanted to identify themselves or give their positions away. "So, what are they going to do next?" Jonas wondered. "Well, this is Raul's country and his call," Jonas thought.

Raul was still staring at the officer, and without looking away, Billy Gator said, "If you are thinking of putting that dog on me, I'll shoot him in a heartbeat, so don't try it."

"No, actually, I was thinking of something different." Raul said very calmly.

"And that would be..?" Gator asked.

" I was thinking that you need to go to your car and radio for backup, and maybe get a shotgun or something to help equalize your position", Raul said, again very calmly.

Billy Gator was looking into Raul's eyes and something scared him. He saw a killer in those eyes, and that, for the first time in a long time, truly scared him. He started backing up slowly towards his car as he was keying his mike and calling for backup. He went to his trunk and was fumbling with the key to open it. Probably to get a shot gun, Raul and the others figured.

Raul pushed the button on his watch and told King to go to the officer and tell him that he was an asshole and to drop the gun. King immediately stood up and walked slowly towards the officer. Billy Gator saw him advancing, dropped his keys and started to take out his pistol. He was very nervous and having trouble getting the large, probably .44 cal. revolver, out of its holster. "Stop him or I'll kill him, I swear it!" Billy Gator yelled.

Raul was smiling, and King looked at Billy Gator and calmly said, "Drop the gun, asshole."

Billy Gator looked like he was in shock. He took his hand off his pistol and was pointing at the dog. "That....that dog... he...he just talked. That's....that's not possible! He just called me an asshole... I heard him!" Raul then commanded King to fart and knock out the cop. King farted, and Billy Gator was staring at him in disbelief as he fell to his knees.

King looked right at the officer, who was now face to face with him, and said, "say goodnight, asshole." Billy Gator hit the sand like a sack of shit and lay still, sleeping like a baby.

Johnny Deerchaser was laughing, almost uncontrollably. "I have wanted to see that jerk get his for I don't know how many years. Do you know how many times he has arrested me for fighting, and thrown whisky and beer on me then taken me to jail? Well, I'll tell you, I haven't had a drink in almost ten years and I can't remember the last physical altercation I was involved in. But every time that bully sees me, he arrests me, just because he can."

Jonas looked puzzled. "Why do you put up with that kind of treatment, if I might ask?

This is the twenty first century; you don't have to stand for that kind of harassment."

"Maybe in Switzerland", Johnny Deerchaser said, with sadness in his voice. But still today, in this great and large country of ours, there are places where the White Man shits and uses the nearest minority to wipe his ass, and that is just the way it is."

Jonas was just shaking his head in disbelief. Raul smiled a little and thought to himself, "Great analogy he had made about the minorities. As sad as it was, Raul knew Johnny Deerchaser was dead right. "Let's get out of here before some more cops come and find this shitbag sleeping next to his car."

Johnny Deerchaser put up his right hand and asked, "Might I ask a favor of the two of you, in the interest of retribution?"

"As long as you are not going to kill him, I don't care what you do." Raul said, as he and Jonas were loading the equipment back into the Hummer.

"Oh, heavens no; I would never do that. I am a peaceful man. But don't you think a 'little of what's good for the goose is good for the gander' is in order?"

Raul and Jonas were smiling as the giant Indian splashed whiskey all over the Corporal. He splashed it on his face and mouth, and the cop involuntarily coughed it out, but did not wake up. He took out his gun and fired all of the five shots that were in it; some into the trees, one into his car, and a couple into the buildings. He wiped the gun clean and placed it in Billy Gator's right hand. He wiped the bottle clean, and threw the empty down on the ground next to Billy Gator and smiled. "It will take his back-up at least thirty minutes to get here. They use the Sheriff's Office or Highway Patrol. Half of them can't even find this place, so we have plenty of time."

As they were turning onto the Alley, headed back to the hotel, Johnny Deerchaser asked, "May I use one of your cellular phones, please?" Jonas handed him a phone and Johnny punched 911. "Yes.... I'd like to report a drunken Fish and Game Officer shooting up the fishing camp at Gator Break. How do I know he's a cop? Simple.... he has a uniform on and threatened to lock up anyone who pissed him off. No dear, my name is of no importance. I believe this officer is crazy and would seek revenge." Johnny smiled and hung up. "Thank you and bless both of you. You two have made an old warrior very happy on this day of retribution."

Raul smiled and told him in Navajo, "Anything I could do for a great warrior on his path of life would be an honor."

Johnny Deerchaser placed his hand over the seat and on Raul's right shoulder. Raul felt a chill run through his body. It was as though Grandpa had just placed his hand on him. Jonas looked at Johnny and saw he was in what looked to be a trance. His pale blue eyes were open, looking straight ahead. Jonas' mouth dropped open as Johnny Deerchaser spoke. "You are a great man, my son; there is pride in the heavens as I walk. Your sons will be proud of you." Johnny removed his hand and there was complete silence in the Hummer.

Raul looked at Jonas and smiled; he knew Grandpa had just spoken to him, and it was time to accept Jonas as his son. He reached over and put his right hand on Jonas left shoulder. He squeezed his shoulder a little and said, "That was your Great Grandfather speaking, and he was one of the greatest warriors I have ever known. He was a Windtalker in the Great War. When there is time, I will tell you more about him."

Jonas' eyes were wet with tears when he looked at his father. "Will you tell me more about my mother as well? Grandpa Borge told me things, but I know there is more."

Raul was smiling and nodding to Jonas, when Johnny Deerchaser interrupted.

"Grandpa has very strong medicine and he is very wise. I know he talks to you. Let me ask you, where is your other son?"

"I don't have any other sons; Jonas is the only one. Why do you ask me that?"

Johnny smiled and replied, "Grandpa said your sons would be proud of you, that's why."

Raul was staring into the roadway ahead. It was starting to get dark and the headlights from other cars were now coming at him. "Grandpa says a lot of things. A lot of them don't make sense. Besides, I'm too old to start raising more kids now." Just as he finished speaking, the clear skies over Alligator Alley lit up as a star shot from the left side of the roadway across to the right and disappeared into the night.

Johnny Deerchaser laughed. "That shooting star just said differently. A shooting star from left to right means a son will be born to a Great Warrior Chief."

"Well, there you have it; I'm a CIA assassin, not a Great Warrior Chief, - so get off it," Raul replied.

"As you wish. Today's assassin, tomorrow's Chief. Nothing more to say", Johnny Deerchaser said, smiling, as he leaned back in the seat. They all noticed a car approaching at a high rate of speed with the headlights flashing and a blue light blinking on the dashboard. It looked like a Fish and Game Supervisor, headed for the camp. The Florida Highway Patrol must have already reached the camp, and, finding Corporal Gator in his condition, called for a supervisor. The three of them laughed, and Johnny commented as the car sped by, "Boy, wouldn't I like to be there, listening to that Skin-Head scumbag try to talk his way out of this one."

Jonas turned around to him and asked, "Aren't skin-heads supposed to be bald? That guy had a full head of hair."

"Bank robbers seldom wear signs saying they are bank robbers, but give them enough time to show their colors and hold onto your wallet", Johnny said in a philosophical tone.

"Boy, I just love this 'Indians wisdom' thing", Jonas said with a grin.

They were all laughing as they passed through the toll plaza and turned South on US 27 towards Miami and the hotel.

When the three of them arrived at the hotel and entered the meeting room, they found Ricky and George already talking with an attractive blonde. The woman was in her early thirties; well built and as indicated, very nice looking. Ricky noticed the three of them first. "Hey, how did you do in the swamps?" he asked.

Before Raul could respond, Johnny Deerchaser interrupted and told them he was going to catch a ride back to the reservation, if that was the plan. George then looked up and told him that he was still in Raul's custody and wouldn't be released until the mission was over. Johnny looked at him and replied, "So does that mean I sleep with him, or what?"

"No, of course not", George replied. "However, you do have a room in this hotel, and you can't leave it without Raul or one of us. So - restaurant, pool or your room. What else do you want to know?"

"Probably the obvious question at this point would be what is the room number and where is the key?" Johnny asked.

"Oh, yes, of course. I have it right here. Now, no drinking and don't disappoint me, Johnny. I'm out on a limb here for you", George said, kind of condescendingly.

Raul picked up on that quickly and felt bad for the way this warrior was being treated. Johnny said nothing and let it run off his back. Raul took the key from George and handed it to Johnny Deerchaser.

"If you need to do anything or go anywhere, I'm at your service. Rest well, my Seminole brother." Raul placed his left hand on Johnny's shoulder and tapped his chest with the other. This was a Navajo sign of true admiration for another warrior. Johnny responded in the Navajo language, and said to Raul, "you have my respect and admiration as well, my Navajo brother."

Jonas was wearing a broad smile as he understood. George had a rather stupid look on his face because he had no idea what had transpired. And Ricky; well Ricky kind of expected anything from Raul at this point in their long friendship, so he said, or showed, absolutely nothing. He did, however, know that for Raul to show this kind of respect for another man, this man had to have really impressed him somehow.

Johnny left for his room and Raul turned to the attractive blonde with shoulder length hair. She had been crying and looked a bit tethered. Ricky filled them in as to what had happened this morning.

It seemed that the woman who had been murdered by the Colombian and Tony Jr. was, in fact, the housekeeper. She had been, within a year or two, the same age and pretty close to the same size and build. Unfortunately for her, she was also a blonde with shoulder length hair. Stacey Cunningham could not have hired a better double to be in her house during the day. Raul wondered if she planned it that way, or if it was a true coincidence. Stacey had told them that she had to go to the dry cleaners this morning because she realized the dress she wanted to wear was never picked up with the rest of the cleaning. The house keeper, Gloria, had shown up at eight thirty for work, and it was about nine when Stacey told her she was going to pick up the dress. She told Gloria to expect Rebecca, and to tell her that she would be back quickly. While she was out, she decided to run to the jewelers and pick up her watch that she had left for repair. She didn't plan on being gone more than a half hour to forty five minutes. She was leaving the jewelers when she got a call on her cell phone from her neighbor, Diane. She wanted her to know that as soon as she left, her housekeeper had a couple male visitors in the house. If she was partying while she was supposed to be working, Stacey should know about it. Stacey told them that she got scared after the call from Diane, so she called the house and got no answer. Ricky had asked her why she would have gotten scared because of a seemingly innocent call like the one she had received from her neighbor. At that point, she had come clean about her entire past and her relationship with Don Carlos. He had been using the house in Weston as his American base, and her job was to act like his wife and run the American operation. She had been kidnapped in Bogota four years earlier and taken to the compound in the jungles by Leticia. She had worked in the camp and the laboratory for six months or so when Don Carlos took a liking to her and promoted her to his assistant. She lived in the house with him, serviced only him and supervised the girls working in the lab. She did that for about a year and a half when Don Carlos got this American base idea. He had guests who she picked up at the airport, and they stayed at the house. She ran errands for him, and did whatever he told her to do. She basically ran the American base for him.

When George asked her why she just didn't go to the police and escape, she just looked at him. "I had a very good job. Don Carlos paid all the bills, gave me a nice, no, a beautiful home in a Country Club and a checking account with money in it all the time. Not to mention my no-limit credit cards. Would you have left that?"

George had no answer for that question. Ricky then told her that she must realize by now that Don Carlos knows something is up and wants her dead. Her only chance for making it out of this alive was to cooperate with them and help them put him away.

"You have to promise me one thing before I can help you," she said.

"What?" Ricky asked.

"You have to promise me that you will kill him. Not wound him or take him into custody. Unless he is dead, my life is not worth anything. I won't be able to live anywhere that he couldn't get me. You have got to understand what I have done to survive, and I don't want to lose anything now".

Raul looked at her; he wasn't sure if he wanted to feel bad for her, or punch her in the face for not caring about the housekeeper. She had definitely become a tough woman, from all that had happened. "How much money is hidden in the walls at the house in Weston?"

Stacey, as well as everybody else, turned and looked at Raul. "How do you know about that?

"WAG" Raul answered. "Now tell me."

"Somewhere between seven and ten million dollars. Is WAG a special branch of the CIA?"

"Let me assure you that I will do everything in my power to carry out your wishes with regard to Don Shitbag Zalazar, but I am going to need your assistance to accomplish that. Can you do that?" Raul asked.

"Absolutely, as long as you are protecting me," she replied.

Ricky leaned over and whispered in Raul's ear. "You took a wild ass guess about the money?" Raul looked at him and winked.

"Good", Raul said. "Now that that is taken care of, I have a special request of you. Call it another deal if you want. I'm going to ask my intelligence coordinator to fax me a list of addresses and names of the girls I freed in Leticia, as well as the camp. I want you to divide up the money in the walls amongst all of you and send them checks. Will you do that? Because if you do, I won't be forced to contact the IRS criminal investigations or have the money seized as illegal assets."

"I guess I have no choice, do I?" She was all smiles and nobody knew why.

George was bothered by the smiles. "What's so funny? We're not getting the joke here."

"No sir, you misunderstand. I am not laughing. I am admiring those two." She was pointing at Raul and Jonas. "You two are the ones who wrecked his night club in Leticia and blew up his compound in the jungle. You freed the girls. I applaud you; however Don Carlos is not so pleased. Just so you are aware, he put a ten million dollar bounty on each of you, and your families."

Raul was just staring at the woman. "What exactly did Don Carlos say to you about the incident in Leticia?"

"You call it an incident? He was so mad that he broke furniture and spent the night on the phone, putting contracts on both of you and anyone you care about. I'd call that more than an incident. He said you cost him close to five hundred million dollars, and you would pay. In fact, he said specifically, 'that Navajo Ghost Warrior prick' was going to pay and pay a lot".

"Do you know where he is right now? His helicopter landed at North Perry airport at five o'clock this afternoon," Raul said.

"Well, I know for sure he won't go back to the house, but he has another apartment in Hollywood. I don't know exactly where it is, but I think it is on 142 Avenue, North of Sheridan St. He got that apartment in my name also, but never took me there so I don't know anything about it. Look under Stacey Princeton and you will probably find it. He doesn't think anyone would ever know about his 'safe house'."

Ricky spoke and asked her if she had any idea what he was up to and when he was going to do it. She told them that Don Carlos planned to blow up the football stadium on opening day. He had told her it was payback for what the government had done to him. She also told them that he had a back- up set of plans hidden in the house in Weston. She told them that she would have to go with them to retrieve the files because they would never find them, even if she tried to explain. "He hired this old German guy to build this special furniture that had all these secret compartments and secret hiding places. The guy was really good, and nobody would ever find the compartments, unless you knew where to look."

The four of them decided to take Stacey back to the house and retrieve any and all information they could. It would be much quicker and less messy than tearing the house and furniture apart. They were amazed when they got to the house. It was still taped off as a crime scene and the bed room was still a bloody mess, but the body was gone. Except for the mess in the bedroom and the black fingerprint dust all over the house, the house looked normal. Stacey went to a large armoire in the guest bedroom and twisted the lower right leg on the unit. A mirror on the wall next to the cabinet opened. Inside was a shelf with papers, maps and stacks of money. "Take all the papers you want" she said, "but remember our deal."

"Anymore compartments?" Ricky asked.

"As a matter of fact…" she said, walking into the office that had been built into the house. She went to the bookcase and pulled on an encyclopedia. An entire section of the cabinet opened, revealing a small room, about eight by eight square feet. This room was also full of money and documents. The most important of these documents was a detailed map of explosive locations at Pro Player Stadium for the opening day game.

The paperwork also detailed manpower plans from the training camp and how they would be used at the game. The manpower documents listed all the soldiers in his camp, along with their photographs and assignments. 'What a gold strike!" they thought. Now they had to decide whether an attack on the camp was really necessary, or if they should just wait and catch the bad guys as they came to the game. They couldn't find specifics on how the explosives would be planted inside the stadium; however, four of the soldiers on the manpower list showed that their employment was at the stadium. They needed to hit the camp before the game on Sunday.

Ghost Warrior

Security at the game could arrest the employees when they arrived, and also catch any stragglers who they didn't get at the camp. Where was Don Carlos going to be during all of this? They couldn't let him get away again. "Find that address in Hollywood", Raul said. 'We need to go there and see what he has". After another fifteen minutes of searching, Ricky asked Stacey where she put the old files on the house and properties. She went to a staircase that led to a loft room above them. "Extra bedroom for guests", she told them. She went to a piece of molding on the wall and lifted it. A section of the wall opened, revealing a small storage space. "These records are two years or newer. Anything else is in storage."

"This will do just fine", Ricky said, and crawled into the space. There was a light inside and he turned it on. He went to a box labeled 'property taxes'. There it was - a tax bill, but the address and name had been whited out. Ricky left the crawl space and went to the computer.

On the bill was a property identification number, used by the Broward County Property Tax Assessor. Ricky referenced the number and there it was. Right down to the apartment number. "Got it!" he shouted. "But the name on this location is Betty Friedman, Do you know this woman?"

"Not at all. I've never heard of her," Stacey replied.

"I'll have Sarah run this name and address and find out who and where she is," Ricky replied. With that, they closed up everything, took the records they needed and returned with Stacey to the hotel.

Ricky's phone rang as they entered the meeting room. It was Sarah, and she was reporting on what she had discovered. "Betty Friedman, age 82 years, lives at 14790 N. 142nd Ave. Apartment 618. She is a widow, lives alone with no known living relatives. Her husband, Stanley, died a year and a half ago of apparent natural causes at the age of 86. I'll send you a detailed list going back to New York. Long Island, North Shore, to be specific, if you want," she advised.

"No, that won't be necessary," Ricky told her. "But answer one question, if you can, for me."

"Shoot boss, I'm all ears," she responded.

"Can you track this Betty Friedman's banking and credit for the past, say, two years?"

"Already done. She has an active bank account at Hollywood Federal Bank, a MasterCard, a Diners' Card, and a Platinum Visa from Hollywood Federal. All active, as of last Monday. No activity in the past five days."

"Thanks kid, I'll get back to you. Good job", Ricky replied. "Zalazar killed this woman and had someone assume her identity. He had her move in the apartment and become her. I'd bet on that. George, get me two female agents. DEA, FBI, ours - I don't care. Just make them sweet and very likable to little old people. Can you do that in the next hour?"

"It's three-thirty in the morning, Ricky…." George said hesitantly.

"Your point is what?" Raul interrupted.

"Nothing sir, I'm right on it".

"What a bunch of whiners they got here!" Raul said to Ricky.

Ricky looked at Raul. "Actually, he's a pretty good agent. He needs a little more time on the job. But all in all, he holds his own."

"Good, then let's take him to the camp when we raid it today, and if he pisses himself it will be on your leg. How's that for a little more experience?" laughed Raul.

"Sounds like a plan. My bet is that he will be there when we need him", Ricky replied.

Jonas turned to Ricky and said, "You know, my father is a pretty good judge of what a man has or doesn't have."

Ricky's mouth fell open. "Your father? I mean it's pretty obvious, but nobody would talk about that. What happened?"

"You know that drunken Indian everyone here talks about?" Jonas replied.

"You mean that Johnny Deerchaser fellow? Because if that is who you're talking about, that's no drunken Indian. I know your father too well not to know about his respect for people. And he respects Johnny Deerchaser."

"Well, he cleared up some issues between us, and, as the Indians say, 'made the stars easier to see in the sky", Jonas said as he placed his hand on Raul's shoulder.

Raul squirmed a bit. "Ok, let's get down to business here," he said, clearing his throat. "We need a plan for this camp. So let's plan."

George returned in about twenty minutes and announced, "Carrie Winters and Joan Trumph will be here by 5:30am. They are both FBI agents assigned to the Miami office."

By five-thirty the two female agents had arrived at the meeting room. George introduced them to Raul, Ricky and the rest of the crew that was working in the room. Raul handed them a printout and told them the plan. He wanted them to go to the address listed and talk to the other tenants. The apartment complex is home to mostly senior citizens, so showing up at seven-thirty on Saturday morning isn't going to bother them. He wanted them to talk to the residents and get intelligence about the apartment in question; find out who lived there and what, if anything, was going on. The two agents were to pose as social workers, checking on Mrs. Friedman and her welfare. Schmooze these people and they will tell you two anything you want to know. "Before we go into that apartment, I want to know what to expect. We will have an FBI SWAT team on standby and take a good look at this picture". He handed them a picture of Don Carlos Zalazar.

"If he is at the building or on the grounds, you call us and let us know. Do not…. and I repeat… Do not try to apprehend this guy. Save him for SWAT; no matter how good you think you are as agents, this guy will kill you in a heartbeat. He is totally ruthless and places no value on human life. I'm not trying to scare you, just make you aware. If he is in the apartment when you check it, be sweet social workers, but don't go into the apartment. Save this guy for SWAT. We clear on this?"

"Yes sir, we will do exactly as you say," they both responded simultaneously.

"Good, then I expect to hear from you within two hours. Get going."

The two agents left and George put the SWAT team on standby at a location six blocks from the apartment complex. The plans for the raid on the camp were ready and now they were just awaiting word from another SWAT team from DEA and some agents from the FBI, CIA and Homeland Security. They wanted to have about fifty agents for the raid, as they were expecting anywhere between seventy-five and one hundred soldiers at the camp. By 7am they were loaded and meeting places and time had been coordinated. Now they just had to wait for the two female FBI agents to report what they had found. As they were waiting, the door to the meeting room opened and a stocky, short, balding man walked in. He was wearing a suit that looked like it had been slept in, and his tie was opened at the top. "Hey, I'm agent Jim Walker from the Florida Department of Law Enforcement. The Governor called me this morning at about 3:00 am and told me there was going to be a raid on a terrorist camp out in the Everglades today. He wanted us to provide some assistance. "

"Might I ask you how you were made aware of what's going on here?" Ricky asked.

"Oh, sure, some friend of the Governor's called him and said we may need some support, so here I am with an FDLE SWAT team. I have about thirty-five guys and equipment downstairs waiting for you to tell us what to do. We are at your disposal."

"Some guy called?" Raul asked.

"Yeah, some guy up in the Government; you know, a boss of some sort. He's got kick; I know that because the Governor doesn't jump for just anybody."

"And you do or don't know this guy's name?" George asked.

"Sure, Jeb Bush. Everybody knows that", Agent Walker responded.

"Not the Governor, the guy who called!" George sighed in exasperation.

"Oh, sorry. Yeah, it was some funny name… you know, not a normal run of the mill name, but something really different. Give me a minute."

Raul looked at the agent and asked, "Was it Hector Lightfoot, by chance?"

"By golly, that's it, how did you know that?" Agent Walker replied, eyebrows raised.

Ricky laughed and added, "it must have been that WAG thing again."

George, Ricky and Jonas were laughing and agent Walker just stood there looking at Raul, unsure of what was going on.

Raul pulled out a map and showed it to the Agent. He pointed out where the meeting point was going to be, and told him to take his team there and wait.

Carrie and Joan arrived at the complex shortly before seven thirty. They were stopped at the front gate. They flashed ID's quickly and told the guard they were from health services, here to check on one Betty Friedman in apartment 618. The guard shrugged and opened the gate. "That was certainly easy", they said to each other. They parked in a guest spot and walked towards the pool area at the center of the complex. The first person they met with was a little elderly lady, probably late seventies, early eighties. She introduced herself as Selma Goldblatt and said she was a board member and wanted to know how she could be of assistance. Carrie told her they were with health services and were here to check on Betty Friedman.

"Just like the Government! A day late and a dollar short. Betty Friedman moved out of here and went back north, about two or three years ago, if my memory serves me correctly. As a matter of fact, she sold her place to her cousin Beatrice Friedman, and she lives there now, with her grandson Carl."

Agent Joan Trumph looked at the little old lady and asked, "When was the last time you saw Carl or Beatrice, do you remember exactly?"

"Of course dear, I remember exactly. It was exactly four days ago. Carl was...., no, wait... it was yesterday."

The agents watched the lady carefully. Finally Carrie asked, "Mrs. Goldblatt, do you know what day today is?"

"Of course I do, silly, today is Saturday. The reason I hesitated was because four days ago I spoke with Carl and Beatrice down here in the court yard. I didn't see either of them again until yesterday morning when I saw Carl. He had a bag, you know, like a suitcase. Anyway, he was getting into his car and he had the strangest look about him."

"Strangest look?" Joan asked.

"Yes. I said 'good morning, Carl', as he was putting the bag in his car. He didn't answer me. I got closer and said good morning again, and asked how his grandmother was doing. He looked at me very strangely, and told me she was dead tired and not to bother her today. I was offended, I don't bother anyone, and it's not my nature."

"Then he just drove off?" Joan asked.

"That's his spot right there. See, it's empty."

"Selma, do you know what kind of car Carl drives?" Carrie asked.

"No dear, I'm afraid I don't. I can tell you it is white and some kind of Sport Utility car. It does, however, have a funny tag on it."

"Funny tag? Is it a Florida tag?" Carrie questioned

"Oh yes, dear. It is a Florida tag alright, and it doesn't have numbers. It just says 'CLAW' on it. Isn't that funny?"

Joan was on the cell phone to Raul, and reported what they knew. She told them they wanted to check the apartment. There was a possibility that the resident was dead and they wanted to verify their suspicions. Raul copied the information on the tag, and told them to standby until a uniformed officer arrived. "Get back to us as soon as you have identified who is living in that apartment", Raul told them.

Ricky was collecting the maps and last minute paperwork necessary for the assault. He asked Raul, "Are you ready to head out towards the camp and meet with the swat troops and get started?"

"Just about", he replied. "Let's do this.... you, George and Jonas head out there and I will meet you in about an hour and we'll hit the place. I want to run by North Perry Airport first and check on something."

"You got it."

And the three of them left for the designated meeting location out off of US 27.

Raul pulled into North Perry Airport and saw what he was looking for. Don Carlos' Helicopter was parked just outside the hanger. The rotor covers had been removed and the wheels were chocked. The chopper was obviously ready to go at a moments notice. Raul could see the pilot in the hanger office drinking coffee with a young lady who worked behind the counter. They were engrossed in a conversation of some sort, and the pilot was not watching the helicopter. "Perfect", Raul thought to himself. He went to the chopper, did what he had come to do, and placed a radio transmitter under the passenger seat.

Agents Carrie and Joan were now standing at the front door to apartment 618. They were accompanied by two Hollywood police officers who were probably from the SWAT team, but without all of the equipment on. They knocked on the door and got the response they had expected... none. The complex manager had keys to everyone's apartments in case of situations where an elderly resident was sick or had passed away during the night. He handed the key to Carrie and she opened the door. There was silence in the apartment and nothing seemed disturbed. They moved into the first bedroom, and everything was fine.

The bed was made and nothing out of place; so far so good. The next bedroom was a different story. There was Beatrice, or whatever her name was, lying on the floor face down in a pool of blood. The blood had poured out so heavily that her face seemed submerged in the blood-soaked carpet. The body was that of an elderly woman, from what they could tell, but it was difficult, as this sadistic maniac had torn her face off.

When they turned the body over and discovered her face had been removed, Joan turned away quickly, and came as close as she ever had to throwing up at the scene of a crime. She regained her composure and noticed a blood-spattered letter that was lying on the bed. She read the note out loud. "By now you have discovered that I have a second residence here in your country. It doesn't matter because I have moved and Grandma has stayed behind. Your CIA has cost me a great deal and so I am forced to retaliate. I will destroy as much in your country as you fucks have wrecked in mine. Get ready because I am just beginning. Oh… and you can tell my friend, Mr. Lightfoot, that I have already made plans to blow up his farm and kill what is dear to him. Before you leave don't forget to look in the closet. 'FACE IT, SOME THINGS HANG AROUND FOREVER'. Goodbye for now, you incompetent imbeciles."

Joan looked at Carrie, and then they both looked at the uniformed officers. One of the officers opened the door to the walk-in closet, and there was Grandma's face, hanging on a hanger tied to a string, attached to the light. The policeman jumped when he saw the sad looking face staring at him.

"God damn, this guy is really sick!" the young police officer yelped.

Raul was driving west on 595, headed for the designated meeting place on US 27, when his cell phone rang. It was Agent Carrie Winters. "Yes sir, this is Agent Winters, and we have entered the apartment and found the woman who was staying here. She has been murdered, apparently by this Don Carlos Zalazar. He is not on the scene and witnesses have told us he left sometime yesterday morning for an unknown destination. Something more interesting than that is a letter we found at the murder scene."

"Damn", he said to himself, "these FBI agents talk like they are writing a report." He laughed to himself, "getting into their pants would probably take a six page report with a supplement". He regained his composure. "Yes, Agent Winters, what does the letter say, in brief?" Raul asked.

"In brief, sir, it says he's going to blow up your pig farm and kill someone dear to you. He says, in the letter, you have wrecked his world and he is retaliating. Sir, do you have a pig farm?"

"Thanks", Raul said as he slammed the cell phone shut and skidded to the side of the road.

He turned on the monitor in the dash of the Hummer and saw Sarah. "Sarah, can you hear me?!" he yelled.

"Yes Raul, what's the matter?" she asked.

"Get Epi to the monitor right now; it's important."

Sarah turned and Raul could see her calling to Epi. Epi's face appeared on the monitor. "What's wrong, is somebody hurt?!" she yelled, almost in a panic.

"No, nothing like that, but there is a problem. This Zalazar fellow is planning an attack on the farm. He left a note at a murder scene describing an attack on the farm and his plans to kill someone close to me. That's got to be Angelita. Epi, I need to know she is safe." Raul voice was showing a little stress, which was totally out of character for him.

"Raul, calm down, this guy is trying to push your buttons and it looks like it's working. First of all, Angelita is here in the bunker and her cousin is with her. She's still a bit under the weather so they came back here yesterday. She is resting right now, so stop worrying about that. Secondly, our security cameras picked up two men with a LAS rocket launcher at the perimeter. The Marines assigned to security caught them both, and I had a couple of agents from Colombian Intelligence talk to them. After about an hour they admitted that Don Carlos Zalazar had hired them to blow up the farm. Colombian Intelligence took the two back to the Department of Administrative Services office in Bogota. So, chalk up another one for the good guys and go get that son-of-a-bitch. And one last thing; and I think I speak for all of us here when I ask. Please do us all a favor and eliminate this wacko Zalazar, because I, for one, am totally tired of screwing around with him."

"Got it... let me see what's in the wind for Mr. Zalazar", Raul replied. "Oh... and let me add, you're doing a hell of a job back home on the farm. Keep up the good work! See ya' soon."

The screen went blank and Raul continued west on 595 towards the Everglades and today's business. He arrived a little while later, and everyone was already in place. Ricky got out the map and they reviewed one last time. Jonas and George had taken the FBI SWAT Team, along with the other available agents, and had followed Johnny Deerchaser in airboats. Five, including the Indians. They were going to enter the camp from the South and use the path that Raul and King had created earlier. Ricky told Raul that Jonas and George had, including themselves, thirty-two agents in that group. The Florida Dept. of Law Enforcement's SWAT Team was standing by at the big truck stop on US 27 and they also had two Huey Helicopters with them They had set them down in the median and the Highway patrol was assisting with traffic.

"Well, do you think they have created enough commotion to tell the world that we are here? Just maybe everyone in that camp will be expecting us", Raul commented.

"Well, the gas station is a ways south of here, so maybe not. But there is something else you should know about it," Ricky said hesitantly.

"And that would be…....?" Raul asked as he was putting on his gear.

"The FBI as well as FDLE insists on offering the inhabitants of the compound an opportunity to surrender before we attack."

"Get the fuck out of here! They want to warn the people in the compound that we are coming so they can be ready? These people probably outnumber us by fifty men and we should warn them and eliminate surprise?!"

"That's what they are saying. Their policy dictates warning them."

"Not a problem, get them on the radio and tell them I'll give them the advance warning. Tell those agents I promise, I'll give the people in the camp notification that we are coming."

Ricky just looked at Raul and they smiled at each other. Ricky knew Raul way too long and way too well; he knew Raul wouldn't roll over for this kind of 'tell them you're coming before you surprise them' crap.

Ricky keyed his mike and notified everyone the assault was a go and that the team with Jonas and George would move in first on Ricky's command. The second team with the helicopters would be activated after the initial assault had begun and it was safe for them to set down or use rope drops. Ricky and Raul had driven off the roadway and down the one-lane dirt road, about fifteen miles. They parked and hid the Hummer. As Raul was getting King out, they both heard a helicopter headed towards them, coming from the southeast. It was traveling at a rapid rate and headed directly for the camp. Raul turned to Ricky after looking towards the sky. "My bet is that's Zalazar in that chopper. That's the one that was parked

Ghost Warrior

at North Perry, and that tells us he just flew over that FDLE SWAT team at the gas station. I wonder if the guys in the airboats had a chance to hide before he approached?"

Ricky was already on the radio to the FDLE agent. "Walker, come in, can you read me?"

"Agent Walker here, what's up? Are we ready so soon?"

"No, stay put. What I want to know is if that white and green helicopter flew over you?"

"Sure did, he flew over, swung around and did a loop, then took off. At first we thought it was a Sheriff's helicopter, but then we noticed no markings. Is there a problem with it?"

"It flew right into the camp we are about to raid. Yes, I think there is a problem. Get ready right now!"

Raul was watching the front of the camp through his binoculars. "Jonas!" he called into his mike.

"Go ahead! And before you ask, we heard the chopper coming and got into the sawgrass before he came over. He didn't see us, I'm sure of it."

"Good job, are you in place right now?" Raul asked.

"We are", Jonas replied.

"They are already expecting something; they have opened up two of the Quonset huts and are pulling out something, it looks like a.... Oh, great, he's got anti-personnel rocket launchers and anti-aircraft missile launchers. It looks like they picked up on the helicopters and SWAT team. I can't get an exact count, but it looks close to seventy-five troops with automatic weapons."

Jonas keyed his mike. "Raul, are you ready for us? Because I can get clear shots on the truck drivers and launch operators."

"How many shots you need?" Raul responded.

"Six shots max, to start."

"After the first explosion, cap the lead truck driver then the operator. That takes care of the anti-personnel vehicle. Cap the second driver and then any operator that gets in the launcher on the first truck. After the third explosion send the troops in. Remember, stay in the marked lines. That field is loaded with mines."

Before Jonas could respond, another voice came on the radio. "This is Special Agent Clark from the FBI. We are obligated to advise them that they are under arrest before we just attack them."

Raul was getting ready to unload on this guy, when Ricky put his hand up, signaling that he would handle it. While Raul was getting in place, Ricky keyed the mike and very calmly spoke.

"Agent Clark, this is Agent Nelson from the CIA. I understand your protocol; therefore, before you stand up and get your ass shot off, please give a contact number to Agent Borge or Agent Backner so we can let your supervisors know that you were the one person possibly killed here today for absolutely no reason."

After a brief moment of dead silence, very sheepishly the agent responded. "Fuck protocol, we're ready when you are."

Raul smiled at Ricky. "Very well put, Blue Coat. And now, welcome to the dance."

That was when Raul detonated the first charge. They watched as the driver of the first vehicle slumped over the wheel of the topless vehicle. The Quonset from which the vehicles had just emerged no longer existed, nor did the fence on the right side of the compound. The operator of the first launcher flew backward in the seat as the bullet struck the front of his head. He leaned to the right and fell from the vehicle, which was still coasting forward. The second driver's head exploded inside the vehicle's cab, as the second explosion evaporated another Quonset hut. This hut had been stocked with ammunition and gasoline. The initial explosion set off a secondary explosion that shook the camp. The SWAT snipers were assisting Jonas and making the assault through the swamp side of the compound much easier for the FBI and the other agents. Raul detonated two more buildings and Jonas was busy picking off operators as they attempted to fire anti-personnel rockets at the agents crossing the field. Raul was watching the compound through the binoculars and saw Don Carlos emerge from one of the bunkers. He was, once again, followed by two men dressed in green military uniforms. The two men with him were yelling orders to the troops and directing more men to get into the missile launcher. Men were hesitantly climbing into the seat and being shot by the snipers. The situation inside the camp had really become pathetic.

Don Carlos yelled to someone inside a bunker next to the one he had emerged from, and a small man dressed in a green uniform exited. He was holding what looked like a detonating device in his hands. "What are they up to?" thought Raul. Just then the little man started detonating. They realized what he was doing too late. He was detonating the mines in the field where the FBI SWAT team was shooting it out with the troops in the compound. The first set of mines that exploded sent four agents flying into the air. The second set of charges killed two more. By this time, Raul had set up his rifle and Ricky was calling in the FDLE SWAT team helicopters. Jonas had seen the little man with the detonator, but could not get a clear shot at him from his position. Besides, if he got distracted they would get a man in that anti-personnel launcher and all hell would break loose. The FBI snipers were trying to get a shot at this guy, but each time they tried they exposed themselves more and were taking heavy fire themselves. The agents in the field were trapped and destined to die if Raul did not do something and quickly. He detonated the last of the pre-set charges and it blew up the bunker behind the little man with the detonator. With that explosion the man was sent flying forward and the detonator came out of his hands and hit the dirt. The agents in the field had a moment's reprieve, but couldn't take advantage. Fire from the camp had intensified, and they were pinned down and in desperate need of backup. The little man stood up and wiped himself off. He bent over, picked up the detonator and stood back up.

As he was turning the charge switch, he looked at Don Carlos and smiled. That was when the left side of his head blew open. The little man stood for a moment looking at Don Carlos with his mouth open and a look of shock on his face. His black rimmed glasses were still sitting on his nose and the detonator still in his hand. Blood ran from the little man's nose as he dropped the detonator and fell forward. Don Carlos was now in Raul's scope; a perfect head shot. Just as Raul took the shot, Don Carlos dropped and the bullet struck one of the two men who had been following him. The bullet hit the man dead center on the chin and came out the back of his neck. He flew backwards against the remaining bunker and was sitting on the ground with his legs spread, eyes still open. Don Carlos was now running, with the other man in front of him acting as cover. They ran to the helicopter and the pilot who Raul had seen at the airport started the engines. He had been waiting in the chopper for Don Carlos to make his get away. The FDLE SWAT helicopters were now hovering at the front of the compound and the team members were coming out sliding down ropes.

Raul looked at them and said to Ricky, "These guys are pretty impressive, once they have their shit together."

Ricky looked back and asked Raul if he knew Zalazar was getting away. Raul smiled.

"That's exactly what he thinks, I'm sure, but what he thinks and what is real is not always the same thing, now, is it?"

"Excuse me, but once again you are making absolutely no sense", Ricky said.

At this point, the troops in the compound were throwing down their weapons and surrendering. The FBI and other agents were moving in, making the arrests.

Don Carlos' helicopter had lifted off and was starting to move away from the compound when Jonas keyed his mike. "Do we need to get to the airport and head this guy off, or what?"

Raul responded. "Patience. He's not going anywhere we can't pick him up. Excuse me while I make a call."

Jonas was staring at his radio and Ricky was staring at Raul. Raul opened his cell phone and dialed a number.

The phone under the seat where Don Carlos was sitting started to ring. "What is that?" he shouted. No one in the chopper had a clue; Don Carlos found the phone and opened it. "Who *is* this?" he demanded.

"This, you crazy, demented fuck, is Raul Lightfoot. I just wanted a moment of your time to let you know what a true sick piece of shit you are."

"I may be all those things you say, but I am the one who has blown up your pig farm and eluded you and your little buddies. So you see, Mr. Navajo Ghost Warrior, you lose once again."

"If you're talking about the two losers you sent to the farm two days ago, DAS intelligence is bonding with them as we speak, so that's another thing you fucked up. And as for getting away once again, are you really sure about that?"

"What do you mean? I'm up here, flying away, and you are down on the ground wishing you had caught me. So you lose!" Don Carlos laughed a deep, robust guffaw.

"Really?" snarled Raul. "If you listen real hard, you worthless rat bastard, you will hear the beeping noise under your seat. Yes, that's your worthless, sick life beeping away."

Don Carlos had the phone open, and Raul could hear as he asked the pilot what that beeping noise was, just before the helicopter exploded in the sky over the Everglades.

Ricky watched the explosion and smiled. "Looks like you put enough C-4 in that chopper to blow that sick son-of-a-bitch to hell. They ought to be picking up pieces for days."

"Couldn't have happened to a sicker piece of shit, and a more deserving wacko. Call your girlfriend back at the farm and tell her today's concern is history. And tell Angelita I'll be home with my son in a day or two."

"You got it, I'm on it right now", Ricky said with a big grin.

The clean up went smoothly, but what a waste of life this had been. All these youngsters who had been suckered in by that sick man and had died here today for nothing more than Don Carlos' ego.

By the end of the day, eleven law enforcement agents had died and seven more were wounded. And these were the light casualty numbers.

Inside the compound fifty-two men were dead, twenty-seven injured, along with thirty-two more that had been arrested and were facing Federal capital murder charges. "What a brutal way to destroy your life for nothing", was the sentiment amongst the survivors on both sides.

As Ricky, King and Raul were getting back to where they had hidden the Hummer, an army-style Jeep pulled up with George and Jonas. Jonas smiled and said, "On the way over here I found something on US 27 that I thought might be of interest to you". He handed Raul a clawed glove. It felt like something was inside it.

"It feels like his fingers are still in it. The good news is, because he was nuts enough to put this thing on while he was in the chopper, we have fingerprints for a positive ID. "

George chimed in. "The fingers, of course, will go to the lab for ID, but I'm sure the glove can be relinquished to Raul. After all, he deserves it for tracking this guy as much as he did. Oh, and by the way, the female FBI agents contacted me and told me that the coroner had lifted prints from the woman in the apartment. An Interpol check showed they belonged to a Russian woman named Olga Potovic. She has a sheet and has been trouble for us for about six years. No real loss there. The only sad thing is that there is nothing on the old woman who lived there originally. We are assuming that they killed her and dumped her somewhere, but we will keep looking. Who knows?"

By six o'clock that evening, Raul, Ricky, Jonas and George were sitting in the bar of the hotel, trying their best to put this day behind them. Raul was starting to get a buzz and decided he would go to his room before he fell over drunk, right there in the bar. As he was getting up and arguing with George over who would pay the bill, his cell phone rang.

"Angelita! I was just on my way to my room to call you. You feeling better? Great! Yes, we are all coming home tomorrow. Yes, I'm anxious too. What is it? What's wrong? No, you can tell me now." Raul stood at the table with a blank stare and everyone at the table was looking back at him. He was mute.

Ricky, concerned, took the phone from Raul. "Angelita, baby doll, what's wrong? Oh my God, I don't believe it! I am so happy for you and this stick in the mud is happy, too... he just doesn't know how to say it! Raul, take the phone and tell her how much you love her."

Raul took the phone and turned from the group. Everyone at the table was looking at Ricky. "What? Why are you looking at me?" he laughed. "You mean because I'm going to be a Godfather? That's right, Angelita is three months pregnant. That's why she has been in Bogota with her cousin. She's been visiting a doctor. And you'll never guess what it is."

Jonas was all smiles and he and Raul looked at each other. "It's your other son".

"How did you know that?" Ricky asked.

"It's a Navajo thing", Raul answered, a big grin forming on his face. As he was turning towards Ricky, he did a double take. He swore he had seen Grandpa standing in the doorway of the bar. When he looked again, Johnny Deerchaser was walking into the bar. Johnny was unaware of the conversation that had just taken place, but walked up to Raul and hugged him.

"Shooting stars make even the skeptical in life believers. Congratulations from one old warrior to a warrior chief. The great spirits have blessed you with two sons to be proud of you."

For the first time in all the time he had known Raul, Ricky thought he saw a tear in his eye, but far be it for him to comment on that. He hugged Raul and congratulated him. "You need to call Hector and tell him. But then again, knowing you Indians, he probably already knows. Well, I think I'll go up and call my honey. Good night."

George told them he would see them off at the airport, and headed for home. Everyone went to their rooms for a well-deserved night's rest.

Morning came and the meeting room was still active. They were still a bit anxious about the opening day game. The football stadium was packed, as is the case when the Dolphins play and security was as tight as it could be without scaring the fans. Bomb dogs had covered the entire stadium a minimum of three times, and every fan had been checked with detectors and sniffed by the dogs. None of the fans seemed to mind. Since September 11th, people in this country were now used to security precautions. The employees who had been listed on the manpower lists of Don Carlos were absent from the stadium. This was because two were deceased and two were in Federal custody. They were not even missed at the stadium, and kickoff was on time.

Everything had been loaded into the transport by three o'clock and Jonas, Ricky and Raul were going over flight checks with Red Tucker. George drove up and Johnny Deerchaser was in his car with him. They said their goodbyes and the giant Indian handed Raul a copy of the Miami Herald. "Page two has a story you might find amusing. It has to do with just rewards."

On the plane home Raul opened the paper to page two. The story read, "Fish and Game Officer Fired and Institutionalized." The story went on to talk about how Corporal William Gator of Fish and Game had become so stressed from the pressures of his job that he had consumed an excessive amount of whiskey and discharged his weapon for unknown reasons. All this while he was on duty. He had told his superiors that he had been trying to arrest a poacher when the guy's dog started talking to him and expelled gas that made him pass out. He didn't know why he was drunk, or who shot off his gun. He had been discharged from service and sent to South Florida State Hospital for Psychological evaluation. Raul laughed to himself. "Sometimes people *do* get exactly what they deserve. Score one for the Giant Indian Warrior."

CHAPTER VII
THE EMERALD WITCH

If people believe that evil exists amongst mankind, and I believe they do, then that brings up the question, "Do angels walk among us as well?" When evil lashes out at mankind and brings the world around us crashing down, who then sifts through the rubble and stands to defend the good of mankind? I believe these persons to be the Angel's Warriors.

Raul and Angelita had been married six months and twelve days on the night their son was born. Angelita had told Raul upon his arrival from the Miami assignment that she believed marriage was a Western World formality, and since she knew there would never be another woman in Raul's life, marriage was kind of a moot point. Still, Raul felt that because a new son was coming to him, via her, a formal marriage was appropriate.

The wedding was a traditional Navajo Indian wedding, and out of all the people who attended the function, Hector, Raul's older brother, was probably the only person who truly understood the significance of the ceremony. As Angelita had requested, the wedding was at the farm with a few friends and family present. It was, as it should have been, a more than special day. Angelita wore the gown that her cousin Maria had made especially for the occasion. Sewn inside the dress was a label that had made Angelita cry a little when she read it. The label was simply stated. Angelita on her wedding day from Maria. Cousins by birth, sisters in life. She had hugged Maria so tightly that Maria pulled her away and warned her not to hurt their son. They were as close as any sisters had ever been.

Angelita's dress was so special because it was not a typical white, all fluffy expensive wedding dress. It was, however, a white Indian maiden wedding dress, of which Raul had supplied a picture for Maria's seamstress. Raul had been dressed in traditional Navajo attire; buckskin pants with a beaded buckskin shirt. He was the grandson of a Navajo Chief and that had entitled him to wear the Chief's Chest-plate of Beads - a great honor amongst the Indian Nations. Hector, as the older brother, by rights had the first rights to the Chief's formal Indian dress, but Hector had opted to get married wearing a tuxedo in a Baptist Church, located in Annapolis, Maryland. Not very Indian, to say the least, and as a result he had passed his birthrights on to his younger brother, Raul. Hector had, however, brought with him an Elder from the tribe who officiated and performed the wedding ceremony. The newlyweds looked perfect together. Raul at his six feet, muscular build, with his shoulder-length jet black hair and pale blue eyes. Angelita had told him from the day they met that his Navajo complexion and features made him look kind of Colombian, but a little different. 'Special', as she called it.

And Angelita… what could be said of this beauty? Five- feet six inches tall, slender and as beautiful as any woman could be. She had soft features, with coal black hair that traveled to the center of her back, and those lovely, big dark brown eyes. She was three months pregnant at the time, but with barely an outward indication. Her perfect face was radiant as she stood with Raul in the circle of friends, accepting the commitments of a Navajo bride.

June had been a perfect month for the wedding in the mountains of Colombia. The air had a chill, but very acceptable. There was no rain, plenty of sunshine, and all their close friends. Maria and Epi, along with Sarah, had worked frantically to make everything perfect, and they had succeeded. Raul, on the other hand, had spent his time with Ricky and Jonas as well as Hector, upon his arrival, sitting on the front porch discussing the pleasures of life with one another. Raul didn't need any last minute encouragement or assurances that he had made the right choice with Angelita; he already knew it and nothing would ever change his mind. Ed had told them how disappointed he had been for not being able to attend the wedding, but he had been called to Washington to present classes and assist scientists there in the construction of robots. As a result, Ed had taken King and gone to Washington four days before the wedding.

The wedding had gone well and the day had been perfect. That was then. Now it was the night of November 11th, at eleven o'clock. It had been extremely cold in the mountains the past few weeks, even for November. The temperature had descended well into the single digits and some nights even below. There had been hail storms, unlike any in the past. Golf ball-sized hail had struck all over Northern Colombia and thousands of dollars in damage had been reported in Bogota alone. People were hesitant to walk in the streets or stay outside for any length of time because of the storms and how quickly they approached. The weather bureau had been unable to predict the storms because there had been no storm paths to follow or systems to keep in check. The skies would be clear and sunny and all of a sudden the hail started from out of nowhere. This was followed by the sky turning not just dark, but black. Visibility was not even an issue; there just wasn't any. Planes had to be diverted away from El Dorado airport in Bogota and every person in the northern part of the country seemed to have changed their lifestyle to correspond with the possibility of a hail storm. The other very noticeable phenomenon was the extraordinary amount of lighting strikes that had been occurring on a regular basis. Animals had to be sheltered and watched continually because of the amount of dead cows, goats, pigs and other wildlife that had suffered from the strikes. The odor from the rotting corpses was gagging at times. Needless to say, between the instant hail storms and the very dangerous lighting strikes, the people of Northern Colombia had reverted to becoming hermits out of self preservation.

The people prayed and the churches remained open twenty-four hours a day. The churches had taken in as many homeless as they could accommodate, and the government was working continually to get people off the streets. The people of Colombia were asking themselves as well as each other the same question, "Is God mad at us for some reason that we are unaware of?"

The grandfather clock that Raul had bought Angelita shortly after Grandma had died struck midnight. Angelita had been in labor for eleven hours and still the baby, their son, refused to emerge into the world. Angelita had wanted to have the baby at the farm instead of the hospital in Bogota. She had told Raul she wanted a natural childbirth at home and there was no other option. Raul loved this woman more than life itself, and if that is what she wanted, he knew she had a good reason. Raul had asked Ricky to bring the doctor from Bogota to the farm, and he had been more than happy to accommodate him. The doctor was as German-looking as could be. His hair, before turning gray, had been dirty blonde and his eyes were a grayish kind of blue. He was very fair complected and a stocky man, who stood about five feet nine or ten inches and went about one hundred ninety pounds. The doctor's name was Harold Von Richter and he had been Angelita's obstetrician from the day she had gone to Bogota to visit Maria seven and a half months ago. Angelita had commented more than once how funny Spanish sounded coming from the doctor, but given his history it was as natural as could be. The doctor's parents had fled Germany at the end of World War II, as did so many, probably because his father was a German officer and feared reprisal in his home country after the war. Mrs. Von Richter had been pregnant with the doctor when they arrived in Bogota in December of 1945. In March of 1946 the doctor had been born in Bogota, Colombia. As a result of this, the good doctor spoke fluent German as well as fluent Spanish, and to add to his list of accomplishments, he went to medical school in California and had mastered the English language before attending. The doctor would tell you in any of the three languages, 'never judge a book by its cover'. "And right he was," Raul had thought so many times.

Maria and Epi were in the bedroom helping the doctor with this very long delivery. The winds had now started to blow even harder, and thunder and lighting started to appear in the sky. Giant flashes of lightning crossed the sky, and deafening cracks of thunder pounded. "Here comes the hail", Ricky told Raul as they patiently waited together for the baby to be born. Jonas had returned to Switzerland shortly after the wedding, and because of the horrendous weather conditions, had not been able to get back for the baby's birth. Hector had also sent his apologies, as he could not be there, either. "Just you and me", Ricky had told him.

Ricky and Raul patiently waited for any sign of activity in the bedroom. Nothing was happening, so Raul sat down on the sofa and closed his eyes for a moment; after all, he had been awake a whole lot of hours, just waiting. He was physically and mentally exhausted, and the soft couch felt so relaxing.

He felt himself drifting into a deep sleep when all of a sudden the front door of the house flew open and there was a little old man standing in the doorway. The old man was only about four feet high and looked to be every bit of a hundred years old. He was dressed in rags and his skin drooped and hung on his weathered skeleton-like frame. His head was abnormally thin and he had only a whisp of gray hair left on it. His eyes were probably the eeriest part of the encounter. They looked red and seemed to glow. "I'm looking for the blue-eyed Indian", he said.

Raul and Ricky both stared at the man in disbelief. "How did you get in here?" Ricky asked. "How did you get past security? This is impossible - the cameras, guards, sensors...."

Raul looked at Ricky and then at the little man. "Why have you come here tonight, and who sent you?" Raul demanded.

The little old man did not respond and Ricky moved toward him. Before Raul could stop Ricky's advance, the little old man put up his right hand with the palm facing outward. Ricky flew backward against the wall and was knocked unconscious.

"I did not come here to hurt you. You know that, don't you?" the old man asked.

"I do", Raul responded. "The persons responsible for the storms sent you, didn't they?"

"She did, and you must listen to her before it is too late."

"Her?" Raul repeated. "Listen to *her*, you said. It is a woman who has caused all this havoc?"

"She wants your son. She believes your son is her son and you must give him to her. If you don't, she has vowed to destroy Colombia. And she will. She is very powerful and you can't fight her. She destroys or takes anything or anybody she wants. Humans are helpless to resist her. You have never fought a power such as this one. Surrender and give her what she wants. I beg you, for the people, I am your friend, and I can help you."

"You still haven't told me her name or where I can find her; and why should I trust you, anyway?"

"She is the Emerald Witch and she will find you; you cannot go to her. Her army would crush you. They are not like soldiers you have fought in the past."

"Does this Emerald Witch have a name?" Raul asked.

"Of course, her name is Marivela Paquade, but that will do you no good. She can be whatever or whoever she wants to be. What is a name?"

"Well, first of all, let me just say that my son is not even born yet, and after he is I am damn sure not giving him to some old battle-axe that thinks she is a witch. And by the way, what is your job? I mean, besides coming out on nasty nights to make absurd requests and give ridiculous warnings for this woman, what do you do?"

"I serve at her request, and when she wants me, she calls me."

"She calls you from where? I mean, where do you live, close to her?" Raul questioned.

"You are quite the detective, I see. Well, let me tell you this, so you will have something to ponder while you are giving the witch what she wants. I reside in Chiquinquira on a small hilltop named Mount Christian."

"I know that area. What are you, a wise-ass or something? Mount Christian is a big cemetery. Nobody lives there, not even the caretakers. The rumor is that it's too scary up there and nobody goes there, especially after sunset. Folklore is that the dead wander aimlessly at night on that mountain. So you figure you can come here, however you got in, and tell me this bullshit about living on Mount Christian and I will be scared enough to do whatever you say. It's time for you to leave before you get hurt."

"I will leave at her request, and as for hurting me, you can no longer do that. I have been hurt in the past, long ago but never again by a mortal. The Witch Paquade's son will be here in seven minutes, at exactly the stroke of twelve thirty. That is when I must take him."

"That may be what you think, but that's not going to happen. Besides, I'm done listening to you and all your bullshit". Raul moved towards the little man in the doorway, and as he did he felt a pressure in his chest like he had never felt before. It was as though a gigantic horse had kicked him. He, like Ricky, flew backwards against the wall. But unlike Ricky, who was still unconscious, Raul had remained conscious. Raul was trying to stand up but couldn't move his legs. He was sitting in a prone position with his legs spread open in front of him. He could see them, he just couldn't move them. There were now three minutes before the minute hand would cross over the six and strike twelve thirty. "What am I going to do?" Raul thought. "I can't just sit here and watch this - whatever *it is* - take my new son".

"If only a great warrior was here to help", Raul said out loud, almost conceding to himself that he had failed. In that instant Raul couldn't believe his eyes. He truly believed he was hallucinating. He watched as a golden arrow head emerged from the chest of the little old man in the doorway. The little man's red eyes started flashing like a traffic light on red caution. As Raul was staring at the shape in the door it started to dissipate. The little old man was literally falling to pieces, but the pieces were disappearing before his eyes. It took exactly three minutes for whatever it was in the doorway to vanish. Raul knew it because the clock struck twelve thirty and he could hear his new son crying. Miguel Marques Lightfoot was finally here. As the feeling in Raul's legs returned and he was starting to get off the floor, he saw the most peculiar thing through the open door way.

Just past the porch in the front yard was a paint pony with an Indian Warrior sitting atop of it. The Indian was wearing a full dress war bonnet and a loin cloth. He was holding a golden bow and a quiver full of golden arrows. Stuck in the ground next to the horse was a golden lance with three war feathers tied to it. The Indian was wearing a War Chief's Breastplate of colored beads and, most shocking of all, were the pale blue eyes that watched him as he approached. Raul was just staring at the Indian, trying to understand if what he was seeing was real or a figment of his imagination. The Indian then spoke in the Navajo language. He told Raul to accept the bow and arrows and carry the lance as well. He must fight this witch to the death. He also told him something very strange, something he had heard from Grandpa. "Protect this woman and your son; they are very important to the Navajo people. You must, as I know you will, defend them with your life."

As Raul was standing in the front yard he suddenly realized two things. First, when the clock struck and his son was born, the storm stopped. It was now calm and the sky was full of stars. Secondly, as he was looking at the War Chief, it dawned on him that this was the War Chief in the picture he had been given. This was the Great Navajo War Chief 'Lightfoot'. He still looked as he did in 1868 when the picture had been taken.

Raul felt humbled by the presence of this Chief and promised, "I will fight to the death, this demon witch, but I ask that the great spirits of the Navajo past help me in this battle that I will face."

"You are truly the Chief I believed you to be," the warrior on the horse said to Raul. "My powers are yours and the Navajo that is in you, is with you. Trust yourself and no one else. This foe has trickery that mankind has not seen." With that, the horse turned and the Indian rode slowly out of the farm and disappeared.

When Raul re-entered the house Ricky was standing at the door to the bedroom waiting for the women to come out with the baby, or let them in, or whatever. He was excited. "Oh, there you are! I thought you went to take a leak or something!"

Ricky had no recollection of what had happened, Raul thought. He also thought that was good because he had to fight this one alone, and he knew if Ricky thought for a minute that he needed help, he would be right there. He didn't want to get Ricky killed, so this was best. It was also good that Ricky was so excited that he never noticed Raul bring in the bow, arrows and lance and put them in the closet. The less anyone knew, the better.

Finally the door opened and there was Angelita, lying on the bed and holding the baby. The baby was healthy and had come out screaming. He weighed eight pounds, nine ounces, had jet black hair already, and as far as anyone could see, was another clone of Raul's. The other very noticeable feature was his pale blue eyes, just like his father's.

As Raul looked into the room at Angelita where she was holding the baby, he noticed that there was a radiant light emanating from Angelita, as well as her new son. It looked light sunlight coming through the window and bouncing off of them. "But that's impossible, it's twelve-thirty in the morning", Raul thought.

Angelita saw Raul frozen in the doorway and motioned for him to come in. She hugged and kissed him, and showed him Miguel Marques Lightfoot. "I want to introduce you to the Navajo Ghost Warrior", she said proudly with a smile.

Raul's emotions were at an all-time high; this was his other son and he was so proud. He bent over and whispered to his newest son. "Rest easy, little warrior, nothing will harm you. I promise."

Angelita didn't even look up at Raul when he said that. He knew that she already knew what had happened. Everyone else had left the room, and Angelita looked up at Raul with those beautiful eyes and said, "You must kill her, or we, as well as many other people, will suffer from her hand. She is the most evil of all witches and thrives on the plight of others. She is in the Muzo Valley and has called to our son twice before his birth. The Muzo Valley was a beautiful place once long ago. Now it is desolate and nothing survives. The only thing that lives there is her army of evil. No birds sing there nor butterflies live there. It is a valley of death dominated by this evil witch. The forests are black in this area and nothing is what it seems.

Raul asked her if she knew what had happened before the baby was born, and of course she did. She told him that the Warrior had given him the weapons to fight this evil being and that there was one last thing he needed. She reached under the pillow on the bed and handed him a golden dagger. The most amazing thing about the dagger was the handle. Imbedded into it was a picture of their son. "How could you have possibly put a picture of Miguel on the handle of this knife?" he asked.

"I didn't. Before I went into labor an angel appeared in my room and handed it to me. I accepted it, but I had no idea what it meant until she told me that this dagger must pierce the heart of the wicked witch, Marivela Paquade. While I was in labor I saw very clearly what had happened to you and Ricky."

"Ricky has no recollection of what happened out there, and it's best not to tell him, don't you think?"

"I agree. When must you leave for the abandoned mines?" she asked.

I'm going to pack some things, see if I can get Ed to part with King, and then I'll be off. Best guess would be an hour or two. I am most concerned about protecting you and the baby. My problem is that I'm not really sure quite how."

Angelita smiled and touched Raul's cheek. "Go and fight the evil. Don't worry about Miguel and me; we have our own protection."

"What are you talking about, your own protection?" Raul asked.

"She will protect us." Angelita was looking past Raul towards the window.

Raul turned and jumped. Angelita put her hand on his chest and immediately calmed him. He needed to be, for what he saw. At the window was a beautiful woman, dressed in white with huge white wings. Looking at her, Raul sensed she was the purist thing he had ever seen. The angel had waist-length blonde hair and crystal blue eyes with a soft white complexion. She had a jeweled crown on her head and was holding a jeweled handled golden sword. The sword was in her left hand facing downward, and her right hand was out stretched with her palm up. Raul was hesitant to believe what he thought he heard the angel speak. He could have sworn she smiled at him and said, "Godspeed, and may He be with you." He looked back at Angelita and then back towards the window. The angel was gone. When he turned back to Angelita again, she smiled. "We are safe, so don't worry. Go and slay the beast; we will be here anxiously awaiting your return."

As he was leaving the bedroom, Raul stopped and turned back towards Angelita and asked, puzzled, "Do you have any idea why this witch wants our baby? I mean, out of all the babies in the world, why did she decide to screw with us?"

"It's a bit hard to explain, but I'll try. The witch doesn't really want Miguel. What she wants is Miguel's spirit. You see, Miguel is very special because he carries the eternal flame of goodness in his spirit. Miguel will do great things in his very long life, and this disturbs the forces of evil, which are represented by this witch, if that makes any sense. The evil Witch Marivela Paquade is also known as the Emerald Witch, because she lives with her army in the abandoned emerald mines. Legend has it that this woman was a child, playing in the mines about one hundred years ago. It seems that while her parents were working in the mines they neglected to pay attention to what she was doing and she fell from a ledge into a hole into the earth. The hole was very deep and the little girl's body was never recovered. Many workers claimed to have seen the little girl during the following years but nobody ever touched her or talked to her. As the years passed, the mine closed, but people have sworn over the years that they continued to see Marivela walking in the mountains and in the forests around the mines. And now, people swear she is over a hundred years old. She has cast spells on people and supposedly raised the dead from their graves and brought them into her army. The people of the Muzo are scared to death of her, and swear she is true evil. Be very careful of her, my love; she changes form at will and can be anything or anyone she wants to be. Her cunning trickery is unsurpassed by anything we know. She is now so old and dying, so she believes that Miguel's spirit will rejuvenate her. Raul, you must stop this woman before she can spread her evil and infect more lives."

Raul was staring at the lovely mother of his newest son without a reply. Finally he spoke... "Angelita, why do you know so much about this evil power? Who told you all of this and why have I never heard of her before today?"

Angelita smiled as she cradled Miguel. "Raul, my love, I know what I know because it is time for me to know. The angel told me this. You have never heard of her before now because there was no need. But now you must destroy this creature. The angels have also told me this."

"They didn't, by chance, drop any hints as to how I am supposed to kill it, did they?" he asked, with a hint of sarcasm.

"You must pierce its heart with the dagger in your hand. The angels will be with you, and we will help you. You will have the strength of the Heavens with you, but you must never surrender your faith; that is of the utmost importance."

Raul couldn't help but notice that as Angelita spoke, the radiant light that had surrounded her and the baby earlier had returned even stronger. He did not miss something she had just said. "The angels will be with you, and WE will help you."

"What did she mean by WE?" Raul thought to himself. "I know this woman is special to *me*, but is it possible that she is special to the world as well? Could it be that his Angelita is an angel in disguise?" He didn't want to even think about that at this time. He looked down at his right hand and realized he was holding the dagger with his son's image facing his heart. He kissed his wife and newborn son, and headed towards the door.

He went to the closet and gathered the bow, quiver and lance. He put them carefully into the Hummer along with his crossbow and some other equipment. After that, he went through the bedroom and into the tunnel to the bunker. At the wall, he looked into the hole which was there and his eye was scanned. The wall slid open and he was granted access. Ed was working at his desk when Raul approached. "Off on another quest?" he asked as soon as he noticed Raul. Raul smiled and Ed opened the door to a large cabinet and King came out. Ed handed Raul the special watch and three pens. "These pens each fire a rocket. Each rocket will take out an area the size of this bunker. So here are three pens, that's forty five thousand square feet of pure destruction. I trust that will make your day complete."

Raul smiled and went with King over to Sarah's desk. Sarah looked up. "Raul, I have something for you, just a minute". She opened a desk drawer and took out a five inch- long silver tube, about a half inch in diameter. "This is a special laser light. If you shine this into the eyes of anything, it will be temporarily blinded and give you time to get close enough to kill them."

"How long is it good for? I mean, how many shots do I get with this?" Raul asked.

"It has a seven minute battery life, but you can recharge it in the Hummer with this adapter."

"Anything else I need before King and I take off?" Raul questioned.

"Take this container and don't lose it. The tablets in it are very important. Carry the container around your neck with the attached chain."

"And what is this?"

"This witch will use everything she has against you. When she blows violet dust at you and you breathe it, take a capsule immediately. The dust is designed to make you hallucinate and the capsules in the container will void that reaction. Here is your transmitter and phone. I don't think they will work in that area, but take them anyway. Raul, be careful, she is very dangerous. Good luck and keep in touch, if you can."

Raul left the bunker thinking to himself, "This was the most unusual send-off I have ever gotten from these people. And how did they even know where I was going or what the mission was? I spoke with Angelita and went straight to the bunker, and they already knew. This is so fucked up I don't even want to ask. I'm out of here."

Raul didn't see Ricky or Epi anywhere, and so he and King got into the Hummer and drove away from the farm, headed for Muzo in the Department of Boyaca. The sky was unusually dark, even for three thirty in the morning, he thought. The one good thing he could see was that the storms seemed to have subsided, at least for the moment. Off in a distance he could see lighting flashing in the sky. It was like fire bolts shooting from one side of the sky to the other. "That's funny", he said to King, who he had activated to respond to questions and was sitting on the front seat next to him. "All this lightning and not a single crash of thunder. No rain or hail either. What do you think of this weather system, does it suck or what?"

King was panting and moving his head back and forth like he was searching for something. "You know, boss, I think if you look really close at that sky you will see that nature's storm path is a little off course right now."

"What the hell are you talking about, and where did this 'boss' stuff come from?", Raul asked as he looked at King.

"Master Ed programmed a more extensive dialog into my computer bank last week, and he told me 'boss' was a correct response when addressing you. Am I correct?"

"Sure, sure. Whatever floats your boat, I don't care. What about the storm path?"

"Boss, I don't have a boat, and if I did why would I float it now? Secondly, the storm is occurring all around us but not on us. Haven't you noticed?"

Raul hit the brakes and stopped the Hummer. "Don't take everything so literally, OK? And try to pay attention!". Then to himself, Raul muttered, "What the hell is wrong with me? I'm arguing with a robot, for Christ's sake. Get a grip on yourself!"

King was just watching Raul and shaking his head slowly. Finally he said, "Boss, get out of the vehicle and look around us, and tell me if you have ever seen a storm like this before."

Raul got out and looked at the sky. He couldn't believe what he was seeing. The lighting and the hail was striking the ground all around him. Golf ball-sized hail was hitting the ground and the trees, as well as bouncing off the nearby houses. "What the hell is going on here?" he said out loud. "This can't be right; the storm is all over the area except for where I am. How can that be?"

Just as he finished asking himself all these questions that he knew he couldn't answer, a face appeared in the sky above him. It was like a hole opened up in the sky and bright, warm sunlight came pouring through. He looked at the face closer and saw it was the same angel that he had seen in the bedroom. She was smiling at him and told him to proceed on with his task and not to think about the storms, as they wouldn't affect him. "You are a warrior of the heavens now and the heavens will guide you", the angel told him. Her face disappeared, but the warm sunlight remained. It was November 12 in the mountains of Northern Colombia, and it had to be eighty degrees where Raul and King stood.

Raul looked at King, who was just sitting on the front seat pretending not to notice anything. "Well, what do you think of that, Mr. 'smartest dog I have ever talked to'?"

"Like I have heard you say so many times before - this is really fucked up. But how do you argue with an angel? Guess we just need to get on down the road and see what happens."

"Where do you come up with that crap? I am going to have to have a serious conversation with Ed when we get back."

"That would be assuming we get back, if I'm not mistaken", King answered, looking at the roadway ahead of them.

Raul just stared at King for a moment and then got back into the Hummer. "Try not to be so damn optimistic, you're getting me all teary-eyed."

"I'm afraid my computer bank doesn't understand what you just said. Could you explain that in a more definitive manner?" King responded.

"Good, see you're not so smart after all are you, Mr. 'I'm The Smartest Robot Dog In The World'."

King turned towards Raul and made a whining sound. "Ouch, that hurt every bit as much as a fried diode in my computer bank."

The both stared straight out the front windshield as they drove towards Chiquinquira. For some reason, when Raul and King arrived in Chiquinquira there were no storms or lightning. It was now about seven thirty in the morning and it actually looked very nice outside. Raul stepped out of the Hummer and felt the warm sun already shining brightly in the sky. The air was chilly, about fifty degrees, but it was nice. No storms, no hail, just sunlight. Raul got back into the Hummer and drove to a gas station that had just opened for the day.

"Good morning", Raul greeted the attendant with a smile. "Could you fill the truck up with high test for me, please?" And the attendant smiled back and nodded in compliance. The attendant was about sixteen years old and couldn't stop staring at the Hummer.

"Sir, please, could you tell me what kind of vehicle this is? I have never seen such a truck in my life. Is it from America?"

Raul chuckled and told the boy what the truck was and that yes, it was from the United States. The boy wanted to see inside the Hummer, and Raul knew it. But King was sitting on the front seat, taking up most of it, and the fact that the boy was very apprehensive about talking to Raul any further kept him from asking.

Raul saw this as a good opportunity to make a new friend and maybe find out a thing or two about Muzo. "Nice day today, isn't it? Looks like maybe the storms are done for a while?" No response from the boy. Raul thought for a few seconds and then said, "Listen, if I raise the hood could you check my oil and water? I don't want to get all greasy."

"Absolutely, sir. Let me do that right now."

"OK, this was working", Raul thought, "the boy has a big interest in the truck. Let's work that." Raul popped the hood and the boy climbed up into the engine compartment. The boy's eyes were the size of half dollars. He was obviously excited to see the engine of the Hummer. As the boy touched things, the computer in the dash turned itself on and announced that foreign objects were under the hood of the vehicle and there was a danger of vandalism or sabotage. The boy hadn't heard the computer talking, and Raul turned it off before he did. As the boy was securing the hood, Raul asked him if he wanted to see inside the car. The boy hesitated. King obviously scared him and Raul spotted that quickly. "King, shake hands with the boy! Show him you are harmless". King shook hands and panted, and the boy was satisfied he was safe in the car with the big dog. The boy sat in the truck, in awe of its dashboard and interior. After a few minutes, the Hummer's special fifty-gallon gas tank was full and the gas nozzle clicked off. The boy jumped out of the truck and went to the rear.

He hung up the handle and took the money Raul was already handing him.

"I'll be right back with your change, sir", the boy said as he started to hurry away.

"Hold up a minute!", Raul shouted to him. "Listen, can you tell me where a good restaurant is in this town, and also how far it is to Muzo?"

"Nellie's is the best restaurant and it opened the same time as we did. It's just one mile straight ahead on the right. You can park in front so you can watch the truck. I'm sure many people have already noticed it, and believe me, they are not all nice people. If I were you I would leave the dog inside. He is so big that maybe the thieves would think twice about trying to break into it."

"Thanks, I appreciate the information. And how far did you say Muzo was from here?" Raul asked.

"I didn't sir, and that is because Muzo is not for tourists. It is for miners. The town is very rough, and outside the town is even scarier", the boy responded.

"I thought I would go there and look for Emeralds. Isn't that where they are?"

"There used to be a lot of Emeralds in that area, but not so much anymore. There is much more trouble there than there are Emeralds. Believe me, if you go there, you will probably not come back. Many people never come back from there."

"Why is that? Are there a lot of guerillas and paramilitary there, or what? Or is it just bandits?" Raul continued questioning.

"The guerillas and the paramilitary don't even go to that place. Bandits, there are bandits all over Colombia, but that is not why the people never return. The reason people get lost in that area is Marivela Paquade." The boy seemed to actually shudder as he said the name.

"Is there something special about this Paquade woman, or what?" Raul asked as innocently as he could, pretending not to already know the answer.

"I can't even talk about her, sir. If she hears me she will take my soul-to-be in her army of the dead." The boy then quickly turned away and ran into the office to get the change.

An older man came out of the office with Raul's change and said he was the boy's father. He asked Raul why the boy was so scared and what Raul had said to him. Raul told the man to give the change to the boy and that all he had done was ask the boy for directions to Muzo and the mines in the forest.

The man turned white as a ghost and said in a pleading tone, "Please, sir, change your mind and don't go to that place! That place in the forest is evil and if Marivela Paquade catches you there she will claim your soul, because if you are determined to go to that place you won't need it any longer. We will pray for your spirit." The man returned to the office, never looking back at Raul.

Raul looked at King as he got in the Hummer. "Well, after a chat like that I certainly need breakfast, don't you agree?"

"Absolutely, Mr. Navajo Ghost Warrior," King replied as he laughed.

"Very cute. Did that come from the 'I can be an asshole' program that Ed must have installed in you?"

King looked like he was smiling and answered, "Paybacks are a bitch, aren't they, boss?"

"I don't know", snarled Raul. "Let me check into my 'go fuck yourself' program. Yes, there it is, go fuck yourself."

"As smart as you are, you must realize that that is a very stupid saying. You do know that fucking yourself is physiologically impossible, don't you?" King replied.

"No shit, Sherlock, nobody's getting anything past you today, are they?" Raul smiled.

"Absolutely not, my dear Watson; absolutely not."

Raul thought this dog was just too incredible. He smiled at King and blew him a kiss.

All the spaces directly in front of the restaurant were occupied. There were two farm trucks and seven bicycles. The only spot Raul could find to park the Hummer was behind the restaurant, off the roadway. "Well, this will have to do", he thought as he set the knock-out alarm system. He left King activated, sitting on the front seat, and went inside.

As he sat at a table, he could smell the beans and onions cooking. He ordered his favorite dish of beans and rice with two sunny-side up eggs on top. The waitress brought him a cup of what he thought was the best coffee he had ever tasted. He asked her where they got their coffee from, and she just smiled and told him that the cook has a little farm outside of town and he grows his own coffee beans. The waitress seemed a bit more talkative than the boy in the gas station, probably because she was a bit older and didn't scare as easily. She introduced herself as Catherine, and when Raul made a crack about her looking like a teenager, she smiled, leaned over and hugged his shoulders. She told him how sweet he was, but that she was really way past that on her last birthday. She did, however, feel like a teenager. "She must rake in the big tips", Raul thought. "Great personality and really knows how to make people feel like tipping big." As he was waiting for his breakfast he couldn't help but notice how strikingly pretty the waitress was. She stood about five feet five inches, probably went about one hundred and twenty pounds. She had a knock-out shape, complimented by her shoulder-length chestnut brown hair and her soft looking pale skin. She definitely didn't belong here. She was Anglo all the way. When she brought his meal she smiled at him. She had a perfectly shaped mouth with beautiful white teeth. The only strange thing that really jumped out was her eyes. One was medium brown and the other was dark blue. Raul had heard of that kind of genetic trait, but had never seen it before. Raul was staring at her and she looked back and asked, "What's wrong, don't you like your breakfast?"

"I don't know, I haven't tried it yet, but it looks delicious. I have to ask you something, if it's not too personal…"

"Go ahead, what can you ask me that a hundred other guys haven't asked before you?" she replied with a smile.

"Let me say this first. You have got to be the prettiest woman in this town, and so far you win the prize for personality. That said, why are you working as a waitress in a restaurant in this town? I guess what I mean is, you could be on the cover of a magazine and live in a fancy apartment in Bogota, if you wanted. I noticed you don't have a ring on your finger so I'm assuming you're single. What could possibly hold you here?"

She stared back at Raul, thinking for a moment. "Catherine had a husband once; he was a miner in the Emerald mines at Muzo. I don't know if you believe in witches or not, but she took Catherine's husband. Not him, just his soul. He is up there in the mines, but it's not *really* him, if you understand. As for the restaurant, she owns it. Her grandmother was Nellie and she left it to her mother. When she passed, Catherine got it. So now you know Catherine's life. I hope it didn't scare you too much."

"Can I ask you what witch you are talking about, and why you are talking about yourself in the third person?"

"It's no secret. It's the only witch we have. Marivela Paquade, The Emerald Witch. I don't want to sound too bitter, but that bitch - and I didn't say 'witch' that time - has screwed up so many lives between here and Muzo, everybody has lost count. Now, about the third person thing.... Not everything you see is really what it is. Understand?"

"Not at all. But why don't the people here do something about her? They can't all be afraid. You don't seem to be afraid. Fight her."

"It's not that simple - I wish it were. But there is hope if the priest is right about what he said that God told him yesterday."

"You have a witch and a priest who talks directly to God. This is quite the town, isn't it?"

"You can be skeptical if you wish, but look outside for a moment. You see how beautiful it is out there?"

"It does look pretty nice, doesn't it?" Raul answered as he turned to look out the window.

"The priest told us yesterday that God told him that on the hour the baby angel was born, the weather would clear up and return to normal. Well, he told us that at eight thirty last night, and sure enough, at twelve thirty last night on November twelfth, the weather cleared up."

"So where is this baby angel?" Raul asked, somewhat hesitantly.

"Nobody here knows that, and that is because he has to be protected from that nasty witch. She wants his soul, especially. But we do know one thing for sure."

"And that would be……..?

"The priest also told us that the angels were going to send their warrior to kill the witch. You see, the baby angel's mother is an angel who lives on earth. Do you believe that angels live with us here on earth?"

"I suppose anything is possible. Sure, I believe that", Raul answered, making every attempt to conceal any hint of emotion.

"I know you do, and I, we, the people in this town, believe strongly that the warrior is already here in the town. He arrived this morning, because Mr. Diaz, the man that owns the gas station, told everyone."

"Let me guess. He talks to God as well, and passes it on to the townspeople."

"No…. he put gas in the warrior's black, very strange, truck. One like no one here has ever seen. He said the man has a giant German Shepherd dog with him."

Before Raul could even respond to Catherine's conversation, the cook came running from the back of the restaurant where the kitchen was located. "Cathy, come quick! There is a black truck behind the building! Pablo, the local thief, tried to get into it and the car knocked him out! I swear the car is magical!"

Everyone in the restaurant ran to the kitchen to see what had happened. Everyone except Catherine. She stayed at Raul's table while he nonchalantly ate his breakfast.

"You cannot drive all the way to the mines where Marivela Paquade is, but you can come very close if you go the back way." She spoke softly. "I can and will show you this route. Do not trust any other person who looks like me when you get to the forest. You must remember this."

"And how will I know the difference?" Raul asked, turning his right palm up in a motion of questioning.

"Look into my eyes. I know you have noticed the color difference, but look deeper."

Raul stared into her eyes and almost fell off of his chair. The brown eye showed Angelita's face and the blue eye showed Miguel's face. The images were perfect. Raul sat there in a state of mild shock. "You're not really from around here, are you?" he asked.

Catherine smiled. "The Emerald Witch does not know what Miguel looks like because one of your ancestors killed her messenger. Only the angels know, and when you look into my eyes and you see him, know that this is the baby angel. Marivela Paquade can't duplicate his face. In five minutes the real Catherine will come to your table. This is the Catherine who everyone but you has seen this morning. When you leave, I will be waiting in your Hummer with King."

Raul did a double take when the other Catherine appeared. She fit in this town, all two hundred and ten pounds of her. Nothing more had to be said. Raul paid the bill and left a hefty tip, which brought a smile to the lips of the real Catherine. He noticed that the smile displayed two empty spaces where teeth had once been.

"Ok, out to the car to fight the witch. At least I have an angel keeping me company. At least I *think* she's an angel. Maybe I won't think about it at all", he said to himself as he walked around back to the Hummer. Next to King, inside the Hummer was sitting the beautiful angel. On the ground, knocked out, was Pablo. Raul moved him aside and got into the truck.

As he turned the key, Ed's voice came on inside the car. "I activated the alarm on one attempted intrusion. Subject should be lying outside the vehicle and the local police have been notified. I would also like to add that interior radar has sensed another being in the vehicle, but strangely enough I cannot detect another warm body. As a result I would advise you to keep on the lookout for something."

"This is quite the car you have here. It talks, knocks out intruders, and heaven knows what else it can do."

"I'm positively sure that heaven knows, along with any representatives that may be here at present", Raul said dryly, looking straight out the windshield as they drove onto the street.

King was sitting between them, looking back and forth at each of them. "Boss, do you think Angelita has any idea that you have picked up such a looker?"

"King, try to show a little couth and some indication of manners. And to answer your question, you can bet your robotic ass she knows Catherine is with us."

"Nice company", King replied. "So listen, sweetheart, you here for the whole trip or just a ride down the street?"

Catherine smiled at King and answered. "Be careful, if you think those thoughts you are thinking, I may have to have a thought or two and they may fry your stimulate board."

"Check!" King said. "I'm just the family pet along for the ride. Oh, and that pet part can be taken literally, if you so desire."

Raul was shaking his head. "King, give it a rest." And as they were driving towards Muzo, Catherine was scratching the top of Kings head, right between his ears. She was smiling as she looked out the windshield and King was panting and started that dog drool thing Ed had installed.

As the three of them drove out of the city towards Muzo they noticed the people start to change. They went from normal-acting people to strange, and, in some cases, very strange. Raul asked Catherine if she had noticed the same thing, and she had. She told them that many of the people he was seeing were really inhabitants of Mount Christian and they were just wandering the earth as lost souls.

"What you are telling me is that these are 'zombies'? I'm a bit confused. I thought zombies only came out at night. This is nine-thirty in the morning", Raul responded.

Catherine looked at the poor creatures and then said, "I'm afraid that you, like too many Americans, watch too much television. You see, in real life, a soulless creature can't determine anything, especially what time it is. These poor soulless creatures are simply wandering at the beckon call of an evil being. In this case it happens to be Marivela Paquade."

"So what do we do about them? I mean, are they a threat to us? Do we have to kill them, or what?" Raul asked.

"First of all, they are already dead, so killing them is a bit redundant. To stop the creature from attacking, we can do various things to put them in a state of limbo. You see, until you destroy the evil witch, these poor creatures can't reclaim their souls and move on to the other world. So your options are: first, you can shoot them with the golden arrows. That stops them as long as the arrow is in them. Second, we can set them ablaze. They can't recuperate from that. Third and final is cut their heads off. As long as they can't find it they can't re-attach it. Oh! And before I forget, if you shoot them with the bow, hit them in the heart or where the heart used to be…that's important."

"These are the options I get from an angel!", Raul stated in near disbelief. "Anybody ever piss you off when you weren't an angel? Oh… and before I forget, what if I run out of arrows? And what the hell are you going to be doing while I'm fighting these 'already dead' things?"

"To answer your first question, you won't run out of arrows, and the answer to your second question is, I'm not allowed to fight, I'm here in a supply and logistics capacity. The fight is you and the dog against them. But I will do everything I can within my power to help in my own way."

"So I do all the fighting and you supply me with arrows. And I also have to watch out for your a… I mean, backside."

"Raul, let's get this out of the way right now. First of all, my ass is not your concern. Secondly, I died one hundred and thirty seven years ago, your time. The difference is that I died a happy soul and took it with me, unlike these creatures. But if you do your job, many of these poor creatures will become angels because you will have restored their souls to them. That's a lot of points for you with the big guy. So, ask me the question you look like you want to ask, and then get your ass in gear."

"Right... my question. Oh yeah. You're an angel, so what are you doing swearing? I thought you had some kind of holy standards or something?"

"Grow up and get with the program. And don't worry about my standards or anything else about me. These 'zombies', as you call them, are the least of your problems. They are here mainly to scare people away. When you get close to the witch you are going to see problems, and I mean *big* problems. So get your head together and be ready for anything. Got it, soldier?"

Raul acknowledged what she had said and looked toward where she was sitting. To his astonishment, she had vanished. King was looking back at him, but Catherine was nowhere to be seen. "Oh, this is great", he said to King. "We are somewhere on the back road to Muzo, we don't know for sure exactly where, and the angel books." Raul hit the brakes on the Hummer as the road abruptly ended. He looked out the windshield and couldn't believe his eyes. There in front of him was a Paint Stallion, the identical horse Chief Lightfoot had sat upon when he gave Raul the weapons. Raul and King got out of the Hummer and the horse walked over to them. The horse was wearing Navajo war paint and an Indian blanket on its back. He also noticed something else, hanging next to the horse's main. It was the jeweled sword the angel in the bedroom with Angelita had held. It was in a leather case that looked to be maybe a hundred and fifty years old. It appeared as though it had been made by an Indian Maiden for her warrior. He recognized the Navajo markings on it as well. He looked into the horse's eyes, and didn't know why, but he started a conversation with the large animal. He asked the horse if it talked, if maybe it was another angel, or if there was anything about it he should know. His apparent trance was broken by King, who walked over to him and pushed him with his body. "Hey, snap out of it, boss! You look really stupid talking to a horse. That's not Mr. Ed, you know."

Raul was just staring at King. This dog was becoming more real every day. "This is impossible", he thought to himself. Raul hung the lance, bow and quiver on the horse. He was holding the cross bow as he jumped on the back the horse. Raul couldn't help but notice that as the morning progressed, the temperature was climbing rapidly. It was eleven o' clock in the morning and it was already every bit of eighty degrees. The air was dry and the sun was steadily getting hotter as it beat down on Raul's neck. By now Raul was wearing only his jeans, a strap t-shirt and jungle boots. The golden dagger with the picture of his baby son on the handle was tucked securely in the belt of his equipment bag, which was strapped tightly around his waist. As he rode the Paint horse through the forest, King followed behind, watching everything from the ground level. Raul had taken his cell phone out of the bag as they rode, and tried to contact Sarah to let them know he had reached his destination. He looked at the screen on the phone. 'No signal'. "I thought that wasn't supposed to happen, with this fancy system they installed", he said out loud. King heard what Raul said and responded.

"Remember, nothing grows, lives or works in this God-forsaken place. Take a look around if you don't believe me."

He did just that and discovered that what King had just told him was as true as it could be. The trees appeared dead and the ground looked as though it had suffered the trauma of volcanic erosion. It was all charred black, with no grass or leaves. Nothing green was living in this forest. He also noticed that there were no birds singing or small animal life of any sort. "What kind of a place is this shit hole?" he asked King.

"Don't know for sure, boss, but maybe this is what a bad death looks like on the other side."

"Bad death, as opposed to a good death? I was under the impression until today there was no such thing as a good death or bad death. Dead is dead, what else can you say?"

"You don't really have to say anything. Just look around this 'shit hole', as you call it."

As they moved further into the forest, Raul had the feeling they were being watched. He asked King to check his sensor and see if he could feel a presence. King responded with a negative. He did, however, tell Raul that even though there was no body warmth in the area, his sensor was picking up movement of some sort on their right side.

It took about five minutes more until a giant being stepped from the trees into the roadway. This thing in front of them was at minimum eight feet tall, and probably weighed five hundred pounds. It was unshaven, really ugly and didn't look like it had an ounce of body fat on it, just muscle. Raul totally ruled out any kind of physical altercation with this thing, and had decided to shoot it when he did a double take on the face. After a second look, Raul discovered that this thing was a Cyclops, having just one eye in the center of its forehead. It stood in the roadway, but made no aggressive moves towards Raul or King. Raul noticed it had only a club in its hands. The club was the size of a small tree, and in the hand of a giant of that size it could wield a lot of damage to a recipient. "Well, what's it going to be?" Raul asked the creature. No response. "Now what?" he thought. He then commanded the dog, "King, walk towards it and let's see what its intentions are!"

King looked at Raul as he walked by. "Thanks a lot for this assignment. If he hits me with that club in the right place, he will totally destroy my circuit boards and that will sure teach you, won't it?"

"Will you shut up and stop whining? He won't get a chance to hit you, I promise!", Raul yelled to King as he passed.

King was mumbling, and Raul couldn't believe what this dog had started to do and say recently. King looked back at Raul and said in a low voice, "easy for you to say."

Raul was busy watching the one-eyed giant while he loaded a Golden arrow into the cross bow. King walked up to the giant and stayed just clear of a swing with the club. King barked but did not growl or show aggression. They needed to see what this thing wanted. The giant just stood motionless, watching King. Finally King sat down and started panting. The giant slowly reached behind his back and withdrew something. Raul couldn't see what it was, so he raised the cross bow and aimed it at the giant Cyclops. It paid no attention to Raul, opened a canteen of water and poured some into his hand. He extended his hand towards King. "Nice doggy, I won't hurt you, I promise", said the giant, in a most friendly tone. "I would love to have a friend like you, but no one wants to be friends with something as big and ugly as I am. Do you want to be my friend?"

Raul had not taken his eyes off the creature and still didn't trust him. "What's your name and what do you want?"

"My name is Samuel, and I'm stuck in purgatory. Why I am here, I have no idea, other than an hour ago an angel named Catherine - what a looker! - came to my meditation spot and told me I could earn my way out of purgatory if I showed dedication to someone or something. So here I am, and as they say, your wish is my command. She told me your name is Raul and you are a warrior of the angels. You must be pretty tough to get that job."

"Exactly how do I know this is not a trick to get me off guard?" Raul asked.

"Again, I have no idea, I'm just here to help, not think. But if I understand correctly, it would be very hard to catch you off guard, just by the nature of your job". The giant Cyclops continued very matter-of-factly. "By the way, how do you like killing people for a living? The reason I ask is because in seventeen twenty two I was an assassin for William of Stonely. He was a Lord of a Manor somewhere in England... that doesn't really matter now, anyway. My point is that I did everything I was told without question, and because I was very good at my job, I died an old man in bed. The problem was, I woke up with this God-forsaken eye in the center of my head, sitting at a meditation wall in purgatory. Where's the justice, I ask?"

"If you know Catherine, the angel, answer a question for me", challenged Raul.

"Shoot, but I don't mean that literally, you understand."

"What color are her eyes, and what's different about them? Get the question right and maybe I'll believe you. Get it wrong and I will shoot you where you stand."

"Feisty human, aren't you? When Catherine appeared to you, she had a blue eye and a brown eye with the faces of two angels in them. I don't really know who they are, but they are special, I think."

"Two angels, you are sure of that?" Raul asked.

"I guess I would stake my life, if that's what you call it, on it", the giant replied.

"Fine. How far to the witch's cave, or tunnel, or wherever it is she is at?"

"Sorry, bloke, I just got here myself. I have no idea where Her Ugliness is. But what I do know for sure is that when I dropped in I saw about a hundred of those 'zombie' things gathering at the cemetery. My guess is there isn't a dance over there, so they are probably coming this way."

"King, go find out how many there are and how far away they are", Raul ordered.

King stood up, turned to Raul and said, "Got it, boss; be right back."

Samuel looked astonished. "The dog talks? They have come a long way in the past few hundred years, haven't they?"

Raul ignored the question and asked, "What kind of weapons, other than the club, do you have?"

"I guess I could breathe on them; that should knock them over", Samuel said, laughing.

"That's it? Just a club? I can't *wait* for this fight."

Samuel, without saying a word, swung the club at a tree and the tree actually exploded. It flew into a thousand pieces.

Raul's eyes were twice their size when he looked at the impact of the club. "Now *that's* a club", he said with a grin.

"Personally, I was always a battle-axe kind of a guy, but Catherine gave me this club and told me to strike the heads of the creatures when they attacked. I guess she wants them in limbo to determine their fate once you have freed their souls from - what's her name? - the pearl queen, or whatever the hell she is."

Raul smiled and stood waiting with Samuel for King to return. While they waited, Raul wanted to get a close-up picture of what they were dealing with, so he touched the screen on his watch. "King, video eyes

Ghost Warrior

on", he ordered, and the screen lit up. Samuel was watching everything Raul was doing with amazement.

"What is that little thing on your wrist there?" he inquired.

"It's a wrist watch that also does some other neat things", Raul replied.

"A wrist watch, is that like a sun dial or wall piece?"

"If that is what you used to tell time, then, yep."

As they were discussing the watch, King stopped at the cemetery and Raul as well as Samuel could see well over a hundred creatures gathered and apparently communicating in some form. The creatures appeared to be in a big circle and someone they couldn't see was inside, talking to them.

"King, get closer, I need to see who or what's inside", Raul ordered.

King moved closer to the group. He edged his way among them almost unnoticed as the creatures were intently listening to whoever was inside talking. As King got closer, Raul saw for the first time what his enemy looked like. "What the fuck?" he said out loud. "That's Catherine; that can't be. Catherine is the witch. Oh, man, this is too screwed up."

Samuel was staring at Raul's watch. "I don't think that's Catherine."

"What are you talking about? Of course it's….." Raul looked at the watch and the witch was pointing at King and telling the creatures to attack the dog. "Catherine knows King is a Robot!" Raul exclaimed .

The creatures started at King and his defensive functions automatically kicked in. He began growling to warn and try to scare off aggressors. When that didn't work, the biting started. King was pulling body parts off these creatures, but they continued coming at him. Raul watched for a moment and then commanded King, "Discharge knock out gas- now!" King started farting and the creatures backed away. They didn't know exactly what he was doing, and they became apprehensive. "Expel lethal gas now!" he ordered. King commenced to act as though he was taking a dump. The creatures started screaming and covering their eyes. The gases weren't killing them, but they sure didn't like it much. It seemed to be affecting their vision and sense of coordination. They started falling down, one after another. The witch started screaming at the creatures to kill the dog as they continued to scream, apparently in pain. Finally, the witch could see this tactic wasn't going to work and fixed her eyes on King. She looked like she was thinking for a moment, then raised her right arm above her head and brought it down crashing to her side. With that, a tremendous bolt of lighting flew from her finger tips and right in King's direction. It was incredible, but King seemed to sense what the witch was going to do before she did it. As her arm was coming down, King side-stepped behind two creatures that had been trying to attack him, but now were very busy wiping their eyes, instead. The bolt of lighting struck the two creatures head on, and with that, they burst into flames. As they were burning they ran screaming into the nearby pack of creatures, who were busily wiping their eyes from King's gas attack. King's video eyes were still activated and Raul and Samuel could see that there were now about seven or eight of the creatures on fire, running around in the group. The witch seemed momentarily confused as to just exactly what had occurred from her blast of lighting. When she realized the consequences of the actions which were meant to be directed at King, she became furious and raised her hand once again. King was standing alone with no cover this time; he would be a direct hit, for sure, unless he did something. Raul yelled into the watch. "Attack the bitch; do *not* let her fire another bolt of lighting at you!"

With that command, King was off the ground and flying towards the witch. King had been a good forty feet from her, but his springing mechanism was so powerful that he could easily jump the forty feet. The witch was stunned. She had never expected that a dog could jump so far so fast, and be so powerful. The witch recovered quickly and in an instant turned herself into a large black raven. The raven was about two and one half times larger than a normal raven would have been; nonetheless, she was now a raven and was flying above the pack of creatures. King landed with such force that he hit the empty space where the witch had been with a crash. He rolled on the ground and got up growling. Raul looked at his robot dog and couldn't believe his eyes. King landed and recovered exactly, to the smallest detail, like a real German Shepherd would have. Ed had surely outdone himself. By the time King had landed and rolled to an upright position, Raul and Samuel had arrived at the cemetery.

Samuel looked at Raul and smiled. "When a good fight won't come to you, you must hasten to get to it." Samuel raised his club and waded into the back of about seventy-some creatures that were still standing. Some had recovered from the gas and some were still wiping their eyes. A few were even slapping out fires on their bodies that the burning ones had caused when they bumped against them. Raul was loading golden arrows into his crossbow and shooting at the creatures. Samuel was busy striking head wounds to the creatures, and King was tearing and biting at them. They were in one hell of a battle now and they knew it. Raul noticed one really peculiar thing as he was loading and shooting the golden arrows. No matter how many arrows he shot, the quiver remained full. Catherine was true to her word about keeping the supplies coming. But then again, what kind of an angel would lie to you? Raul laughed out loud, right in the middle of fighting for his life. He was laughing as he thought about an angel telling lies and then trying to convince the Big Guy that they weren't lies.

The creatures were falling all around them as Raul hit them with the golden arrows and Samuel swung his club. Raul couldn't believe the force of the club Samuel was swinging. He hit these creatures and their heads exploded, like they had been struck with a forty-five caliber bullet at close range. The battle raged on and Raul was starting to get tired. King was chasing creatures and biting them with such force they looked like they were afraid of the dog as they attacked Samuel and Raul. Raul looked back towards Samuel and could see the giant's eight foot frame was now covered by creatures. The creatures had started climbing and jumping on Samuel's back and arms. Raul watched as the giant fell, landing on top of a pile of dead creatures. There were still twenty or so tearing at Samuel and Raul could hear him crying out to him. "Kill the bastards.... I'm finished.... blow us all to hell now!"

Hearing the giant's screams, Raul took one of the three pens he had been given by Ed and fired it in the direction of Samuel and the attackers. The blast from the explosion knocked both Raul and King off their feet. When Raul stood, he saw a giant hole where Samuel and the creatures had been fighting. There were no more creatures left, but Samuel had vanished as well. King walked over to Raul and rubbed against his leg. King actually looked sad, like he had lost a friend. "Well, aren't you one hell of a robot?" Raul knelt down and scratched his ears. King was making a whining sound like he was crying over the loss of Samuel. A new friend, short lived, but a friend, indeed. He had gone to the mat for Raul, and Raul would never forget that. Raul looked up at the clear sky and said out loud, "My friend, I hope you are in a better place now. And if anybody asks, you showed your true allegiance today and you surely have my vote."

Raul had no sooner finished speaking when the sky seemed to open up and through the parted clouds there was a large ray of bright light. The light was so bright that Raul had to turn away and cover his eyes. When the light subsided, Raul uncovered his eyes and looked up. There stood Catherine, as lovely as before. "Spend no more time pondering the eternal fate of Samuel. He has shown his allegiance and received his reward. Samuel rests in eternal bliss until such time as he may be called to return to the mortal world for a purpose."

"I am truly glad to hear that," Raul responded. "He was a good man, and deserved some good fortune. Can I ask you, does the poor guy have to be in eternal bliss with that ugly eye thing going on, in his face? What I mean is, he is so big and really stands out, so does he have to be so ugly too? That doesn't seem quite fair to me."

"He came to earth for acceptance as well as allegiance. His acceptance by you was not based on looks but rather by his motives and intentions. I believe your first thought was that because he was so big, a physical fight would be out of the question, and that if he was aggressive you would have shot him for aggression, not for ugliness. Am I correct?"

"You are." Raul nodded.

"Well, that's heavenly. Ok, move on and rid this world of that evil witch. Oh, and by the way, that was really an excellent call when you recognized so quickly that the witch was trying to steal my identity. I mean, picking up on the fact that she didn't know the dog, which was good. Many of the angels were surprised that you did that so quickly. Bravo!" With that, she disappeared.

Raul felt a nudge at his back and there was the horse; it was obviously time to move on.

Raul was riding along, doing a recap of events in his mind. Two exploding pens remaining, along with his bows, knife and a quiver full of arrows. Not to mention the sword he hadn't even taken out of the case yet. King was walking alongside the horse and Raul looked down and asked him what the exact temperature was. It felt like the closer he got to the witch's tunnels the hotter it was getting outside. King looked up and advised that the temperature had now reached one hundred degrees and was still rising as they spoke.

Raul looked down at King once again. "I wonder how hot it actually is in the tunnels where this old battle-axe lives?"

King looked up and replied. "Based on conditions provided and the mathematical computations of the degree pattern so far, I would estimate the temperature to be…. pretty fucking hot!" Then the dog started laughing.

Raul couldn't help but laugh himself, but he still could not believe the responses and human-like things this robot dog was saying and doing. They almost seemed impossible. More and more, the robot dog seemed like it was becoming a real dog, but with a human personality and voice. "Stop that thinking right now," he said to himself. "That kind of thinking is totally insane and is not normal."

As Raul rode along in the direction of the abandoned mines he couldn't help but wonder what lay ahead. What was his next challenge to be, and would he be ready for it? It was about five seconds later when King advised him that his sensors were tracking some sort of animal ahead of them, about three hundred yards away. The animal or whatever it was appeared to be stalking them and waiting to attack. Raul asked about size, shape, or some type of specifics, but King had no answers because he noted that the animal's shape kept changing. "Boss, every time I get a fix on it, it changes. All I can tell you for sure is that it's quite nasty and it is not our friend. Watch your ass; this thing is trouble."

Raul dismounted and took the golden bow and arrows with him. As he was turning to head towards whatever was in front of him, the sword and case fell from the horse.

King ran over and picked it up with his mouth and followed Raul. "I think Catherine wants you to take this with you," King said after Raul had taken it from his mouth.

"You think so? I guess I should be lucky she didn't throw it at me," he said with a smile.

King looked around almost in a panic. "Boss, I think I'd be real careful what you ask for around these angels. I'm not sure if they have a sense of humor or not."

"Good point. By the way, did you take an extra-strength smart pill today, or what?"

"No, I've always been this smart. Why do you ask?"

"No reason in particular; it just seems that you are not quite yourself today", Raul answered in a concerned tone.

"Well let me see," King replied, "here we are in the middle of this God-forsaken forest, being attacked by Zombie creatures, chased by a very nasty witch, making friends with a giant Cyclops, and all of this is at the whim of some seemingly unpredictable angels. How's your anxiety level?"

"I see your point, but robot dogs don't have anxiety levels. So what's up with you? You have a glitch or something?"

"I've got your 'glitch', hanging. What makes you think I don't have feelings, too? I have programs that you can't even imagine. Maybe, just maybe, there is an anxiety program deep inside me that is affecting me. So how about a little consideration?"

"Consider this, my mechanical mutt. How about you get your anxious ass up the road, so I can look through your anxious video eyes, and see what the hell is up there. I swear, of all the robot dogs in the world, it figures I'd get the one with a fucking anxiety problem."

"Ok, Ok, I'm going. I get your point. Try not to be so pushy. I may have a delicate condition that you're unaware of."

As King was leaving, Raul muttered under his breath, "Delicate condition, my ass. Maybe I'll shoot you in the ass with one of these delicate golden arrows." Raul was chuckling to himself.

King, without turning around or stopping, simply responded, "I heard that, and it wasn't very nice. I may be forced to remember that at a future date."

Raul watched the screen on his watch as King walked along the trail. The trail was covered with what looked like charred ashes and, once again, no living vegetation. Only dead-looking trees and bushes lined the sides of the narrow pathway. "What a depressing looking place", Raul thought to himself as he looked at the screen. All of a sudden King stopped and sat down. Raul studied the screen and all he could see was that in front of King was a small black cat, rolling around playing in the pathway with what looked like a sponge or rubber ball of some type. King was steadily watching the cat, not moving or advancing forward at all. "What is it?" Raul asked King anxiously. King was all business now as he studied the kitten.

"It doesn't have a molecular structure of any type known to man. My best guess is that it really isn't there at all, it just looks like it is."

"Stay put and keep watching it, I'm getting closer." Raul was in the dead trees and bushes, stooped over, moving swiftly towards the thing in the pathway. As he approached the side of the path where the kitten was playing, he put an arrow in the bow and watched. The cat stopped playing and stood up, tail up and ears back, arching its back at King.

King showed absolutely no reaction to the cat, which stopped and stared at the dog. After a minute or two the cat slowly turned to the right, where Raul was hiding behind a dead tree. The cat looked at Raul's location then back at King. Back and forth for what seemed like an hour but in reality was about twenty seconds. Finally, the cat blew a bolt of fire out of its mouth at the dog. King tried to side-step the flame, but it caught the right side of his face and burned the synthetic fur down to the web matting below it. King retaliated by jumping straight for the cat at a full-force lunge. As soon as he struck the cat it vanished and King was standing in the pathway alone. "That was a great trick!" King commented, approvingly.

"How much damage did the fire do to your systems?" Raul asked, concerned.

"No interior damage to my circuit boards or anything like that. I have a slight blur in my right video port. I believe I can adjust the circuitry and correct the problem," King responded.

"Did you by chance see where that cat went after it fried your face?"

"No, it disappeared after I jumped it; I'm not really sure where it went...wait a minute, that friggin' bird is back. You know, the raven after the witch....oh shit! It's coming straight at me! It thinks it's a dive bomber or something like that." King sounded in a bit of a panic.

Raul was watching and not believing what he was hearing from his robot dog. He detected a bit of anxiety in his response. "Is that possible?" he asked himself. He was watching the video screen on the watch and saw the raven headed straight for King. He had to do something and quickly. Raul jumped out from behind the tree he was using as cover and fired one of the golden arrows at the raven. The arrow passed through its left wing. When the arrow struck the bird it started to tumble, and it appeared to lose its aeronautical coordination and was floundering in the air. The raven hit the ground with a thump, and immediately changed into the witch. Raul had another arrow already in the bow and the bow string was cocked. He fired the arrow at the witch, who by this time was standing and looking directly at him, hands on hips. The witch screamed and held up her right hand as if she was stopping everything with that action. The arrow passed through her hand and grazed the side of her head. She screamed again and looked at the hole in her hand. She then brought her right arm up and then crashing down, the way she had at the cemetery. This time nothing came out of her fingertips. Raul apparently had incapacitated her with the arrow through her hand. Raul was in the process of loading another arrow into the bow when the witch changed back into the raven and started to fly straight up in the air. He released the bow string grasp by the two fingers on his right hand and the arrow shot forward towards the raven as it ascended.

So close, but a miss. The arrow grazed the underside of the raven as it flew higher into the sky.

Raul was watching the bird as it circled, well out of reach of another golden arrow. The raven circled for about a minute and then stopped in mid-air and stared at Raul and King. As it was looking at the dog and his master down below, the raven transformed before their eyes. It took the shape of a child with angel's wings. "I'm just a baby angel, would you shoot an angel? I take comfort in the fact that you may not." The angel then very slowly, and what seemed cautiously, lowered itself towards the ground. As it ever so gently touched the ground, Raul could see that the raven had taken the form of a little girl, but had added angel's wings to the shape. The little girl was about seven or eight years old, very pretty with golden blonde curly locks. The angel's eyes were pale blue; the color of Raul's own eyes. The angel looked up at Raul and asked very softly, "Why would you shoot me? I mean you no harm. You have come to my home to kill me, but I don't understand why. What have I done to you? Can you truthfully answer that? Before this day, you did not know of my existence. You did not have hatred for my being. But on this day you feel hatred and wish me harm; you even wish me dead. But I think you have no good reason for this, just the word of another angel, who said I must die. Do you kill beings just because one person tells you another must die?"

Raul watched the thing in front of him very carefully. This was no angel; this was a pure form of evil, using anything at its disposal to lure him into a weak, unprotected moment. This would be the time it would strike. Not when you were protected, but when you felt secure and were most vulnerable. Raul decided to play this to his advantage and try to 'trick the tricker', so to speak. "I think you have me all wrong, little angel. I'm not here to kill anything good in life. Why, good things bring green grass, flowers, butterflies and singing birds. Good things bring happy little kids who sing and dance, and play throughout the day. What I feel sorry for is the poor little child who is playing, minding her own business, when evil reaches out of a hole in the ground and pulls her in, because that's what evil does. It sucks you in and tries to take everything it can from you. Then, when it has every good thing it can get from you, it kills your existence and tosses your soulless body away, or better yet, decides to keep your wondering corpse around as something to be amused by. It has you walk around like a zombie, acting on every command or whim it has. Do you know anybody whom that might have happened to? I think maybe you do, and if you do, then you know fully well why I kill evil every chance I get. And to further answer your question, nobody has to tell me what evil is, because evil smells like evil and looks like evil. Everybody knows that if you are standing in a pile of what looks like shit and smells like shit, guess what?"

The thing in front of him stared silently at him. Raul thought he saw sadness in its eyes, or maybe even a tear. But there was something else in those eyes as well. Rage. And any second this….whatever it was….would attack him. That second came at the very end of that thought. The baby angel's face changed from a pretty little girl into a horned and clawed gargoyle, as it lunged at Raul. Raul dropped to the ground as it passed over him. One of its claws scratched his forehead above his right eye. Blood was running into the eye and down his face. The gargoyle turned, took off into the air and the sky instantly turned black. No stars, no moon, but pitch black. King ran over to where Raul was lying and spoke.

"Boss, you OK? Did that thing hurt you bad? Can I help? Tell me what you need!"

"What I need is for you to shut up for a minute. You are a goddamn robot! What is with all the compassion and 'I'm the closest thing to a real partner you have' crap?"

"Because, Mr. Navajo Ghost Warrior, I *am* the closest thing to a real partner you have, so why don't you stop being so damn bitchy about it and accept it?"

Before Raul could respond to the latest round of verbal sparring, King interrupted his thoughts with a timely observation. "There is something with three heads coming down this trail and he is not your friend, so you might want to consider getting your ass off the ground and hiding until we see what it is we are going to have to fight now."

"Good point, but how can we fight it if we can't see it. It's pitch black out here."

"Maybe that means that hopefully it can't see us either. These trees here good for you?" They both jumped off the roadway and behind a tree.

Raul and King waited while Raul watched his video screen. King had automatically switched to night vision when the lights went out, so anything his sensors picked up would be relayed through King's eyes. They waited patiently, and nothing. "How close was that thing you felt, anyway?" Raul asked King.

"It was close. Maybe a hundred yards or so. It should have been here by now."

And just then they both heard the noise behind them.

It was a gigantic snake; a python, or something like it. The difference was that it had three heads and was spitting from all of them. Raul could feel this thing breathing down his neck. It was too close. He reached into his bag and took out a flare. The snake was snooping around in the trees and bushes, smelling for its prey. The prey being Raul, and he knew it. "King", he whispered, "Bark at this thing and get it to look over here."

King barked and the snake did just that. It stuck one of its heads right in King's face. King stood fast, without moving. The snake, not knowing what King was, decided to test him. Raul was counting on that. As soon as the snake opened the mouth on the face in front of King, Raul lit the flare and stuck in its mouth. The snake instinctively swallowed, thinking it was food, and within seconds its eyes were glowing and it was screaming. Flames shot from its large nostrils and smoke was literally coming out of both sides of its head. It was the head in the center that Raul saw brighten up from the flames of the flare. The other two heads on the snake were poking into the trees, searching for whatever had hurt it. Raul had the large sword out and called to the snake. The snake looked at him and plunged one of its two remaining heads towards him. At that moment Raul swung the sword, cutting the large head from the body. A greenish-yellow substance squirted from the decapitated neck of the beast as it fell, lifeless, to the ground. The rest of the beast, having only one functioning head and neck remaining, was swinging it back and forth in pain. One of its heads was gone and the other was on fire. Raul pulled the bow string back on the golden bow and released a golden arrow. The arrow pierced the under side of the remaining head and exited the top of its mouth. The snake could not open its mouth to strike or bite. The remaining head stood upright about twenty seconds and then toppled to the ground with a crash. Raul and King both looked up as the sky brightened and the sun came back out. They also noticed the raven sitting in a tree on the other side of the pathway. The bird was glaring at them and finally spoke. "So, you fuckers think you can challenge me, do you? You are really starting to piss me off and you won't like that, I can assure you."

Raul looked at the bird and fired another golden arrow. "Sit on *this*, bitch!" The arrow struck the limb the bird was sitting on and Raul could see that it had truly startled the witch.

"Bastard!" the bird screamed as it flew off the branch. "I'm not done with you yet and take comfort in knowing that when I *am* done with you I am going to your farm and kill your pig angel wife and steal the baby angel!" Raul shot another arrow at the raven and was shocked himself to see how far into the air the arrow actually traveled. The arrow whisked past the bird, who had believed it was out of reach, and startled the witch so much it started to tumble once again. Before Raul could get another arrow off, the witch regained her balance and flew off, shouting obscenities at Raul and King.

"I think we pissed her off!" Raul said with a chuckle. Raul and King stepped back onto the pathway from the trees and Raul whistled for the horse. The horse walked down the trail slowly towards them and Raul pondered their next move. "Well, we can't be that far from the tunnels, so let's get going", Raul said out loud and they started walking. Raul was leading the horse and King was leading the way down the path. All of a sudden the ground started to shake and they could all feel the earth move as something approached them from the opposite direction. Something very heavy was walking in their direction and it was knocking the trees over as it approached.

Raul motioned for the horse to run back down the trail, and he and King jumped into the trees once again. As they watched the trail they saw it coming. "Not another giant!" King exclaimed. "Well, I wonder whose side he is on."

This particular giant was even bigger than Samuel, in fact more than twice as big. It had to be at least twenty feet high and about eight hundred pounds, Raul figured. "Was this what the witch was sending out next to fight them?" Raul wondered out loud. The giant stopped in front of where Raul and King were hiding. He appeared to be looking in their direction but wasn't seeing what he wanted to, so he started knocking trees out of the way until he found both of them. Raul had the bow already pulled and an arrow in place. "That's it?" the giant asked with a laugh. "No fire, no lighting bolts, none of the normal shit I've had to put up with most of my life. All you got is that dinky little bow and arrow. What are you, some kind of Indian or something?"

"Well now that you mention it...." responded Raul. "And who might you be, friend or foe?"

The giant smiled. He was a stout looking young man who looked to be about twenty five years old. But who really knew for sure, lately? He was clean-shaven and actually fairly good looking for a kid his size. He had fire-red hair, very white skin, bright blue eyes, and surprisingly enough, a pleasant smile. "Let me introduce myself. My name is William H. McBonney, but you can call me Billy, for short. Get it.....for short?

Never mind, it's not important. What is important is that the bitch on the broom has two very nasty gargoyles and a very big dragon that protects her house. She has retreated to the tunnels and is waiting to ambush you with anything she can. You should know that you have been more effective as a combatant than she ever expected. As a result, she is not a happy person. A good analogy would be, if you took all my ex wives, put them on brooms - where most of them belong, I might add - and gave them a double dose of PMS without their support checks. This would come close to how nasty this particular witch is going to get now. I was minding my own business, chasing about in the heavens when this knock out angel calls to me. 'Billy', she says, 'I would like a favor from you, if you could.' One look at this beauty and I could do anything. 'What do you need, sweetheart?' I asked. 'I am sure I'll have time for you'."

"Listen", Raul said. "You are a pretty big guy, so the last thing I want to do is insult you. So could I just ask you simply to knock off all the bullshit and get to the point? I have a job to do and not a whole lot of time, so, please."

"Absolutely no offense taken. Here is my story and the reason why I'm here. By the way, did you notice your dog is kind of fucked up? I'll bet that hurt, didn't it boy?"

"Boy *this*," King replied. "It looks worse than it is."

"Did I just hear your dog talk? That is too cool. Anyway, the Angel Catherine asked me to come here and fight the dragon with you. After she told me what the mission was she asked me if I needed anything. So I told her that if I had to fight a dragon I wanted to be twenty feet tall and about six hundred pounds of pure thunder."

"Might I ask you where you are from and what kind of experience you have fighting anything?" Raul replied.

"Absolutely. I'm from the Bronx, you know, the one in New York. I was the heavy weight golden glove champion in the tri-state area. I would have gone pro for sure if I wouldn't have gotten my ass shot off in Vietnam in nineteen sixty eight. I was a forward air controller, or FAC, as we called ourselves. You were military, so I know you know that we used to jump into red zones and call in air strikes. Charlie didn't like us much. Any of us, for that matter. They used to put big time bounties on our heads. And I mean *on our heads*. If somebody could kill one of us, they would cut the head off the body and Charlie paid them a hefty penny for it. They used to put them on poles to show the world how tough they were. At least I went out fighting and didn't get taken alive like some of the poor guys. Those pricks used to keep them alive for days just so they could torture them. Boy, what I wouldn't give for a mission back there now; a little payback might just be my cup of tea."

"How did you know about the gargoyles? Did you see them, or what? asked Raul.

"Actually, I did. About a half a click up the path here is an entrance to a tunnel. The average person would think these two gargoyle things are just stone statues. You know, like some Inca palace or some shit like that. Anyway, when you start to enter the tunnel they come to life and try to bite you or eat you….you know what I mean."

"They attacked you?" Raul inquired.

"Got that right. One of those nasty little mother-fuckers reached around and bit me on the arm. See?" Billy showed them a giant set of teeth marks on his left forearm. "Well, that really hurt, so I punched the Shit right in the face. The old one-two. Now he ain't got no teeth to bite nobody no more. I wasn't a Golden Glove champ for nothing, you know."

King addressed the group by asking what a klick was. Billy responded by telling him that it is a little more than a half mile. He then asked King how he learned to speak so well. Raul interceded and explained that King was a programmed robot and that he had been built especially for Raul by a computer genius. Billy looked at Raul for a minute or two and then asked what his specialty in life was. Raul thought for a moment then figured, "what the hell, I'm talking to a guy who has been dead for almost forty years."

"I'm an assassin for the CIA, so I guess I make my living killing people," Raul advised him matter-of-factly.

Billy seemed unfazed. "How do you kill people? I mean, do you look them in the eye as you kill them, or do you hide in a hole or tree and wait for some unsuspecting idiot to be walking his dog and you cap him or her? I'm just curious."

Raul had to think about his answer. He had capped people from distances and sometimes long distances. He had looked some of his targets in the eye. Raul thought for a minute and then answered. "Billy, on the question of killing people.... you, yourself, were killed by someone. As a result you are not a heavyweight champ of the world, or a lot of other things. So, do you think there is a right or wrong way to kill someone, or is it something we do because we picked a side and stayed with it? Kind of like a Forward Air Controller who gets on the radio with coordinates so a plane can drop a bomb on a bunch of soldiers, or whoever happens to be in the way. Dead is dead and I don't guess it much matters how you got that way, now does it?"

Billy looked at Raul with admiration in his eyes. "You know, I asked the Council of Angels why you were the Angels' Warrior and they simply said 'because he is'. And you know what? Now I know what they meant by that. Sir, I would be glad to go and kick some ass with you whenever you are ready!"

Raul smiled at the giant and announced, "Ok then, Pilgrim, saddle up and let's get riding."

"John Wayne! I loved that guy. Was he great, or what?"

"He was a personal favorite of mine," King responded.

Billy did a double-take and said, "Your dog watches movies? Too cool!"

Raul looked down the pathway where he had sent the horse and saw it standing there. Atop the horse was Chief Lightfoot, holding a War Lance. The Chief did a double-pump in the air with the lance, gave a war cry and disappeared, along with the horse.

Raul, King and the giant Billy turned and walked towards the entrance. Billy's head was at tree top level for the most part, so he kept watch and advised of the progress as they walked along the pathway. Fifteen minutes or so passed and Billy shouted down to Raul and King. "Ok, guys, we're here! I see the two gargoyles and the tunnel opening." The three of them stood a safe distance from the stone statues. Raul placed an arrow into the bow and Billy led the way, with King bringing up the rear. The gargoyle on the right sprung to life first and jumped from its stone pedestal onto the ground in front of them.

    The gargoyle was about twice as big as Raul, but only a little more than half the size of Billy. The second gargoyle came to life and stayed on its pedestal, just watching the three of them, as well as the other gargoyle. The first gargoyle was standing upright and its wings were fluttering. It was levitating about one foot off the ground, staying in one spot with its very nasty-looking claws extended, and growling at them while displaying a mouth full of large teeth. Billy made the first move. He reached out and grabbed the gargoyle by the throat and started to squeeze. The gargoyle was gasping for air, but managed to make a fist with its right hand and sent it crashing into Billy's chest. This knocked Billy backwards and onto the ground. It had also knocked the wind from him, and he was trying to recuperate when the second gargoyle jumped from its perch and landed on his chest. When it opened its mouth to growl, it displayed a vacant space where the very large front teeth had been. The gargoyle on the ground was holding its throat and trying to catch its breath as well. By now, the one on Billy's chest had opened both of its hands, exposing long, sharp dangerous claws. Billy had a hold of the arms of the gargoyle on his chest as the second one started fluttering its wings again in an obvious attack mode. Raul pointed the arrow in the bow at that gargoyle and released the string. The arrow sailed over the head of the gargoyle on Billy's chest and struck the other one in the left eye. The arrow penetrated deeply and the scream of the gargoyle could be heard for miles. It shrieked in pain and was attempting to pull the arrow out of its eye when the second arrow hit. This arrow struck the gargoyle in the throat, just below its chin, and penetrated deeply as well. This silenced the screams of the gargoyle, but it was still moving. The gargoyle on Billy's chest was watching its partner with what appeared to be concern. It stopped attacking Billy just long enough for him to throw the gargoyle off of his chest and get to his feet. Before this gargoyle could respond to Billy's action, Billy had pulled a tree out of the ground and sent it crashing down on the gargoyle's head. It fell to the ground, dazed and nearly unconscious. Raul sent a third arrow into the chest of the second gargoyle, hoping that if this thing had a heart, he had just struck it with the golden arrow. The gargoyle stopped moving and stood motionless for a moment. Then its head started moving rapidly back and forth, for about a minute. Finally, as quickly as it started moving, the head stopped and the entire gargoyle burst into flames. The burst of heat was so spontaneous and hot that Billy, as well Raul and King, jumped back. The second gargoyle started screaming, but not from the pain of injury but more from the loss of its mate. It was attempting to take the tree which was pinning it down off its chest when Billy grabbed its neck and snapped it. The creature fell lifelessly to the ground. It was less than a minute later when this gargoyle suddenly burst into flames and disappeared as well.

"Well I guess that takes care of the gargoyle problem", Billy observed with a chuckle in his voice.

"Don't count your dead gargoyles too fast," King responded as he looked towards the tunnel entrance. Billy and Raul looked towards the entrance as well, and there they were; two new stone gargoyles in the exact same spot the ones they had just fought with had been.

"Ain't this some bullshit", Billy exclaimed as he ran towards the entrance. Raul and King could do nothing but watch as Billy grabbed the first stone gargoyle and tore it loose from its perch. Billy stood in front of the tunnel holding a lifeless stone gargoyle. "It would be safe to assume that I'm a bit confused at this point", Billy said, wrinkling his huge brow. He then set the stone gargoyle back on the perch and patted it on the head. "You guys coming, or what?" Billy yelled out as he stooped over to enter the tunnel.

Raul and King followed, and as King walked by the stone gargoyles he barked. "What the hell are you doing?" Raul asked.

"I'm trying to act like a real dog, if you don't mind, thank you very much." King answered very indignantly as he strutted by them.

Billy started laughing and said to Raul, "Is your dog queer, or what? He kind of sounds like a fag sometimes when he talks."

King looked up at the giant, who was still bent over as they entered, and growled. "Go fuck yourself, Shorty!" he snapped.

Raul started laughing at King. "I thought you told me that was impossible. Change your mind, did you?"

King stopped and looked at Raul. "Hey, twenty-foot giants and stone gargoyles that come to life and attack you are impossible, too. But isn't Casper there about twenty feet tall? And, if I'm not mistaken, we just got in a hell of a fight with two stone statues."

Billy was finally able to stand up. He stretched and they could all hear his back crack when he twisted it to the left then to the right. "Hey, Pooch, my name is Billy. Who is this Casper fellow?"

"Obviously, the name-caller doesn't read. Casper happens to be a very famous cartoon ghost. You never heard of 'Casper, the friendly ghost'?"

Bill started laughing very loud and faced Raul. "Well, aren't you lucky to have an intellectual gay robot-dog with an attitude! Looks to me like you need to slap the programmer, first chance you get."

Raul was beginning to wonder if Ed had done something funny to King's program and if he was back at the farm laughing about it right now.

"Well!" King yelled out, "With Billy there yelling and laughing so loud, I guess a surprise attack is out of the question. What is our plan?"

The three of them were inside a cavern that was at least forty feet high, with little ledges and what looked like holes or little caves all along the inside walls. They walked a little further into the cavern and noticed that in the center of it was a gigantic hole filled with some substance unknown to all of them. The substance was bright green and looked very thick. Raul asked King to do a sensory visual and odor identification. All King could report back was that the substance had an oil base and the composition of Jello. The substance wasn't moving or bubbling, it just filled the hole. As the three of them continued walking, King advised Raul that he was picking up density particles in the small caves above them. "These particles have vision capabilities, but no thought processes. Hand and eye coordination, but their motor skills are limited. In short, they remind me a lot of Casper, up there ahead of us." Raul couldn't help himself - he just started laughing. He had to hand it to Ed; King had developed a personality, and quite a good one, at that.

Billy stopped and turned around. "Is your dog ragging on me? Did I hear a faint trace of insult in the air? Well, good for you, Pooch, you scored!" Billy started to laugh even louder.

Raul looked at the big man and thought to himself how great it was that Billy could throw insults with the best of them, but he also took them well. Catherine had sent him a good-natured giant, and boy, was he glad of that!

They continued on through the giant cavern, feeling eyes on them the entire time. They came upon a giant crevice in the wall, and further investigation revealed that the split offered a pathway into another chamber. Billy suggested that the crevice was like a giant doorway in the wall. As they passed through it, Raul could have sworn he heard someone call his name. Not just someone, but someone special; a voice from the past. A voice very close to him. "King, did you pick up a voice just now?" Raul asked.

"No boss, nothing; just us Pilgrims. Why do you ask?"

Before Raul could answer King, he saw what he thought he had heard. It was Mandy Borge. She ran past him and disappeared. Raul knew it was Mandy; it smelled like her, it looked like her, it was her. Except it couldn't be; she was dead. But then again – "so is everyone here," he remembered. Mandy Borge, Jonas's mother, had died in a bombing incident in Palestine many years before.

"Boss, why are you stopping? What are you looking at? And, if I'm not being too personal, is there any specific reason you just turned as white as a ghost?" King asked.

With that comment, Billy stopped and looked back at Raul. "What's up, Chief, something wrong I should know about?"

"That fucking witch is playing with my head. She may or may not know it, but she is starting to piss me off! So if I find it necessary to scalp the bitch, she should know that she brought it on herself."

"Man, don't let her get to you. Shitbags like her thrive on that crap. I remember Charlie used to do things to try to piss us off. You know, like kill little kids and throw them at us. Just anything they could think of to try and make us mad. They knew that a man filled with anger doesn't have room in his head to think clearly about the job at hand. Thus, you have a foe easier to beat. You know that saying…. about how a madman kills himself while his enemies cheer him on."

King looked up at Billy inquisitively. "You made that up, didn't you?"

"You mean about Charlie and the little kids? No, that shit happened."

"Not about Charlie. About the 'madman' thing," King responded.

"Oh that, well it sounded good, didn't it?"

"You're a real prophet" King replied.

They continued on through the crevice and into another chamber. This one was not as large as the one prior, but still a good size. This chamber was special because the walls were lined with emeralds. The emeralds were everywhere; sticking out of the walls, lying on the floor, just everywhere.

"Well, this is a multi-million dollar room if I've ever seen one!" Billy blurted out.

"Something is wrong; this has been way too easy to get this far," Raul commented.

"Yeah, where is that broom-stick woman?" Billy asked.

Just then they heard crying. They started looking around for where it was coming from. They discovered the sounds were coming through a wall deeper into the cavern. Billy started hitting the wall with his fists and the stones started flying. He was desperately trying to get to the source of the crying. Finally he broke through the wall and disclosed a separate little room. There were five small children dressed in rags. The children were all Vietnamese and looked to have been beaten up and thrown into the room. Billy started into the room and he stopped dead in his tracks. He stepped back out of the room and looked down at Raul and King. The big man had tears in his eyes. Raul climbed up to the hole Billy had made and was repulsed by what he saw. Inside the room, along with the children, were five poles with the heads of young men on them.

"I know every one of those guys; they were all my partners in Nam. Those kids, I've seen them before, too. These are some of the kids they killed."

"Billy, this isn't real! The witch is doing this to play with you, just like she did me. She's using our bad memories against us. Come on, we need to blow this off and get going. Don't let her do this to you."

"You're right and I know it, but this is really playing dirty." Billy replied, disgusted and angry.

"Yes it is, but you know what? We are going to fuck with her a bit ourselves. Right now!"

"I'm ready; what do you have in mind?" Billy asked Raul.

"How about we start with this? King, go into the first cavern and expel enough knock-out gas to affect the things in the holes. When you are done with that, take a toxic dump in the green pit out there."

King smiled at Raul, and left to follow orders.

"Why do you want him to take a dump in the green pit?" Billy asked, confused.

"I'm not really sure, but I have this feeling that if there are any slimy things living in it, they won't appreciate the toxic dump, will they? By the way, don't you think it's a little strange that we haven't seen the bitch on the broom yet?"

"That is strange, isn't it?" Billy acknowledged.

King had been gone for about five minutes when the screaming started. The holes in the walls had been storage spaces for zombies who the witch had not called on as of yet. It would appear that this was her 'reserve army'. The zombies were now rubbing their eyes and stumbling all around inside the cavern. Some had fallen from their spaces in the walls and were lying on the dirt floor, rubbing their eyes as well. King had returned to the group by this time and was standing in front of the crevice in the wall, making it possible for Raul to see through his video eyes and determine what was actually occurring in the other chamber. Suddenly King jumped back and yelped. This caught the attention of both Raul and Billy. "That is what real dogs do, not robot dogs!" Billy yelled to Raul. Raul was just staring at King, who was lying flat on his stomach with his front paws pulled up under his chin. The dog eyes were fixed on the chamber. Oddly enough, his video cameras had ceased to function and Raul had no idea what had caused the dog to act like this. Raul decided it was time to go see for himself, and went into the crevice, followed by Billy.

When Raul and Billy entered the crevice King stood up, and the three of them watched as a very large ball of entwined tentacles emerged from the green pit. The ball was connected by a large, single trunk which was supporting a mass of tentacle arms. As the arms opened, they gazed in horror at what they saw. Each arm had a head and a face at the end of it. Each face had no other features except a mouth with large vampire-like teeth. The mouths of the blank faces were opening and closing, snapping at anything that might dare to come close enough. The trunk rose up about fifteen feet into the air and each tentacle, ten of them to be exact, extended close to twenty feet from the trunk. The tentacles were moving continuously, in and out, up and down and from side to side. They were plucking the wandering Zombies off the floor and pulling them into the pit. As the Zombies sank into the pit, its face would appear on the blank head, and then disappear. The faces continually changed as each one was pulled into the pit.

"We are in for one hell of a fight now," Raul said as he grabbed the angel's sword from its sheath.

Billy put two of his giant fingers on Raul's shoulder and said, "No, partner, *we* are not in for a fight here. I'm in for a fight, not you. I was sent here to fight this thing. Hold the angel's sword up, if you would, please."

"What are you talking about? We're in this together! Grab a big rock or something!" Raul yelled to him.

"Not this time, this is *my* dance." Billy touched the angel's sword in Raul's hands and it magically grew to ten times its size. "I want to thank you for carrying this thing all the way here for me; I do appreciate it. Oh, and it's been a piece of heaven working with you." Billy then charged the heads.

"So, this is the witch's idea of a dragon, is it?" Raul said out loud.

Raul could not follow Billy into the chamber because between the knock-out gas and lethal gases which King had expelled, the air was thick, vision was limited and the fumes still present were extremely lethal. Raul did notice that for some reason it wasn't affecting Billy at all as he charged the dragon's heads with the angel's sword swinging back and forth. Raul and King could both hear yelling and screaming coming from the pit, but were unable to determine exactly who, besides Billy, was fighting in the chamber. As the smoke cleared they saw clearly what the problem was. The dragon's faces had turned into the faces of Billy's friends from the past. They were calling to him and begging him not to kill them. Meanwhile Billy was busy fighting off zombies as well as bites and strikes from the dragon's fangs. Now that Raul could see, he started shooting golden arrows into zombies and making it easier for Billy to fight the dragon.

"Christ!" Raul yelled, "There has got to be a hundred zombies in this room!" The zombies were hanging on Billy's legs and jumping onto his back. They were clawing and biting the big guy while he was busily fending off attacks from the dragon's ten faces. Raul continued shooting at the zombies, but he wanted to do more. "But what?" he thought. "I need to drop more of those zombies to give Billy a fighting chance."

"Hey, boss, how about I run out there and start pissing on the zombies legs? I think the acid will eat away at their feet and legs and drop them like flies!"

"Great idea, King. I think that's exactly what we need at this point of the game." Raul replied.

Raul continued taking shots at the zombies climbing on Billy, and King ran into the room totally unnoticed by the zombies. He ran up behind them one by one, lifted his right leg and sprayed acid on their legs. The zombies actually started screaming and fell to the ground. Raul could see their legs and feet being eaten away by the acid as they thrashed around on the dirt floor of the chamber.

Between the acid spraying techniques of King and the exceptional good arrow shooting of Raul, the zombie problem was eliminated in swift order.

Billy continued swinging the giant-sized angel's sword at the dragon. He had already cut off three heads and they were lying on the ground at his feet. There were still seven more heads, still biting at him with their vampire-sized teeth, and Billy wasn't looking very well at this point. His arms, back and legs were dripping with blood from all the bites, and Raul could tell he was in pain. Raul started shooting the golden arrows at the dragon, but as they hit the creature the effect seemed to be minimal. Raul was hitting the tentacles with the arrows, but he needed to get closer and try to hit the thing in its faces. He moved into the chamber, coughing from the gases that were still lingering. He stood about twenty five feet from the pit and placed another golden arrow into the bow's string, then drew the string back. He moved closer to the pit and one of the faces spotted him. The tentacle at first had the face of one of Billy's friends on it, but as it noticed Raul the face changed to Epi's face and it started calling out to Raul for help. Raul moved a little closer and then the tentacle struck at him. The giant fangs were headed straight for Raul's head in an attempt to decapitate him. Just as the fang-filled face got within four feet of Raul, a giant foot kicked it right in the mouth. Billy had seen the tentacle move towards Raul and was waiting for the right moment. Billy's kick was so forceful that the tentacle as well as the face was stunned. The faces starting changing rapidly, almost as though the head of the tentacle had become short-circuited. That instant was when Raul let the bow string go and the arrow sailed from the bow and struck the tentacle's rapidly changing face, right between the eyes. The arrow sunk clear up to its feathers and the face stopped changing. It was the face of a little girl, with pretty blue eyes and rosy red cheeks. The face screamed when the arrow hit and she started crying. Less than a minute later the face and head burst into flames and the little girl disappeared. The tentacle fell to the ground and lay with the other three headless arms of the dragon.

Six more to go, and Billy was showing signs of fatigue from swinging the sword and from all the blood loss. Raul continued shooting at the faces, but the heads were extremely fast and he was having no success at hitting any of them in the face. That seemed to be the only place the arrows appeared to affect the creature, and Raul knew he wasn't getting the job done.

Finally Billy yelled to Raul. "Get out of here! I can't fight this thing much longer and it's getting the best of me. Run, get the dog out, too!"

Raul was being driven back towards the crevice by the strikes of the remaining six heads. The tentacles seemed to be growing longer and the deadly fangs were getting closer and closer. Raul called to King and the dog ran towards him. One of the tentacles tried to snap at the dog and Raul took a shot.

It proved to be a lucky shot, as it struck the face in the right eye. This face, like the previous one, changed as it screamed. This time it changed into Raul's own face. It was like he was watching himself die. Less than a minute later, that head also burst into flames and the tentacle fell lifeless to the chamber floor. The dragon was now playing with Billy, and Raul and Billy both knew it. Billy decided to start striking at the trunk of the beast to see if that had any affect on its power. The problem with this tactic was that Billy had to move closer to the heads and there were still five attacking him. As Billy moved in to strike the trunk, one of the heads came crashing down on his right shoulder. The face bit into the flesh and tore it away. Raul could see the bones in Billy's shoulder. They had been shattered as he sunk the sword into the dragon's trunk. All of the remaining five heads screamed at the same time. All of the faces started changing rapidly, but they were not bursting into flames. They were becoming more vicious with each biting attack. Billy was being bitten to death and Raul had to do something to stop this monster. As the five remaining heads grabbed Billy and started sinking into the pit, Raul took out the second of three exploding pens and fired it at the trunk. The trunk submerged and Raul thought it had gotten away. Then came the sound. The sound was like someone's stomach growling but amplified a hundred times. He and King looked at each other as they realized that there had been an explosion inside the pit. They simultaneously jumped for cover inside the crevice. At that moment, the pit exploded. Green substance erupted like a volcano and the chamber was covered in what looked like green Jello. Raul counted ten tentacles without heads lying on the floor of the cavern, and he supposed that the massive green chunks stuck to the walls had been the trunk. "Well, the Exorcist has nothing on us when it comes to green shit, now does it?" he asked King.

"Well, Boss, I have to believe that the evil Marivel Paquade has got to know we are in the building by now."

Raul swore that King was chuckling as he said that. "No, that's impossible; dogs don't laugh", Raul said to himself as they walked back into the Emerald-filled chamber.

"Well, what now?" King asked Raul as they walked along.

"I think we just have to continue on into these tunnels and see where they lead us. That witch has got to be hiding here somewhere. I can't believe that she would just walk away. So, I guess we are going to have to see what else she has in store for us. You up for that?"

"Mister, I am up for anything. That is why I'm such a stud!" King replied, again with what appeared to be a laugh.

"I have been meaning to ask you what happened to your circuitry. You are supposed to be a robot, but lately I'm seeing this kind of dog, kinda human tendencies. What's up with that? Did Ed do something funny to your program, or what?"

"The way I see it," King replied, "You are seeing exactly what you want to see, and hearing exactly what you want to hear. Nothing more, nothing less."

"You see, that's what I mean. What kind of an answer is that? You are a robot, are you not? However, you are continually talking to me like some kind of human partner."

"Does that bother you? Has the way I have acted troubled you?" King asked, lifting one ear and eyebrow as he looked inquisitively at Raul.

"No, it doesn't bother me. What it does is spark my curiosity somewhat. One minute you are a robot. The next minute you act like a real dog. The next minute I'm not sure if I'm having a conversation with a robot or myself. You have a programmed answer for that?"

"Ever thought that maybe you are?" King answered as he moved in front of Raul.

"You see, that's exactly what I mean. Your answer made absolutely no sense whatsoever. And I……what was that?"

King stopped and they both noticed that whatever light they had a few moments ago was fading. "King, activate your lighting system!"

Both of King's eyes lit up with the power of one hundred watt halogen bulbs. There was nothing in front of them but more darkness. They were entering the deepest part of the witch's tunnels. The tunnel started to feel damp and muggy, and they could see what looked like large black and white worms crawling along the walls of the passageway. The wormy-looking things were about a foot long and their eyes glowed red in the light King was giving off. They both stopped and studied the creatures. They were about six inches in diameter with a slimy looking substance covering their smooth bodies. Raul took a closer look at one of them and discovered the head of the worm, like the dragon, contained the face of a human. These faces, however, were not changing. They were the faces of agony and despair. Raul was staring at one of the worm's faces and saw it was the face of a little boy, about twelve years old. The face had very sad brown eyes and it was crying without making a sound. Tears were rolling down the cheeks of the little boy's face and it was trying to speak.

"Can you help me, sir? I'm stuck in this body and I can't get out. Please look at me. Can you help me?"

Raul, against the warnings of King, moved closer to the face to try to hear what it was saying. Raul was about a foot from its face when it instantly turned into a serpent's face with large yellowish-green fangs. The face leaped at Raul and bit him on the right side of his neck, sinking its fangs deep into his flesh. Raul could feel a hot burning substance being transferred from the fangs into his body. He instantly grabbed at the thing attached to his neck, but he was getting weaker by the second. His strength was rapidly leaving his body and he could feel himself falling and falling.

It was a very large black hole and he was falling into it. Before he went unconscious, he heard the worm scream as the fuzzy image of King's face was clamping his jaws on the creature's back. Raul felt the fangs leave his neck, tearing at his skin as they pulled away. Raul was still falling and couldn't stop himself. He knew he had violated his primary rule. He had gotten too close to the enemy. He was going to die for that violation, and there was absolutely nothing he could do about it. Sensing he would soon hit the bottom of the hole, he knew he would be lifeless and helpless to defend his Baby Angel as well as his beloved Angelita. As he was falling he saw Grandpa. Grandpa was crying and chanting for him in Navajo. His mother and father were standing with him in a circle. They each had a rattle and they were shaking them as they chanted. That was a death chant and Raul knew it. Raul then saw Billy Dirtyface; the first man Raul had ever killed. He was wandering aimlessly and bumping into the walls of the hole. Raul also noticed that he had been scalped by someone. Raul had wanted to do that, but hadn't. Maybe his strong desires in life had been carried out in Billy Dirtyface's death. Is that possible? Be very careful for what you wish for; be very careful! This was flashing in Raul's head like an old eight-millimeter film. "Who will I see next", he thought. "Are all the people who I have killed, or been responsible for killing, going to flash in front of me now? Why haven't I hit the bottom yet? It seems like I have been falling for hours."

All of a sudden Raul felt like he was no longer falling, but simply suspended in mid-air, almost in a state of limbo, just waiting. "But for what?" he thought. It took a minute to realize what was happening, but finally it hit him. Catherine was holding him. She was cradling him like a child, effortlessly. Raul's eyes were closed and in the distance he heard Catherine telling him, "Raul, open your eyes and look at Mandy."

Raul did as he was told and saw Mandy, as beautiful as she had been when they first met, over twenty years before. She spoke to him softly. "Raul, you have accepted Jonas and you have made me very happy. Jonas is not only your first son, but he is you in many ways. After you there was still you, in Jonas. Listen to me now. You have another son, and Miguel is very important as well. You know that Miguel is an angel, as is Angelita. They are very important to the forces of good on Earth. They must not be harmed or touched by evil. You understand this, don't you?"

Raul looked into her beautiful eyes and answered. "I do understand, but what can I do now? I made a mistake and let everybody down. I knew better than to trust anything. I broke that rule and now it has taken my life."

"You have shown compassion, wisdom and strength in these past few days. At this moment you showed the ability to trust. It has not killed you, it has made you stronger. You must now go back. Your task still awaits you."

"But I'm dead, I can't go back. I sealed my own fate," Raul replied.

At that moment, Mandy disappeared. Raul, with surprise and shock on his face, was desperately looking all around to find her.

"She is gone", Catherine said. "Raul, you must make a decision. But first you must know that you cannot determine your own fate. Your fate is in the hands of a much greater power than you can imagine. The Council of Angels wants you to return and continue to fight the witch and her evil."

"But how can I do that now? You just told me I can't determine my own fate, so how do I get out of this hole?"

"Want and desire. If you want it, you will fight for it. If you desire it strongly enough, your will and determination will crave your return. Then, and only then, will you have it."

"I do want to return and I will fight this Evil. On this I give the Council of Angels my word."

"The word of the Angel's Warrior is a strong force. I will return you now."

Raul felt the upward force as Catherine raised him out of the hole. He felt a warm touch on his neck and the burning and bleeding suddenly subsided. Raul then felt somebody wipe his face with something that felt like a wet rag. He opened his eyes and saw the "wet rag". King was standing over him, whining. No, actually his robot dog was crying and licking his face. "Give me a break!" Raul yelped. "You're going to drown me!"

King's face lit up. "You came back! I can't believe it! You came back! Oh, thank God!"

"You can say that again. Hey, you are a robot. What the hell are you doing crying? Robots don't cry"

"Yeah, and real men don't eat quiche, but I've seen you eat it. Besides, I was worried."

"Really? I'm touched that you care so much."

"Well, it's not so much *you*, but I'm not quite sure how to get back to the Hummer, and if you died I could be lost! Then look at the thousands of dollars your good old Uncle Sam would lose."

Raul could see very clearly that King was laughing. "Your concern for my safety is too gratifying. Oh, and could you stop laughing? Remember, I still have the detonator button for that pack of explosives tucked into your ass, or did you forget that?" Raul was laughing now, and he could see that King was truly ecstatic to have him back.

"I'm betting you'd get a real bang out of that, right?" King asked, indignantly.

Raul started laughing as he was getting up. "The only time I ever even think about it is when you start talking out of your ass."

"Ouch, that's another one of those straight-to-my-heart shots. That troubles me that a man of your stature would stoop to such low shots. Once again, I stand by your side a hurt partner."

"Oh, for crying out loud. King, here is a flash for you. You are a ROBOT. You don't have a heart, and I'm not that little old Italian guy, Giuseppi What's-his-name, and you are not Pinocchio. Now let's go find that witch and fry her ass, OK?!"

"Nag, nag, nag. You're back what, three minutes, and already there you go with the pushy, bossy stuff. No chance you could just ask nicely? You might not know this, but I got the worm that bit you. You're welcome."

Raul looked as King lit up the area where they had been when he had let his guard down and paid the ultimate price for it. There on the ground were at least ten of the big white worms, all lifeless and displaying large teeth impressions on the back of their heads.

"You said you got the one that bit me. I see a bunch of them on the ground. Which one bit me?"

"Does it really matter? I couldn't remember, so I killed as many as I could before all of the little bastards ran into their holes. Is there a problem here? Because if there is, I fail to see it."

"Absolutely, positively not! You did a fantastic job and I thank you with all my heart." Raul bent over and grabbed King's ears, then kissed him on the nose.

"Well, you are most welcome." King started laughing and added, "By the way, you don't know where I had my nose last, do you?"

Raul started laughing and pretended to spit. "Give me a minute to focus; remember, I've been dead for the last few minutes."

They were both chuckling as King led the way down the dark pathway. The blast of fire that the witch had hit him with earlier had damaged his right eye more severely than either of them had suspected, and after a hundred yards or so down the dark pathway, the eye started to dim. Raul looked into the monitor on his watch, and the video portion of the right eye had failed completely.

"King, scan your interior functions for other problems." Raul ordered.

King stopped, and after approximately two minutes reported. "Right eye video terminated. Hearing and sensory perception on the right side deteriorating rapidly. My right eye lighting is at twenty percent and holding. Other than those few items everything else is functioning at peak performance. Not to worry boss, I'm good to go. By the way, how are *you* functioning after your temporary set back?"

"Just fine, my nosey pooch. How far down this pathway can you see?"

"Funny you should ask that. This pathway is starting to get narrower and narrower, and up ahead it goes into a hole in the rock wall. That would be about a hundred feet in front of us."

"I'm starting to develop a phobia about these holes and pits, and basically about all this slimy shit that evil seems to dwell in. Go up to the hole and light it up so I can see what's in it, or where it goes, or what fucking stupid creature is waiting to fight with us next!"

"Got it!" And off the dog went with no other comment. It was almost like King could sense Raul's frustration, or just the fact that he seemed kind of tired at this point.

King approached the hole and stuck his head in, turning to the right so Raul could get a video track from the left eye. King lit up the hole and they both just stared at the little girl standing in the small passageway. Raul was staring at his monitor and King, directly at the little girl.

"Back out of there now, King! That's the witch and she is up to something." King started to back out of the narrow little passageway and then suddenly stopped.

"Boss, she just turned around and ran out the other end. She is laughing and playing in the next chamber."

"Can you see the next chamber very well?" Raul asked as he approached the opening to the passageway.

"Not very well, but looks like a.......I'm sorry, Boss, but what the hell is that?" King responded, hesitating.

Raul was standing behind King at this point, and they both moved slowly through the small entrance and into a giant child's playhouse. "This is a people-sized dollhouse!" Raul exclaimed as he looked around.

The room was the size of a normal room, but was appointed with all the necessary furnishings of a little girl's dollhouse. The other unbelievable thing about this dollhouse was its dolls. They were all people, or at least had been people at one time. All the dolls in this family, excluding the little girl in the passageway, were mummified humans. There was a mother, father, brother and sister. Even the family dog and cat were mummified.

The little girl was skipping around the table where the four mummies were seated. She was singing a nursery rhyme and laughing. "Roses are red, violets are blue. Get ready now, because the witch wants to eat you!" This was a little girl who was singing, laughing and skipping, and not the witch. Raul picked up what the witch was up to. This was either a deceased young girl who the witch had animated, or she was a local who was either lost or had been kidnapped. If the latter was the case, Raul's heart went out to her, because this evil Emerald Witch had driven this little child to madness.

Raul wanted to try something. He moved into the room in clear view of the little girl. "Sweetheart, can you hear me? What is your name? Are you lost in the mine? Do you need help?"

"So, you want to help me? You want to know if I am lost? You want to know my name? Do I, will I, am I? You are really a nosey cock-sucker, aren't you?" Suddenly the sweet little girl had transformed into a snarling, sarcastic young woman right before Raul's eyes. "Do you want to know about my sexual habits as well? Do I do this, do I do that, am I a spitter, do I fuck dead things? What else can I help you with? Want to play, Mr. Navajo Ghost Warrior?"

"Well, let me just add this," Raul said very calmly, with a smile. "Are you Marivela Paquade, the Emerald Witch, or just one of her stand-in, worn-out emerald mine pigs? Because no matter how pretty you try to be you are still a pig on the inside, and this Navajo really doesn't care if you blow dead guys or not." With that, Raul retrieved a golden arrow from the quiver hanging on his side. Before this thing in front of him could move, transform or do anything, he had the arrow locked into the bow string and pulled taut. He released the string and the arrow sunk deep into the chest of the creature in front of him. The thing looked at him and started laughing; a high-pitched, wicked laugh.

"You can't kill me, I am Marivela's daughter, and I know that nothing can hurt me. Now it's my turn." The creature took two steps towards Raul, and King jumped in front of him in a protective move. Before either of them could do anything else, the creature in front of them screamed. "God, this fucking arrow hurts! Mommy! This nasty man killed me with one of those fucking angels' arrows. Mommy, it burns, come and help me!" Just then blood started running out of the woman's eyes. As Raul and King watched, fixed on this creature, her head started rocking back and forth from left to right. Back and forth, as she screamed vulgarities at Raul. The woman's head suddenly stopped rocking and again she screamed, "Mommy, help me!" Within seconds her head started spinning around on her neck, and about five revolutions later it stopped and exploded. The young body of this "woman" fell to the floor of the dollhouse.

Raul didn't want to even look at the body, but King stopped as they walked by it, heading to the door. "Hey boss, check this out."

He stopped and turned around. Looking down, he saw the head on the body had been replaced with Angelita's face. Even though Raul knew this was one of the witch's nasty tricks, he felt a sharp pain run through his chest.

They both looked up when they heard the scratchy voice screaming at them. "I'll bet that bothers you doesn't it?" This was followed by a high-pitched howling laugh. The noise was coming from the out side the house they were standing in, and it the voice belonged to Marivela Paquade.

Raul laughed right back at her. "No, bitch, killing your daughter doesn't bother me at all. I just can't believe that you have a daughter."

"Why is that? I have many things. You've seen some of them. And there is even more waiting for you. And when this is all over, I'm going to your pig farm and steal the soul of your new son, remember?!"

Raul was truly bothered by this, but knew that he couldn't show it. He couldn't give this witch one inch. If she thought that she could push his buttons, she would continue to do so. He had to remain cool and try to turn her own trick on her. "Hey, skag, I have to believe this pig of yours that I just killed was adopted. I know she wasn't something you gave birth to."

"Why do you think that? If I want a daughter I will have a daughter. I get anything I want. Including the soul of your new baby." She started laughing again, the same high-pitched, wicked laugh.

"That is the most obnoxious laugh I have ever heard. You must have gotten it from some Hansel and Gretel story. Oh, and back to my point. As ugly as you are, just exactly who or what would ever fuck you long enough to make you pregnant? Even on a bad drunken night, you're not going to get some guy that hard up."

That accomplished exactly what Raul wanted. The witch was furious. She started yelling and screaming so loud that the walls of the dollhouse started to shake. After a few minutes of that, King looked up at Raul. "Looks like you have been able to piss her off sufficiently."

They both looked through the front window of the house and saw the witch looking inside. Had she grown to a giant size, or had they shrunk when they entered the dollhouse? That question was answered in a flash. The witch swung her hand at the front wall sending the window, as well as the front of the house, crashing into small pieces. Raul and King jumped for cover as glass and wood flew everywhere.

"Hello in the house!" the witch called. "Can that Ghost Warrior son-of-a- bitch come out and play? Oh, and bring that pathetic excuse for a mutt with you! My cat wants to play with him. I hear little black pussies really light him up!" The witch started laughing again.

Raul looked at King. "I guess the dance is about to start. My partner is the one with the terrible B-grade movie laugh, and yours will be the little black kitty, according to Miss Ugly. You ready?"

"As ready as I'll ever be. I think it is time to show that cat what a pissed- off German Shepherd is capable of." King replied, appearing to snarl.

The two of them walked through the rubble and out the front of the dollhouse into the front yard. As soon as they cleared the house, they looked back and saw a little child's dollhouse sitting on the dirt floor behind them. Scattered in the dirt next to it were a family of dolls, including a mother, father, brother, little sister and….the young woman Raul had killed.

Even the cat and dog were now dolls. Nothing was mummified like before; everything was toy, like you would find in a real child's dollhouse. But when Raul looked closely at the young woman whom he had shot with the golden arrow, he saw it was still lodged in her chest. Raul also noticed that the face of the girl had changed once again. It was no longer Angelita, now it looked like a generic California surfer girl. Long blonde hair, blue eyes, over- done doctor-made boobs, and a twenty- inch waist. "Yep, all she needs is a surf board and the Beach Boys singing in the background", Raul told King as they looked back.

Raul and King continued walking away from the area where the dollhouse was into another part of the forest. The sun had returned and it was bright and warm. In fact, it was hot. King advised that the temperature had reached one hundred and ten degrees and was slowly climbing. Raul still had the golden bow and the quiver full of golden arrows. Catherine had told him earlier that she would supply the arrows he needed, and she had kept her word. No matter how many arrows Raul shot, there were always fifteen arrows in the quiver. Raul had the golden dagger with the picture of Miguel on the handle tucked securely into his belt. A quick re-con of the rest of his equipment revealed one exploding pen, a small amount of C-4 plastic explosives, one detonator and something he had not packed. Raul took a slingshot and six golden balls, the size of bunkers in a marble game, out of the bag. "Where did these come from? I didn't pack these. King, did you put these in my bag?"

"Never seen them before. Let me smell one of the balls." Raul put one of the golden balls under King's nose. "Pure gold", he sniffed, "but I detect something in the center. It's small, but there is something that is not gold in the center." King sniffed again. "Got me. It's not an earthly substance, for sure. I can't tell you what it is, or does. Sorry."

"Well, I must need it. I just don't know why yet," Raul said with a shrug as they continued walking through the hot, barren forest.

They had been walking for approximately thirty minutes, surrounded by silence, other than their own voices. They soon came upon a large stone chair, sitting on a stone platform, six steps above the ground. The chair was flanked on either side by three large statues. The statues were about the size Billy had been, some twenty feet high. They were statues of what looked like Roman Soldiers, dressed in armor with those steel helmets that had feathers down the center resembling a Mohawk haircut. The chair was empty and the statues were stone. "What exactly did that witch have in mind?" Raul thought to himself. King barked as the black cat walked from behind the stone chair. He then started to growl, moving his front legs alternately up and down.

Raul observed King closely; he was doing things he hadn't done before. He was not acting like a robot, but rather like a real German Shepherd. King was dropping back on his rear legs in an attack mode. Just then, what looked like Catherine came from behind the chair and sat down in it. She looked at Raul and spoke. "Raul, we have to talk. The Council of Angels has decided that the battle with the witch is no longer necessary. She is in her own domicile and there really isn't any need to molest her more than we have. We believe she has learned a valuable lesson, and will no longer attempt to steal the soul of the Baby Angel. As a result of this decision, the angels would like you to leave Muzo, and take the dog with you. And leave the golden bow and arrows; the Council would like them back."

Raul was staring at this woman who looked like Catherine. "So Catherine, what is my dog's name and do you remember what it was about him you liked so much?"

Before she could answer, King sat down and looked up approvingly at Raul. "You go, boss! You know this isn't Catherine, I assume."

"I certainly have my suspicions," Raul responded. "So Catherine, what was his name again?"

The woman in the chair studied Raul for a moment, and then replied. "Raul, my sweet Warrior of the Angels, look into my eyes. They are the secret to your mistrust. You see, one is blue and one is brown; these eyes are full of love. You must trust me."

"Lady, those eyes are full of shit and have no idea what love is, so stuff it!" A voice behind Raul and King answered this woman in the chair. Raul and King spun around to see who had sneaked up on them so quietly. There stood another Catherine. "Turn back around and don't take your eyes off that sneaky bitch in the chair."

Raul took an instant to mentally process what was happening. "King! Rear scanners! Give me an optical scan behind us."

As the second Catherine was about to say something, King's ears turned around. "Negative on the scan behind us, or in front of us. Duplicate false readings."

Without saying a word, Raul spun around, withdrew the dagger and plunged it into the chest of the woman behind him. The scream was piercing and horrendous, and both of the imitation Catherines were shrieking together. The one behind him was clutching her chest and had fallen to her knees. The one in the chair burst into a mass of spinning black smoke and dissipated. The thing behind them was still screaming as Raul and King watched it turn from a beautiful replica of Catherine to a very old, decayed corpse. The skin was turning brown, then black, in front of their eyes. Its hair fell from the head in clumps and its teeth and eyes fell from the face. Maggots crawled from the eye sockets and it started to wreak of death. As the creature in front of them finally turned into a mass of black ashes on the ground, King looked up at Raul. "Do you think that was the witch? Do you think we finally got her and this is over?"

Before Raul could answer, the cat jumped into the stone chair and yelled to them. "Not on your life, you stupid shits! Did you think you could kill ME that easily? I love to fight humans; they are such a stupid prey!" The cat then started to transform into the witch. First, she was a little girl with big brown eyes and long brown hair. Then she rapidly started maturing, and as she did the faces of all the souls she had stolen started appearing on her face. It was like ads on the internet; the faces changed rapidly and seemed endless. Finally, an extremely old, frail-looking woman with long gray thinning hair and a wrinkled face was revealed. This woman looked every bit of one- hundred-plus years old. She was dressed in a long burgundy colored robe and looked like she weighed maybe eighty pounds. She was sitting slumped in the large stone chair.

Raul thought she looked almost harmless with the very sad-looking brown eyes. Now, the question in his mind. "Was this the real Marivela Paquade, or another trick?"

"Let me introduce myself. I am Marivela Paquade, also known as the Emerald Witch. As you can see, I am old, and because you are such a formidable opponent, I will let you see that much. We are, however, not finished, you and I. And before this day is over one of us must die here. You-who is attempting to save your son, the so-called 'Baby Angel'. And yes, by the way, I do have a hard time buying that. Just wait until he is two years old and the devil in him comes out", she said with a laugh. "Then there is myself, fighting for my life. Unfortunately for you, I need the soul of that little devil, your son, to survive another one hundred years. So, there you have it. Anything to say before we begin? Oh, and I get to cheat, and you don't!"

With that, she shot a bolt of lighting from her right hand and hit King right in the side. The robot fell to the ground and remained still. It looked like someone had just turned him off. Still, Raul felt a pain as he watched his partner fall, then a sense of rage and revenge entered his mind.

Before Raul could determine the witch's next move, she flung her left arm in the air and the stone statues started to move. Six giant Roman soldiers to fight with. "You may now kill this varmint!" she ordered the statues.

Raul had come to expect anything from this witch, but he didn't think the arrows were going to get the job done. He fired one at the first giant soldier. He hit it about waist high. The soldier yelled and pulled the arrow out of his side. The soldier then threw the arrow back toward Raul. The arrow flew past Raul, glancing off his left leg. The arrow stuck in the ground next to him, but when he looked down the pain shot up his leg into his hip. There was a small trickle of blood that he could feel running down his leg. His pant leg had a small tear in it and blood had seeped into the cotton around the wound. Raul knew he needed to do something and quick, but what? He was about to be trampled and his arrows were flying back at him.

"Raul, are they not like Goliath and you like David?"

"Well, that has got to be Catherine. I'm about to get my ass kicked and there you are with a proverb for me to dwell on. No time right now, I'm looking for a place to hide."

"Did I not tell you I was your supplier? Shoot for the face and I will help guide you."

"Shoot what for the face?" Then it hit him; the sling shot and the six bunkers. Raul took out the weapon, loaded a golden ball in it, aimed at the lead soldiers face and pulled back the sling. He fired the first shot and it hit the soldier right in the forehead. That was when Raul found out what was in the center of the bunker. As soon as the bunker hit the giant's head, it exploded and so did its target. The bunker blew the giant's head completely off of its shoulders. The exposed open neck started blowing dark red blood straight up from the hole in the shoulders. The giant stood for a moment, and then before he could fall, returned to stone and crumbled straight down from its own weight. The next two soldiers were taken out in the same fashion within two minutes of each other.

The witch was now standing in her chair, screaming at Raul. "You fucking cheater! You got those Goddamn angels to help you! That's cheating and you know it! Stop fucking cheating and fight fair! Jesus Christ, I can't believe what a fucking cheater you are! The rules were really clear and simple. I get to cheat and you don't!" The witch was screaming at the top of her lungs and then she raised her right arm as Raul jumped behind a pile of rocks, which had been one of her soldiers. The arm came crashing down and a tremendous bolt of lighting hit the pile of stone in front of him. The stone exploded and the ground shook. Raul lowered the sling shot at the witch and loaded a golden bunker in it.

"No!" yelled Catherine, "that will not work on her, don't waste the bunker. You need it."

Raul raised the slingshot and fired it at the next soldier. This soldier was closer to the witch, and when his head exploded it blew the dark red blood all over the witch and her chair.

"You son-of-a-bitch, you have ruined my dress not to mention my hair-do!" She turned to the remaining two and yelled, "Any chance you two idiots could charge that motherfucker together, before he has a chance to shoot both of you?! Christ almighty, you are as dumb as rocks!"

Raul started to laugh; he couldn't help himself. He had moved from his spot behind the crumbled soldier when the witch was yelling at the remaining two. They, along with the witch, were looking for him. He had the slingshot ready and jumped up and called to them. "Hey, stupid, over here!" When the two giants turned around, he fired at the closer of the two. Raul couldn't believe what happened next.

The first giant side-stepped the bunker and it struck the one behind him right in the left eye. Same effect as the others - explosion, lots of blood, and the witch got covered again and the giant soldier turned to stone and crumbled. The remaining soldier, however, did not look at the witch, giving Raul a chance to reload. Instead he charged Raul's position.

Raul was trying to load as quickly as possible, and dropped the golden bunker into the pile of stone rubble. He was frantically searching for the bunker as the giant charged. Raul could hear the witch screaming at the top of her lungs. "Get him, get the bastard, charge him, and kill the fucker!" Then the giant tripped over one of his fallen stone comrades. He fell to the ground with an earth-shattering crash. The ground shook once again and Raul bounced in the air. When he landed, he saw the bunker between two pieces of stone on the ground in front of him. He picked it up and placed it in the slingshot. He stood just as the giant soldier was standing, and raised his giant sword to attack again. The giant's arm with the sword was raised high and he was yelling when the bunker hit him right in the mouth. He looked at Raul with eyes as big as giant cymbals, just as the bunker exploded. Just as before, it took only a few seconds before the massive blood flow stopped and it turned back to stone and crumbled to the ground.

The witch screamed at Raul just as her arm came crashing down, releasing another bolt of lighting. "You bastard, you have destroyed my army and now it looks like it's just me and you, Mr. Navajo Ghost Warrior!"

Raul jumped behind one of the crumbled stone soldiers just as the fiery bolt of lighting swept across his back. He felt the heat and then the burn, which had set the back of his strap t-shirt on fire. He rolled over on his back and put the fire out, but the pain from the burn was excruciating. Nothing to do now but keep out of her way and wait for a shot at her. The witch was laughing and hadn't even left the chair where she was still standing. "Come on out, Mr. Warrior, I've got something for you."

With that, she sent another blast over his head and into the ground behind him. Hot sparks and embers flew up and struck him on the back of his neck and shoulder. The sparks made burn marks the size of cigarette burns and shot pains through Raul's entire body.

Raul had to do something, and quickly, before the witch either killed him or escaped. He was tired of chasing her, and had decided this was going to end here and now. "You are a pathetic old hag!" he yelled. "All you got is those wimpy lighting blasts of yours, and I'll bet when you were fifty years younger they had some kick, but now they go along with the Pampers you probably have to wear!"

Raul was waiting for the reaction. He had observed that every time she fired a bolt of lighting, it took her about five to six minutes to regenerate enough kick to fire another one. Now the trick was piss her off enough to throw some more fire and then take his shot.

"So, you think I'm old and don't have it anymore, do you, you little pestilent piece of shit! Well, maybe I'll wait for you to stick your head up and put a bolt of fire in one of those baby blues of yours. I'm sure that would burn you up!" And she started laughing and howling again.

"Please, please, Marivela, could you please stop laughing? The fire bolts are easier to take than that silly laugh of yours. You're killing me with that alone! Hey, maybe you could market that stupid laugh, along with your ugly face. Yeah, we could market hemorrhoid cream. You could be the ugly hemorrhoid that is a pain in everyone's ass, and tell them about a fantastic cream that would shut that obnoxious mouth of yours. What do you think, maybe we could sell that?" Raul was still behind the crumbled stone with the bow in his hand and a golden arrow loaded, just waiting for the Emerald Witch to get mad enough to fire another bolt of lighting.

"I got your hemorrhoid cream right here, you sneaky little fuck. See how you like this. Maybe you will piss your pants and need a diaper yourself." With that she raised both arms and sent them crashing down to her sides, releasing two bolts of fire-laced lighting. The bolt struck the stone Raul was hiding behind and sent it flying into the air in thousands of pieces. The blast was so strong that Raul also went flying backwards. He landed about fifteen feet further back than he was, but still had the bow in his hand and the arrow was still set in the string and ready to fire. When he landed, it wasn't with a crashing thump on the ground because he had landed on King, who was still lying motionless on the ground. Raul looked at King and the rage returned. He then looked at the witch and noticed that the double whammy she had just sent had taken a toll on her. She was now sitting in the chair, no longer standing, and looked totally worn out. She looked up at Raul, and started to move out of the chair. She had thought that the last bolt she had sent his way had done him in and was shocked to see him standing with the bow in his hand. As she attempted to flee to her left, Raul fired the golden arrow at her. It struck her robe just above her left shoulder. Raul and the witch were both surprised to see that the arrow actually stuck into the stone chair.

"You can't kill me with that stupid bow and arrow! What's wrong with you? I'm Marivela Paquade, the Emerald Witch; arrows don't hurt me." She then tried to flee, but discovered she was stuck to the stone chair by her robe, which was pinned via the arrow to the back of the chair.

Raul was now walking towards her with the dagger in his hand. "No bitch, the arrow won't hurt you, but I did want you to see up close a picture of my newest son, Miguel. Oh, I'm sorry, you know him as the Baby Angel. Here, get a really up-close and personal look." With that, Raul threw the dagger at the witch's chest. The dagger struck its mark and Marivela Paquade screamed.

The dagger had penetrated her chest clear up to the handle, and on the handle the last thing she saw before she started to decay and fall apart right in front of Raul's eyes, was the picture of Miguel Marques Lightfoot, the Baby Angel. The witch crumpled into black dust and was no longer a threat to anyone; just a pile of dust. Raul watched as the entire forest started to come alive right before his eyes. The trees were now green, and flowers were growing and blooming as he watched. The squirrels and birds started to appear. The forest had once again become beautiful in front of Raul's eyes. He also watched as what looked like flashes of soft light left the forest, headed toward the heavens. The souls that the Emerald Witch had captured were now released and heading home. This was a good day, Raul thought to himself. Then he looked past the piles of rocks that still remained on the ground and saw King, still lying motionless on the ground.

He went to King and laid him on his side and opened his internal compartment. Everything inside the dog had been burnt to a crisp. Raul couldn't do anything to help King. He wouldn't leave him here; he would carry him home and have Ed repair him.

Raul was still suffering from the injuries the witch had inflicted on him and didn't have enough strength to lift the over-sized robot dog. Raul sat down next to his partner in frustration. "Don't worry pal, we are both sitting here until I get the strength to carry you out of here. You are going home with me, I promise you that." Raul sat down next to his motionless friend, exhausted.

"Raul, what's wrong? The Council of Angels is very pleased with you. You have defeated the evil witch and freed many souls to return home. And as for you personally, you have secured a good future for your newest son."

"Nothing is wrong, Catherine, I'm just sitting here resting; kind of gathering my strength."

Catherine, who had appeared as Raul was talking to King, said. "Raul, I can heal your wounds, if you would like. Would that help you with your problem?"

"What problem? I don't have a problem. I don't need you to do anything for me. I'm fine. I just need a moment to rest." Raul replied defensively.

"What about King? Are you going to leave him here and come back for him?"

"Nope, I going to rest up and carry him out of here. This is my partner; he goes where I go."

"He's a pretty heavy robot. You are going to need a lot of rest to carry him, don't you think?"

"I've got time." Raul said as he looked at King.

Catherine bent down, kissed Raul on the forehead and petted King on the top of the head, scratching him gently between the ears. "We all thank you, Raul. You and King are truly the Angel's Warriors. Go home and see your newest son." With that she vanished.

Raul felt a lot better and looked down at his leg. The cut from the arrow was gone. He then noticed that his back was no longer burning or hurting him. "I feel good enough to take you out of here", Raul said to King. Raul took one last look at the chair where the witch had been sitting and noticed the dagger was gone. "Catherine must have taken it with her", he said out loud.

"Yeah, but she sure is a honey, isn't she?"

Raul answered without thinking. "She sure is." Then he realized that King had said that. He turned around and looked at King. He was perfect; no signs of wear or abuse from the witch. "You alright to walk, I mean, how are you feeling?"

"Never felt better, and I mean that. Everything is functioning at full throttle."

"Well, good, then let's get out of here. What do you say, partner? Raul looked up to the sky and spoke out loud. "Thank you, Catherine, I owe you one." The two of them started walking and walking. It seemed like this forest would never end. Then Raul heard Ricky calling him.

"Raul, Raul wake up!" Raul could feel someone shaking him. "Hey, man, wake up. It's happened, you have a new son!

"What...., what are you saying?"

"I'm saying, get up, man, you fell asleep. You have been sleeping for the past hour or so. I didn't bother you because you were so worn out, but you need to get up and go see your new son!"

"Right, right. I must have fallen asleep." Raul said almost in a daze.

Ricky hugged him and congratulated him. "Man, that must have been some kind of dream you had when you were sleeping. I swore you were arguing with someone and ready to kill them. Did you have a nightmare, or what?"

As Raul was headed for the bedroom and his newest son he murmured, "A nightmare or something; I'm not really sure what it was." Raul opened the door and did a double-take. There was Angelita, holding his new baby son. Raul swore he had seen a halo of light behind them when he opened the door. "That's crazy", he said to himself, and walked over to his wife and son.

Angelita showed Raul the baby and said, "Miguel Marques Lightfoot, I want to introduce you to the Navajo Ghost Warrior."

Raul smiled at his new son. "Well, aren't you a little angel."

Angelita smiled as well and said, "You have no idea." She held the tiny finger of the little baby. "You are my little baby angel, aren't you?"

Raul was looking at his son, who had the prettiest blue eyes, and swore he was smiling at his mother. Ricky knocked on the door. "Can I come in?" He entered the room holding something. "I can't, for the life of me, tell you how this happened, but a woman showed up at the door while you were napping and left this for you. I thought it was really neat so I wanted to show you." He held up a golden dagger with the picture of a baby on the handle.

Angelita looked at the knife's handle and exclaimed, "Oh, my God, this picture looks a lot like Miguel, doesn't it?"

Raul looked at Ricky and asked him to describe the woman who brought the knife.

"She was late twenties, early thirties. Dark hair and a real knock-out. I mean beautiful, light skin, and gorgeous eyes. In fact, they were really kind of neat."

Raul stared at him. "Let me guess, one was brown and one was blue, and she said her name was Catherine."

"Well, yes. She said she was just passing through and wanted you to have this in celebration of your little angel. How would you possibly know her name and about the eyes?" Ricky asked. "Next you are going to tell me that you know the future and what's going to happen next."

Raul smiled and looked at both of them. "No, I'm just like you; I'm just sitting here wondering what's going to happen next."

EPILOGUE

We all have our "demons". Demons, small or large; but demons nevertheless. No soul alive, of adult age, can truthfully say that they are free of guilt for every action taken in their life. Maybe it is guilt for the cruel, harsh words once spoken which caused irreparable damage. Or the boss who is begrudgingly forced to terminate an employee; knowing well the financial hardship this will cause the individual and his family. The careless driver, whose momentary lapse of attention causes a tragic accident which injures or kills another. The police officer, who, justifiably or not, fires the fatal bullet at the alleged criminal.

Some of us keep these demons buried deep within ourselves, pretending to never feel any ill effects from their existence. Others acknowledge these intruders from time to time, yet in general do not allow them to affect their daily lives. Then there are those who live in constant torment, plagued by guilt or misery for the path they have taken in their life.

Raul's demons awoke on an evening of pure physical and mental exhaustion. They came to him on a night which preceded what was to become one of the most joyous occasions in his life. Perhaps it was from guilt for finally being so completely happy; he may have felt undeserving of such fortune. In one night of fantasy and surrealism, Raul came to grips with the truth about his work and his mission in life. He had never acknowledged publicly, or to himself, the extent to which he questioned the morality and righteousness of his chosen career. But from somewhere deep inside his soul, those doubts and inhibitions began to surface and manifested themselves at a most vulnerable moment in his life.

Will Raul be able to keep his demons from resurrecting and intruding again? Will he be able to live a peaceful existence with his beloved Angelita and family? Or will he be a tormented soul for the rest of his days? Will that night forever change the direction of Raul's path in life?

Only time will tell....